Keigo in
Modern Japan

Keigo in Modern Japan

POLITE LANGUAGE
FROM MEIJI
TO THE
PRESENT

Patricia J. Wetzel

University of Hawai'i Press
Honolulu

© 2004 University of Hawai'i Press
All rights reserved
Printed in the United States of America
09 08 07 06 05 04   6 5 4 3 2 1

Library of Congress Cataloging-in-Publication Data

Wetzel, Patricia Jean.
 Keigo in modern Japan : polite language from Meiji to the present /
Patricia J. Wetzel.
   p. cm.
Includes bibliographical references.
 ISBN 0-8248-2602-7 (hc : alk. paper)
 1. Japanese language—Honorific. I. Title.
PL629.H65 W47 2004
495.6'5—dc21

                                         2003013833

University of Hawai'i Press books are printed on acid-free
paper and meet the guidelines for permanence and durability
of the Council on Library Resources.

Designed by Kaelin Chappell
Printed by The Maple-Vail Book Manufacturing Group

For Elizabeth

CONTENTS

ACKNOWLEDGMENTS

I am grateful to many people and institutions for their support during my writing of this book. For funding, I thank the Japan Foundation, the National Science Foundation, and the Japan–United States Friendship Commission through the Northeast Asia Council of the Association for Asian Studies. For hosting me in Japan while I carried out research, I owe thanks to the Kokuritsu Kokugo Kenkyūjo (Kokken), the National Institute for Multimedia Education (NIME), and Waseda University. Dr. Seiju Sugito, of the Kokken, has been especially helpful over the years, having provided me with my first opportunity to go there as a visiting researcher in 1991, as well as critical advice and much-needed direction over the years. More recently, Dr. Yasuo Yoshioka of the same institution, has been immensely helpful, sharing his knowledge with me each time I made even the smallest request. Similarly, Professor Yoshikazu Kawaguchi, of Waseda University, was kind enough to read earlier drafts of this work and had many valuable suggestions. Had I not had access to the Kokken and the Waseda libraries and the excellent advice of their resident scholars, I could never have completed this project. For advice on the intricacies of language policy, I thank Professor Sachiko Ide of Japan Women's University, Professor Megumi Sakamoto of Tokyo University of Foreign Studies, and Mr. Toshio Nomura of the Bunka-chō. Others who have read earlier drafts and given me valuable comments on my work include Steve Nussbaum, Miyako Inoue, Akiko Kawasaki, and Jane Bachnik. Chapter 1 is based on a paper that I presented at the November 1995 Festival for Eleanor H. Jorden held in Portland, Oregon. For the translations of the Japanese, I have had generous help over the years at Portland State University from Nobuko Murakami

Chalfen, Kōichi Sawasaki, Masa Suganuma, Yōko Takeda, and others. The final draft might never have seen the light of day without the superb assistance of Keiko Ikeda.

Elizabeth Hengeveld, to whom this work is dedicated, shares my love of language and of Japan, and is always willing to hear me go on at length about both. Sometimes she even agrees.

Acknowledgments

INTRODUCTION

Grounding

[handwritten annotation: Is Wetzel's search for the "final vocabulary" of keigo?]

This book is the story of two searches for vocabulary. One is my own; the other takes place within the field of language study. It begins with a phenomenon that, for better or worse, is known in modern Japan as *"keigo." Keigo* is known variously in Western accounts as "honorifics" or "honorific language," "linguistic politeness and formality," and/or "polite forms/style." In trying to write about *keigo*, I found myself in the triple bind of writing about a very complex linguistic phenomenon as well as about the Japanese vocabulary used to describe that phenomenon—and doing so in another language, English. This entire enterprise reflects my struggle to bring the vocabulary that is *keigo* and the language that is about *keigo* to English. *[handwritten annotation: Oh wait ...]*

The second search is approximately one hundred years old and involves two approaches to the study of *keigo*. One of these takes place within American structuralism and its successors, including transformational-generative grammar. The other approach begins with Meiji grammarians' efforts to define a grammar of spoken Japanese, including *keigo,* and their successors' efforts to define just what falls under the umbrella of *keigo*. The fact that the two approaches go into the enterprise with different assumptions about the nature of language and very different descriptors affects their end products.

Ask Japanese speakers on the street today if they know what *keigo* is, and the answer will be a resounding yes. A hundred years ago, the response is more likely to have been no, or at the very least, "What?" The word *"keigo"* was invented by Meiji scholars to describe something that presumably already existed but had never been named. Along with that naming came *keigo* ideology. In

1

some sense *keigo* is a modern construct that serves an important ideological function. Its contemporary identity is a product of historical processes that begin in what I call the "Big Bang" of *keigo* ideology: *kokugo seisaku* 'language policy', which began with the <u>*Kokugo Chōsa Iinkai* of 1902</u>.

If *keigo* ideology did not exist before Meiji, how did it come to exist today? What was the cloud of raw materials out of which it formed? What stages has it passed through? How is its contemporary shape different from the primordial mass from which it emanated? And how did it happen that the primordial mass has passed from a timeless state of perfection to a state of decline?

If one presses modern Japanese speakers to talk a little more about *keigo*, they will probably indicate that it is an important component of what it means to function as an adult in society, that they wish they could use it more skillfully, or that they wish the younger generation could use it more skillfully— that *keigo* today is *midarete iru* 'in a state of disarray'. They will talk about *keigo* in terms of the social fabric within which it functions. Their views are echoed and elaborated in a self-help, "how-to" genre. *Keigo* how-to takes its place alongside other kinds of Japanese how-to, and makes use of the same images, the same constructs, and the same view of the Japanese cultural landscape as do other kinds of how-to in Japan.

If Japanese speakers are asked to pin down more explicitly just what *keigo* is, certain vocabulary and certain descriptors will start to repeat themselves. Words such as *jōge-kankei* 'vertical relationships', *otona no shakai* 'adult society', *miuchi* 'insiders', *omoiyari* 'consideration', and *aite* 'other(s)' will recur in matter-of-fact pronouncements, as if these words had the power to explain how *keigo* works. Borrowing from the philosopher Richard Rorty, I call these words, which speakers cannot divide into any more subtle constructs, *keigo*'s "final vocabulary." By asking Japanese speakers to explain *keigo* and pressing them for an explanation of what, to them, is second nature, one comes up against the boundaries of common sense. It is often charged that modern Japanese young people cannot speak properly or correctly. This, in turn, is often taken to mean that *keigo* is somehow dying. Nothing could be further from the truth: *keigo* is alive and thriving, and its profile emerges in the conventions of common sense. The analysis of common sense entails a discussion of Japanese language ideology as it is embodied in regularities of practice.

The audience for this book is the student of Japan in the broadest sense of the word. For anyone specializing in Japanese area studies, I hope to demonstrate the richness that language can bring to the analysis of Japanese culture and history. For beginning language students and those with just a passing interest in Japan, I hope to reinforce the importance of language to our understanding of an unambiguously modern, but most assuredly not Western, country. For linguists with a comparative interest in Japanese, I hope to illustrate the place that *keigo* holds in the *kokugogaku* 'Japanese linguistics' canon.

Keigo is too often seen as an appendage of Japanese grammar whose analysis takes second place to more pressing questions that originate in Western formalism (processes associated with reference, reflexivity, anaphora, person, and the like). Such questions indicate principally what is important and interesting to the investigator in scientific inquiry. The Japanese are much misunderstood as being simply polite. To find politeness woven into the structure of the language reinforces this stereotype. *Keigo* is about much more than politeness or respect. It is a barometer of how people understand themselves and others; it serves to structure discourse and interaction; it abides change as much as any aspect of language ever could or will; and it is not going away. If ever there was a linguistic window onto the depth, complexity, flexibility, and variety of Japanese culture, *keigo* is that window. It is critical to examine all of these things in the historical and social contexts within which *keigo* is used by Japanese people.

Just What Is *Keigo?*

The word *"keigo"* is usually translated into English as 'honorifics' or 'honorific language'. But the term "honorific" regularly does double duty. It refers both to the category as a whole and to a subset of the category that exalts or "honors" the addressee/referent. This points up immediately the problem inherent in translating the Japanese vocabulary of *keigo* into English. The range of terms having to do with politeness, formality, respect, and social identity that have been brought by Japanese scholars over the years to the struggle to describe *keigo* are a marvel of semantic nuance, and the term "honorific" is only the beginning of the problem. I reserve this term for the narrower of its two meanings, using it to refer to a specific subtype of the broader category *keigo* 'polite language'.

This first sticking point brings up, too, the realization that terminology is not simply a matter of translation. It is, of course, possible to translate the Japanese received analysis of *keigo* into English, and this is frequently done. But the classical Japanese analysis has its roots in pre-Saussurean philological grammar and was profoundly unsatisfying to the American structural grammarians who set out to (or were given the assignment to) describe the world's non-Indo-European languages in the mid-twentieth century. It is not surprising that an analysis of the binary features that distinguish *keigo* emerged from that intellectual movement in a 1964 article by Samuel Martin called "Speech Levels in Japan and Korea" (Martin 1964). In his article, Martin presented *keigo* as a series of choices: formal *(-masu/-desu)* or informal, depending on the speaker-addressee relationship; polite or not polite, depending on the speaker-referent/bystander relationship; and if polite, humble (self-oriented) or honorific (other-oriented), depending on the affiliation of the sentence subject. All of these he set out in a tidy two-axis paradigm (see Table 1). That analysis competes with

Table 1. *Martin's analysis of* keigo *depends on a series of binary choices: formal–informal, polite–not polite, humble–honorific. Here, the verb* kaku *'write' in six forms.*

		Informal	Formal
Polite	Honorific	*o-kaki-ni naru*	*o-kaki-ni narimasu*
	Humble	*o-kaki-suru*	*o-kaki-shimasu*
Plain		*kaku*	*kaki-masu*

the native paradigm, which has its roots in classical grammar as carried to Japan by scholars in the late nineteenth and early twentieth centuries. Japanese speakers learn in their *kokugo* 'Japanese language' education that *keigo* is hierarchically organized (see Figure 1). The differences between these two might not seem to be of any great consequence to the nonspecialist, but different intellectual stances toward the object of study flourish in these two approaches. It matters very much which one the inquirer takes to be truth.

This oversimplified description might lead the reader to conclude that *keigo* is not so very complex, but it is critical to keep in mind that these examples represent only one predicate type (nominal and adjectival inflections parallel the verbal forms), and that suppletive and competing forms proliferate. Take the verb *shiru* 'know, find out':

Plain	*shiru*	*shirimasu*	
Polite-honorific	*gozonji (da)*	*gozonji desu*	'(I/you) will find out'
Polite-humble	*zonjiru*	*zonjimasu*	

The humble form *zonjiru* is unrelated morphologically to the plain form *shiru* (it is suppletive), and this is true, according to Martin (1975) for about thirty of the (of course) most commonly used verbs. Moreover, the honorific form *gozonji da* is built on the stem of the humble form *zonjiru* and constitutes a nominal predicate type, not a verbal one, so its inflections follow the nominal paradigm.

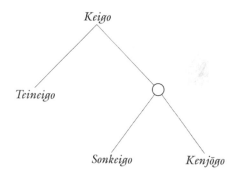

Figure 1. *In the established Japanese account (used in Japanese* kokugo *instruction), keigo is a matter of two major bifurcations.*

As if this were not enough, *shiru* takes the following present progressive/ perfect *-te iru* forms:

Plain	*shitte iru*	*shitte imasu*	
Polite-honorific	*shitte irassharu*	*hitte irasshaimasu* or	
	gozonji (da)	*gozonji desu* or	
	gozonji de irassharu	*gozonji de irasshaimasu*	'(I/you) know'
Polite-humble	*shitte oru*	*shitte orimasu* or	
	zonjite iru	*zonjite imasu* or	
	zonjite oru	*zonjite orimasu*	

That is, both parts of the plain *shitte + iru* combination constitute verbs, and either may be manipulated to make it honorific: *shitte → gozonji* or *iru → irassharu*. Moreover, *gozonji da* is by definition honorific, but there is a more polite form of the copula *da*, which is *de irassharu*. Substituted for *da* in the already honorific *gozonji da*, it is as if *gozonji de irassharu* were doubly honorific, which in some sense it is. Similarly, either part of *shitte + iru* may be manipulated to make it humble: *shitte iru → zonjite iru* or *shitte iru → shitte oru*. Or both may be changed: *shitte iru → zonjite oru*, which again makes the final product in some sense doubly humble.

It often seems that most attention is focused on the verb in *keigo*, but the other two predicate types also inflect for politeness—the nominal (1) quite readily and the adjectival (2) less so:

(1)	*Tanaka-san da*	*Tanaka-san desu*	
	Tanaka-san de irassharu	*Tanaka-san de irasshaimasu*	'(I/(s)he) am/is Tanaka'
	Tanaka-san de gozaru	*Tanaka-san de gozaimasu*	

(2)	*atarashii*	*atarashii desu*	
	atarashū gozaru	*atarashū gozaimasu*	'(It) is new'

The adjectival pattern is antiquated (especially the form *atarashū gozaru*, which might be heard today in a period drama, but nowhere else) and is now most frequently to be found in ritual expressions such as *ohayō gozaimasu* 'good morning' (< *hayai* 'early'), *arigatō gozaimasu* 'thank you' (< *arigatai* 'fortunate, blessed'), and *omedetō gozaimasu* 'congratulations' (< *medetai* 'happy, auspicious').

Outside the realm of inflected forms, Japanese reflects a complex system of morphology, including personal reference and address forms, that correlates closely with *keigo* proper. The prefixes *o-* and *go-* figure in both honorific and humble paradigms, as shown above, but they extend far beyond this in their conventional application to nominal and adjectival elements and in their function of making the speaker sound more refined, intelligent, respectful, sophisticated, deferential, feminine, or all of the above. Personal reference is well known to be a tricky matter and is often avoided altogether in Japanese.

But the structural properties of *keigo* are only the tip of the iceberg. Usage—the how, when, where, and why of *keigo*—is a source of constant comment among the Japanese, eliciting all manner of criticism and consternation, but rarely indifference.

By its nature *keigo* represents the Japanese linguistic response to the boundary between self and other, much as person does in Indo-European languages (Wetzel 1995a). I do not talk about me and mine *(uchi)* in the same way that I talk about those who are *not* me or mine *(soto)* (Wetzel 1984, 1994a). In Japanese, such differences can be measured either vertically or horizontally. Superior-subordinate relationships are the clearest example of vertical difference; degrees of social intimacy characterize horizontal difference. But difference and distance are highly nuanced and culture-specific. Contextual features of the relationships among conversational players that impinge on perceived difference include: venue, benefaction, in-group/out-group relationships, and just plain what's at stake. Demographic features that come into play include age, gender, area of geographic origin ("dialect"), socioeconomic class, and profession. No wonder, then, that non-native speakers, along with the Japanese themselves, are stymied in the face of linguistic choice.

Keigo is often associated with the rigid, highly stratified social structure that is Japan. On the other hand, in both academic and popular accounts, Japan's "traditional" social structure is fast becoming outmoded, with a corresponding assumption that all the cultural and linguistic artifacts that accompany it will fall by the historical wayside. But the traditional view of Japan as a rigid society is soundly refuted by its adaptation to the tremendous social and political upheaval of the last 150 years; it is an adaptation that has not been without rupture, but what Western culture or nation can lay claim to a consistently smooth transition from one era to another, particularly in the shift to modernity? If we know anything of language, it is surely that its conventions are infinitely adaptable. What's more, the idea that the Japanese could simply shed *keigo* assumes that there is a linguistic space that is *not-keigo*. Such an assumption constitutes a serious misunderstanding not only of *keigo* but also of Japan.

CHAPTER 1

Keigo in Linguistics

The Two Traditions of *Keigo* Research

Research on Japanese *keigo* emanates from a broad spectrum of theoretical models and perspectives. Among Western (primarily but not exclusively American) linguists, this includes the structural delimitation of *keigo* categories (Jorden 1963, Martin 1964, 1975, Miller 1967, 1971), the syntax of honorifics (Harada 1976, Kageyama 1999, Shibatani 1978), and pragmatic and sociolinguistic research (Hendry 1990, Ide 1982, 1989, Okamoto 1995, 1998, Wetzel 1994a, 1994b). Within the Japanese *kokugogaku* paradigm, there have been repeated attempts to finalize the taxonomy of *keigo* (Ōishi 1975, Tsujimura 1992) as well as to tie *keigo* to a larger system of linguistically mediated relationships that includes not only politeness behavior, but also, at the other end of the spectrum, the acts of cursing and insulting—so-called *taigū-hyōgen* 'expressions of consideration' (Minami 1987, Kikuchi 1994, Kabaya, Kawaguchi, and Sakamoto 1998).

These Western and Japanese categories are recognized here for heuristic purposes. Clearly there is overlap between the two groups, especially since the Japanese linguistic tradition harks back to the intellectual influences that poured into Japan from Europe and the United States during the Meiji Era. The differences between them are far more salient in Japan than they are in the United States or elsewhere for the simple reason that *kokugo* scholars' work is largely unknown outside Japan. Japanese awareness of developments in Western theory clearly affects linguistic research in Japan. Indeed, many Japanese linguists are trained and/or work at American, Australian, and European institutions. But the different concerns of Western and Japanese analyses of *keigo* are identifiable and reflect underlying epistemological differences.

American Structuralism

For the most part, contemporary theoretical American linguistics, which is taken here to be transformational-generative theory and its offshoots, does not concern itself with the problem of discrete categories; this is a structuralist question. Structuralist linguistics, in contrast, held among its objectives the definition of discrete categories and the interplay of those categories and the elements within them in a system. Structural accounts, needless to say, also continue to serve as the basis for teaching grammars.

Among the early elaborations of Japanese polite forms is Martin's 1964 account, which holds that "speech levels" function on two axes: an axis of address and an axis of reference. The two options on the axis of address are essentially identical to what are variously called formal/informal forms (Jorden 1963), direct/distal style (Jorden and Noda 1987), and *teineigo* in Japanese (but see Ōishi 1975 and Minami 1987): that is, any inflected form that ends in *-mas(u)* or *des(u)*. The axis of reference, according to Martin, offers a primary choice between polite and neutral, and a secondary choice, if polite, between humble and honorific.

Miller (1967) took Martin's account and expanded it under the rubric of "special and notable utterances," differing from Martin's treatment in a number of ways. The first is one of terminology, not substance: what Martin calls "exalted" forms, Miller terms "elegant." But Miller recognizes two additional categories of politeness, reserving the term "exalted" for an older pattern of honorification based morphologically on the verb *asobasu,* and adding to the stock of elements a "respectful" level whose morphological formation is identical to the passive. The difference among the competing honorific forms as Miller sees it is one of degree (of politeness), not of function.

It is worth noting that in Martin's initial analysis of the axis of reference, the trigger for humble, neutral, and exalted forms is taken to be the sentence subject (409). But in his 1975 *Reference Grammar of Japanese,* Martin alters his analysis to recognize instead "exaltation devices," which show deference on the part of the speaker and which are of two types: subject exaltation (honorific forms in his earlier analysis) and object exaltation (humble forms in his earlier analysis). The question of which element of a sentence triggers honorification is not argued.

Table 2. *Miller's 1967 analysis of "special and notable utterances," including alternating morphological derivations of honorifics.*

Humble	*o-* . . . *(-i) suru*	Elegant	*o-* . . . *(-i) ni naru*
Neutral	*(-r)u*	Exalted	*o-* . . . *asobasu*
Respectful	*(-r)areru*		

(But the notion of distinct subject and object honorification is later adopted by Harada (1976) and Shibatani (1990) and is one of the more interesting ideas in *keigo* studies.) Martin's choice of terminology parallels (and perhaps foreshadows) that of Comrie's (1976) more general classification of axes of linguistic politeness: speaker-addressee, speaker-referent, and speaker-bystander.

In structural analysis, then, the grammar of politeness in Japanese revolves around a series of binary choices: formal or informal (speaker-addressee relationship); polite or not polite (speaker-referent/bystander relationship); if polite, humble (self-oriented) or honorific (other-oriented). This approach differs from native Japanese descriptions of these forms, reflecting the structuralist orientation.

SYNTACTIC ISSUES

Contemporary theoretical linguistics has not been concerned to any large degree with analysis of Japanese polite forms. Syntax forms the cornerstone of contemporary analysis, and there are few or no perceived syntactic problems posed by these forms. One exception to this is the question of which sentence element triggers honorification. This is not usually perceived to be a problem for syntacticians working on *keigo,* since the idea that there are two processes at work, one of subject honorification and another of object honorification caught on quickly and continues to predominate. Nonetheless, if sentence roles—at least subject, and perhaps object—do constitute a trigger, the theoretician should define those roles, whether in configurational or nonconfigurational fashion (Whitman 1982, Hale 1983), by some sort of thematic relations (Foley and Van Valin 1984, Kuno 1980) using "nuclear" and "peripheral" sentential roles (Fillmore 1977); or in terms of sentence particles (Shibatani 1978). I argue that the role of the object is irrelevant; *keigo* is better explained as being triggered invariably by the subject, however defined.

Harada (1976), Shibatani (1978), and others distinguish between (a) *sensei ga watakushi ni okaki ni narimashita* 'The teacher wrote it to me' and (b) *watakushi ga sensei ni okaki shimashita* 'I wrote it to the teacher'. Assuming separate processes of subject and object honorification, *okaki ni narimashita* 'wrote' in (a) is triggered by the appearance of *sensei* 'teacher' as subject, while *okaki shimashita* 'wrote' in (b) is triggered by the appearance of *sensei* as indirect object. For the most part, object honorification is indirect object honorification. The difference is an important one, for it requires that for every "humble" *(kenjōgo)* form, there be an indirect object (sometimes elided) in the sentence. Yet while it is relatively easy to claim that every predicate takes a subject or even an object, it is not so easy to claim that every verb takes an indirect object, which is precisely what must be posited to account for humble forms. The alternative is to suggest that only instances of humble verb forms reflect an underlying indirect object—a very ad hoc solution.

The case might be made that intransitive verbs do not for the most part take a humble form:

- *Ni-ji ni otsuki shimashita.*   'I arrived at 2:00.'
- *Omodori shimashō ka?*   'Shall I go back?'

This situation could derive from the fact that there is no indirect object to trigger the form. A better argument can be made, however. Humble forms are derived morphologically by means of the transitive verb *shimasu* 'do', and they are not different in kind grammatically from transitive compound verbs based on nominals such as *benkyō-shimasu* 'study', *kekkon-shimasu* 'get married', or *shippai-shimasu* 'fail'. It stands to reason that intransitive verbs (*tsuku* 'arrive', *modoru* 'return') do not participate in a transformation that would alter their underlying transitivity. The honorific form, in contrast, derived through the intransitive verb *naru* 'become', maintains the intransitive nature of an intransitive verb:

> *Ni-ji ni otsuki ni narimashita.*   'S/he arrived at 2:00.'
>
> *Omodori ni narimasu ka?*   'Will s/he go back?'

There are examples of intransitive humble verbs, but these are suppletive forms:

> *Ashita mairimasu.*   'I'll be here tomorrow.'
>
> *Ni-kai ni orimasu.*   'I'll be on the second floor.'

It would be difficult to argue that *mairu* 'come' and especially *oru* 'be' take indirect objects. These verbs constitute convincing evidence that humble forms are not triggered by an (indirect) object. Rather, it makes more sense to allow the subject to trigger both humble and honorific forms. It is the speaker's relationship with the subject that determines whether the verb will be honorific (subject is speaker's out-group) or humble (subject is speaker's in-group).

Such a solution poses other difficulties, however, including just what constitutes a subject in Japanese. We must account for the role of *sensei* in the following sentences (among others):

> *Sensei ga okaeri ni narimashita.*   'The teacher went home.'
>   'It was the teacher who went home.'
>
> *Sensei wa okaeri ni narimashita.*   'The teacher went home.'
>   'As for the teacher, s/he went home.'
>
> *Sensei mo okaeri ni narimashita.*   'The teacher also went home.'

Insofar as *sensei* plays the same role vis-à-vis the verb *okaeri ni naru* 'go home' in these sentences, that role must be identified. Within transformational-generative grammar, it is not clear whether any configurational definition of subject can be provided for Japanese (Whitman 1982, Hale 1983). But Fillmore's (1977:94–124) description of sentences in terms of nuclear and peripheral elements defines subject not by its configuration, but as the nominal element that ranks highest in the nucleus of a sentence. Martin (1975:52–70) goes on to provide criteria for recognizing not only the inclusion of subject and object in the nucleus of a Japanese sentence, but the ranking of these two elements within the nucleus as well. Within a discussion of "focus particles," the "backgrounding" particle *wa* (no translation) and the "foregrounding" particle *mo* 'too', he points out that *wa* and *mo* can follow any of these other particles:

e wa/mo	*e* 'to'
ni wa/mo	*ni* 'to, for, in'
de wa/mo	*de* 'in'
kara wa/mo	*kara* 'from, because'
made wa/mo	*made* 'up to'

But they cannot follow the particles *ga* or *o*.

•*ga* /*wa*/*mo*
•*o wa*/*mo*

That is, peripheral elements are backgrounded or foregrounded by adding *wa* or *mo*:

Tōkyō e itta.	'S/he went to Tokyo.'
Tōkyō e wa itta.	'S/he went to Tokyo (at least).'
Tōkyō e mo itta.	'S/he went to Tokyo, too.'

But when nuclear elements are brought into focus, *ga* and *o* are "suppressed," according to Martin (1975:53):

Yasuko ga kaerimashita.	'Yasuko (is the one who) returned.'
Yasuko wa kaerimashita.	'Yasuko (at least) returned.'
Yasuko mo kaerimashita.	'Yasuko also returned.'

Closer examination of the subject and object roles in Japanese provides reason for assigning primacy of subject over object. As Martin points out, almost any predicate can take a subject, but many do not take objects: witness the series of Japanese transitive/intransitive verbal pairs (*shimeru/shimaru* 'close', *akeru/aku* 'open', *katazukeru/katazuku* 'clean up'). Additional evidence comes from neutral sentence order, in which the subject precedes the object, as well as in the tendency for ellipsis and thematization to affect subjects more often than objects (Martin 1975:58–59).

Numerous other problems revolve around the role of the subject in Japanese. Shibatani (1978:55) offers examples of sentences in which, at first glance, it appears that some sentence element other than the subject triggers a polite form:

a. *sensei no o-nakunari ni natta koto*   'that the teacher has died'
b. *Sensei ni shakkin ga takusan o-ari*   'The teacher has a lot of debts.'
   ni naru.

There is, to account for the first of these, a well-known conversion of the subject marker *ga* to *no* in subordinate clauses. In other words, (a) is recognized as related to *sensei ga o-nakunari ni natta koto* 'that the teacher has died'. As for (b) above, Kuno (1973:88) suggests that there is a process of "*ga/ni* conversion" where NP_1 *ga* NP_2 *ga* VERB constructions can change in many instances to NP_1 *ni* NP_2 *ga* VERB.

There are problems, however, in stating just what unifies the set of verbs that can undergo *ga/ni* conversion. Martin's (1975:194–198) solution is to recognize a "grammar of existence, location, and possession" in Japanese that includes verbs such as *aru* 'be, exist'. The grammar of existentials, locatives, and possessives is recognized as problematic across languages (Anderson 1971, Asher 1968, Bach 1967, Clark 1970, Fillmore 1968, Hannay 1985, Lumsden 1988, Lyons 1967). The Japanese situation, in which a *ni*-marked noun triggers politeness, is comparable to postverbal accord in English (for example 'there is/are'), where verb accord does not depend on the surface subject. That nonsubjects can be involved in agreement phenomena is therefore more a comment on a particular class of predicate than on the rules of subject agreement.

The notion of a subject trigger for politeness also makes it easier to account for contemporary "misuse" of polite forms. Even a cursory survey of so-called mistaken usage makes its clear that speakers are more likely to err in using humble forms than they are in using honorific ones, both humble and honorific forms apparently being reinterpreted as simply polite. A single trigger for polite verbs would facilitate the linguistic account of all these phenomena.

Sociopragmatic Issues concerning *Keigo*

A good deal more effort has been expended on the sociolinguistics and pragmatics of *keigo* than has been given over to questions of where *keigo* belongs in the grammar or how it is to be treated syntactically. I perceive three main threads of discourse about *keigo* in contemporary discussion. The first and most obvious has to do with usage and attitudes—how much people use *keigo*, who uses it, when, where, why, and how. The second concerns *keigo*'s relationship to what has come to be known as Japanese "women's language." The third deals with *keigo*'s ancillary function(s) in structuring discourse. The first two of these are hopelessly intertwined in both the popular imagination and the research record, so that they cannot always be distinguished.

Keigo study gained greater momentum with the boom of interest in Japan that accompanied its economic ascendance, yet, despite the developments in socio-linguistics that took place in the 1970s, remarkably little solid evidence came out of that boom about when, why, and how people use *keigo*. A good deal of fieldwork relied on self-report studies that asked informants what they would say in a given situation. Examples include:

1. Hill, Ide, Ikuta, Kawasaki, and Ogino's (1986) large-scale comparative study of Japanese and American politeness, which relies entirely on questionnaire-generated data for its conclusions on use.

2. Ide's (1989) survey asking men and women three questions about their use of *keigo:* (a) their assessment of the politeness of forms of the verb 'go'; (b) their assessment of whether it was appropriate to use certain forms to certain addressees; and (c) their choice of forms for various addressees. In Ide's view, "deference and demeanor" explain rules of linguistic conduct.

3. Research in English that relies on fieldwork carried out in Japan within *kokugogaku*. Shibamoto's (1987) citation of a *Kokuritsu Kokugo Kenkyūjo* survey found that "there are many nominals in Japanese to which women either always or more often than men, attach the polite prefixes *o-, go-,* or *oni-* ... giving their speech a more refined, or polite, tone" (28). While admitting that the self-report methodology used in the study was not entirely reliable, Shibamoto nonetheless concluded that Japanese "women's speech is more polite than men's" (33).

There are serious, well-known methodological flaws inherent in extrapolating from self-report to actual usage, but self-report studies continue to inform the Western understanding of *keigo*. Holmes (1995), for example, states unequivocally that "Japanese women are required [emphasis added] to express themselves with more deference than men. . . . They use a wider and more complex range of honorifics than men, and they are particularly sensitive to the complex contextual factors which determine polite usage" (22). Not only is this statement inaccurate; it misses the complexity and texture of the Japanese linguistic experience. Wading through the literature on Japanese linguistic behavior in search of accurate information can be a tricky process.

A great deal of commentary on the nuances of *keigo* usage ties *keigo* to broader cultural phenomena. Miller (1994) views *keigo* as a barometer of modernization. Hendry (1990) suggests that honorific language "goes with the make-up and the type of attire chosen when the occasion demands" (116). Shibatani (1990) skirts the problem of explaining *keigo* practice with the generalization that "the honorific system appears to be ultimately explainable in terms of the notion of (psychological) distance" (379). While doubtless this is the case, it doesn't satisfy as an explanation of behavior, and one is left with the circular question of what causes Japanese speakers to feel psychological distance. So it is that (with notable exceptions, discussed below) the accuracy of pronouncements on *keigo* usage goes unverified by corresponding experimental evidence from behavioral studies.

It is true that many of the claims generated by questionnaire-based research have been confirmed by careful study—for example, the claim that women are more sensitive to linguistic norms than are men. But more often than not, sweeping generalizations about Japanese polite language have at least been refined by further study, as the norms of any language are much more complex than the simple correlation of form *(keigo)* with demographic variable (gender) can explain. My own (Wetzel 1994b) investigation into Japanese attitudes toward (as contrasted with usage of) *keigo* illustrates the complexity of the relationship between language and demographic factors such as age, dialect, and gender. In a listening task where subjects heard honorifics used both correctly and incorrectly, female listeners emerged as far more sensitive to usage than did male listeners: 91 percent of women noticed mistaken usage, compared to 50 percent of men. Just what such sensitivity represents is a matter of interpretation. Labov (1991) has suggested that women lead men in rejecting linguistic changes as they become recognized within the speech community, but my 1994 study did not determine whether Japanese women evaluated mistaken usage negatively or not, only whether they had taken note of it. The same study found that listeners of both sexes judged male speakers more critically than female speakers. Somewhat paradoxically, it also determined that women tend to be more forgiving of mistaken usage than are men. Finally, all listeners judged speakers who used incorrect *keigo* to be more polite and more affable than those who used language correctly. Across all demographic categories (dialect, age, gender), Japanese listeners formed a positive image of people who used *keigo,* even if the speakers were mistaken or unsuccessful in their usage (effort apparently counts). This reiterates the findings of studies conducted in other Indo-European languages: neither linguistic consciousness nor linguistic behavior is easily ascribed to isolated demographic features like gender, age, or dialect.

Something that self-report questionnaires provide—and that goes almost entirely unremarked— is important information about attitudes and ideology. When asked what they would say in a given context, Japanese people are remarkably accurate at providing the "correct" answer (where "correct" is in accord with "standard language"). But there is a dire need for research that measures the disparity between behavior and attitude. What factors lead people to believe in or behave in accordance with ideological norms? What factors lead them to believe or behave in opposition? Ideology is too often dismissed as being simply coercive, yet not every instance of "nonstandard" language belief or behavior can be interpreted as a slap in the face of ideology. Such issues do not, so far, have a place in anyone's research agenda.

Probably the best known, and yet most misinterpreted, feature of Japanese outside Japan has to do with the notion of "women's language." The party line on women's speech is captured neatly by Miller's (1967) contrast of female and male speech in his description of a garden scene, and the accompanying generalization that the distinction between men's and women's speech is an important part of speech levels *(keigo):* "Women make more use of the deferential prefix *o-* and of elegant and exalted verb forms than do men" (289).

The pairing of honorifics with women's mode(s) of expression has a long history in Japan, and it was not a great leap for that association to catch the imaginations of Western scholars. It has been argued that both the idea of women's language and its staying power with regard to Japan is a reflection of Orientalism. What would never pass critical muster in the analysis of a more familiar Indo-European language has become part and parcel of the beliefs surrounding an Asian language such as Japanese. Japan's role in promoting the idea of women's language is great; the category has its origins in the processes of linguistic standardization and universal education that characterized Meiji Japan. Inoue (1996) points out that gender was actively targeted by the Meiji state in order to regulate citizens' behavior. Especially critical was compulsory education based on the ideal of *ryōsai kembo* 'good wife and wise mother' derived from Confucian teachings. "The emergence of Japanese women's language can be located precisely in the linguistic modernization process through which, as in standard Japanese itself, some voices were elided and others were elevated, and reconstructed to be 'women's language'" (Inoue 1996:75). The characteristic patterns of this women's language were promulgated in literature as well as in government-sanctioned teaching materials, quickly finding their way into the popular press. Women's language so captured people's (women's) imaginations that it continues today to elicit from native speakers of Japanese a reaction of familiarity and, often, insecurity about their own ability to meet society's expectations.

What is to be made of this category of Japanese women's language today? It is a contentious area. Among other things, it is still said that women use more honorifics—in both a wider range and with greater frequency—than do men (Ide 1990). But some of the most significant criticism of attempts to describe the parameters of women's usage comes from the work of Okamoto (1995, 1998, 2002) and Matsumoto (1996, 1999), who maintain that the received story of *keigo*—that is, the description set forth by linguists who attune themselves only to the standard language—is skewed. The linking of politeness and age, of politeness and gender, indeed of politeness and the Japanese themselves, is, Okamoto (2002) observes, "based on the hegemonic ideology of language, gender, and class" (18) and is not borne out by observations of actual linguistic behavior. Echoing this, Matsumoto contends that Japanese speakers have a wide range of stylistic variations open to them; to tie gender or age inextricably to any of these is to deny agency to speakers. The hold of "standard Japanese" on the academic imagination does limit the understanding of many people's lives. But critical (in the sense of "critical theoretical") approaches to *keigo* usage have failed thus far to go the additional step of historicizing their commentary. Whence comes the standard language of Japan? What is the chronological narrative of Japanese language, from which both usage and the popular and academic awareness of *keigo* emanate? How is its hegemony over Japanese people's consciousness of themselves and their language attained and maintained? Is Japanese one more language like all the rest? Or do its non-Western roots give it a character that might enable the blazing of alternative paths to modernization and out of its dilemmas?

Finally, in pointing out that a research agenda is ideological, one is not demonstrating that it is false, only that it contributes to the reproduction of relationships of power. My investigation cannot take on the question of what courses are available once the ideological character of a particular enterprise has been exposed. But it can locate *keigo* in a larger picture of Japanese history and culture, and give it depth and definition beyond the one-dimensional notion that it simply reflects politeness and that women are, in turn, bound by the constraints of society to be polite. In many circumstances, *keigo* has nothing whatsoever to do with politeness; and once the notion that deference always underlies *keigo* is cast aside, its ideology becomes much more complex.

KEIGO'S ANCILLARY FUNCTIONS

Studies in text and discourse analysis have yielded tremendous insight into the multifaceted character of *keigo* in Japanese and promise a much fuller picture of this complex linguistic phenomenon. It should come as no surprise that *keigo*'s potential for structuring discourse should extend beyond its paradigmatic role(s), as other formal features of language have been shown to function in similar ways. Perhaps the best-known example is that of anaphora, whose resolution in discourse is one of the most common problems of research in Natural Language Processing (NLP) (Chafe 1970, Grosz, Joshi, and Weinstein 1995, Walker, Iida and Cote 1994). I have argued that the deictic nature of *keigo* (Wetzel 1984, 1994a) opens the potential for its participation in the same sorts of discourse phenomena that characterize the deictic elements of English and other languages. In Wetzel (1988a) I used close analysis of a television talk show discourse to demonstrate how "reference spaces" in Japanese depend on *keigo* elements for their perspective and implicit reference. This replicates Grimes' (1983) findings in English, where the pronoun "it" may be used multiple times without any question as to its referent.

There is also substantial work that focuses specifically on the *desu/-masu* axis and its correlation with discourse structure. Ikuta (1983, 2002) finds that shifts between *desu/-masu* and non-*desu/-masu* style open a supportive or illustrative context space, where "context space" refers to "a series of utterances that taken together constitute a unit or whole, such as the event-recounting portion of a narrative" (McLaughlin 1984:271). In the same vein, Cook's (1996, 1998, 2002) examinations of *desu/-masu* shifts in school settings demonstrate close connections between *keigo* and activity types like *happyō* 'presentations, announcements'. *Keigo* is not alone in this capacity. The linguistic forms Cook calls "affect keys" (sentence-final particles, vowel lengthening, rising intonation, coalescence, and voice quality) combine with politeness to characterize text types. All these features, according to Cook, create social meanings, and they must always be considered in light of the social activity or human interaction in which they are embedded.

Maynard (1993), too, spotlights the *da* versus *desu/-masu* distinction and draws heavily on Japanese *kokugogaku* scholars for examining its participation in what she terms "discourse modality." Discourse modality contrasts with propositional content, which is the central concern of most (Western) research. Discourse modality "directly expresses the speaking self's personal voice, on the basis of which the utterance is intended to be meaningfully interpreted" (39). This modality has always, Maynard asserts, been a fundamental concern of Japanese *kokugogaku* scholars. It goes beyond sentential boundaries and includes both attitudes that might come through independent lexical items and those expressed by discourse structures and other pragmatic means. Its relevance to *keigo* study comes, for Maynard, in the motivation for mixing *da*-style with *desu/-masu* in a single conversational turn. Echoing Cook, she discovers that the shift is determined by two factors: immediacy and directness of expression, and internal or external narrative perspective. In conversation *da* endings tend to appear in abrupt remembrance or sudden emotional surge, in expressing internal narrative point of view, and/or in echo questions or jointly produced utterances (159).

The Great Divide

Such is the state of *keigo* study in English (primarily American) linguistics. Its twists and turns parallel the vagaries of Western theory—from structuralist categorical problems, to transformational-generative syntactic issues, to broader sociolinguistic and pragmatic concerns—and are informed by the same fundamental questions about the nature of language, what a formal grammar should include, and what the limits (and limitations) of theory are. Although many of the scholars I have cited are themselves Japanese, the *keigo* narrative that is available in English is fundamentally Western; there is remarkably little input from the Japanese *kokugogaku* tradition into the Western intellectual account. The opposite, however, cannot be said, as *kokugogaku* has been influenced in large and small ways by importations from Western theory. The result is a large gap between the Western understanding of *keigo* and the Japanese *kokugogaku* understanding of *keigo*.

CHAPTER 2

Keigo in Kokugogaku

Not surprisingly, *keigo* consumes much more energy in Japanese linguistic circles than it does in American or Western theory. The history of *keigo* study from Meiji onward is fraught with twists and turns that reflect both politics and theoretical development. From the outset, and continuing even into contemporary theory, Japanese linguists have had an overriding concern for taxonomy— that is to say, delineation of the whole category of *keigo* in addition to its subdivisions. The *kokugo* theory *(kokugogaku)* that underlies *keigo* analysis in Japan was not originally based on structuralism but rather on the Western tradition of philology and etymological analysis. *Kokugogaku* is by no means immune to the influence of linguistic developments outside Japan, but its foundations and its concerns demonstrate a very different perspective from that of Western linguistics.

Beginnings of *Keigo* Study

There was no (native) Japanese study of *keigo* until the Meiji period (Nishida 1987:208). Ōishi (1977:207) observes that occasional comments appear about language that is polite as early as the *Manyōshū* (ca. A.D. 770), but the Japanese scholarly community did not fasten on such language as an object of study. The native Japanese paradigm actually has its origins in Western linguistic analysis; it was developed and refined from the Latin-based Western linguistic methodology carried to Japan by missionaries and other emissaries such as the Portuguese and the Dutch, among them Iao Rodriguez (1561–1633), Jan Hendrik Donker Curtius (1813–1879), and Johann Joseph Hoffman (1805–

1878). Rodriguez included a section entitled *Meirei-hō no samazama na teido ni tsuite* (Regarding various levels of the imperative) in his 1608 *Arte da linguoa de Iapan* (Japanese language arts). He did not give names to the levels, but rather illustrated them by examples associated with relationships and contexts. Arranged on a scale of least polite to most polite, they included the following forms of *ageru* 'give', most of which are no longer seen or heard today:

1. *agai, ageyo*
2. *agesashime*
3. *agesai*
4. *agesasemase*
5. *agerarei*
6. *oageare*
7. *oagearao*
8. *agesaserarei*
9. *oagenasarei*
10. *oagenasareu* (Rodriguez 1608, cited in Kojima 1998:62)

Rodriguez's explanation, such as it is, is set out in terms of grammatical person. The forms in (1) above, for example, are used for servants *(meshitsukai, geboku)*, while the forms in (3) are what parents use toward children, and so on.

Rodriguez's work is interesting for its parallels in later native analyses that took grammatical person as their starting point (Kojima suggests that modern linguists who prefer the analysis of *keigo* through person hark back to Rodriguez [59–61]). But as Ōishi (1977:207) points out, the work of Rodriguez had little or no impact on Japanese grammarians—at least those who built the early analysis of *keigo* (and *kokugo*) in Meiji Japan, because his writings were unknown in the country. In fact, he was banished to Macao during Tokugawa Ieyasu's prohibition against Christianity (Nishida 1987:217). The Japanese really had little or nothing at stake in analysis of their own language until two things happened.

First, Western influence made linguistic difference salient. This does not mean that there had been no foreign influence in Japan until Matthew C. Perry's arrival in Uraga Bay in 1853. Obviously, Chinese influence in Japan over the centuries had been extensive. According to Nishida, there is mention of *keigo* in the historical record of interchange with China. But contact with China was primarily a matter of importation of written artifacts into Japan, and there was little effort on the part of the Chinese either to learn or to analyze the Japanese language. The situation changed, however, with Perry's arrival in Tokyo and the onset of industrialization.

Second, a system of universal education became a priority. Both Western influence and the need for universal education became critical in the Meiji period.

The Seeds of Change

The impact of Western intellectual tradition on the analysis of *keigo*, according to Miller, actually derives from the writing of Basil Hall Chamberlain, who called Meiji Japanese grammarians' attention to the system of speech levels. Miller observes that Chamberlain's 1888 statement, "It seems advisable to gather together under one heading all the leading manifestations of a habit of speech, without proper mastery of which it is impossible to speak Japanese with any approach to correctness," elicited a profound response from the leading figures in late Meiji and early Taisho Japanese language scholarship (Miller 1971:609). Scholars who were in the vanguard of *keigo* study often approached their subject by romanticizing it: "*Keigo* is a refined custom of deference for us Japanese" (Yamada Yoshio). "*Keigo* is a manifestation of the thoughtfulness *(omoiyari)* in (our) national character; it is a very precious thing" (Matsushita Daizaburō) (both cited in Ōishi et al. 1983:61).[1] *Keigo* figures prominently in the grammatical analysis that was part of linguistic standardization in Meiji Japan. Since the late nineteenth century the Japanese have speculated about the nature of *keigo* and tied it in various ways to accounts of Japanese grammar.

Even as the analysis of *keigo* was being carried out in Meiji Japan, the terminology of analysis was being invented. Whether that terminology was borrowed whole cloth from analysis of Western languages (e.g., using person) or was manufactured from Chinese morphology by native grammarians, it is indisputable that *keigo* posed special problems, as it represented a class of linguistic forms heretofore unencountered in the West. The history of *keigo* study demonstrates the process of the construction of linguistics itself in Japan. No grammarian remained untouched by Western theory, but Western theory alone was unequal to the task of untangling *keigo*.

The Meiji Surge in *Keigo* Study

Tsujimura (1992:112), in examining the history of *keigo* studies, contends that there have been three basic theoretical approaches to the analysis of *keigo*: according to (1) person *(ninshō)*, to (2) meaning *(imi)*, or to (3) target *(taishō)*. These three provide a frame for the history of *keigo* studies.

ANALYSIS OF *KEIGO* THROUGH UNDERLYING PERSON

The first systematic description of *keigo* appeared in 1892 (Meiji 25) with Mitsuhashi's *Hōbunjō no keigo* (Vernacular *keigo*). As Nishida (1987) observes, the influence of Western grammar is immediately evident in Mitsuhashi's reliance on the categories of person for defining two basic *keigo* categories: *tashō-keigo* (other-reference *keigo*) and *jishō-keigo* (self-reference *keigo*):

- *Tashō-keigo:* When self *(onore)* respects the person s/he is talking to *(ni-ninshō* 'second person') or some person(s) who come up in the conversation *(san-ninshō* 'third person'), these forms are used in regard to that person or any things, behavior, etc. that pertain to them. Examples: *'kimi'* (you), *'on-koromo'* (clothes), *'tamau'* (grant), *'zasu'* (sit), etc.

- *Jishō-keigo:* When one respects the person one is talking to (second person) or some person(s) who come up in the conversation (third person), these forms are used in regard to self *(jiko)* or any things, behavior, etc., that pertain to self. Examples: *'yatsugare'* (I), *'tatematsuru'* (offer), *'haberi'* (attend), *'-sōrō'* (copular form). (Mitsuhashi 1892, cited in Nishida 1987:230)[2]

Tashō-keigo is similar but not identical to what came later to be known as *sonkeigo,* and *jishō-keigo* is similar but not identical to what came later to be known as *kenjōgo.* The terms *tashō-keigo, jishō-keigo,* and *ni/san-ninshō* were coined at the time in order to translate the Western concepts of grammatical person and reference *(shō* is the same morpheme throughout, meaning something like "call" or "evoke"). Mitsuhashi was the first, but certainly not the last, to rely on the categories of person for analyzing these forms (Tsujimura 1992:113). At least four other grammarians, following Mitsuhashi, relied on person for their analysis. They include Yamada Yoshio (1924) whose *keigoron* 'keigo theory' explained *keigo* as a grammatical phenomenon. This is significant, Tsujimura (1992:31–32) points out, because an ongoing debate centered on whether *keigo* was a grammatical *(bumpō)* or lexical/semantic *(goi)* phenomenon. Other scholars who followed the person-oriented lead were Ekoyama (1943), Ishizaka (1951, 1957), and Tsujimura himself, a prolific scholar of *keigo* studies.

For his own approach, Tsujimura (1992) takes as a point of departure his 1963 work, *Keigo no bunseki ni tsuite* (Regarding the analysis of *keigo*), in which he followed Tokieda (1941) in drawing a central distinction between *sozai-keigo* 'referent *keigo*' and *taisha-keigo* 'addressee *keigo*'. My translations of these terms echo contemporary Western linguistic theory. Here is Tsujimura's definition of just what Tokieda meant by these terms in 1941:

- Referent *keigo (sozai-keigo) Keigo* with a connection to the material within the expression

  (1) Higher-ranking subject *(jōi-shutaigo)* (= *keishō* 'honorific titles'). *Keigo* that raises the status of or indicates respect for the grammatical subject's *(shutai)* action(s) and/or condition(s). Usually used in regard to the people and things that are made referents for the topic or those included in the expression. Typically, this is what is called *sonkeigo.*

  (2) Lower-ranking subject *(kai-shutaigo)* (= *kenshō* 'humble titles'). Language that lowers the status of or humbles the subject's actions and/or condition(s).

Usually used in regard to the people and things that are made referents for the topic or those included in the expression. Typically, this is what is called *kenjōgo*.

(3) Beautified language *(bika-go)* (= *bishō* 'beautified titles'). Language that beautifies the material within the expression. Usually called *teineigo*. Most of the time it is used with the object's *(taisha)* awareness, but there are also occurrences where this is not absolutely the case.

• Addressee *keigo* (respect titles). Shows a feeling of respect for the receiver of the expression *(hyōgen-juyō-sha)*. Different from referent *keigo* in that one must infer the addressee *(taisha)*. (Tsujimura 1992:88–89)[3]

This is the first time that *bikago* (or *bika-hyōgen* 'beautifying expressions') was used as a separate category and specialized term for *keigo;* the category was picked up later by Ōishi and is often recognized as a discrete kind of *keigo* even today. Tsujimura (1992) has not abandoned his 1963 analysis and illustrates how it compares to the more generally recognized categories of *teineigo, sonkeigo,* and *kenjōgo* in Figure 2.

From the modern perspective, it is interesting that the debate over where within grammar *keigo* should be analyzed took place even before the rise of structuralism, let alone the debates within generative theory as to at what level of the grammar various phenomena were handled. Japanese accounts do not, by and large, search for deeper theoretical issues in choosing among competing analyses. Rather, the Japanese analyses demonstrate the Sino-Confucian

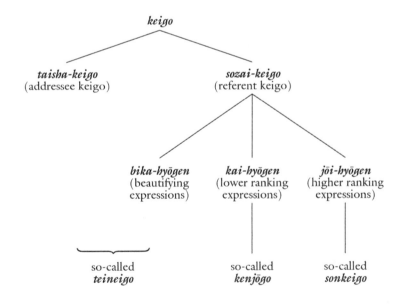

Figure 2. Tsujimura's (1992:227) juxtaposition of his 1963 analysis with the three most widely recognized categories of keigo *today—teineigo, kenjōgo,* and *sonkeigo.*

tradition of cataloguing, re-cataloguing, and detailed taxonomy. Concern within the Japanese academy seems to lead inexorably to the question of how wide to cast the net of *keigo*. Early analyses focused their efforts on establishing a technical vocabulary for research, although even at this stage one can foresee the question of just what these terms refer to arising.

ANALYSIS OF *KEIGO* THROUGH MEANING

By "analysis through meaning," Tsujimura apparently means that description of language is articulated through the language of the experience of politeness (for lack of a better word). This approach took people's understanding of how social relationships work and used its vocabulary to describe *keigo*. Part of the problem in translating the development of *keigo* study, as well as the structures to which social studies of Japan often refer, is capturing the useful nuances of the lexicon. Meiji linguistic scholars were faced with the daunting task of using a Western instrument (linguistic theory, such as it was) to delineate a phenomenon that had had no place in descriptions of language until that time. (This problem has not been entirely eradicated in contemporary theory.) The range of vernacular terms, as well as terms that could be (and were) coined using Chinese morphology, is impressive; the search for a metavocabulary for description was very much a part of *keigo* studies during Meiji and beyond.

Yoshioka's (1906) *Nihon kōgohō* (Grammar of spoken Japanese) presents the first systematic book-length study of *keigo*, according to Tsujimura. Employing a term that combines the morphology of *sonkei* 'respect' and *kenjō* 'humility', *keiken-dōshi* 'honorific-humble-verb(s)', Yoshioka divided verbs into three categories: (1) *dōsa o uyamatte iu* 'saying/voicing the action respectfully', (2) *dōsa o herikudatte iu* 'saying/voicing the action humbly', and (3) *sonzai o teinei ni iu* 'saying/voicing the existence politely'. Although Yoshioka's analysis itself did not catch on, this three-way division is the basis for the modern tripartite analysis of *keigo* into *sonkeigo* 'honorific', *kenjōgo* 'humble', and *teineigo* 'formal'. It also appealed to other scholars. Uchiyama Kaoru (1928) proposed a similar three-way division of meanings into *sonkei, kenjō*, and *teichō* (the first two are the familiar honorific and humble; the last is translated here as "courteous"); and Hashimoto Shinkichi (1935), whose forum as professor at Tokyo University made him an influential teacher of teachers and contributor to textbooks that included *keigo*, presented another three-way division defining forms as *sonkei-suru iikata* 'way(s) of speaking that indicate respect', *kenson-suru iikata* 'way(s) of speaking that indicate humility', and *teinei ni iu iikata* 'way(s) of speaking that indicate politeness/care'.

Tsujimura suggests that Hashimoto's position as an educator led to the eventual adoption of this particular model in such Mombushō (ministry of education) generated textbooks as *Chūtō bumpō—bungohen kōgohen* (Middle

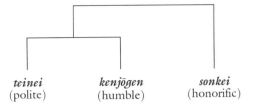

Figure 3. Saeki's (1953) presentation of keigo *categories as a successive subdivision (cited in Kojima 1998:14). Note the absence of names for the higher nodes.*

teinei   kenjōgen   sonkei
(polite)   (humble)   (honorific)

school grammar—Written language and spoken language) (Tsujimura 1992:112–113). The final subdivision of *keigo* into two groups with three subdivisions was taken by Saeki (1953) in a grammar for high school use (Kojima 1998:14). Saeki's presentation of *keigo*, endorsed by the Mombushō and promulgated in the educational system, is the now familiar model represented in Figure 3. Although Saeki's system arose from what Tsujimura calls analysis of *keigo* through meaning, it cannot be said that it represents Japanese people's understanding today. Hashimoto's approach is taken by the *kokugo* to be grammar-driven, according to Tsujimura, and Saeki's adaptation is a starting point. But most contemporary accounts are much more interested in what the category *keigo* encompasses than in where *keigo* belongs in the grammar. Thus, Tsujimura's third categorical basis, target, creeps into most contemporary analyses of *keigo*.

ANALYSIS OF *KEIGO* THROUGH TARGET

The third and final approach that Tsujimura recognizes takes as its point of departure the target of respect *(keii no taishō)*. The earliest proponent of such an analysis was Mitsuya Shigematsu in a 1902 paper entitled "Kokugo ni tokuyū na bun no san-tai" (Three types of special sentences in Japanese) and a 1908 book called *Kōtō Nihon bumpō* (Advanced Japanese grammar). In *Kōtō Nihon bumpō*, Mitsuya proposed four categories (and four new terms) for describing *keigo:*

1. *Sonta-keigo* 'respect-for-other(s) *keigo*'
   Sonta-keigo, which indicates respect for the other, is used to indicate that respect for the other as subject, the other's belongings, actions, or state

2. *Jihi-keigo* 'self-humbling *keigo*'
   Jihi-keigo humbles the self *(jiko)* as subject, the self's belongings or actions

3. *Kankei-keigo* 'relational *keigo*'
   Kankei-keigo demeans anything related to the self's actions

4. *Taiwa-keigo* 'conversational *keigo*'
   Taiwa-keigo, in order to indicate respect for the listener(s) *(chōsha)*, makes language more careful/courteous *(teinei)*. (Mitsuya 1908, cited in Tsujimura 1992:117–118)[4]

Mitsuya's contemporary Matsushita Daizaburō focused on preparing grammars for the wave of foreign students (primarily from China) coming into Japan (Nishida 1987:234). In 1901 Matsushita produced a volume entitled *Nihon zokugo bumpō* (Colloquial Japanese grammar),[5] in which he joins other grammarians in utilizing the overarching term *"taigū"* (rank), in this case to cover three categories, one of which is subdivided.

> *songū* 'respectful/honorific treatment'
> *shutai-songū* 'honorific treatment of subject'
> *kyakutai-songū* 'honorific treatment of object'
> *taisha-songū* 'honorific treatment of listener'
> *higū* 'humble treatment'
> *futeigū* 'negative treatment' (Matsushita 1901, cited in Tsujimura 1992:118)

The morpheme *-gū* in all of these terms means something like 'treat, deal, receive'. I take this as one early indicator that Japanese grammarians recognized very early on that a satisfactory analysis of *keigo* was not going to come out of consideration only of linguistic elements.

Categorical Issues

While government-sanctioned textbooks and the popular press might present the phenomenon of *keigo* as an incontrovertible matter today, there is still a great deal of disagreement in Japanese linguistic circles over just how to designate the Japanese forms reflecting politeness. This, in turn, has always been an issue that accompanies questions about what should be included in Japanese polite language. While Mitsuhashi was analyzing *keigo* and cataloguing its various forms, Okada (1900) was addressing the topic of *taigū-hō* 'the grammar of rank', which he divided into five categories:

- *keigohō* 'honorific language'

    When speaking to a superior *(meue no hito)*, language that shows one's respect *(sonkei)* for everything that has to do with that person

    Examples: *onamae* 'name', *go-ryōshin* 'parents'
- *kengohō* 'humble language'

    When speaking to a superior, language that shows one's humility *(kenson)* for everything that has to do with oneself

    Examples: myself, my wife, my house (hovel)
- *gōgohō* 'haughty language'

    When speaking to an inferior, language that shows one's disdain *(keibetsu)* for everything that has to do with the other

    Example: *konata* (for oneself)

Keigo in Kokugogaku

- *higohō* 'vulgar language'

When speaking to an inferior *(meshita)*, language that shows one's disdain for everything that has to do with that person

Examples: *sono kata* (for the other person), *aitsu* (for outsiders)

- *heigohō* 'common/ordinary/neutral language'

When speaking to someone equal to oneself, language that does not show any hint of respect, humility, or disdain for anything that has to do with that person or oneself

Examples: *ware* (for oneself), *chichi-haha* (for people's parents). (Okada 1900, cited in Tsujimura 1992:132)[6]

According to Tsujimura, Okada's work marks the introduction of the term *taigū*, which became popular as a technical term, went out of fashion, and then came back again after the Pacific War in the analysis of *taigū-hyōgen*, the preferred technical expression of many contemporary linguists. There has been continuing speculation over the relationship between *keigo* proper (which is usually taken to encompass *sonkeigo*, *kenjōgo*, and *teineigo*), and the range of linguistic and paralinguistic behaviors that touch on *keigo* in some fashion *(taigū-hyōgen)*.

In this meaning, it is appropriate to subsume the entire honorific-humble class *(keihitō)* under the appellation *"taigū-hyōgen."* The word *"keigo,"* after all, is limited to those expressions that are used in regard to subjects who are regarded as higher ranking.

But that being said, in fact the class of *keigo* is not that easily limited. I think most people would have no quarrel with the notion that words such as *irassharu, mōshiageru, desu, masu*, and *okao* are to be regarded as *keigo*, but among personal pronouns such as *anatasama, anata, anta, otaku, kimi, omae*, and *kisama*, it is impossible to distinguish which is *keigo* and which is the opposite. It may be all right to say that *anatasama* is *keigo* while *kisama* is derogatory in the standard language, but one is hard pressed to answer when asked which is the neutral term. (Tsujimura 1992:50)[7]

This shifts the burden of definition to *taigū-hyōgen*, which is no less a challenge than *keigo*. Such are the arguments that underlie Japanese grammarians' continuing discussion of *keigo* taxonomy and the boundaries of classification.

In the sample of scholarship reviewed here, the following Chinese and Japanese morphemes are combined and recombined in an effort to define *keigo:*

son 'respect'
    sonkei 'respect'
    songū 'respectful treatment'
    sonta 'respect for others'
    kenson 'humble'

kei, uyamau 'respect'
    sonkei 'respect'
    keigo 'respect language'

keii 'respectful'
   keshōi 'respect titles'
   uyamau 'respect'
ken 'humble'
   kenjō 'humble'
   kenson 'humble'
   kenshō 'humble titles'
hi, iyashimu 'humble,' 'demean'
   higū 'humble treatment'
   jihi 'self-demeaning'
   iyashimu 'demean'
ta 'other'
   tashō 'other person'
   sonta 'respect for another'
ji 'self'
   jishō 'self'
   jihi 'self-demeaning'
   jiko 'self'
gū 'treatment'
   taigū 'considerate treatment'
   songū 'respectful/honorific treatment'
   higū 'humble treatment'
   futeigū 'negative, inconsiderate treatment'
teinei 'polite, courteous'

Some of these caught on; others were limited in use to the scholars who coined them. It is a challenge in translation to distinguish the shades of meaning that characterize all these Japanese tropes for dealing with politeness—respect, humility, courtesy, deference, and so on. It is also a challenge to avoid placing them unwittingly in some sort of Western framework that carries with it intellectual baggage. Is *"taisha"* to be translated as 'other', 'listener', 'addressee', 'object', 'target', or something else? In the modern mind, the choice of translation creates an immediate and unwarranted commitment to some epistemology. Meiji grammarians owed an intellectual debt to Western grammar, but they were by no means bound by it. The struggle of these early scholars sheds light on the process of category reification and a priori nature of most terminology used in the social sciences, especially in linguistics.

Contemporary Japanese Linguists

After the Pacific War, Japanese grammarians seemed to come together for a brief time on their analysis of and terminology for referring to *keigo*. From approximately 1950 onward, grammarians adhered to Saeki's analysis of *keigo* as a three-part system and were consistent in their use of the terms *sonkeigo, kenjōgo,* and *teineigo* to refer to these. There was at last a sense of continuity and completion in the analysis. This must have owed much to the fact that government policy for teaching *keigo* in the schools had to be settled and materials produced posthaste. The idea, however, that grammarians ever actually agreed is probably postmodern nostalgia. All, or almost all, *kokugo* scholars writing after the war take Saeki's analysis as their point of departure; yet, academics being what they are, and language being what it is, agreement on *keigo* was never meant to last. Even as the "unified theory" was established, speculation on *keigo* analysis and vocabulary began to expand once again.

Three modern linguistic accounts of *keigo,* all entitled simply *Keigo* (by Ōishi Hatsutarō 1975, by Minami Fujio 1987, and by Kikuchi Yasuto 1994), appeared approximately ten years apart and show the state of contemporary argument about Japanese (in general) and *keigo* (in particular) within the Japanese academy. The authors represent succeeding generations of Japanese linguistic thought: Ōishi was born in 1911, Minami in 1927, and Kikuchi in 1954. They espouse differing ideologies of language and illustrate the continuing lively interest in *keigo* and all its manifestations. They also demonstrate that discussion in Japan reflects different philosophical underpinnings from those of Western linguistics.

ŌISHI (1975): LOOSENING THE PARADIGM

Ōishi's (1975) *Keigo* is one of the most frequently cited works on the subject of honorifics. It takes as its point of departure the received analysis—the analysis that forms the basis for what is promulgated in the educational system—and fills in its particulars. Ōishi spent the bulk of his career as a resident scholar at the National Language Research Institute (Kokuritsu Kokugo Kenkyūjo). After the Pacific War, it took some time for the Japanese academic engine to start publishing again. Kindaichi Kyōsuke produced an important volume entitled *Nihon no Keigo* (Japan's *keigo*) (1959); likewise, Tsujimura Toshiki produced his *Gendai no Keigo* (Modern *keigo*) (1967). But Ōishi's book *Keigo* is a distillation of much of the research that had been carried out on *keigo* and was an attempt to present a unified account. This is hardly accidental; Ōishi was associated with a Ministry of Education think tank, and the ministry produced any number of position papers on language immediately following the war. Thus Ōishi, in keeping with the received story of *keigo,* divides it into:

Honorifics *(sonkeigo)*
Raise the status of the person who is the topic of discussion, regardless of whether that person is the addressee or some third party. [See Figures 4 and 5.] Used in speaking about the person him/herself under discussion, that person's location, or that person's behavior, character, or condition.[8]

Humble forms *(kenjōgo)*
Kenjōgo expresses respect for the other or the listener by lowering the status of (humbling) the self or self's side [See Figure 6.] [Ōishi 1975:89][9]

Polite language *(teineigo)*
Language that indicates an attitude of respect on the part of the speaker for the hearer [See Figure 7.] (Ōishi 1975:93)[10]

Figure 4. Ōishi's (1975:89) diagram for sonkeigo *that raises the status of the listener. Note that* wadai no hito *and* kikite *are the same (b).*

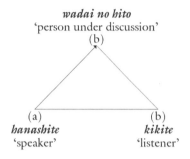

wadai no hito
'person under discussion'
(b)

(a)   (b)
hanashite   **kikite**
'speaker'   'listener'

Figure 5. Ōishi's (1975:89) diagram for sonkeigo *that raises the status of the person under discussion. Note that* wadai no hito *(c)* and kikite *(b) are different people.*

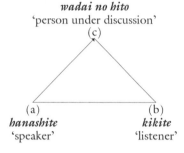

wadai no hito
'person under discussion'
(c)

(a)   (b)
hanashite   **kikite**
'speaker'   'listener'

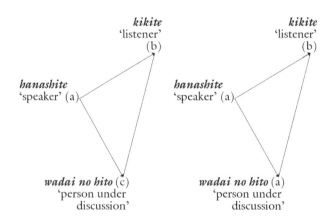

Figure 6. Ōishi's (1975:89) diagrams of two possible scenarios calling for the use of kenjōgo *'humble forms'. In the first, the speaker (a) has some connection to the person under discussion (c); in the second, the speaker (a) is identical to the person under discussion (a).*

Elegant language *(bikago)*
Language that indicates the quality or beauty of what is said. A consciousness of the listener may also underlie this, but essentially *bikago* serves to demonstrate the quality of the speaker's language. (Ōishi 1975:95)[11]

Ōishi's work is important because it represents the academic institutionalization of the received analysis of *keigo*. The scope of the four categories is given full definition. *Sonkeigo*, for example, includes not only the predicate paradigms recognized as honorific *(o/go-...ni naru, -[ra]reru, de irassharu)*, but also titles *(-sensei, -buchō, -san, -sama)*, such forms of deictic reference as *anata, donata, kochira, sochira, (kono) kata*, and the prefixes *o-* and *go-*. The second category, *kenjōgo*, includes not only the predicate paradigm recognized as humble *(o/go-...suru)*, but also such referents as *watakushi* 'I' and *temaedomo* 'we', self-deprecatory terms like *tonji* 'my son' and *keisai* 'my wife', and the humbling prefixes *hei-* and *gu-* (1975:88–91). The primary forms of *teineigo* are *desu, -masu*, and *de gozaimasu*, but other forms include *gozaimasu, yoroshii, -te mairimasu* (as in *ame ga futte mairimashita* 'it began to rain'). Clearly, forms such as *de gozai(masu), mairimasu, itasu*, and *mōsu* have been assigned to both *kenjōgo* and *teineigo*. Ōishi explains this by saying that they serve two different purposes (94).

It is hard to imagine a modern theoretical linguist tolerating the sort of category overlap that is allowed in the Japanese analysis. This is compounded in *bikago*, which is said to include the forms classed as *sonkeigo, kenjōgo*, or *teineigo* as they are used to demonstrate quality. It also includes such euphemisms as *naku naru* 'pass away' (as opposed to *shinu* 'die'), *yasumu* 'rest' (as opposed to *neru* 'sleep'), and *osumoji* 'sushi'. *Bikago* is interesting for its foreshadowing; the canonical categories of *sonkeigo, kenjōgo*, and *teineigo* are what Japanese learn in the educational system, but Japanese linguists have long struggled with the form-function distinction in *keigo*. *Sonkeigo* forms do not just serve to indicate difference in rank or respect. Coming to terms with the uses of *keigo* in actual discourse is a central problem in analysis. Ōishi solves this with the inclusion of a third kind of *keigo*, whose function is simply to sound elegant/cultured/educated. This function of *keigo* confounds linguists, causing a proliferation of categories in the *keigo* taxonomy.

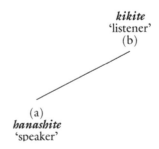

kikite
'listener'
(b)

Figure 7. *Ōishi's (1975:93) diagram of the relationship between speaker and other in using* teineigo.

(a)
hanashite
'speaker'

In a discussion of *"agame no hyōgen"* (expressions of respect), Ōishi demonstrates a typical strategy for distinguishing between linguistic form and function. *Agame* is a word whose meaning is close to 'reverence', but as a technical term it will be translated here as 'respect'. Clearly struggling for a vocabulary to define the governing principles of *keigo*, Ōishi, like others writing about *keigo*, feels free to invent a new idiom, and this freedom of invention is what distinguishes the various accounts one from another. This may be a reflex of the personal nature of Japanese academic writing and of the influence of the Confucian tradition. But my point is that what is going on is primarily a struggle over taxonomy, and that includes the question of what to call the twists and turns in that taxonomy. The Japanese progression of taxonomies for *keigo* is every bit as telling about intellectual ideology as are Western exchanges over the existence of universal grammar. Scholars' disagreement about technical vocabulary offers a window on what is really at stake—a commitment to view the world in one way or another. The range of rhetoric that has been used to describe *keigo* points up changes in both the Japanese consciousness of how society functions and the role of language in relation to that society.

Within, *'agame no hyōgen'*—"This is after all the primary reason for using *keigo*. Whom does one respect?"—he distinguishes four sources of respect:

- Respecting *(agameru)* rank *(chii)* or ability *(nōryoku)*

  One uses *keigo* when talking to or about those people one respects either because they occupy a high social rank or because they possess extraordinary ability or credentials.

- Respecting those who are dominant *(yūi)*

  One uses *keigo* when talking to or about people one respects because they are in a dominant position.

- Respecting those to whom one is indebted *(onkei o ataeru)*

  One uses *keigo* when talking to or about people one respects because one is indebted.

- Respect for humanity *(ningen no sonchō)*

  One uses *keigo* in order to show respect for the other when that feeling comes from a respect for humanity.[12]

What marks this description, in contrast to Minami or Kikuchi, is the salience of hierarchy. But there are other factors in addition to hierarchy:

2. Expression(s) of difference *(hedate)*
   - Lack of courtesy *(bu-sahō)*, familiarity *(shitashimi)*
   - Failure to appear at an arranged meeting (for marriage)
3. Expression(s) of formality *(aratamari)*
   - Language for public circumstances *(ōyake no ba)*
   - Difference/formality in the service of respect *(agame)*

4. Expression(s) of dignity *(igen)*, decorum *(hin'i)*, disdain *(keibetsu)*, sarcasm *(hiniku)*
   - *Keigo* used out of a sense of superiority *(yūetsukan)*
   - Women prefer *keigo*

5. Expression(s) of closeness *(shin'ai)*
   - Closeness rather than respect *(sonkei)*
   - One more thing

   [There follows a citation from a novel by Dazai Osamu called *Shayō* (The setting sun) in which family members use *keigo* toward one another, and the mother, as a model for her children, toward herself.] It seems certain that there are not many places where the mother says *"nasatte..."* about herself these days.... But here we have a household in which the position of the parents is taken as absolute, and the expression of respect is shown by the parents themselves. (from Ōishi 1975:58–70)[13]

Ōishi's strong appeal to tradition ties him firmly to the prewar generation of scholars. But his nostalgia is also part and parcel of his inclusion of factors such as *onkei* 'indebtedness' as determinants of respect. "Whom does one respect?" There is less concern for what *keigo* is than for what triggers it. Many Japanese linguists attempt to catalogue the contexts of *keigo* usage as *taigū-hyōgen*. So although Ōishi is not a linguist who emphasizes *taigū-hyōgen* or sees *taigū-hyōgen* as the ultimate question for *keigo*, this work indicates that far less about *keigo*'s function is taken for granted than it was when the primary object of inquiry was the mere forms of *keigo*.

MINAMI (1987): OPENING THE PARADIGM

A leading contemporary Japanese *keigo* theorist and, like Ōishi, a career resident scholar at the government National Language Research Center, Minami's work was instrumental in moving the discussion of *keigo* firmly toward the more general phenomenon of *taigū-hyōgen* 'expressions of consideration'. Minami begins by addressing the question of what can be included under the umbrella of *keigo no kan'i* 'the range of *keigo*', and he casts his net very wide indeed. He does this by creating a distinction between form *(keishiki)* and content *(naiyō)*, producing the classification system seen in Table 3.

Keigo in its narrowest sense is limited to A, according to Minami—that is, specialized language that conveys respect, humility, or politeness. But there is more to the story than this. Using his feature analysis to gather under one umbrella the varied analyses of *keigo* to date, he suggests that B, C, and D are identical to what Ōishi (1975) called *keii-hyōgen* (respect expressions). What traditional Japanese language analysis calls *taigū-hyōgen*, he says is D, while *taigū-kōdō* refers to E and F. The broad definition of *keigo*, then, according to Minami, takes in the entire range of B through F, and can be typed according

Table 3. Minami's feature grid for keigo no kan'i *'the range of* keigo' *(Minami 1987:15). Minami suggests that all* keigo-*like behavior can be characterized by form of expression and content of expression. He assigns plus and minus features to each kind of characteristic and the various subcategories fall out by design.*

	Form of Expression			Content	
	Exclusive linguistic elements	Ordinary linguistic expressions	Nonlinguistic expressions	Honorific, humble, polite, etc.	Coarse, arrogant, etc.
A	+	–	–	+	–
B	+	–	–	+	+
C	+	+	–	+	–
D	+	+	–	+	+
E	+	+	+	+	–
F	+	+	+	+	+

to form: *gengo-hyōgen* 'linguistic expressions', *hi-gengo-hyōgen* A 'nonlinguistic expressions A' (those with a connection to spoken language), and *hi-gengo-hyōgen* B 'nonlinguistic expressions B' (those with no apparent connection to spoken language, such as clothing, facial expression, etc.) (Minami 1987:17).

"Linguistic expressions" take as a starting point the four narrowly recognized categories from Ōishi, but expand to comprise no fewer than twenty-two varieties:

1. *Sonkeigo.*

2. *Kenjōgo.*

3. *Teineigo.*

4. *Bikago.*

5. Abusive or derisive language: What was previously called "minus *keigo*," including -*kusaru* 'stinks/smacks of', -*yagaru* (derogative modal), *kozoume* (derogative reference for young boys), *aitsu* (derogative reference; 'that slob'), etc.

6. Arrogant expressions: these used to be included in "minus *keigo*," including -*te tsukawasu* 'I'll let you do', -*chōdai suru (arigataku chōdai shiro)* (humbly receive; 'Take it, and be thankful to me!'), *aresama* 'dear me', etc.

7. Various forms of address outside those offered thus far, especially which factors enter into the equation and under what circumstances. These include: whether to say (or write) given-plus-family name, just family name, or just given name.

8. Kinds of interjections and responses, including *naa, na, nee, ne, oi, oioi, kora, korakora, moshimoshi, anō, ūn, ee,* etc.

9. Kinds of final particles and response particles, such as *naa, na, nee, na, ka, kai, wa, ze, zo, no, yo, saa, sa.*

10. Choice of vocabulary in general, including choice among Japanese, Sino-Japanese, and borrowed vocabulary, and choice between spoken vocabulary and written vocabulary.

11. Whether the structure of the sentence is to be spoken style or written style also becomes an issue, such as the choice between *Kinō wa asa roku-ji ni okite, T-chō ni dekaketa* and *Kinō wa asa roku-ji ni oki, T-chō ni dekaketa* (both 'yesterday I woke up at six o'clock and went over to town').

12. Appropriate use of commands, demands, prohibition, invitations, and the like, including choice among the imperative, verbal *-te* alone, *nasai -te chōdai, -te ku-dasai* ('please do…'), etc.

13. Length of sentence.

14. Whether to use sentences with omitted elements or to use fully formed sentences without omitted elements.

15. Whether to use indirect, euphemistic speech style or direct speech style.

16. Whether to use expressions that humble oneself or not.

17. Similar to the foregoing, whether or not to say some words (e.g., preliminary remarks) or take note of what speaker is going to say.

18. There are units bigger than the sentence or vocabulary, and these also have relevance in discussions of *taigū-hyōgen*.

19. On second look, there are also problems surrounding the form of expression— that is to say, elements of sound or superficial elements, such as the choice among *-chau, -chimau,* and *-te shimau* (all 'end up doing').

20. Whether to use spoken style or written style. This question differs from (11) in that it refers to the medium to be used, not the choice among linguistic forms themselves: whether to carry out a task by telephone or letter, for example.

21. It is thought that there are also situations where choice of linguistic form (dialect) is systematic, as well as situations where one segment (for example, pronunciation alone) is systematic, and there are various levels of difference among these.

22. A more general problem is that of whether one talks or not (writes or not) to a counterpart, in other words whether to carry on linguistic communication at all. (Minami 1987:17–26)[15]

Nonlinguistic expressions with a connection to spoken language, include:

23. Response sounds used in speech, such as the in-drawn breath with tongue against front teeth that is typical [Minami says] of men's speech.

24. Formal, stiff tone(s), informal tone(s), the strong tone of an angry voice, etc.

25. Laughter that accompanies conversation.

26. Things in/of the face that accompany talk, such as frowns, distortions of the mouth, and the like.

27. Eye movement.

28. Movement of the arm(s), hand(s), head, and the like accompanying speech.

29. The way physical distance is established between those involved in speech.

30. The way intervals are spaced in speech.

31. What will be the medium of communication?

32. The form/type of script characters, the style of characters, the character script itself, etc.

33. The form of copies, including if this is done in horizontal or vertical style, typeset, or freehand.

34. The means for copying, as in whether to type, write, use a word processor, and so on.

35. Material(s) for copying: whether to use a brush, a ballpoint pen, or a pencil. (Minami 1987:26–29)[16]

Nonlinguistic expressions that have nothing to do with the spoken word include:

36. Clothing.

37. Whether or not to put things on [take things off] the body [hats, gloves, shoes, makeup, beard or mustache, etc.].

38. The endless other things needed to keep oneself neat.

39. Things that do not accompany linguistic expressions but appear on the face, such as frowns, sideways looks, glares, and the like.

40. Forms of laughter that appear without accompanying linguistic expressions, such as smiles of recognition across a distance, snorts, scoffs, and so on.

41. Attitude, manners, behavior.

42. The act of letting others go first, seen when entering and leaving a room or getting on and off transportation.

43. Etiquette at mealtime.

44. Hospitality to clients or guests.

45. Various behavior(s) when associating with others. (Minami 1987:29–30)[17]

Minami is certainly on to something in recognizing the interrelatedness of all of the sign systems involved in the foregoing communicative behavior. He might easily be headed in the direction of saying that there is no space in Japan that is non-*keigo*, but that would be a decidedly antiformalist tack to take (see Chapter 5). From the formal linguistic standpoint, one can only ask what is not *keigo* in response to such a broad interpretation.

The influence of modern Western scholarship is evident not only in the feature analysis, but also in Minami's incorporation of *okurite* 'sender' and *ukete* 'receiver' into his analysis of *keigo*, where earlier analyses had used the terms *"hanashite"* and *"kikite."* Minami suggests that three characteristics of *keigo* should always be taken into consideration:

1. There is a deference/solicitude *(koryo)* on the part of the sender *(okurite)* for/ toward some object of concern *(taishō)*.

2. This deference/solicitude is usually mirrored in a kind of "appreciative attitude" on the part of the sender.

3. Such a deference and an appreciative attitude are basic; there is a concern *(hōka-teki taido)* for how one treats the object of discussion, and there is a proper use of expressions to reflect the different ways that one could treat the object. (Minami 1987:66–67)[18]

Just what constitutes "concern"—especially whether it is a conscious or an unconscious process—is not clear. Crucial is the notion that speakers have particular relationships with the people around them, both in the speech event and in the narrative event, and that language use hinges on these. This notion is reinforced when Minami defines the factors or elements that enter into deference. Those are:

Participant(s) *(sankasha)*
Sender(s) *(okurite)*
Receiver(s) *(ukete)*
    Direct (primary) receiver(s) *(matomo no ukete)*
    Peripheral receiver(s) *(waki no ukete)*
Concerned party/parties *(kankeisha)*
Agent(s)/initiator(s) of action *(dōsashu)*
Patient(s)/recipient(s) of action *(hidōsashu)*
Content of communication *(komyunikeishon no naiyō)*
Circumstances *(jōkyō)*
(Minami 1987:68)[19]

The parallels with Comrie's (1976) analysis of speaker-addressee, speaker-referent, and speaker-bystander honorifics are striking, as are the parallels with Brown and Levinson's (1987) analyses of politeness phenomena. In an attempt similar to theirs at classifying politeness phenomena in Japanese, Minami defines six functions of *keigo* in communication. Calling it *keigo no hataraki* 'the work of *keigo*', he suggests that *keigo* functions in:

1. Initiation (or discontinuation) of social relationship(s)

2. Maintenance/upkeep of social relationship(s)

3. Maintenance/upkeep of social status

4. Conveying important/essential information

5. Coercion, appeals to the addressee, and the like

6. Expression of aesthetic value(s) [which may, after all, be the primary purpose of all *keigo*, as all *keigo* use has an element of this] (Minami 1987:136–138)[20]

Minami contrasts with Ōishi in bringing a wide range of linguistic behavior under the *keigo* umbrella. Although Ōishi recognized that language that was the linguistic opposite of *keigo*, which he termed *hikeigo*, could not be ignored in grammar, he nonetheless drew a strict line between *keigo* proper and other uses of forms that serve as *keigo*. Unfortunately, by allowing *bikago* into the general category of *keigo*, both Ōishi and Minami may have let the camel's nose into the tent. This is not because *bikago* is the opposite of *keigo*—it is not—but because of the repetition and redundancy to which it gives rise. Once an element appears in multiple categories, the lid is off the category constraint, as is clearly seen in Minami's work. Principled though he may be, he has moved from classifying linguistic forms to cataloguing linguistic functions.

KIKUCHI (1994): ABANDONING THE PARADIGM

Kikuchi represents very forcefully the view of many modern young Japanese linguists that the governing object of study ought not to be *keigo* as such but rather the overarching category of *taigū-hyōgen*. Without an understanding of how *keigo* fits into that broader classification, one cannot account for *keigo* itself. But what is *keigo*? In response to this question, Kikuchi says:

> It is often said that *keigo* are expressions that demonstrate "respect" *(keii)* or "politeness" *(teineisa)*, but that respect is not simply limited to "heartfelt respect" *(kokoro kara no keii/sonkei no nen)*. For example, the common pattern is the case where an employee speaks about the company president within the office when s/he is aware of the surroundings, s/he uses *keigo*. Once having left the office, however, s/he does not usually use *keigo* when speaking about the boss. It is hard to imagine that this sort of employee has "heartfelt respect." There are those who recognize that it does not suffice to say that *keigo* are expressions of respect.
>
> But even in the case just mentioned, it seems reasonable to say that the act of using *keigo* at the office shows at the very least one kind of "respect" toward the president. As we have seen before, it is not simply a matter of having a grasp of vertical relationships, and there is always the possibility if one doesn't want to use *keigo* to choose not to use it (with the knowledge, of course, of the social sanction that may accompany such behavior). It can also be said that, ruling out the foregoing choice and using *keigo* to further one's aims is another kind of respect expression. To put it more theoretically, using *keigo* is an expression of one's aim to show respect, and in that sense *keigo* functions as one kind of expression of respect. In the end, it is "respect," but from the vantage point of the *taigū-hyōgen* mentioned earlier, this much more narrowly defined thing called *keigo* belongs under the rubric of *taigū-hyōgen* that carry a *"taigūteki imi"* (respectful meaning):
>
> 1. *"Ue"* (Raises the status of the person under discussion as "higher ranking");
> 2. *"Shita"* (Lowers the status of self's side as "lower ranking"). This can also be understood as "courtesy" = "politeness" + "formality";
> 3. *"Teinei"* (Extends "politeness toward listener[s]") (Kikuchi 1994:70–71)[21]

This would seem to indicate that Kikuchi has no quarrel with the three established structural categories that emerge from the Meiji tradition and in fact, his

Keigo in *Kokugogaku*

succeeding analysis takes these as givens. But Kikuchi's approach should resound with the Western functional school of linguistics because he insists that the function and not the structure of language is what must be accounted for. Functional linguistics starts from the social context and looks at how language both acts upon and is constrained by social context. It thus views speakers as agents who interact with the world by means of language. Speaking "like an employee," for example, is not a structural but a sociocultural question, and is as such open to negotiation. This is precisely Kikuchi's stance in his description of *keigo*. Speakers can certainly choose to use *keigo* or not, and part of being a Japanese speaker is knowing the repercussions of either option. Such information, Kikuchi says, is not a function of *keigo* but of *taigū-hyōgen*, the category that he inherits from his Meiji predecessors. What, then, are *taigū-hyōgen*? According to Kikuchi, "Basically, we call *taigū-hyōgen* those numerous expressions that say the same thing but that are used differently depending on how one regards the people and things that are the topic of the conversation; the listener; and the context....This *taigū* is basically the same as the *'taigū'* of 'That company treats (= pays) well' and 'executive compensation'" (Kikuchi 1994:19–21).[22]

I have elected to translate *taigū-hyōgen* as 'expressions of consideration' here in large part because of the vague nature of the Japanese word *taigū*. What I have tried to capture by using the word "consideration" is both this vagueness (still a valued trait in Japanese culture, including academia) and the focus on relationship rather than participants that is important in the Japanese analysis. Rampant Westernization notwithstanding, the Japanese still value very highly the ability to attune self to other(s). This theme emerges again and again in popular accounts of *keigo* (see Chapters 4 and 5), and it is not surprising that it forms the cornerstone of academic analyses of *taigū-hyōgen*.

That being said, Kikuchi's definition above, insofar as it attempts to set the structural stage for a functional analysis, is profoundly unsatisfying. Kikuchi offers no criteria for determining what it means to "say the same thing," a question that philosophical linguists have long wrestled with without reaching a satisfactory conclusion. In any event, *taigū-hyōgen* are divided into six "types" *(taipu)*, according, Kikuchi says, to their meaning:

1. Verticality *(jōge)*
2. Politeness ↔ roughness *(teinei ↔ zonzai-ranbō)*
3. Formality ↔ ease/crudeness/arrogance *(aratamari ↔ kudake/soya/sondai)*
4. Elegance ↔ vulgarity *(jōhin ↔ hizoku)*
5. Partiality *(kō-o)*
6. Benefaction *(onkei no juju)* (Kikuchi 1994: 24)[23]

The types, in turn, are governed by an array of "factors" *(fakutaa):*

I. Social factors

    A. Location as well as topic

1. Makeup of the location....Refers to the speaker, the listener (conversational partner), and third parties in that location (not the direct conversational partner but people who are within earshot).

2. Nature of the context....Usage is quite different depending on whether the context is written style or spoken style. Even though one may not use *keigo* in a particular spoken situation, one uses it when the context is written....It is not unusual to find such situations where the participant makeup is the same, but the language changes.

3. Topic. Those who make up the context (as well as their families and the like), but also third parties who may not be present.

B. Interpersonal relationships. The interpersonal relationships within the confines of A—"those who make up the context" or "people and things under discussion"—are a very important factor in language use.

1. Vertical relationships: Among interpersonal relationships, vertical relationships must surely be the single most important factor affecting language use.

2. Positional relationships....

   a. The position of settling debt/the position of incurring debt (benefactive relationships)...

   b. The position of holding authority/ the position of having to entrust authority to the other (authority/subordination relationships)...

   c. The position of strength (dominance)/the position of weakness (inferiority) (power relationships)...

   d. Seeming positions of settling debt/the position of incurring debt (pseudobenefactive relationships)...

   e. The position of having to be aggrandized up/position of having to aggrandize the other (pseudoauthority/subordination relationships)...

3. Relative familiarity....Needless to say, usage changes depending on whether the relationship is a close one, or an acquaintance who one does not know well, or someone one does not know because one has just been introduced.

4. In-group/out-group relationships

II. Psychological factors

A. Intention of consideration. The speaker has a grasp of and calculates social factors and uses *taigū-hyōgen* in accordance with them.

1. General intention of the consideration. Most generally speaking, the intentions underlying *taigū-hyōgen* are: "expressions of aggrandizement/ ordinary or average expressions/expressions that treat the other lightly," or "polite (polite, dignity-maintaining) expressions/ordinary or average expressions/malicious expressions"....Most work to convey the intention of "recognizing vertical relationships in language use," but...it is not un-

usual to find situations where the speaker's intention is "to dare not to follow conventions appropriate to vertical relationships."

2. Grasp of the "benefaction"....There are also situations where speakers' intentions are not in strict accordance only with "vertical relationships" but rather with "benefaction" or "power."

3. How relative distance in "familiar relationships" is understood....This depends on the speaker's intention regarding "degree of distance to be employed."

4. Grasp of *"uchi"* and *"soto."*

5. Special intentions....There are also *taigū-hyōgen* that might be chosen in those situations which serve to convey the intention of "some emotion or addition of color in sarcasm/meanness/jest and the like."

6. Situations in which speakers talk before considering any of these intentions.

B. More background factors.

C. Considered from the viewpoint of skill in expression and effective transmission. (Kikuchi 1994:30–57)[24]

It is illustrative to compare Kikuchi's taxonomies with Minami's. The major difference between the two appears to be at a more or less theoretical level—that is, what of *keigo* is a matter of structure and what is a matter of pragmatics. At a micro level, there is less to distinguish the two accounts. Both seem compelled to bring into the analysis of *keigo* all imaginable features of context that can possibly affect language use—speakers' intentions, medium (written versus spoken), relative position—distinguished by recognized categories within Japanese culture (*onkei* 'benefaction', *jōge* 'vertical', *ningen-kankei* 'interpersonal relationships', *uchi/soto* 'in-group/out-group')—and the like.

There are striking differences between Japanese and Western accounts of *keigo*. Such differences appear in the selection and cataloguing or classification of data, in the manner in which description is refined, in the place of theory in argumentation (for the Western researcher, all else hinges on this), and in the role of the observer or the theoretician. The procedures and concerns that the two sides consider acceptable tell a great deal about their respective intellectual traditions.

The story of *keigo* in the Japanese academy is in large part the story of a search for vocabulary. The Meiji scholars who embarked on the formal description of the Japanese language took most of their tools of analysis from translations of Western analytical terms, using words like *meishi* 'noun', *dōshi* 'verb', and *daimeishi* 'pronoun'. But they found no counterpart for *keigo* in the grammars they emulated, the descriptions of Latin, Greek, and vernacular languages that themselves clothed Western theories about the nature of language. Grammarians may have found neat parallels for nominal, verbal, pronominal, and other "traditional" elements of Western language in Japanese,[25] but *keigo* called for a good deal of innovation on the part of *kokugo* scholars. The development of *kokugo* grammar around *keigo* offers an opportunity for modern scholars to observe the development of a descriptive model unhampered (or at least less constrained) by the rigidities of already established theory.

In Japan the idea of *keigo* coalesced around its grammatical treatment which included nomenclature. But just as swiftly as questions of grammar and nomenclature seemed to have been settled, their analysis proved inadequate to grammarians, so that *keigo* analysis has continued to evolve. In large part this is because Japanese grammarians have never been of the notion that linguistic analysis should disassociate language from context. Contemporary pragmatics and semiotics probably have more in common with recent Japanese accounts than does either structural or generative linguistics. *Keigo* in particular strains any view of language that isolates form from context and function. From the Western perspective, however, Japanese analyses very often lack rigor; categories proliferate in the absence of a stated theoretical framework that might control speculation. Japanese scholars themselves offer no criteria by which they might be judged.

The theoretical accounts form the backdrop for an examination of *keigo* in Japanese culture and society. From the very beginning, Japanese grammarians' speculations on the epistemology of their enterprise have focused on the place of language (and *keigo*) in the formation of the nation *(kokka)*. There is an abiding concern for embedding language within a much larger picture of Japanese tradition and history, namely, what it means to be Japanese. From the outset, Japan has had a hybrid way of thinking about language that includes, among other things, a concern for the contextualization of the person vis-à-vis others. What often sounds like mystification on the part of Japanese scholars emerges from an intellectual tradition that sought to situate Japan in the world. That tradition includes not only the work of such scholars as Mori Arinori, Yanagita Kunio, and Mori Ōgai, but also that of *kokugo* scholars like those mentioned here.

All Japanese today have some consciousness of *keigo*. It is part of the *kokugo* grammar to which they are exposed as they make their way through the school system. Language—including *keigo*—is a frequent reason for sanction in everything from the *kurabu-katsudō* 'club activities' of junior high school to the job interviews of new college graduates. How can we characterize *keigo*'s place in Japanese society and culture? How does Japan argue about *keigo*'s role and meanings? What are the venues, both formal and informal, in which this discourse is carried out? What other aspects of Japanese society and culture come to play in arguments over *keigo*? What do Japanese people, the professional linguists and the ordinary citizens, profess to believe about their own language? The answers to such questions are possible only because *keigo* has joined the ranks of other grammatical phenomena as an immutable formal category. But countless questions remain and are being argued even as *keigo*'s interface with culture and society is negotiated and renegotiated.

CHAPTER 3

Inventing *Keigo:*
Standardization

There is increasing interest within contemporary linguistics in what Cameron (1995) has called "language intervention"—attempts on the part of outside agencies to affect speakers' linguistic behavior through overt commentary or instruction. Language intervention embraces everything from governmental policy to popular commentary. Language is fodder for editorializing of the sort practiced by professionals like William Safire in the United States and Suzuki Takao[1] in Japan. Yet it requires no particular expertise; even amateurs can participate—witness the comments of ordinary citizens whose opinions appear from time to time on the editorial pages of any newspaper, and now on the World Wide Web. To judge by Aristotle's *Art of Rhetoric,* intervention in linguistic matters is as old as humanity. As Cameron observes, questions of language are a time-honored field for contending arguments about the way the world ought or ought not to be.

Ultimately language intervention is about ideology. How do linguistic form and use tie to notions of the person and the social group? To ethnic identity? To socialization? To gender relations? To the nation-state? All of these have been the subject of inquiry by, for example, Atkinson and Errington (1990), Fairclough (1989, 1992, 1995), Schieffelin, Woolard, and Kroskrity (1998), and Kroskrity (2000). In the case of Japanese, little has been done that addresses language ideology directly, although the work of Kondo (1990), Bachnik and Quinn (1994), Maher and MacDonald (1995), and Gottlieb (1996) touches on it.

A particularly potent form of language intervention—and hence ideology— is called "standardization." In the traditional account, language standardization is simply a by-product of the formation of national identities. It is a natural utilitarian response of society to the perceived need to improve communication—large masses of people who are involved in economic activity must at least understand the standard even if they don't speak it themselves. In the revisionist account, standardization reflects the prevailing ideology and is one vehicle by which an elite maintains the power status quo. Access to language defines a "linguistic market" (Bourdieu 1991), a system of rewards and sanctions that endows particular forms of language with greater or lesser value. The political underpinnings of standardization are not at issue, but what standard language represents is. I am not sure that the traditionalist and the revisionist views on this question are completely incompatible. Certainly it is true that, at the turn of the twentieth century, Japan viewed standardization as a natural outgrowth of its development into a nation-state, but the twists and turns of language standardization in Japan represent far more than the relatively simple process of becoming a modern political entity.

Japan's case is marked by circumstances that identify its place in the world at the end of the nineteenth century. A foreign script (Chinese *kanji*) was in common use for writing a hybrid language *(kanbun* or *sōrōbun)* at the expense of any agreed-upon oral or written vernacular. Beginning with the Meiji Restoration, and through concerted governmental efforts, Japan did manage to come to a consensus on standards for language, including *keigo,* that, for better or for worse, still continue to be negotiated. *Keigo* is only one stage on which Japan's modernization is played out.[2] Script may be an even better gauge of the political and social questions that accompany language intervention in Japan.[3] But *kanji,* after all, were imported from China; *keigo* is native to Japanese. And *keigo* is also a spoken phenomenon first and foremost. So when arguments arise over the ability or inability of the Japanese population to cope with spoken language convention, *keigo* is always at the fore. When discussing what language reflects about individual character, upbringing, socialization, gender relations, and even ethnic identity, *keigo* is unparalleled in the burden it has been assigned. How it came to assume this role is to be found in the history of its standardization. (How it maintains it is the subject of Chapter 4.) The story of *keigo* tells much about how social institutions respond to change and, in the process, themselves undergo transformation. It can also tell how a society negotiates and renegotiates the ideals, values, and beliefs that language represents.

Meiji language reform: Standardization

Concerted intervention into language in Japan, including the conventions of *keigo,* begins with the Meiji Era's movement to standardization. The scholars who engineered the "story" of *keigo* (outlined in the previous chapter) had adapted the conviction, common among Western scholars, that linguistic sta-

Inventing *Keigo*

bilization is a precursor to modernization: "It is only civilization and culture that can bind together into one the parts of great community....A written literature, the habit of recording and reading, the prevalence of actual instruction, work yet more powerfully in the same direction; and when such forces have reached the degree of strength which they show in our modern enlightened communities, they fairly dominate the history of speech. The language is stabilized, especially as regards all those alterations which proceed from inaccuracy; local differences are not only restrained from arising, but are even wiped out, so far as the effect of education extends" (Whitney 1875:158).

Such western accounts were well known within Japanese intellectual circles and are reflected in the writing of such scholars as Ueda Kazutoshi (1867–1937), Hoshina Kōichi (1872–1955), and Tokieda Motoki (1900–1967). Ueda spent three and a half years as an exchange student in Germany (1890–1894) and returned to his native Japan deeply influenced by the Allgemeine Deutsche Sprachverein (German Language Society) and the notion of *Sprachnation* 'national language' (carried over to Japanese as *kokugo*) that he had learned about there (Lee 1996:118). In 1895 Ueda published a paper entitled *Hyōjungo ni tsukite* (Regarding standard language), in which he observed that, because advanced European countries like England, Germany, France, and Italy had in due course developed and established standard languages, it behooved Japan to nurture a beautiful, polished standard language as well. Ueda is credited with instigating the association of the term *"hyōjungo"* with Japanese, as well as with deciding that the Tokyo speech would serve as the standard, even before he was given responsibility for guiding governmental policy (Sanada 1991:91–92). He is also credited with having set up the first course of study in linguistics at the Imperial University. Among his graduates were Hoshina and Tokieda, who reflect the ethos of their mentor and age: "*Kokugo*, besides training the national character and cultivating quality in the citizen's spirit, is in and of itself a thing of immense influence" (Hoshina 1901:1).

But scholars had their work cut out for them. Until the middle of the nineteenth century, writing in Japan had matured around the representation of *kanbun*, a Sino-Japanese hybrid that had little to do with the spoken language(s) of Japan. In a break with the past whose importance cannot be overemphasized, a movement known as *gembun-itchi*, usually translated as 'unification of written and spoken styles', emerged in Meiji Japan to promote the representation of vernacular Japanese in writing, that is, to unify the written and spoken languages of Japanese. A core group of influential scholars succeeded in drawing attention to the hindrance that written Japanese posed to the accelerated spread of information, a crucial realization for the emerging Japanese state. The only solution, these scholars insisted, was to effect dramatic language reform in key areas (Twine 1991:74).

A precondition for the unification of written and spoken language was the absolute necessity of standardizing spoken Japanese grammar and usage. At the beginning of the Meiji period, 250 years of the Tokugawa policy of regional isolation had resulted in a society so highly segmented that dialects and stylistic variations flourished.[4] Members of the *gembun-itchi* movement saw the need for linguistic unification of the oral code *(kōgo)* as a prerequisite to any reform of the written one. The role of *keigo* in this *gembun-itchi* is not a large one, as there was no tradition of *keigo* analysis. Even the word *"keigo"* did not exist in Japanese until it appeared in the work of Natsume Sōseki and Mori Ōgai (*Nihongo hyakka daijiten* [1995]). At least intellectuals knew what *keigo* was; the morphology of *kei* 'honorific' and *go* 'language' is transparent. But the chronology presented in Chapter 1 shows that *keigo*'s analysis and its place in the Japanese linguistic canon were not yet established. Yamada's grammar of *keigo*, *Keigo-hō no kenkyū* (Research on the grammar of *keigo*), was not published until 1924. If *keigo* had any role in *gembun-itchi*, it was precisely because it was a spoken phenomenon, as worthy as any other aspect of the spoken language of being represented by script. In 1890 Mozume Takami produced a paper that offered seven arguments for the unification of spoken and written language, including the fact that "Japanese contains much *keigo*." But there was nothing like universal agreement on what was meant by Mozume's *keigo*, and its morphological inflections and paradigmatic analysis were terra incognita. The legacy of *keigo* had yet to be invented.

By the turn of the twentieth century, sufficient pressure had been brought to bear by those in favor of linguistic standardization that the Meiji government decided to establish a governmental body whose charge was the supervision of language reform. In 1899 the government commissioned a Kokugo Chōsakai (National Language Investigative Panel) to begin addressing questions of reform, but the first frontal assault on *kokugo* issues came under the purview of the Kokugo Chōsa Iinkai (National Language Research Council; hereafter Iinkai) established in 1902 within the Ministry of Education and led by Ueda Kazutoshi. Ivy (1995:75) comments on the politics that underlay the selection of Tokyo as the standard: "But what was to serve as the standard colloquial language that the written language was to reflect? Hundreds of dialects existed throughout the country; spoken Japanese was fragmented and various and bore the marks of locale. The state sought to contain this diversity by establishing a standard spoken Japanese, then bringing written Japanese closer to this colloquial standard. In language as in everything else, the power of the center determined the result: the dominant dialect of Edo gradually became the standard spoken language in Japan."

The ascendancy of Tokyo in the standardization process simplified many issues (though it continues to rankle even today in many parts of Japan) but by no means solved all the problems of smoothing out the language's rough edges. According to Twine (1991:71–72), for example, when language reform began there were no fewer than six forms of the copula in common use: *de gozaru, de gozarimasu, de arimasu, desu, de aru,* and *da. De gozaimasu* was already commonly used by the upper classes, and the need was felt for a form somewhere between it and the plain *da* or *de aru.* Early on in the reform movement, *de gozaru,* a form used by women of the pleasure quarters, was recommended and adopted by many writers. *De arimasu* also appeared in many works of popular fiction, but did not spread, Twine says, because it competed with the form *desu. De arimasu* was a more polite form of *de aru,* which, along with *da,* was used extensively outside the pleasure quarters by men and women of all ranks. *Da,* in fact, became the standard plain form in Tokyo speech after the Meiji Restoration. *Desu* marked the speech of townspeople (samurai and wealthy merchants) in the late Tokugawa period. Sanada (1991:86–88) remarks on the competition among these forms of the copula as they were used by popular novelists. In the third decade of Meiji (1887–1897), a succession of novels appeared that gave momentum to *gembun-itchi.* Within a two-year span, Futabatei produced a novel *Ukigumo* (Moving clouds [1887]), using *da,* and another work, *Nozue no kiku* (Chrysanthemums in the far-off fields [1889]), using *de arimasu,* while Yamada published *Kochō* (Butterflies [1889]), using *desu.* Two years later Ozaki's *Ninin nyōbō* (Two wives) used yet another form, *de aru.* According to Ozaki, *da* was too blunt and *de gozaimasu* too polite, while *de aru* carried a neutral tone. The *gembun-itchi* movement had begun.

The Iinkai was assigned four initial tasks:

• To investigate script reform, especially as regards adopting a phonetic (sound-based) script

• To conduct an investigation into adopting *gembun-itchi*

• To conduct an investigation into the phonemic structure of the language

• To conduct an investigation of dialects in order to create a dialect atlas and recommend a standard language *(hyōjungo)* (*Kokugogaku kenkyū jiten* 1977:31).[5]

In pursuit of the investigation of dialects, it did not take long for the Iinkai to embark on a major survey of spoken language, including polite language (Kokugo Chōsa Iinkai 1903). The survey methodology used by these early scholars was the same as that used to create dialect atlases in Europe. That paradigm viewed dialects as radiating outward concentrically from a center. The results of the Japanese survey, conveniently, showed Tokyo to be that center, which served to push it even further into the vanguard of standardization.

The Iinkai's survey took the form of a series of thirty-eight questions whose purpose was to determine preferences among competing inflections. The questions included elicitation for forms of *keigo: nasaru, kudasaru, -masu,* and *desu:*

Select those you use from among the following conjugations for the *nasaru* and *kudasaru* of *goran-nasaru* and *okiki kudasaru.*

nasari(mase)	*nasare*		
nasara(nu)	*nasaru*	*nasareba*	*nasarau*
nasare(te)(ta)(tai, taku)	*nasai*		
kudasari(mase)	*kudasare*		
kudasara(nu)	*kudasaru*	*kudasare(ba)*	*kudasarau*
kudasare(te)(ta)(tai, taku)	*kudasai*		

(Kokugo Chōsa Iinkai 1903:xx)[6]

History does not have much to say about the consciousness that underlay this question about polite language. The formal description of *keigo* was at this time still very much in its infancy, so by contemporary standards, the forms that investigators chose to include in this and successive surveys are paradigmatically incongruent. Were there neat dialectal lines that scholars knew would emerge in the survey's results? Or did the designers simply select four of the most commonly used forms and hope for the best? Given the state of linguistic investigation at the time, indeed as it was imported from the West, a little of each is a distinct likelihood.

The Iinkai's survey was distributed to teachers in each school in the prefectural system around the country (Bunka-chō 1999a:417), and the results were published three years later in a two-part paper called *Kōgo-hō chōsa hōkoku-sho* (Report on the investigation into spoken language grammar) with an accompanying atlas, *Kōgo-hō bumbuzu* (Spoken language grammar distribution atlas) (Kokugo Chōsa Iinkai 1906a, 1906b).[7]

But by all accounts there was considerable dissatisfaction on the part of both members of the Iinkai and the government sponsors. The entire project had been rushed, and not everyone involved in the project had a firm grounding in dialectology. The results were, therefore, unreliable. In 1908 a second survey was developed and sent out. This second survey included ninety items, and this time asked specifically if respondents used or had heard of a wide variety of polite forms (note the choice of the technical term *"keii"* in the heading):

Keii o hyō-suru gozukai, ikaga
What about those forms indicating respect?

Watakushi mo kaimasu.
I will also buy it.

Watakushi mo mairimasu.
I will also go.

Okashi-mōshimasu.
I will borrow it.

Watakushi ga o-hanashi-mōshimasu.
I will speak.

Kono gohon wo chotto o-kari-mōshimasu.
I will borrow this book for a bit.

Inventing *Keigo*

Nani o o-kai -nasaru no desu ka.
What will you buy?

Kyō wa dono o-meshi o omeshi-nasaimasu ka.
What will you wear today?

Sonna ni ikumai ka o-meshi asobasu to oatsū gozaimashō.
It must be too hot to wear so many clothes.

Doko e oide asobashimasu.
Where are you going?

Kochira e oide nasaru hō ga yoroshū gozaimashō.
Would it be better to come here?

Sore de oyoroshū gozaimashō.
Will that be all right?

Sendatte no ohanashi no shina wa osagashi ni narimashite mo gozaimasen deshita deshō.
You wouldn't be looking for the thing you spoke about the other day.

Konata wa taisō oshizuka de gozaimasu ne.
This one would be very quiet, wouldn't it.

Kono tegami o yonde kudasai.
Please read this letter.

Tegami o kaite kudasai.
Please write a letter.

Hon o kashite tsukaasai.
Please lend me a book.

Tegami o kaite okureyasu.
Please write a letter.

Nani o kai naharu.
What are you buying?

Nani o kiki yahattana.
What are you listening to?

Erō nigiyaka ya omahen ka.
Don't you think it is awfully noisy?

Hon o yomu shi.
I'll read a book.

Kashi o kū shi.
I'll eat sweets.

(Kokugo Chōsa Iinkai 1908a:440–441)

The results of this second survey took the form of two position papers appearing in 1916 *(Kōgo-hō)* and 1917 *(Kōgo-hō bekki)*. Of interest here is the commentary on polite forms:

Honorific-humble *(keijō)* auxiliary verbs are used to show respect in speaking *(uyamatte iu)* or politeness in speaking *(teinei ni iu)* about an action.

Sensei no iwareru tōri	As the professor says,
mō korareru koro da.	it is time for him/her to come here.
Kanari takaku tobimasu.	It flies rather high.

Also, as is evident from the following, honorific-humble verbs can be used as auxiliary verbs.

O-ukagai mōshimasu.	I will ask.
O-maneki itashimashita.	I will invite them.
o-yasumi asobasu yō ni	in order to rest
asa hayaku o-oki nasaru nara	if you get up early
yoku o-tazune kudasaru o-kata	people who visit often
O-uke tsukamatsurimasu.	I will try.

(Kokugo Chōsa Iinkai 1916:51)[8]

The term *"keijō,"* created by the Iinkai, combines the *kei* of *keigo* and *sonkeigo* with the *jō* of *kenjōgo*. This term is not seen elsewhere.

Perhaps as important as these research findings themselves was the critical role they played in the development of educational policy and materials. This, after all, is the central role of any national language academy. The Iinkai and its work were behind the earliest language instruction primers for teachers in the schools of the prefectural system. The first of these, *Tōkyō-go keigo-hō ryakuhyō* (Tokyo *keigo* summary) (Kokugo Chōsa Iinkai 1908b), is representative in its clear message that Tokyo was to serve as the standard: "This document was prepared with regard to *keigo* at it is used in Tokyo. This can only be called a summary; it is inclusive of the language used in multiple contexts *(baai)* and by multiple classes *(kaikyō)*, save only that the language is that used by those in the middle class in such-and-such a context when the person is talking to ordinary *(dōtō)* people and/or when the person is talking to higher-ranking *(meue)* people. Thus it should not be thought that these are the only styles to be found in Tokyo style; there is a wide variety of speech styles, it must be clear." (Kokugo Chōsa Iinkai 1908b:2)[9]

This constitutes the first *keigo* policy statement made by a government entity that I have found. In addition to naming Tokyo as the standard and justifying its choices of forms on the basis of scientific evidence, the *Ryakuhyō* provided guidelines for three levels of language, taking grammatical person as an analytical point of departure:

We list the language that self *(jiko)* uses in order to show the action(s) of other *(aite)* or anything else pertaining to other when other is equal *(dōtō)* to self—ordinary language *(jōgo)*; we list the language that self uses in order to show the action(s) of self or anything else pertaining to self when other is superior *(meue)* to self—humble language *(kengo)*; we list the language that self uses in order to show the action(s) of the other or anything else pertaining to the other when the other is superior to self— respect language *(keigo)*. In these tables, so-called self is limited to self or (tangible or intangible) things having a connection thereto; so-called other is limited to the other

Inventing *Keigo*

person or (tangible or intangible) things having a connection thereto. (Kokugo Chōsa Iinkai 1908b:2)[10]

Although *jōgo*, *kengo*, and *keigo* seem to refer to the same trinity later called *teineigo*, *kenjōgo*, and *sonkeigo*, the technical terms continued to fluctuate. But ideologically, the rhetoric of *keigo* policy was focused on the formal aspects of the *keigo* paradigm, including the defining vertical relationship between self and other. It is telling that, even in the early descriptions, the context dependence of *keigo* creeps into the discussion.

The balance of the 1908 document consists of fifty-six tables like the one reprinted in Table 4, supplying complete sample conjugations for the verbs *utsu* 'hit', *kuru* 'come', *suteru* 'discard', *iu* 'say', *suru* 'do', *aru* 'have', and *da* 'be'. It is made clear to the reader that *-desu/masu* forms are desirable. Examples of appropriate usage are given in *-desu/masu*: the honorific and humble forms are recommended for "ordinary use" *(jōriyō)*, and contracted forms (such as *-cha* for *-te wa*) are termed "rough" *(zonzai)* (3–4). The motivation behind these recommendations had to do with the disparity that had arisen between spoken and written language, and the attitude with which written colloquial language was viewed as *gembun-itchi* gathered momentum: "Vulgarity was the charge most often and most bitterly leveled by detractors of colloquial style, who saw the use of any part of the spoken language in writing except certain parts of the lexicon as an offence in itself" (Twine 1991:30). As a result, choice among competing forms for a standard typically tended in the direction of what was perceived to be the more polite, namely, *keigo*. The controversy over the choice of the copula is also telling in this regard.

Even more interesting from the modern critical perspective is a position paper that appeared in Meiji 44 (1911) based on the results of these early investigations. *Kōgo-tai shokan-bun ni kansuru chōsa hōkoku* (Report on an investigation of spoken language forms in letter-writing style) lists forms of

Table 4. *Conjugation of the verbs* iu *and* suru *from* Tōkyō Keigo-hō Ryakuhyō *'Tokyo Keigo Summary'* (Kokugo Chōsa Iinkai *1908b: 6*).[11]

iu 'say'			*suru* 'do'		
Honorific	Humble	Plain	Honorific	Humble	Plain
(keigo)	*(kenjō)*	*(jōgo)*			
ossharu	*mōsu*	*iu*	*nasaru*	*itasu*	*suru*
o-ii-nasaru					
o-ii ni naru					
osshaimasu	*mōshimasu*	*iimasu*	*nasaimasu*	*itashimasu*	*shimasu*
o-ii-nasaimasu					
o-ii ni narimasu					

address and reference for use in epistolary style and includes forty-nine sample letters from around the country. More important, its commentary on *keigo* is limited to a list of areas where errors are likely to occur, including "*keigo o dassetsu-suru koto* 'omitted *keigo*' and *keigo no yōhō o ayamaru koto* 'mistaken *keigo*'" (Kokugo Chōsa Iinkai 1911:59). Ironically, the Iinkai's 1911 direct reference to erroneous and omitted *keigo* belies the now popular notion that *keigo* passed through a golden age when, ostensibly, all Japanese knew their place in a world of vertically structured relationships, and each used *keigo* according to a universal plan. The educational system was in fact the state's most powerful tool in creating a standardized language, but standardization did not take place overnight, there is no evidence that it ever went to completion, and it was not without controversy. It is crucial to recognize that one purpose of standardization was, among other things, to create a "public" language for use among people who do not know each other well in a rapidly modernizing society. Juxtaposed with this is the fact that most ordinary citizens still lived highly circumscribed lives, and that their interactions were limited to a narrowly defined circle of known individuals. Even in the pre-Meiji world that Twine describes, interaction in the capital was so fixed on a day-to-day basis that forms of the copula were readily identifiable as belonging to townspeople or the pleasure quarters. *Kōgo-tai shokan-bun ni kansuru chōsa hōkoku* tells a great deal about standardization in general, as well as about what aspects of Japanese were most in need of it. Those aspects included, naturally, *keigo*. *Kōgo-tai shokan-bun ni kansuru chōsa hōkoku* was taken for quite some time as a point of departure for establishing educational content and policy (Bunka-chō 1999b:32).

Thus began the "scientific" delineation of *keigo* in Japan. For practical as well as ideological reasons, there was an overriding desire to smooth over diachronic linguistic imperfections and to present a unified account of language and society. As conscious as the Japanese were that language should not hinder their progress into the modern world, they were also eager to hold Japanese up as a model for communication. A highly centralized educational system with direct ties to government agencies like the Iinkai played a crucial role in standardizing Japanese and promulgating the standard. The task of instruction in the underlying, nonlinguistic principles of Japanese society are seen in the choice of morphology used to invent guidelines for *keigo* usage in these early documents: *ken-tō, uyamau, tei-nei, kei-go, ken-go, kei-jō.*

Taisho and Early Shōwa

The Kokugo Chōsa Iinkai fell victim to declining revenues and was dissolved in 1913 (*Kokugo kenkyū jiten* 1977:32). Gottlieb (1996) suggests that its dissolution was in part due to opposition from a conservative countermovement whose representatives resisted the reforms (especially in script) that the Iinkai was advocating (13). But although the Iinkai was disbanded, the demands for reform and standardization of the written language were so strong that in 1921 (Taisho 10) a *Rinji* (Temporary) *Kokugo Chōsa-kai* was set up within the Mombushō (Ministry of Education). Thirteen years later, the Kokugo Shingikai replaced it, and that is the name given to the body that adjudicated language policy in Japan through 2001, when as part of a ministerial overhaul the Kokugo Shingikai and matters of language policy were folded into the charge of the new Bunka Shingikai 'Culture Academy.' But the Rinji Kokugo Chōsa-kai and the Kokugo Shingikai were assigned the task of determining kana usage and kanji convention and had no opportunity to carry out field-work on the spoken language (Tokieda 1940:202). The Taisho period was described by leading scholars of the day as "an era in which dialect research came to a standstill" (Tōjō 1932:30) and "the dark days of Taisho when people were asleep to dialect study" (Tachibana 1933:2). The only context within which it was possible to speak of dialects[12] and spoken language convention, was that of *teikoku* 'Imperial Japan', and that word was bound up in *kokumin kokka nihon* 'nationalistic Japan' (Yasuda 1999:142–143).

Language policy as Japan expanded into East Asia with the annexation of Formosa in 1895, of the Liaotung Peninsula in 1905, and of Korea in 1910 focused primarily on *kokugo*'s role in galvanizing a sense of *kokka* 'nation' both internally and among its colonies. Insofar as *keigo* was included in *kokugo* training, its description was in line with *kokugo* ideology. More important, however, attention shifted dramatically to script.

This is not to say that the dialogue on *keigo* came to a halt; Japanese scholars continued to work in earnest on the grammar of the spoken language. But government-sanctioned activity with regard to spoken language came a distant second to other problems of *kokugo* policy, and those other priorities surfaced in the rhetoric of *keigo* in a number of arenas.

Representative of the received story about *keigo* is a Shōwa 16 (1941) Mombushō (Ministry of Education) publication entitled *Mombu jihō*, from which comes *Reihō yōkō* (Important points in manners). *Reihō yōkō*'s target audience is middle school teachers, and though it focuses primarily on behavior, its fifth section, *Kotoba-zuka(h)i* (Language use), makes nine specific recommendations for language:

1. With regard to superiors *(chōjō)*, one uses appropriate *keigo*.
2. For self *(jishō)* reference, one uses the usual *watashi* 'I'. With regard to superiors, it is a matter of using either *shi* 'sir' or the name. With regard to men, it is all right to use *boku* 'I' with equals *(dōhai)*, but not with superiors.
3. For other reference, one uses appropriate titles to superiors according to social

position *(mibun)*. To equals one uses the usual *anata* 'you' or, in the case of men, it is all right to use *kimi* 'you'.

4. When speaking about those outside the conversation *(taiwasha-igai no hito)*, one uses appropriate titles and *keigo* in regard to superiors, of course, but also in regard to others. With regard to superiors, in speaking about those who rank below the superior(s) *(chii yori hikui mono)*, even if the person is higher ranking *(jō)* than oneself, one does not use titles or *keigo*, or alternatively, one simplifies.

5. When speaking to outsiders about relatives, one does not use titles or *keigo*. In general it is exemplary not to use titles or *keigo* in talking about things having to do with ourselves *(jibun)*.

6. In accepting something, one always says *hai* 'yes'; especially when speaking to superiors it is not good to say *ee* 'yes'.

7. Toward superiors one uses *gozaimasu, arimasu, mairimasu, itashimasu, zonji-masu, asobasu, mōshimasu, itadakimasu,* and the like as much as possible. One does not use *desu, morau, kureru,* and the like.

8. In regard to outsiders' things, one attaches *o-/go-*, but we do not use these in talking about our own things. In talking about things in general it is normal not to use them *[o-/go-]*, but there are situations where they are used, depending on the tone or by convention.

9. One uses the standard language *(hyōjungo)* as much as possible. (Mombushō 1941:170)[13]

As far as I can discern, this 1941 pronouncement is the first example of *keigo* "how-to" from a government source. Readers (educators) are expected either to know the paradigms to which it refers or to be able to find them in *kokugo* materials. The key relationships determining language use and behavior remain simple: superior-self *(chōjō/jishō)* and inside/outside *(kinshin/tanin)*. Certain inflections are now passé *(asobasu)*, and it is no longer inappropriate to say *ee* to a superior. But *(u)n* 'uh' has surely taken the place of *ee,* as it is deemed inappropriate toward superiors. The 1941 terms of government-sanctioned how-to include *"keishō,"* which never caught on as a technical term among grammarians or the public. *"Hyōjungo"* 'standard language' as a term has become slightly tainted; it implies that dialects are less than they ought to be. The "politically correct" word in contemporary Japan is *kyōtsūgo* 'common language'. The Mombushō's 1941 document makes it clear that the process of standardization was not considered complete. One almost never sees exhortations in modern Japan to use the standard language "as much as possible." Raising citizens' consciousness of *keigo* and other spoken-language conventions was still a high priority. The finer points of gauging language to context came later.

Within twenty years of the appearance of Yamada's grammar, *keigo* had assumed a mythical place in Japan's portrayal of itself as embodying aspects of culture that set it apart from the rest of the world. Miller (1971) maintains that, during Japan's expansionist period, *keigo* became a political tool used to demonstrate the superiority of Japanese language, culture, and society over those of its colonies. He cites the work of Maruyama Rimpei (1941), a professor at the (now defunct) *Kenkoku* (lit., 'found/construct the nation') University: "Japanese is rich in *keigo;* actually, it seems to be over-rich. For this reason even many Japanese do not understand how to use *keigo,* or use it incorrectly. How much more, then, might we expect persons for whom Japanese is not their native language, as for example, people from the continent of Asia, to feel that the Japanese *keigo* is difficult, and even that it is a nuisance. But the richness of *keigo* is, in one respect, something that has arisen from the special nature of the Japanese race, and hence, it is a vital feature of the Japanese language" (Maruyama 1941:1, cited in Miller 1971: 610).[14] According to Miller, the pressure that Japanese scholars were under to participate in the glorification of Japanese culture is evident even in the preface to Ekoyama Tsuneakira's (1943) *Keigo-hō:*

> Now that the construction of Greater East Asia has become the most pressing task of the day for us, it is only to be expected that the Japanese language should present itself as a much debated issue—to be expected, and to be rejoiced about!...The permeation of the Japanese language throughout the Co-prosperity Sphere will require extraordinary exertion and patience, and it goes without saying that as far as *keigo* is concerned, this must be done in terms of exhaustive knowledge and exact measures. But as a matter of fact, some people today complain about the poverty of *keigo,* while others bewail its over-use, and there is agreement only upon one thing—that *keigo* today is in a state of confusion....In order to solve the problem of how to refine *keigo* even further, and to secure the proper appearance of the divinely endowed Yamato language, it is first necessary to realize scientifically what the proper forms for *keigo* actually are; then on the basis of this knowledge, we must effectively grasp and criticize the present state of affairs.[15] (Ekoyama 1943:1–2, cited in Miller 1971:611)

The extent to which Japanese grammarians advanced the causes of the authoritarian state that Japan had become by the beginning of the Shōwa era, including imposition of the Japanese language on occupied territories like Taiwan and Korea, is the subject of renewed debate in contemporary Japan (Lee 1996, Yasuda 1999), and it has even made its way into English-language scholarship (Tai 1999). It is crucial to ground arguments about Japan's linguistic imperialism in an understanding of the historical forces within which that imperialism took place. The scholarship of the era is only one source of evidence for determining the role of academics in promoting Japan's colonial agenda. Lee (1996) and Yasuda (1999) have made a point of examining correspondence and other written records from members of the intellectual elite, including exchanges between scholars and the government bureaucrats who set language policy. It is clear that educational enterprises, because they operated under government sanction, were co-opted to some extent (Marshall 1992). Dower

(1999) observes, "Only a handful of academics emerged from the war with their reputations enhanced for not having been swept along by the tides of ultranationalism" (233). With regard to *keigo* in particular, it is interesting to examine the process by which *keigo* acquired the ideological burden that it so obviously has today. In the years leading up to the Pacific War, it was not an established linguistic category with a long history of political import. Far from it; *keigo*'s history was still little more than forty years old, a product of the Meiji grammarians of the previous generation who had isolated *keigo* and discovered, to their bewilderment (it seems), that it constituted something extraordinary in the Japanese language. The parameters of that "something" had to be written down and disseminated before *keigo* would be able to carry the weight of representing all that was fine in the tradition(s) of Japanese culture. I suggest that this had not yet happened in the years leading up to the Pacific War. *Keigo*'s story was being written right along with the story of the Co-prosperity Sphere. It is one thing to embark on the enterprise of capturing in paradigmatic ("scientific") fashion the rules and conventions that conscribe a group's linguistic behavior. It is quite another to take an established linguistic tradition or convention and rewrite if for the purposes of the current age. This difference may be what differentiates the modern from the postmodern. *Keigo*, in any event, was very much a work still in progress. The trauma of the Pacific War provided a useful, if unfortunate, rupture in the history of language consciousness. After the war a number of factors came together to contribute to what *keigo* would become. For example, the recovering economy poured resources into educational enterprises, and universal education finally became a reality. With it, the standardization of Japanese grammar can be said to have gone to completion. Moreover, *keigo* joined a host of other Japanese "traditions" whose stories had to be rewritten as a result of Japan's surrender in 1945. At that point *keigo* acquired real salience. Its all-too-brief past became fossilized, and reconstruction was the order of the day. But in order for reconstruction to take place, there had to be stable constructs that would lend themselves to renovation. *Keigo* was about to come of age.

Keigo in the Postwar Period

A dramatic shift in language policy took place at midcentury with the end of World War II. The Kokugo Shingikai, reconstituted in 1950 as the American Occupation came to an end, was given a mandate to carry out any and all activities that might "improve the language" *(kokugo no kaizen)* (Kokugo Shingikai 1998:3). Its first priority was to assist in reversing the damage done by ultranationalism and in rebuilding Japan in a more democratic image (Gottlieb 1995:121). To that end, a new picture of Japan had to be painted, and *keigo* was ideal for the job. Two years after its institution, the Kokugo Shingikai produced its first sweeping pronouncement on *keigo*. Entitled "Kore kara no keigo" (*Keigo* from Now On) (Kokugo Shingikai 1952) and reprinted below as Appendix 1, that pronouncement served the dual function of summarizing the past and setting the tone for the future. It had taken fifty years or thereabouts for Japanese grammar to be standardized and the grammatical classification of *keigo* to become a fact of life. After the war, government policy for the first time directly addressed *keigo* as a freestanding phenomenon. "Kore kara no keigo" is among the first policy statements to emerge from the postwar Kokugo Shingikai. It is reasonable to conclude that policymakers saw *keigo* as a useful backdrop for setting the tone of future language policy. The overriding tenor of "Kore kara no keigo" is conciliatory, as perhaps might be expected from a government authority that was attempting to bring what was viewed first as a feudal and then as an ultranationalistic phenomenon into the present. In a dramatic turnaround, "Kore kara no keigo" portrays *keigo* as, naturally enough, a vehicle for bringing Japan into the impending "new age":

Preface

This monograph selects those problems that are closest to us in our everyday linguistic existence and sets out that form which is thought to be desirable for the future.

Problems related to *keigo*'s future obviously do not stop with these. In essence, problems of *keigo* are not limited to just those of language; rather, they concern whether *keigo* will be unified with the manners and etiquette of real life. So along with the growth of manners and etiquette that conform to the lifestyle of our new age, we hope to achieve sound development of a straightforward and clear-cut code of *keigo* (189)....

In conclusion

The conversation of adults in society *(shakaijin)* is one of mutual equality *(sōgo ni taitō)*, and yet it must contain respect *(keii)*.

On this point, language use between, for example, public servants and the public, or all the various workers in a workplace, should take *desu/-masu* as fundamental, because of its being of a form that is kind *(yasashii)* and polite *(teinei)*....

After the war, clerks and the authorities had already put such language into practice along these lines, but from now on it is to be desired that this tendency achieve even more universality *(futsūka)* (193).

Keigo suddenly assumed the role of helping to unify postwar Japan as a civilized—or rather, civil—country. It continues to play this role in contemporary Japan, both in government policy and in the how-to industry. This function of *keigo* is frequently underplayed, especially in pedagogical treatments. Whether it is one that fits comfortably into people's psyches, or one that can be made consonant with its alternative manifestation as reflective of a highly structured vertical society, is a matter that is not without controversy. One task of the Kokugo Shingikai in this regard is to smooth over inconsistencies and make *keigo*'s new role a palatable, matter-of-fact representation of common sense.

In its postwar incarnation, the standardized form of *keigo* is a given, and any complications are attributed to historical accident:

Fundamental policy

1. Up until now, *keigo* existed as it had developed from past ages, with more trouble-some points than were necessary. From now on, taking a lesson from those excesses and rectifying mistaken usage, *keigo* is something that we want, to the extent possible, to be straightforward and clear-cut (189).

It may be this need to "simplify" *keigo* for public consumption that led scholars finally to agree on its terms of analysis (see Chapter 1). But that is only part of the story. "Simplification" here refers to the eventual elimination of forms most strongly associated with prewar Imperial Japan, notably the last line in what follows:

6. The language of actions

Honorific forms for actions take in three forms. That is,

	kaku	*ukeru*
Form		
I	*kakareru*	*ukerareru*
II	*o-kaki ni naru*	*o-uke ni naru*
III	*(o-kaki asobasu)*	*(o-uke asobasu)*

The model of (I), *-reru/rareru* is misleading and is often mistaken for a passive inflection, but because it regularly attaches to all actions and is, moreover, quite simple, it can be recognized as promising for future use. There is no need to change (II) *o-...ni naru*, to *o-...ni narareru*. The form of (III), the so-called *asobase-kotoba*, should be gradually discarded from what is recognized to be plain, straightforward *keigo* (191).[16]

It is interesting to speculate what might be intended here by "promising" with regard to the *-reru/-rareru* inflection. Contemporary criticism of those who rely exclusively on this form belies the notion that this ever meant complete regularization of the paradigm.

Like a phoenix from the ashes, *keigo* emerges—democratized—from its feudal past. "Until now, *keigo* developed based primarily on vertical relationship(s), but from now on, *keigo* must be based on mutual respect that derives from valuing the essential character of each person....Mistaking the spirit of service, there are those, especially in commerce, who use too lofty honorifics or obsequious humble forms. We should all take a lesson from the fact that, without even knowing it, they miss the point of their own and others' human dignity. It is hoped that all citizens will develop a consciousness of this point" (189). Diachronic dissonance is played down; *keigo* has acquired an integrated history that will smooth (or hide) the seam between the multiple *keigo*s of pre-modern Japan and the account that is set out in "Kore kara no keigo" for public consumption. *Keigo* mirrors the structure of Japanese society: prewar, vertical; postwar, egalitarian. This is not unlike the oversimplified picture of Indo-European social structure contained in Brown and Gilman's well-known 1960 essay on the so-called pronouns of power and solidarity.[17] Brown and Gilman's original thesis—that "differences of power cause V [= *vous*] to emerge in one direction of address; differences not concerned with power cause V to emerge in both directions" (257)—treated power and solidarity as discrete, as opposing ends of a cline or spectrum, presumably with solidarity on the progressive end. Moreover, the proposed shift from a semantic of power to one of solidarity seems to subsume an assumption that unequal relationships are on the decline. But such a conclusion is, in Fairclough's (1989:71) terms, "highly suspect" in light of the evidence from elsewhere that power inequalities have not changed substantially over time. Too, Brown and Gilman's original thesis does not allow for the simultaneous existence of both power and solidarity throughout *tu/vous* history, nor for its continuing into the foreseeable future. The same might be said of *keigo*. Though Japan now sees itself as an egalitarian society, few would argue that it is structured in terms of vertical relationships. The Japanese themselves do not seem to be ill at ease with this seeming contradiction, but it creates problems for theoretical models.

Of related interest is the fact that, in "Kore kara no keigo," women's usage has achieved a dubious notoriety, so much so that it is given parity with the other "fundamental policies": "3. In women's language *(joseigo)*, *keigo* as well as euphemism is used excessively (for example, the overuse of polite prefix *o-*). It is hoped that there will be rectification of this point once women reflect and come to self-awareness" (189). I take this as further evidence that *keigo* serves as an arena for argumentation over much of Japan's modernization. Deliberation about women's status and roles in contemporary Japan is embedded in issues of women's language—and therefore *keigo*—for professional commentators and ordinary citizens alike.[18]

The remaining sections of "Kore kara no keigo" make specific recommendations about usage:

1. *Hito o sasu kotoba* (Referring to people)
2. *Keishō* (Honorific titles)
3. *'-tachi' to 'ra'* (Plural suffixes *tachi* and *-ra*)
4. *'O-' 'go-' no keiri* (Accounting for *o-* and *go-*)
5. *Taiwa no kichō* (Setting the tone of conversation)
6. *Dōsa no kotoba* (The language of actions)
7. *Keiyōshi to 'desu'* (Adjectives and *desu*)
8. *Aisatsu-go* (Words for greetings)
9. *Gakkō-yōgo* (Special vocabulary for school)
10. *Shimbun, rajio no yōgo* (Special vocabulary for newspapers and radio)
11. *Kōshitsu-yōgo* (Special vocabulary for the imperial family)

As analytical categories, these seem arbitrary from the scientific point of view. In fact, they read much more like the tables of contents from traditional *kotoba-zukai* 'language how-to' books. *Keigo* holds little interest for either Japanese scholars or Japanese laypeople as a linguistic paradigm divorced from context. *Keigo*'s value lies in what it tells us about our relationships to others and to society.

"Kore kara no keigo" provided a baseline for the discussion of *keigo* for forty-five years. By 1974 it represented the ideal with which prescriptive grammarians could contrast the disintegrating conventions around them. From the contemporary perspective, "Kore kara no keigo" represents a unity, a convenient curtain for separating the move toward *hyōjungo* from the fall away from *hyōjungo*. Only in postwar textbooks did a unified analysis of *keigo*, the *sonkeigo*, *kenjōgo*, *teineigo* trinity, finally appear.[19] In the textbooks that flowed out of the Mombushō just after the war, *keigo* finally emerged in its modern guise.

Spoken *keigo*

When we speak or write, there are expressions that include a feeling of respect *(sonkei)*, humility *(kenjō)*, or politeness *(teinei)* toward the addressee *(aite)* or third person. This is called *keigo*. For example, if we show this for the word *"iku"*:

Sonkei	*Sensei ga sochira ni ikareru.*	
	Sensei ga sochira ni oide ni naru.	'The teacher is going there.'
	Sensei ga sochira ni irassharu.	
Kenjō	*Asu sensei no tokoro ni ukagau koto ni shita.*	'I decided to visit the teacher's place tomorrow.'
	Chichi mo sensei no tokoro ni mairu sō desu.	'My father says he will also go to the teacher's place.'

Next there is

Teinei	*Sensei ga achira ni irasshaimasu.*	'The teacher is going there.'
	Kyō wa totemo samui desu.	'It is very cold today.'
	Kyō wa totemo samū gozaimasu.	'It is very cold today.'
	Kaze ga shizuka desu.	'The wind is quiet.'
	Kaze ga shizuka de gozaimasu.	'The wind is quiet.'

(Kumazawa 1956:224–225)[20]

Since the 1950s it has been the expectation that every educated person should know what *keigo* is, how it is analyzed, and how it functions. This consciousness continues to be inculcated by an educational system that puts substantial resources into language—including *keigo*—education.

"Kore kara no keigo" served as the basis for the creation of educational materials aimed not only at students, but at educators as well. *"Keigo"* was both the subject and the title of the first of the Bunka-chō's *Kotoba Shiriizu* (Language Series; Bunka-chō 1973), which started off with the proceedings of a *zadankai* 'round-table discussion' featuring nine *kokugo* scholars—among them Ōishi Hatsutarō (see Chapter 2). In three subsequent volumes (Bunka-chō 1986, 1995, 1996) readers can find step-by-step guidance in the particulars of *keigo* as it is taught in the school system and promulgated by the government.

Keigo Today

The late 1990s saw a flurry of activity surrounding *keigo* policy in Japan.[21] Why *keigo* should have come under renewed scrutiny at this juncture is probably more a question of the flow of ongoing policy deliberation than it is any cold-blooded decision motivated by a sense of language decline, although concern for current usage was certainly a factor. There was a strong sense throughout *kokugogaku* circles that things had gone far enough. Natural and inevitable though linguistic change may be, it was time to take a stand, or at least take stock. "Kore kara no keigo" had represented the fulcrum of "acceptable" *keigo* policy for almost fifty years, and it was wearing thin. Japan and the Japanese people had changed; that change needed to be examined and current standards documented. Leadership was in order, as was an overhaul of *keigo* policy. It is probably not entirely coincidental that the projected deadline for policy statements was scheduled to coincide roughly with the hundredth anniversary of the establishment of the first Kokugo Chōsa Iinkai (1901) as well as the fiftieth anniversary of the appearance of "Kore kara no keigo" (1952).

In 1993 the twentieth Kokugo Shingikai convened and was charged with reviewing "language policy for the new age." That charge is outlined in a paper of the same title (*Atarashii jidai ni ōjita kokugo seisaku ni tsuite* [Kokugo Shingikai 1995]).[22] In this paper, the Shingikai singled out three problems for further deliberation. One of these was issues of language use *(kotoba-zukai ni kansuru koto)*.[23] Issues of language use were divided into (1) basic consciousness *(kihonteki na ninshiki)*, (2) importance of the language environment *(gengo-kankyō no jūyōsei)*, and (3) problems of *keigo (keigo no mondai)*. Adopting "Kore kara no keigo" as a point of departure, the twentieth Shingikai made the following recommendation to the next Shingikai: "In 'Kore kara no keigo,' a basic policy was to avoid excess, correct mistaken usage, and use simple, clear language as much as possible. This approach is requested here. In practical life there is no denying that those who avoid excess, correct mistaken usage, and use simple and clear politeness are vital to the enrichment of language" (Kokugo Shingikai 1995:301).[24] The *Shingikai* scarcely rejected the ethos of "Kore kara no keigo." Furthermore, the instructions elaborated that questions of *keigo* should proceed from certain "points of view" *(kanten):* "It is necessary to view *keigo* from the perspective of smoothing communication or suitability of language depending on context. It is not a problem of vocabulary, but rather

Inventing *Keigo*

a matter of appropriateness of entire expressions" (Kokugo Shingikai 1995: 302).[25]

In a 1996 progress report, *Keii hyōgen no rinen to hyōjun no arikata* (Guidelines for standards and conceptualization of polite expressions), the twenty-first Kokugo Shingikai reiterated and expanded on these instructions, setting up two unambiguous charges for itself:

First: consider the variety of *keii hyōgen*

As was previously pointed out, the *keii hyōgen* that people use nowadays are indeed varied. The view presented in "Communication and Language Use" is that contemporary society presents us with a wide variety of options and that human relationships mirror that variety, but beyond this it has become the norm to distinguish *keii hyōgen* according to time and place. It is necessary to judge the variety of *keii hyōgen* with forethought and in the knowledge that they are part of the richness of our national language *(kokugo)*.

Second: consider how to deal with the appropriateness of practical usage

The Shingikai is assigned the task of addressing itself to demonstrating specific standards for *keii hyōgen*. This includes not only correcting errors of linguistic form, but also dealing with the appropriateness of practical usage. That is to say, the Shingikai should provide a guide for practical usage that assigns order among the variety of *keii hyōgen* that are in actual use, establishes, in clear language, criteria for choices among the many alternatives, and provides reasons that those items marked by high misuse are errors. (Kokuritsu Kokugo Kenkyūjo 2000:54)[26]

Arguments about this policy statement inevitably hark back to the original charge and the twenty-first Shingikai's interpretation of it. What was the intent of the original charge from the twentieth Shingikai? How was it interpreted by the twenty-first Shingikai? Was the assignment to provide clear and concise rules for usage, or was it an open one that allowed for discussion of leadership? These arguments play out in responses to the twenty-first Kokugo Shingikai's policy statement, *Gendai ni okeru keii hyōgen no arikata* (Guidelines for respect expressions in the modern age) (Appendix 2).

The titles *Keii hyōgen no rinen to hyōjun no arikata* and *Gendai ni okeru keii hyōgen no arikata* refer not to *keigo*, but to *keii hyōgen*, and this is significant. As might be expected, the presence on the Shingikai of academics who conduct research on *keigo* is abundantly reflected in the very terms of analysis. *Keigo* is no longer limited to the traditional paradigm but has expanded to include the same kind of phenomena included in the works I mentioned in Chapter 1, for example, Kikuchi's *Keigo* (1994) or Kabaya, Kawaguchi, and Sakamoto's *Keigo hyōgen* (1998) (one of the authors of *Keigo hyōgen* sat on the *Shingikai*). This sort of cross-fertilization is more the rule than the exception; the Shingikai does, after all, represent both Mombushō bureaucrats and the finest minds that can be assembled from the country's universities to deliberate national policy.

The influence of these scholars is part and parcel of the Shingikai's work, and it would be more than a little surprising if national policy did not reflect the intellectual positions of contemporary scholars. But by casting the net so broadly, the Shingikai has also weakened its ability to make specific recommendations about correct and incorrect usage. (Whether it could have done so anyway is debatable.) In any event, *Gendai ni okeru keii hyōgen* was taken to task by critics for its laissez-faire attitude toward usage. No specific guidelines are included to give citizens a sure footing for measuring their control of *keigo,* and herein lies the source of debate. The second part of the charge, "The next Shingikai is assigned the task of addressing itself to demonstrating specific standards for *keii hyōgen*... not only correcting errors of linguistic form but also... appropriateness of practical usage," remains, in the eyes of many, entirely untouched. "In this writer's opinion, when it comes to form and practical use, though it may be an old-fashioned metaphor, like the two wheels of a cart, both are necessary. In spite of the fact that there was a request made for specific advice on central forms (especially those that are shaky), it was not carried out, and that is regrettable" (Asamatsu 2001a:46).[27] From interviews with members, I learned that the Shingikai's justification for its stance is that it aims to describe general, not specific, principles for usage and to define the underlying principles of civil interaction. As these scholars point out, attempts to intervene and dictate rules for usage are doomed to failure and invite controversy.

If *keigo* policy is a reflection of prevailing ideology, what does this most recent document and its attendant arguments about the Shingikai's role represent? Is it coincidental that the rift between traditional *kokugo* approaches to language and the attitude of modern linguistics, which claims to be purely "descriptive," has grown more pronounced over the past twenty years? Successive conventions of the Shingikai in the 1990s represent the first time that representatives of these two radically different approaches have had to face off on any substantive issues. Until now, they have existed in parallel universes within the academy, with *kokugo* housed in Japanese language and literature units and linguistics more closely affiliated with departments of English. But the different responses to the latest *kokugo* policy do not divide neatly between *kokugo* scholarship and Western linguistics. Perhaps even more salient is the division in Japan that has parallels in the U.S. and elsewhere between those who favor strict educational standards and those who see the imposition of standards as stultifying to the educational process. As the primary applications of the Shingikai's work are to be found in the educational system, it is not surprising that such questions should find their way into the language debate.

Other factors loom large in the Shingikai's collective consciousness and must surely have had an impact on the final policy statement. The impact of internationalization *(kokusaika)* was prominent in the Shingikai's deliberations. *Kokusaika* became a common buzzword in educational and governmental circles from the late 1980s onward, as Japan's bubble economy burst, and the scope of the global economy expanded ever wider. In education it became clear that the labor force would have to be trained to deal with more kinds of people in more contexts outside Japan. Simultaneously, as Japan's population dwindles, it is faced with an internal labor shortage, leaving it no choice but to come to terms with the influx of foreign labor, an influx that will have a tremendous impact on society in the coming decades. *Gendai ni okeru keii hyōgen* attempts to temper any perceived threat to the status quo by holding that diversity is a recent phenomenon in Japan and is to be valued, not disparaged. In truth, the arrival of large numbers of foreigners during the postwar economic boom has not been a new experience for Japan. In many decades of the twentieth century, foreign influence was enormous, as, for example, during Japan's Asian expansion, with its often forced immigration of labor. Such periods of foreign influence also elicited anxiety, and were also met with calming responses from the government in the form of social commentary and policy.

Another aspect of diversity recognized in *Gendai ni okeru keii hyōgen* comes from regional dialects. These, too, had never disappeared; rather, as the nation pulled together after World War II, regionalism of all kinds was low on the Japanese radar screen. Among the fictions of postwar Japan was the complacent belief that dialects represented little more than remnants of Japan's feudal past. They had no place in the fiction of homogeneity that was the modern miracle of Japan. Within the global capitalist system, however, the role of the nation-state has weakened, and with it the internal bonds that once cemented the nation-state as an entity (see Hirst and Thompson 1996). Language is one of those bonds, and the resurgence of pride in dialect is symptomatic of Japan's composition as a political entity.

Another point touched on in *Gendai ni okeru keii hyōgen* is that "the boundary between men's and women's forms of expression is in a state of flux." Where women's language is concerned, the Shingikai has abandoned a tried and true term that used to reflect popular ideology: *joseigo*, or *josei no kotoba* 'women's language'. Instead the rhetoric focuses on the diffuseness of the line that differentiates men and women, in an apparent attempt to call attention away from the threat posed by language change or instability.

All in all, *Gendai ni okeru keii hyōgen* refrains from fueling controversy or taking on what some might call the hard issues. As Gottlieb (1995:201) observes, there is no social upheaval or trauma to which agents of change—either conservative or progressive—can link their arguments. Accordingly, there is no strong impetus in any direction for making a strong statement by means of *keigo* policy. There may be agreement at all levels that not everyone follows the norms of the standard *kyōtsūgo*, but even the meaning of this is a matter of interpretation. In conservative hands, it can be construed as a lack of respect for the ideology itself—a powerful argument against those who would question or even undermine the ideology by failing (consciously or unconsciously) to follow its norms. In the hands of the disenfranchised, it can be an equally powerful statement that the norms are oppressive. The Kokugo Shingikai's response to the gap between prescription and usage is to adopt an attitude of inclusiveness, denying that there is any real conflict and attempting to bring all factions under a single umbrella— *"enkatsu na komyunikeeshon"*—mentioned no fewer than six times. The message is that disenfranchised are not really disenfranchised, and those who are in charge are not really oppressive. They simply need to promote smoother communication.

Keigo from Now On?

One of the things that happened in the grammatical analysis of *keigo* was that it became narrowly defined, perhaps too much so. Its reification as a grammar category may have been a plus from the scientific linguistic perspective, but, judging by its re-expansion since the end of World War II, it was profoundly dissatisfying to scholars. It is important to heed both the academic account of *keigo,* as argued by Japanese grammarians, and the parallel but independent application of *keigo* standards to all manner of issues facing modern Japan, as addressed by the rhetoric of the Kokugo Shingikai: internationalization, diversity, foreign influence, gender relations. It is abundantly clear from the material of language policy and its implementation that Japan has a great deal at stake in *keigo.* From the initial move to standardization up to the present, it is obvious that in Japan, as elsewhere, language does not fall outside human efforts to enforce conventional behavior. It is the job of language academies like the Shingikai to provide leadership, but they must also make language visible to the public. Shingikai policy touches the average Japanese in myriad ways, both directly and indirectly, beginning with its implementation in the educational system and continuing throughout life in its influence over all those agencies that tell people how to talk and/or write—newspapers and the media, the publishing industry, and popular instruction in how to use language.

CHAPTER 4

The Modernization of *Keigo*

Language intervention in Japan, as elsewhere, is by no means limited to public policy or state-sanctioned practices. There is an industry in Japan whose purpose it is to provide instruction in the commonplace practices of everyday life—the how-to industry, also known as self-help or advice literature. I consider the how-to industry an artifact of modernization. The appropriation of *keigo* by the how-to industry and its subsequent manipulation and portrayal in Japan are consistent with features of modernization that are described by Ivy (1995) as "discourses of the vanishing," by Giddens (1991) as "disembedding mechanisms" and by Fairclough (1995) as "the technologization of discourse." What is the relationship between language intervention as practiced by the how-to industry and actual language practice? Or intervention and the value judgments that people make about language? Or intervention and the wider arena of social practices and beliefs that tie into language? Scholars are only beginning to assess the consequences of changing or reinforcing people's beliefs about or consciousness of language. Intervention has consequences, but those consequences may lie far afield from the original linguistic issue. If language behavior is a performance, then linguistic intervention is simultaneously a discussion of the rules for that performance *and* a performance in itself. How can one look at both aspects of intervention at the same time? To present a complete picture of language, it is surely necessary to address the processes and consequences of attempts to affect linguistic convention. The nature of the relationship between language and people's attitudes and beliefs about it is a complex matter, and investigation into the intervention process itself can only foster understanding of its broader effects.

うっかり + 引力 = キケン

Figure 8. A manner poster from Tokyo's Tei+o Rapid Transit Authority (1997), featuring Sir Isaac Newton sitting among passengers. The caption reads, "Carelessness + Gravity = Danger."

The Concern for Convention in Japan: Parameters of How-to

One cannot board a train, enter public buildings or restrooms, pick up a newspaper, or watch television in contemporary Japan without soon encountering some kind of commentary or exhortation regarding polite behavior. Even to the most casual observer, the concern for appropriate social behavior in Japan outstrips anything that Emily Post could ever have imagined.[1] The loanword *manaa* 'manners' is probably most often used to describe such behavior, although one also encounters words like *echiketto* 'etiquette', *sahō* 'etiquette', *reigi* 'courtesy', *yarikata* 'way to do it', and others. In any station of the private railways in Tokyo there is a designated *manaa posutaa* 'manner poster', visible on the way to the ticket vending machines, that enjoins users to be on their best behavior as they board the trains. In January 1997 I observed just such a *manaa posutaa* (pictured in Figure 8) in one of the stations of the Yūrakucho line of the Tokyo subway system. It featured a cartoon of Isaac Newton seated on a train, apples about to cascade onto his head from the shopping bag of a fellow (female) passenger, as she looked on in embarrassed amazement. The caption read *"ukkari + inryoku = kiken"* (carelessness + gravity = danger), and beneath it, in both Japanese and English (not included here), was the admonition "Please be careful of your belongings on the train." JR (Japan Railway) hung a poster in its commuter trains in October 1996, charging those who use the station restroom with responsibility for leaving it in decent condition for the person who came next: *toire no manaa* 'restroom manners'. In the entrance to its locker rooms, a private fitness club placed a poster featuring a photograph

Figure 9. A book about telephone etiquette, Speak Comfortably on the Telephone *(1994), which promises explanations that will amaze listeners in everything from cordial greetings to the smooth transfer of calls and customer service. "Point-by-point, concise explanation, rich in examples, easy to understand." "When in doubt, use this book." "No embarrassment, no failure, no fear!"*

of an orangutan looking squarely at the viewer, reminding members to watch their *manaa* as they used the facilities. Monthly manner posters on the Tokyo metropolitan subway date back to 1974 and have provided exhortations on everything from smoking to interfering with others on the train.

Modern Japanese bookstores contain a special section of books that offer instruction on everything from manners in general (Chiteki Seikatsu Kenkyūjo 1994, Deguchi and Minagawa 1994), to telephone etiquette (Fuji Zerokusu Sōgō Kyōiku Kenkyūkai 1994; Figure 9), to asking and refusing favors (Fukuda 1996; Figure 10), to speeches, to job interviewing skills (in both male [Matsuura 1992] and female versions [Shūshoku Taisaku Kenkyūjo 1992]), to penmanship (Nomoto 1998) (keeping in mind that Chinese characters are traditionally written with a brush, what happens to them when the writer uses a ballpoint pen is conventionalized and often a matter of some concern for those writing formulaic letters such as thank-you notes or invitations). The range of topics seems endless, but is generally taken to reflect an abiding concern in Japanese culture for social convention: how-to.

On the topic of *keigo,* academic specialists are not the only ones with a history of outlining the principles, rules, and patterns of appropriate usage. Outside the academy there exists a wide range of cultural agencies and industries ensuring that the story of *keigo* stays firmly in the Japanese consciousness. Aca-

Figure 10. A book about requests, How to Ask, How to Refuse: 55 Rules, *by Fukuda Takeshi (1996). "Make it easy for people to say yes! Acquire the ability to say no without hesitation! (Here are) key points of interpersonal politics that you can use right away!!"*

demics appear on the popular media of Japan, which means that they make their work palatable to a popular audience. There is no shame in doing so; in fact it is expected. As a result, the media participate in the demystification of the intellectual, including *keigo,* in a way that Americans would find astonishing. The extent to which such constituencies talk to one another and cross-fertilize in Japan means that even the "academic" understanding of *keigo* is informed by the vernacular—to a degree that would surprise the Western scholar.

In a similar vein, and germane to this discussion of *keigo,* is the propensity for academics to publish handbooks, guides, and other how-to materials in their respective fields. Examples include Araki Hiroyuki's *Keigo japanorojii* (*Keigo* Japanology [1990]), Tokyo University professor Kikuchi Yasuto's *Keigo no sainyūmon* (A re-introduction to *keigo* [1996]), and Ōishi Hatsutarō and Hayashi Shirō's *Keigo no tsukaikata* (How to use keigo [1992]). Araki, who is associated with various prestigious institutions, among them Ritsumeikan University, Hiroshima University, and Kita-Kyushu University, offers Japanese and non-Japanese laypeople alike a glimpse into the unique aspects of Japanese culture and behavior through an understanding of *keigo.* Kikuchi, whose academic account I reviewed in Chapter 2, leads the reader through the specialist's technical vocabulary of *keigo* while simultaneously offering detailed analysis of forms and usage. His work is aimed, quite simply, at those who "are

The Modernization of *Keigo*   69

Figure 11. A book on keigo, *You Can Master How to Use Keigo in 3 Hours, by Shimizu Shōzō and Arimura Itsuko (1999), covering topics "from greetings and workplace manners to business negotiation." This is one volume in what the publisher calls its "ultra-illustrated, easy-to-understand, rookie support series."*

bad at, or want to improve their command of *keigo*" (Kikuchi 1994:iii). Similar manuals abound. At any given time the popular bookshelves in Japan are laden with guides to correct *keigo* usage. These promise to sort out once and for all the difficulties that Japanese face in attempting to speak their own language "correctly."

- *Keigo no tsukaikata ga san-jikan de masutaa dekiru* (You can master how to use *keigo* in three hours) (Shimizu and Arimura 1999; Figure 11)

- *Atte'ru yō de okashi na keigo jōshiki* (*Keigo* common sense) (Muramatsu 1990; Figure 12)

- *Tadashii keigo de hanasemasu ka?* (Can you speak correct *keigo*?) (21-Seiki no Nihongo o Kangaeru Kai 2001; Figure 13)

- *Keigo no tsukaikata ga wakaru hon* (The book for understanding how to use *keigo*) (Noguchi 1992)

- *Keigo ni tsuyoi hito no hon* (The book for people who are good at *keigo*) (Uchiyama 1992)

- *Anata no keigo doko ka okashii! Doko ga okashii?* (Somewhere your *keigo* is odd! Where is it odd?) (Ariyoshi 1989)

- *Mō machigawanai keigo no hon* (The book for no more mistaken *keigo*) (Fukuda 1989)

Figure 12. A book about keigo, You Think It's Right, but It's Odd: Keigo Common Sense, by Muramatsu Ei (1990) offering "180 success tips to deftly impress your audience." "If you don't know these rules, you will surely fail in corporate culture."

Figure 13. A book about keigo from 21-Seiki no Nihongo o Kangaeru Kai (2000), Tadashii keigo de hanasemasu ka? (Can you speak correct keigo?), promising instruction for keigo in the office, on the telephone, and during business visits.

- *Onna no miryoku wa "hanashikata" shidai "aisatsu" kara "keigo" made, shirazu-shirazu ni mi ni tsuku hon* (A woman's charm is in her language: The book for how to unconsciously pick up everything from greetings to *keigo*) (Kanai 1989)
- *Itsu de mo doko de mo tadashii keigo ga hanaseru hon: anata wa mechakucha keigo o tsukatte iru* (The book for always speaking correct *keigo*: *You* are using muddled *keigo*) (Hinata 1989)
- *Keigo o tsukaikonasu* (Getting the knack of using *keigo*) (Nomoto 1987)

Included in all of these materials[2] are the authors' credentials, which means their university and/or corporate affiliations. Their institutional affiliations lend credibility to the enterprise: instruction by an "expert" in how to talk.

The extent to which Japanese in general and the popular Japanese press in particular concern themselves with questions of polite language dwarfs any comparable phenomenon in the United States. Americans simply are not concerned with the questions of language use that Japanese speakers face; there is no paradigm in English whose primary function is to reflect the social relationships between speakers of the language. Similarities may perhaps exist in the consciousness of sexist and nonsexist language that some attempt to foster, but even this is quite limited in scope and general impact when compared to Japanese speakers' concern for and consciousness of language.

A Japanese acquaintance who works for one of the more "respectable" publishing houses characterized this genre of how-to books as "soft." In fact, the better known, more academic presses do not produce or distribute how-to books. Nonetheless, these books and corresponding educational enterprises tell us a great deal about how Japanese view social convention and about how customs are formulated. As Cameron (1995) observes, "In advice literature of all kinds, we see the norms for what counts as acceptable or unacceptable performance spelled out with especial clarity" (169). After all, the aim is surely to present an analysis and use a vocabulary that the greatest number of people will understand or that will appeal to the greatest number of people and, by extension, sell the greatest number of books. It is this capacity to encapsulate cultural norms that is the reason for my singling out of how-to books for scrutiny.[3]

How-to materials in Japan are also part of a larger how-to industry that includes educational enterprises in an astounding variety. As in the United States and Britain, there is an industry in Japan whose self-proclaimed role is to teach people how to talk. Practitioners in this enterprise come from the publishing industry as well as the academy (government monitored and regulated) and private instructional enterprise (not government monitored or regulated). The Tokyo equivalent of the yellow pages has a separate heading for *hanashikata-kyōshitsu* 'speaking classes/schools', although entries can also be found under *semmon-gakkō* 'vocational schools'. The popular press is peppered with articles about and advertisements for *hanashikata-kyōshitsu* that promise instruction in public speaking, job interview skills, and the development of interpersonal *apiiru* 'appeal'. A regular feature of any newspaper is the education listings, where people can go to find instructional opportunities in everything from bookkeeping to running a boardinghouse. The January 27, 1997, edition of the *Asahi shimbun* ran a full page of advertisements under the banner "School Square," including headings for (not in this order):

Speaking *(hanashikata)*	Language, conversation *(gogaku, kaiwa)*
Japanese teacher training *(nihongo-kyōshi yōsei)*	Handwriting, calligraphy
Announcing *(anaunsu)*	Calligraphy instruction
Bookkeeping/accounting	Computers, word processing
Medical office administration	Information processing
Home-building management	Paralegal
Administrative assistant	Public works
Government employment	National qualification
Travel industry	Private tutor
Nurse	Customs, trade administration
Consumer advisor	Small-business consulting
Tracing, drafting, CAD	Computer graphics
Architecture	Interior design
Color coordination	Jewelry
Stained glass	Counseling
Bridal counselor	Sports, health
Welfare mediation	Dog grooming
Coffeeshop, small restaurant	Lodging license

Note that language training takes its place alongside other skills that might further career opportunities. In the case of most language training this furtherance is a secondary skill, one that might not contribute directly or visibly to a person's prospects but that adds what in Japanese is known as *purasu arufua* 'plus alpha' (i.e., that extra something) to the overall personal portfolio. In the case of *hanashikata-kyōshitsu*, it adds "polish," enabling one, say, to negotiate the business scene in such a way as to make a good impression (to get the job, or the contract, or the sale) or to function in the wider social arena that accompanies rising through the ranks. The older a person gets and the higher s/he rises in the company hierarchy, the more s/he is called on to speak at weddings (especially those of subordinates), to chair meetings, to act as master of ceremonies at functions, and to negotiate the interpersonal politics of such groups as the PTA. Under the heading *"hanashikata"* in the abovementioned newspaper advertisement, the reader finds as well potential training in or solutions for: "Nerves, tension, blushing, trembling, stuttering, pronunciation, eye contact, conversation, greetings, meetings, interviews, persuasion, ceremonial occasions, PTA."[4]

In an effort to discover how native speakers talk about language and *keigo* for a native-speaking audience, I enrolled myself in one of these *hanashikata-kyōshitsu* in 1996. I took three courses over a nine-month period: one in public speaking *(supiichi)*, one in social conversation *(kaiwa)*, and one in running meetings *(shikaisha)*. Many of my fellow participants in the *hanashikata-kyōshitsu* had been sent or encouraged by their employers to undergo coaching. The ability to speak smoothly and fluently in a wide range of settings is a matter of serious concern in most Japanese business organizations. This is demonstrated most obviously in the business etiquette training that is a part of the process that new recruits into the workforce undergo as they are brought from the university into the highly structured atmosphere of their companies. Training is not limited to neophytes, however, as became clear from my conversations with others in the classes. Larger companies have the resources to include special sections on language and etiquette in their training for employees; smaller companies contract training out to specialists; individuals can, and do, take matters into their own hands and enroll themselves in self-improvement courses on public speaking. The *hanashikata-kyōshitsu* that I attended served both audiences: the preponderance of its business was not in the open-enrollment classes that I took, but in the training that it did for companies on a contract basis, tailoring programs to the needs and functions of its clientele. It is also not coincidental that the president and CEO of the school that I attended published his own book on speech and communication skills even as I was undergoing classes.

Part of the how-to industry's effectiveness lies in its indeterminate nature, both in membership and in content. Membership requires only a credential, and concerns are not limited to language. Content is organized more by the realities of everyday life than by the formal categories academics might prefer. By stating and restating the conventions for *keigo* usage (or any other subcomponent of appropriate behavior) in everyday parlance and placing them within contexts that "we all understand," the how-to industry reinforces those conventions even as it reassures readers that, by their participation in those conventions, their belongingness in Japan is cemented. The promotion of group cohesion is a central function of such enterprises, maybe as important as the content area itself. For example, as new recruits are brought into the Japanese workforce, it is not unusual for them to undergo some sort of orientation. Seminars and classes are part of the ongoing business of organizations. On the surface, such training might appear to serve only to bring participants up to speed on the skills necessary to carry out their work functions. But in Japan, the enculturation component is rarely overlooked. Those attending a weekend retreat for acquiring job skills can also look forward to playing tennis, going into the bath, and taking part in late-night drinking and karaoke parties. There is even "*seishin* training," whose very focus is spiritual development and development of group cohesion. When I attended classes at the *hanashikata-kyōshitsu*, we often went out together to karaoke bars—where the microphones were set up not for singing but for speech-making, of course. During these outings I asked many members of the group why they had signed up for classes. The obvious (to me at least) answer that they needed speaking skills on the job or at the PTA was rarely forthcoming. It was more likely that they had an opening in their social schedules (one—a Shinto priest—was taking some class or other almost every day of the week). That is, the stated utilitarian aspect of the class as it appeared in the advertisement was not necessarily the participants' main reason for signing up. They seemed to take classes more to make friends and for general self-improvement. This is a remarkable attitude from an American point of view, but in a culture where self-contextualization ("Where do I fit?") carries such a high premium, it is a natural extension of self.

Disembedding and the Technologization of Discourse

The how-to industry has assumed the task of telling the received story of *keigo*. Fifty years after the publication of "Kore kara no keigo," the how-to industry echoes prescriptions from that document. For example, *Bijinesu keigo ga sura-sura hanaseru hon* (The book for speaking smooth business *keigo*) by (Fukuda 1993) reminds us that *keigo* is, at its roots, a matter of civil behavior:

> *Keigo* is originally simplicity itself...but *keigo* follows the principles of language. It has rules and theory. If one studies them and makes them one's own, worries such as "I can't speak clearly," and "I'm just clumsy" will completely disappear.
>
> Language changes along with the flow of its era. But language is a tool of communication and also has parts that cannot be pulled apart from old customs and human connections. In fact, *keigo* carries with it this troublesome baggage.
>
> And so it keeps people at a distance.
>
> But to say that "it's troublesome to learn it little by little so let's just forget it"— isn't that purposely to confuse and keep at a distance the *keigo* that is originally so simple? (5–6)[5]

Meiji forebears might or might not have been surprised to hear that *keigo* was "originally so simple." But in the how-to story of *keigo*, simplicity is critical: "In times past, ranking by social position *(mibun)* was fixed. When speaking to a superior *(mibun no takai hito),* one used honorific speech, and when speaking of oneself *(jibun),* one used humble speech. When speaking about things, one used formal speech. When high-ranking people spoke to servants and the like, in contrast, they attached nothing. This will be explained later, but this is a major point of difference in modern *keigo*" (Asada 1996:9).[6] Such attempts to adapt the history and conventions of *keigo*, from the Kokugo Shingikai to how-to books to *hanashikata-kyōshitsu*, are consonant with features of modernization that Giddens (1991) calls "disembedding," and Fairclough (1995) the "technologization of discourse."

Giddens' notion of disembedding refers to the lifting out of traditional social relations that mark local contexts and their application to abstract systems of large-scale, industrial societies (1991:21). Disembedding is a defining feature of the discontinuities that mark transition from the traditional to modern world, the movement from small-scale systems to large-scale societies. The process of *keigo* standardization exemplifies exactly this: from a premodern cacophony of regional and class varieties, a "standard" was cobbled together for application in a modern nation-state. Though Japan had large cities in the pre-Meiji era, the kinds of relationships that mark modern society in general—impersonal, anonymous, mobile, rapidly changing—were rare. One of *keigo*'s modern roles, for those who master it, is to alleviate the angst associated with the array of human/interpersonal interactions that mark modern life in Japan.[7] Advice for linguistic behavior lays out its instruction in terms of those interactions, not in terms of the forms themselves. A popular "dictionary" of expressions called *Chotto shita mono no iikata* (Trivial expressions) (Pakira Hausu 1990) presents scenes of human relationships and the language with which they are associated: *sewa ni natta* (being in someone's debt), *mono o moratta* (having received something), *jibun no misu o ayamaru* (apologizing for your own gaffes), and so forth. From its introduction:

> There are about 1000 phrases recorded in this little dictionary. Some are casual greetings, others are request patterns that carry with the address a feeling that we are about to incur a feeling of unending obligation. Still others are filled with the antagonism that sometimes accompanies differences in perspective, and yet one can feel underlying the turn of phrase a conscientious effort not to damage the friendship with the addressee/listener. Thus, these thousand are scenes of human relationships. In those scenes, one result of the language used toward the addressee/listener is what happens afterward—the relationship might improve; alternatively, it might deteriorate. Even when they don't seem that significant, words carry the power to transform in subtle ways, to dampen spirits or, alternatively, to indicate greater closeness than anticipated. Those transformations may seem trivial, but it can be daunting to look back afterward and think, "That's when it began."
>
> In the time-honored phrase "trivial expressions" we can hear "in things there are expressions," or, in other words, "in one phrase it is possible to fall either to the left or to the right"; therefore, it also behooves us to be careful of foolish language or insensitive language. We inherit the progressive wisdom that tells us "this is the way you should say it."
>
> As we continue to gaze at this wise expression, it's quite something how a deeper

The Modernization of *Keigo*

and deeper understanding of scenes of human relationships unfolds, and for some reason, we smile. This smile is the smile of gladness that we come to associate with understanding the honesty in something we have heard; in other words, there is some kind of truth included here. This is what we have tried to put together in this little dictionary.[8]

Language that readers know (or come to think they should know) from one network of experiences is generalized to other contexts and is then credited with bringing a feeling of familiarity to both speaker and listener in those other contexts.

Among the disembedding mechanisms that Giddens describes in detail is the creation of "symbolic tokens" like money or language. Language in modern society becomes a resource that can be bought and sold, a medium of exchange, and a kind of capital. Bourdieu (1991) has more to say on the topic of linguistic capital than does Giddens, critiquing contemporary linguistics, for example, in its concern for the competence that constitutes the target of most linguistic investigation. Competence, Bourdieu says, "is of little consequence in the real world since, though it may be adequate to produce sentences that are likely to be understood, it may be quite inadequate to produce sentences that are likely to be listened to, likely to be recognized as acceptable in all the situations in which there is occasion to speak" (55). This is language as capital, and Bourdieu goes on to state that the more formulaic or conventional a situation is, the more likely it is that language will become linguistic capital, a medium for buying or selling one's way in and out (70). Beginning with "Kore kara no keigo" and continuing into the present, Japanese how-to can be counted on to reinforce exactly this point:

> The number of generally used *keigo* expressions is actually quite limited. Honorific and humble forms are frequently confused and mistaken, but if you internalize the other basics of language, it stands to reason that you will also make huge strides in the use of *keigo*. (Gendai Manaa Fuōramu 1996:14)[9]

> In adult society there is this troublesome thing called *keigo*....
> In reality, one doesn't hear so much about people, in the business world, for example, who lost their jobs because their *keigo* was incompetent. And yet there are any number of people who missed the way simply because they misused language....
> If you are to become a full-fledged member of society, you will be required to use "the correct language of adults." (Chiteki Seikatsu Kenkyūjo 1994:3–4)[10]

Language is the means by which one purchases credibility as an adult in society. There are other symbolic systems that go hand-in-hand with language (gesture, body language, and clothing, to name three), but the place of language in how-to books about manners, human relationships *(ningen-kankei)*, and speeches demonstrates the primacy of linguistic capital.

A secondary feature of Giddens' disembedding mechanism is the "expert system," which is a complex of technical accomplishment or professional expertise that organizes large areas of the material and social environments in which people live from day to day (1991:27). Expert systems serve to organize areas of the social environment in which people live. They provide "guarantees" of expectations across time and space. Giddens provides examples of expert systems that include lawyers, architects, and doctors. I add to this the language professionals who populate the how-to industry of Japan. Like lawyers, doctors, and architects, they are "sensei," and the contingent and chimerical nature of that very title yields insight into the nature of what it means to be an expert in modern Japan.

More specifically, Fairclough's notion of the "technologization of discourse" serves to render in detail the expert systems that are the language how-to industry of Japan. The "technologization of discourse" is a process by which institutions intervene in the sphere of discourse practices with the objective of constructing or maintaining the status quo (1995:102). Technologization of discourse, according to Fairclough, is marked by five features, all of which call up images of the *hanashikata-kyōshitsu* and its teachers:

1. The emergence of expert "discourse technologists." These are professionals who are marked by a special, privileged relationship with the knowledge of the sphere in which they intervene.

2. A shift in the "policing" of discourse practices. Technologists are outsiders to the institutions in which they intervene.

3. Design and projection of context-free discourse techniques. The design and redesign of discourse practices aims, to the extent possible, to make them usable in any relevant context.

4. Strategically motivated simulation in discourse. Discourse practices arising elsewhere are grafted onto newly designed or redesigned discourse techniques.

5. Pressure toward standardization of discourse practices. Centralizing and standardizing pressures, which often meet with resistance, are brought to bear on discourse practice.

The accredited professionals who are members of the Kokugo Shingikai, who run the *hanashikata-kyōshitsu*, and who write the how-to books hold special, privileged relationships to the knowledge that they dispense. For hands-on skills in speaking, training is carried out by former radio and television announcers, airline flight attendants, customer service experts, and so on—representatives of fields where the skillful manipulation of language is a sine qua non. Printed materials are produced either by groups whose raison d'être is to provide expert guidance (such as the Twenty-Four Hour Manners Group [Gurūpu 24-Jikan no Manaa] that authored *Manaa bukku* [Manner book] or the Modern Manners Forum [Gendai Manaa Fuōramu] that produced *E de wakaru manaa jiten* [Dictionary of manners through pictures]) or by individual experts whose academic credentials are listed on the flyleaf or copyright page of the book.

In Fairclough's terms, modern discourse practices surrounding *keigo* have grown more and more familiar in contemporary Japan through the "policing" of language and social convention by language professionals. Earlier forms of intervention in discourse practice (for example, the family and its extensions) have been replaced, as Fairclough predicts, by the language how-to industry. Those earlier forms of intervention are, in fact, often mentioned in the how-to materials themselves:

> Recently, the custom of using *keigo* at home has become but a shadow of its former self. Because of this, the number of young people who cannot use it correctly has increased. There are arguments for the abolition of *keigo*, but in average society *keigo* is just common sense. (Gurūpu 24-Jikan no Manaa 1996:23)[11]

> *Keigo* is in a state of disarray. And it's no ordinary mix-up. Two young wives were talking. One said something like, "Oh, it's time to nurse *ageru* ['give' to out-group] the baby." It isn't that she's going to nurse *ageru* someone else's baby. Even though she's going to nurse *yaru* ['give' to in-group] her own, she talks like this. [There follow other examples of misuse, primarily by young people.] There are many people who are of a mind that we should do away with *keigo* or at the very least reform it, especially "progressive" scholars and critics, even many of the teachers at the place I work....But Japanese *keigo* is the Japanese heart, our way of thinking, our way of behaving, our way of assigning value. In short, it is tied deeply to Japanese culture. (Kikuchi 1996:11, 18, 30)[12]

It is hard to find a Japanese speaker who does not agree with the sentiment quoted above. Its acceptance is accompanied by a corresponding embrace, in modern Japan, of the need for intervention on the part of outside agents—who train people in the art of speaking. The how-to materials themselves lay out the standards and principles that are agreed on and serve to guide instruction.

Language standards, once established and widely recognized, can be manipulated—in Fairclough's words, "designed and redesigned." In this sense, the frame that underlay *keigo* in the past has been expertly redesigned for application to the modern situation. It has essentially been borrowed from one social venue and applied not only to modern social structures (business, neighborhood relations, hospital visits), but also assigned the role of structuring discourse itself, as in the following excerpt from *Kotobazukai to keigo* (Language use and *keigo*) within which *keigo* frames the predictable interactions of the business day:

Calling out to the boss *(kachō)*

In using language that incorporates *keigo,* the most important thing is getting used to it. Now that we understand the basic forms, let's try using the following.

First, think of the workplace where you belong as the sort of place where one uses *keigo,* speak in a positive way, and if you make a mistake have someone tell you about it right away so that you can say it correctly. In so doing, you will acquire the confidence to talk with people outside the company as well.

Let's try using the following language in combination with addressing the *kachō*. One wants to get used to it coming out of one's mouth unconsciously during daily conversations.

Kachō! Good morning.
Kachō! I hope you will treat me favorably again today.
Kachō! What time will you be here?
Kachō! Could I have you explain this to me?
Kachō! Is this all right?
Kachō! Could we have you attend?
Kachō! What is convenient for you?
Kachō! So-and-so-division chief is here.
Kachō! I am just back from such-and-such company.
Kachō! I brought the materials to hand in.
Kachō! I will take your bags.
Kachō! I want to ask about such-and-such a matter.
Kachō! What will you have?
Kachō! Is now a good time?
Kachō! I'll do it.
Kachō! Thank you for today.
Kachō! Excuse me for going first. (Suzuki Yukiko 1991:40–41)[13]

The fifth characteristic of Fairclough's technologization of discourse— pressure toward standardization of discourse practices—certainly holds for linguistic convention in Japan. In fact, a whole range of specific examples of standardization can be seen in the discourse practices associated not only with *keigo*, but with manners and etiquette, job interviewing, letter-writing, wedding speeches, and telephoning (see Wetzel and Inoue 1999). Telephoning is an especially good arena for observing how discourse practices are standardized. The structure of a telephone call anywhere is constrained and predictable by its nature—it has an unambiguous beginning and end, it is usually purposeful, and it contains more redundancy than face-to-face conversation, because participants cannot see each other and often don't know each other well. In Japan the pressure to standardize the structure of the telephone call is fraught with appeals to righteousness:

A telephone call is the round-trip exchange of voices. Your first word conveys for better or worse the image of your company. Indeed, just because you can't be seen, you express everything through your manner of speaking and use of language. Your smiling face, your expression, and your attitude all come through. (Noguchi 1992:46)[14]

On the telephone, you rely on your language and voice
On the telephone, you can't see your counterpart. It's very convenient to be able to talk to someone who is in another place while you just stand there, but you can't see what your listener looks like. Naturally, you rely on your voice and language. And if you can't use *keigo* and *keigo*-like expressions, your very character comes under suspicion. (Uchiyama 1992:97)[15]

The Modernization of *Keigo*

Telephone calls, then, are orchestrated, with the norms for *keigo* understood in their coordination with other sign systems like clothes, body movements, and manners and etiquette. From *Bijinesu keigo ga surasura hanaseru hon:*

Make sure that you have memo paper ready
Make the call after having prepared what you want to get across
Keep contractions to a minimum
Answer incoming calls within three rings
Talk about your business within three minutes
When you ask the other party to wait, get confirmation!
Be sure to double-check names and times
Be sure to repeat the matter under discussion
Clear, easy to understand speed!
Replace the receiver quietly   (Fukuda 1993:191)[16]

Even the flow of the exchange is conventionalized, down to the order in which rituals and content are folded into the sequence:

Taking a call	Making a call
Answer within three rings	Double-check the matter you are calling about and the telephone number
Say your company name	Make the call (Check the company name of the person you are calling)
Verify the name of the person who is calling (Always double-check)	Give your own full name and company name
Greeting We are always grateful to you for your business.	Clearly state your business
Ask what the call is about (Don't forget memo paper)	Greet, then state your business
Verify the main point(s)	Make sure that the content has gotten across correctly
Say good-by, and replace the receiver quietly.	Never slam it down.

(Fukuda 1993:193)[17]

An almost identical script is included in the training materials examined by Wetzel and Inoue (1999), and the same language can be found in other how-to books and teaching materials. The utility of the sequence derives, as Fairclough says, from its predictability and its applicability to a wide range of encounters.

Finally, Giddens observes that "stretching" of the social system is achieved through "the impersonal nature of tests applied to evaluate technical knowledge and by public critique (upon which the production of technical knowledge is based), to control its form" (1991:28).

Examples of this in the language how-to industry abound in quizzes, tests, and checks that are included in much of the popular analysis of *keigo*. People are constantly reminded to examine their own understanding of linguistic convention. Below is a quiz used at the *hanashikata-kyōshitsu* that I attended.

I. Correct or incorrect?

1. "Section Chief, did you see (*haiken-shimashita* [humble verb]) this?"

    [Incorrect: The humble form *haiken-shimashita* should not be used in addressing a superior.]

2. "What do you say (*mōsararemasu* [humble verb/honorific inflection]) your name is?"

    [Incorrect: *Mōsararemasu* is an honorific derivation (*-araremase*) combined with a humble verb (*mōs-u*).]

3. "Don't you know (*zonjiagemasen* [humble verb]) anything about baseball?"

    [Incorrect: The humble form *zonjiagemasen* should not be used in addressing others.]

4. "I know (*shitte imasu* [plain verb]) about the president."

    [Incorrect: A nonhonorific form like *shitte imasu* is not sufficient in speaking about the company president.]

5. "Welcome, everyone."

    [Correct.]

6. "Please take out (*o-dashi* [honorific verb]) the paper that you received (*itadaita* [humble verb]) at the reception area."

    [Incorrect: The humble form *itadaita* should not be used in addressing others.]

II. Supply the correct honorific and humble special equivalents.

iu 'say'
kiku 'listen/ask'
miru 'look'
taberu 'eat'
iru 'be'
suru 'do'
yaru 'give'
morau 'get, receive'
kureru 'give to me/us'[18]

Every month, as part of the training, there was a closing ceremony (*shūryōshiki*) for all those who had completed courses at the school. The first part of this closing ceremony was always a one-hour lecture given by some member of the faculty on a topic that touched on communication. The topic for one lecture was *Tadashii keigo no tsukaikata* (Correct use of *keigo*) and was given by the vice president of the school. The content of her speech was consonant with the how-to books: "It is said that language is deteriorating...we are all aware of current popular language and phrases such as *'chō beri-gū'* [really good], *'chō beri-baa'* [really bad], *'nama-ashi'* [stockingless legs], etc. Language is alive, so one expects it to change....But all of these examples of current slang are phrases/language *(kotoba)* that will disappear. What then is *keigo?*" (from my notes). The message was familiar, mirroring the how-to books in content and evaluative stance. In this lecture, as with many of the how-to books, there was a self-evaluation segment—questions that would allow listeners to check themselves on whether they actually had mastered the forms under discussion. We were challenged to judge the sentences in the foregoing as acceptable or unacceptable, then to supply the appropriate humble and honorific forms for the nine verbs listed. Those in attendance answered about half of the items correctly. Four days later, at a Tuesday meeting of a communication skills class, *keigo* was again the theme. Perhaps the instructor had been inspired by the previous Friday's lecture—both because of its content and because of the inability of participants to perform. We began class with the recognition that part and parcel of interacting with people when meeting for the first time is to be polite. "And," the instructor assumed agreement, "there is a minimal level of *keigo* that is called for in such circumstances. What is that level?" While waiting for a response (which was not forthcoming), he took from his briefcase a stack of *keigo* exercises.

Use of *sonkeigo* and *kenjōgo*

Basic form	Sonkeigo	Kenjōgo
iku 'go'	*irassharu*	
kuru 'come'		
iu 'say'		
suru 'do'		
kaku 'write'		
taberu 'eat'		
miru 'look'		
iru 'be'		

Use of *teineigo*

Basic form	Polite phrase	One level more polite
atchi 'over there'	*achira*	
kotchi 'here'		
dō? 'how is it?'		
aru 'exists, is'		
ii yo 'it's all right'		
sō da 'that's right'		

Use of '*o-*' and '*go-*'

When to use '-o' in regard to the other person

The other person's body
The other person's state of health
Things the other person is carrying
The other person's actions
The other person's family or relatives

Use '*-o*' in regard to the actions of those who are affiliated with the other person[19]

Again there were bafflement, frustration, and resignation from classmates in the face of this activity.

One week after the class meeting, there was, as usual, a warm-up activity—this time reviewing what we had covered in the previous class. Individual members of the class were asked to provide specific forms of *keigo:*

- The *sonkeigo* form of *kuru* 'come'?

  The participant who was called on to answer responded, *"Aah… 'kimasu'?"* The correct answer is *irassharu.*

- The *sonkeigo* form of *iu* 'say'?

  The participant who was called on to answer responded, *"Ossharu da to omoimasu"* (I think it's *ossharu*). This was correct.

- The *sonkeigo* form of *suru* 'do'? The response came, *"Nasaru."* Correct.

- The *kenjōgo* form of *suru?* The person to whom this was directed gave the instructor a blank look.

- A more polite *(issō teinei)* way of saying *sō da?* Again, the person addressed drew a blank.

Setting aside for the moment the issue of native speakers' mediocre performance on these exercises, it is illustrative to compare them to exercises taken from published how-to materials. The first example is a "check test" from one of the *keigo* how-to manuals (Noguchi 1992); the second is a similar quiz from the Bunka-chō's pamphlet on *keigo* for teachers (Bunka-chō 1995). It is no strain to see that the information presented about *keigo* in the how-to industry and the standard Mombusho-sanctioned texts is closely connected.

There are two major categories of language in the following. Place an X beside those phrases that you would use for your own actions, and a circle beside those you would use for the other person's actions.

1. *orimasu* ('be' [humble])
   [Correct answer: X]

2. *go-setsumei mōshiageru* ('explain' [humble])
   [Correct answer: X]

4. *irassharu* ('be/go' [honorific])
   [Correct answer: O]

5. *goran ni naru* ('look' [honorific])
   [Correct answer: O]

6. *chōdai-suru* ('receive' [humble])
   [Correct answer: X]

7. *zonjite iru* ('know' [humble])
   [Correct answer: X]

8. *go-annai itasu* ('lead' [humble])
   [Correct answer: X]

9. *omimi ni hairu* ('hear' [honorific])
   [Correct answer: O]

10. *omie ni naru* ('appear/come' [honorific])
    [Correct answer: O]

11. *ossharu* ('say' [honorific])
    [Correct answer: O]

12. *mōsu* ('say' [humble])
    [Correct answer: X]

13. *ukagau* ('ask/visit' [humble])
    [Correct answer: X]

14. *okoshi negau* ('have [someone] come' [humble])
    [Correct answer: X]

15. *go-sokurō itadaku* ('have [someone] come' [humble])
    [Correct answer: X][20]

Choose one

20. *'Toriisogi gohenji made'* to *'Toriisogi ohenji made'*.
    [Your immediate reply: *gohenji* or *ohenji*]

21. *'Shitsurei desu ga, sensei no otaku wa Kamakura de irasshaimashita ka'* to *'Shitsurei desu ga, sensei no otaku wa Kamakura de gozaimashita ka'*
    [I'm sorry, was the teacher's house in Kamakura? *Irasshaimashita* or *gozaimashita*]

22. *'Buchō, kachō ga kyō wa sha ni wa modoranai to osshatte imashita'* to *'Buchō, kachō ga kyō wa sha ni wa modoranai to itte imashita'*
    [Chief, the Section Head said that s/he wouldn't be coming back today: *osshatte* or *itte*]

23. *'Sono ken ni tsuite wa, watakushi kara keii o gohōkoku itashimasu'* to *'Sono ken ni tsuite wa, watakushi kara keii o gohōkoku sasete itadakimasu'*
    [I will do the report on details of that case: *itashimasu* or *sasete itadakimasu*]

24. *'Shachō wa, ano hōkoku ni manzoku sarete ita yo'* to *'Shachō wa, ano hōkoku ni manzoku shite irasshatta yo'*
    [The president was satisfied with that report: *sarete ita* or *shite irasshatta*]

25. *'Mō kore ijō, aite chiimu ni ten o agete wa ikemasen ne'* to *'Mō kore ijō, aite chiimu ni ten o yatte wa ikemasen ne'*
    [We shouldn't give the other team any more points than this: *agete* or *yatte*]

26. *'Yamada-sensei ni yoroshiku otsutae kudasai'* to *'Yamada-sensei ni yoroshiku mōshiagete kudasai'*
[Please ~~give~~ my best wishes to Prof. Yamada: *otsutae* or *moshiagete*][21]

Compare the three exercises reprinted above with the next one, taken from a *kokugo* grammar book (Saeki 1953:79):

Problem
Are the following phrases appropriate?
Sensei mo kono hon o oyomi ni natta ka.
(Caution: Think about the case where a parent asks a child, and the case of asking your teacher.)

Problem
Turn the following into forms showing *sonkei* (politeness), and think about the resulting forms.
kaku   motsu   mou   toru   okiru   tasukeru   ukeru   kimeru   miseru

Problem
Think about forms of the following that would show *sonkei* (politeness).
kiru   kū   shinu[22]

The tasks are hauntingly similar. The *hanashikata-kyōshitsu* and the how-to book exercises should feel familiar—nostalgic—to anyone who experienced the Japanese educational system of the 1950s or 1960s. The consistency in content and form seems almost conspiratorial, which is not surprising. All these agencies talk to each other and function to instill and reiterate the same practices. The question then becomes one of why the story of *keigo* seems so important to these adults at this point in their lives, what is at stake in its portrayal, and how to relate this "modern" account of *keigo* to the "traditional" story that speakers (should have) learned in their compulsory education. The Japanese language how-to industry takes traditional relationships and their associated linguistic conventions and restructures them for contemporary (modern) Japanese interaction—in the company, in the modern urban neighborhood (where most people commute in and out on a daily basis and where few people are native), at restaurants, at funerals, in the morning, at the first meeting, and so on. The quizzes and tests established to teach or measure people's success at internalizing those conventions are themselves standardized.

All Japanese people come into *keigo* instruction with some experience of *keigo*. The problem lies in bridging the gap between their experience of it in their lives and the contexts and relationships that how-to distills and standardizes in these quizzes. The Japanese laypeople whom I observed in the *hanashikata-kyōshitsu*, when faced with the directives and advice of the language professionals who were our teachers, had a difficult time associating what was presented in the classroom with their own experience of language. They were singularly bad at the quizzes even as, in my observations, many of them used reasonably skillful *keigo* in actual interactions. None was as incompetent as their failure at the classroom quizzes would have led me to predict. The extent to which they bought into the portrayal of linguistic convention set forth by the *hanashikata-kyōshitsu* is undoubtedly an issue, but the fact that they chose to take the class indicates a belief that internalizing what was being taught was important. This, too, is typical of modernization, according to Giddens. Most laypeople consult professionals infrequently, but when they do, they have faith in the professionals' "codes of knowledge." In the case of the language how-to industry, these are the grammar and associated conventions of *keigo*. Giddens is clear on another point: the layperson's trust in the expert system does not depend on mastery of the specific content area (27). The uneasy interface between knowledge brokers and consumers could not have a more telling example than the trust put in Japanese *hanashikata-kyōshitsu* and how-to materials in general.

Keigo Nostalgia

It has been observed by social scientists that within Japan's postwar economic boom there arose a nostalgia for the past and an ensuing introspection in pursuit of continuity. In language, as in other cultural institutions, idealizing the past can be instrumental in smoothing over the discontinuities of the present. "As culture industries seek to reassure Japanese that everything is in place and all is not lost, the concomitant understanding arises...that such reassurance would not be necessary if loss, indeed, were not at stake" (Ivy 1995:10).

It is, therefore, no coincidence that *keigo* how-to books began to appear in the 1970s and peaked in the economic boom of the 1980s and 1990s.[23] This represents a wave of *keigo* nostalgia on the part of multiple constituencies, including the generation of Japanese who were brought up and educated just after World War II, during *keigo*'s "golden age," that window when *keigo* saw universal agreement in its analysis and in what it represented, and was instilled as doctrine. Another constituency consists of succeeding generations who are willing to consume products that reassure them about continuity. *Keigo*'s "golden age" was brief, and it is not accidental that it coincided with the fervor of national unity that marked Japan's recovery from war. In the *keigo* how-to that began to appear twenty years later, when the postwar generation began to come of age, there are both a looking back and a recognition, as Ivy (1995) says, "that the destabilizations of capitalist modernity have decreed the loss of much of the past, a past sometimes troped as 'traditional'" (9–10). This nostalgia grows as the postwar generation realizes that succeeding generations no longer learn about *keigo* in the same way. An industry has grown up around trying to recover the unity of the 1950s version of *keigo*, while at the same time preserving the sense of absence that motivates the recovery effort. How-to engages in acts of nostalgia that construct an idealized snapshot of the past "in an attempt to conquer and spatialize time" (Boym 2001:49).

Language intervention, exemplified in Japan's how-to industry, provides an outstanding opportunity to observe the interface between public policy and educational enterprise, between convention and practice, and between history and the present, in addition to providing a window on modern linguistic ideology in Japan. Public and private concerns, as well as individual and institutional interests, all of which have something at stake in language practice, come together in language how-to to forge a remarkably consistent portrait of convention, itself a consequence of historical process. The cooperation evident in the language how-to industry of Japan, while not without dissension, reflects a unity of purpose that those who tout educational "standards" would envy. Beyond this, it adheres to principles and processes of modernization that have been said to accompany the dissolution of tradition and the advent of industry and technology in the modern state.

And yet the agreement that characterizes language convention in Japan reflects a complex of cultural attitudes and beliefs that lies outside the Western, or at least the American, mold: an assumption that vertical relations are harmonious; a concern for the other that simultaneously supersedes and serves self-interest; a conviction that meaning follows form. Do these differences pose a challenge to models that have been developed for Western societies? How can these differences be reconciled, and what do they mean to our understanding of linguistic and other social processes? How will these attributes impinge on the continuing evolution of linguistic convention in Japan?

At the very least it is clear that language does not function or change alone, without conscious human intervention. In Japan as elsewhere, the social and the linguistic are inextricably intertwined, and deliberation over the one has repercussions for the other. Linguistic and social change is not just a matter of progress in a certain direction, but involves contradictions and multiple forces. This aspect of language is underexamined, perhaps because the interaction of forces is so complex as to thwart scientific certainty. In historical perspective, however, the arguments of the past shed light on those of the present and make linguistic modernization one of the most fruitful avenues of investigation for contemporary social research.

The Modernization of *Keigo*

CHAPTER 5

Keigo Common Sense

Keigo convention as it is portrayed through how-to enterprises is not limited to language in the professional linguistic sense but takes in a wide range of social practices that impinge on language use. How-to is rarely, if ever, organized or categorized by the formal features that academics pride themselves on winkling out. In prescriptive guides for *keigo* in Japan, language is held up to the same light that illuminates a myriad of other social practices, and the process blurs many distinctions that language professionals might prefer to make.

Although their underlying aims (and even some of their conclusions) are quite different, what virtually all how-to enterprises have in common is an integrated approach to what I call the "linguistic landscape" of Japan. Anthropologists make use of the term "cultural landscape" to mean a way of seeing human surroundings that emphasizes the interaction between human beings and nature over time. The cultural landscape is a setting for human experience and activity. It is constantly being made and remade by human activities, which gives it significant meanings and values. It may be the countryside; it may be an urban street or square; or it may be a place imbued with a sense of public history (Ingerson 2000). Humans are located physically, as well as psychologically and socially, in conventional worlds that can be described as cultural landscapes. Because it is a cultural artifact, language too constitutes a landscape, a setting for experiencing what it means to be Japanese (or anything else), complete with locators that enable participants to identify themselves and others and to navigate through a shared world. How does one become located linguistically in Japanese? What are the parameters of linguistic form that combine to make up a world that is Japanese, and not English or some other language? This is the linguistic landscape of Japan, language as a place where speakers locate themselves for successive actions. This landscape has serious repercussions for a full understanding of *keigo*, including that (1) formal analysis cannot capture the native speaker's experience of language; and that (2) language must be viewed as tied inexorably to a whole class of phenomena generally (perhaps universally) grouped under the rubric "common sense."

The World before *Keigo*

Long before there was a formal category called *keigo*, there was *aisatsu*. The term *"aisatsu"* has a long history in Japanese and in Japanese language how-to. In an age when there was no word *"keigo,"* instruction in language use entailed instruction in something other than what came to be known as *keigo*. It is easy to find prewar how-to books, magazines, and pamphlets that take language and politeness as their point of departure. Those materials may refer to *kotobazukai* 'language use', *hōmon* 'visiting', and *ōtai* 'reception, hosting',[1] but as often as not they refer to *aisatsu*, as exemplified in materials like Figure 14, which comes from a mass-market paperback entitled *Fujin no kotobadukai mohanshū: Nichijō no ōtai/shōreishiki no aisatsu* (Model language usage for women: Everyday dealings, various polite greetings) (Fujin Kurabu 1932).

Figure 14. A 1932 book about language and social situations for the "modern" woman that makes no mention of keigo: Model Language Usage for Women: Everyday Dealings, Various Polite Greetings.

Another volume, *Aisatu no kotoba-duka (h)i no kihon to naru gendaishiki reigi sahō* (Greetings and language use: The basis of modern courtesy and manners) (Shūbunsha Henshūbu 1933), has similar illustrations.

Such handbooks never mention the word *"keigo,"* let alone anything that approaches formal analysis of such linguistic categories as *sonkeigo, kenjōgo,* or *teineigo*. Rather, they are organized by social situations with their appropriate language.

Everyday greetings *(nichijō no aisatsu)*
Manners and greetings *(aisatsu)* for visits *(hōmon)*
Manners for visitors *(hōmon-kyaku)*
Manners and greetings *(aisatsu)* for celebrations
Manners and greetings *(aisatsu)* for comforting the sick
Manners and greetings *(aisatsu)* in times of misfortune
Manners and greetings *(aisatsu)* at mealtimes
General manners and greetings *(ippan no sahō to aisatsu)*, etc.

(from the table of contents, Shūbunsha Henshūbu 1933)[2]

Redundancy is common, and naming of linguistic categories is superfluous.

Not so very much has changed. One can still find how-to books on *kotoba-zukai* (Suzuki 1991), *ōtai* (Urano 2002), *hōmon* (Nishio 1993), and *aisatsu* (Amemiya 1998, Maruoka 1992, 1996, Urano 1999). But a new category—*keigo*—has joined these. Yet Asada's (1996) *Keigo manyuaru* (*Keigo* manual) demonstrates that the modern formal category is artificial. It is the old-fashioned, functional categories that still hold people's imaginations. A 428-page guide to "using honorifics" (in English; from the cover page), *Keigo manyuaru*'s first 40 topics of a total 150 are all *aisatsu:*

1. When you meet someone in the morning
2. When you meet someone during the day
3. When you meet someone in the evening
4. When you're going to sleep
5. When you meet someone for the first time
6. When you're asking someone out after that
7. When you're going out
8. When you're seeing someone off
9. When you've come back
10. When you're meeting someone who's come back
11. When you meet someone after not seeing him/her for a long time
12. When you go home before others
13. When parting
14. When you ask the other person to go with you
15. When you visit another's house
16. When welcoming a visitor
17. When attracting the other's attention

18. When having a meal
19. When finishing a meal
20. When offering something to the other
21. When you've been offered something
22. When showing appreciation
23. When you respond to appreciation or apologies
24. Showing that you are sorry
25. When showing gratitude
26. When offering encouragement
27. When showing surprise
28. When showing anger
29. When showing sympathy
30. When making requests and demands
31. When receiving requests and demands
32. When trying to refuse requests and demands
33. When refusing requests and demands
34. When trying to give advice
35. Celebrating matters having to do with the other
36. Praising matters having to do with the other
37. Showing consideration for matters having to do with the other
38. Showing consideration when the other is ill or injured
39. Asking after the other's health
40. Wishing for the other's success[3]

The remaining 110 topics list individual verbs, their inflections, and attendant idiosyncrasies. Is this confounding of *aisatsu* and *keigo* unusual? By no means. It is much more the rule than the exception. *Aisatsu* preoccupies *keigo* how-to to a startling degree. From *Keigo ni tsuyoi hito no hon:*

> **The success or failure of business negotiations is decided by language use**
> 1. Visiting a customer—*aisatsu* and self-introduction, presenting your *meishi* 'business card'
> *Suimasen* in what follows is not *aisatsu!*
> A tall young man comes to the door, puts out his *meishi,* and says, "*Suimasen,* I am so-and-so."
> When paying calls, first, let's make *aisatsu* a priority.
>
> > *Ohayō gozaimasu* 'Good morning'
> > *Konnichi wa* 'Good afternoon'
> > *Shitsurei shimasu* 'Pardon me'
>
> Let's think about the goodwill that we convey when we use these with a smile, brightly, freshly, conscious of facial expression and attitude.
> When our expressions are positive, our demeanors are perky and sunny!
> A bright voice comes out of a bright face; a bright voice does not accompany a gloomy expression.
>
> (Uchiyama 1992:46–47)[4]

Keigo Common Sense

One gets a clear, if saccharine, sense of the emotional impact of *aisatsu*. All this advice about *aisatsu* serves as a lead-in to the *keigo* appropriate for business negotiations. Lest any reader persist in thinking these examples merely idiosyncratic, *Keigo: Haji o kakanai tsukaikata* (*Keigo:* Use without fear) considers *aisatsu* fundamental to daily communication *(nichijō komyunikeeshon)*: "In everyday life, we human beings cannot live alone. In order to carry on communication with other people, the simplest, most effective strategy is *aisatsu*" (Uchiyama 1994:43).[5] *Keigo no tsukaikata ga wakaru hon* places *aisatsu* and *keigo* in the same category for purposes of treating people civilly: "*Aisatsu* and polite language together—these are only appropriate as natural behaviors to accompany a warm reception. For the guest/client/customer who feels that s/he has been treated with care, let's think about what that means and how to express it" (Noguchi 1992:77).[6]

Clearly, *aisatsu* is seriously undertranslated as 'greetings'. By its very nature *aisatsu* is much more serious business in Japan than are greetings in English. A term that better captures the function of *aisatsu* might be "discursive bookends,"[7] for the simple reason that *aisatsu* grounds most interactions in Japan. Not only does it lend structure; it also tells the participants what kind of interaction is at hand, who is involved, what their relationship is, and what is at stake. Two examples from the *hanashikata-kyōshitsu* that I attended come immediately to mind. The first comes from the convention of selecting, at the end of each course, one representative from each class to give a five-minute speech before about seventy-five people at a "graduation" ceremony where all students and teachers are in attendance. I was corralled into doing one of these presentations by my first class (the wages of sin—I missed the class where the representative was selected), and the week before the ceremony my teacher offered to assist me with my speech. We arranged to meet an hour before the next class to go over my speech. At that meeting, we practiced m·· *aisatsu* for the speech for the entire hour: stand after being introduced, proceed to the podium, and perform the opening and closing *aisatsu* for the speech: "Good evening, everyone. My name is [bow to the count of three]....Today I would like to speak about [title]. Thank you for listening....Today I spoke about [title] [bow to the count of three]." We rehearsed all this while taking special pains with bowing, pacing, and voice projection. There was no mention of the substance of the speech. It was clear that if the *aisatsu* created the right atmosphere and audience rapport, content would be a non-issue.

In another course I took, this one about conversational skills, the importance of *aisatsu* arose early on (at the second meeting). It was stressed that if one wants to be thought of as *reigi tadashii* 'in accordance with etiquette', then one must attend first and foremost to *aisatsu*. The instructor reiterated that *aisatsu* does not stop with greetings such as *konnichi wa* or *konban wa*. *Aisatsu*, he emphasized, surfaces in all aspects of everyday life *(nichijō-seikatsu)*.

It includes expressions of gratitude and conveys a respectful attitude *(keii)*, goodwill *(kōi)*, and warmth *(shitashimi)*. It comprises not only language, including *keigo*, but also facial expressions or demeanor *(hyōjō)* and actions *(kōi)*. It is, the instructor concluded (with all in attendance nodding sagely), *hanashi no kozeni* 'the small change of conversation'.

Was this instructor telling the members of the class something they did not already know? Not likely. Overt instruction, like printed advice, serves less to instruct than to validate (and perhaps bring to consciousness) what people already know. At the metalevel, how-to provides concrete "scripts" that guide behavior in specially constructed linguistic and cultural frames. Such structures "provide templates of ways in which perceptions, feelings, and thoughts are fused into patterns for action" (Bruner 1986, cited in Ben-Ari 1990:115).

As if reinforcing the deep contextual underpinnings of the social aspects of language, the physical world of Japan is structured so that language activities run smoothly: communicative practices are not limited to linguistic parameters. Conventions associated with the *genkan* 'entryway' are one example. Is it just a coincidence that the *genkan* is almost always provided in a culture where performance of *aisatsu* ranks so highly in the social canon? To take another example from my own experience, I recall an office to which I was assigned on a research stay at an academic institution. The space had just been made over for visiting researcher use, and I was struck by what were considered to be minimal furnishings and their layout in the Japanese setting. Entering a large room, one first saw a small sofa and chair combination arranged around a coffee table. The function of these was for hosting any and all visitors to the occupant's professional space. One does not sit at a desk and chat with visitors in Japan, as is common in the American academic setting. Rather, a separate space, even if visible from the work area, should always be available for entertaining guests and clients. To the left of the entrance to this workspace were a sink, a small shelf unit containing tea and coffee utensils (curtained and out of sight, of course), and a locker for coats and other outside apparel. This constituted the kitchen space. (I have never had an office in Japan that did not have a small sink.) The desks, all three of them, were furthest removed from the door. They faced away from the door and toward the window. Because one never hosts visitors seated at a desk in Japan, the desk setup made sense. There were no extra chairs for congregating around the work stations. I was also at first amused to observe that there were no bookshelves. My immediate American reaction, which I did not share with my hosts: "A sofa, but no bookshelves?" When I asked about shelves, I was told that they could be ordered. I did finally get some, but not before I had internalized the cultural lesson that in the Japanese context a higher priority is placed on creating a space for the dance of *aisatsu* than it did on the necessities of research—like bookshelves. The *aisatsu*

Figure 15. *An illustration by the popular cartoonist Sampei of the body language that accompanies the customary bow in a variety of contexts: (1) To subordinates, waving the hand while in motion; (2) standing greeting for superiors; (3) the classic bow when in motion. From a book called* Last-Minute Manners *(Satō 1982).*

and other language practices that regularly take place in such spaces cannot be separated from the architecture in which they are performed (I use "architecture" here loosely, to describe the arrangement of space around its occupants). In fact, *aisatsu* cannot be performed without a great deal of awkwardness (and foreignness) in, for example, an American office setting. The conventions of office space in Japan do not take shape apart from the social conventions that they serve.

Even in an apparently simple activity like *aisatsu,* there are countless associated body movements and physical dimensions—everything from the language *(osu,* or *ohayō,* or *ohayō gozaimasu)* to the cursory bow that the cartoonist Sampei (see Figure 15) depicts so well, to the space within which it is carried out.

Beyond Formalism

In detailing the dimensions of "communicative practice," Hanks (1996) adopts Bourdieu's notion of *habitus* and offers a compelling framework for pulling out the threads that bind language to its multiple contextual footings. *"Habitus"* has been defined as a set of dispositions acquired through (formative) early experiences, which incline individual actors to behave in certain ways. From these dispositions come practices, perceptions, and attitudes that are regular but not rule-governed (in the theoretical linguistic sense). *Habitus* circumscribes our actions without strictly determining them (Bourdieu 1991:12–13). *Shitamachi* 'downtown' Tokyoites will have different dispositions from those of *yamanote* 'uptown' Tokyoites,[8] and, more broadly, Japanese speakers will have different dispositions from those of English speakers. Hanks (1996:12) uses the notion of communicative practice to refer to those routine, repeated ways of acting and speaking into which speakers are inculcated through education and daily experience. Clearly Hanks is influenced heavily by Bourdieu in this sense, insofar as language is not so much a vehicle for conveying objective information (as the formalist would have it), but rather a kind of performance within which meanings emerge from the inclination of agents to evaluate and act on the world in typical ways—Bourdieu's *habitus*. The burden of mutual understanding rests as much in these dispositions to actions as it does in the shared formal features of language. In this view, language and all its associated features are a form of cultural capital (*hanashi no kozeni*, in the words of my *hanashikata-kyōshitsu* instructor) that people can acquire, compete for, and put to use for strategic ends (Hanks 1996:13). Those who do not share these resources are viewed as impoverished and seriously disadvantaged.

To illustrate this, Hanks (1996) begins his critique of formal linguistics by examining an ordinary conversational exchange with which I will take copious liberties and render here in Japanese. It takes the form of an exchange between husband and wife.

Q: *Shimbun, mada konai?*   Q: Newspaper not come yet?

A: *Genkan yo.*   A: In the entryway.

On first glance, there is nothing extraordinary about this exchange. The husband might pick up the newspaper from its usual place in the *genkan* and then go in to breakfast at the kitchen table. The rest of the morning can proceed as it always does: he drinks his tea, has a piece of toast and perhaps a boiled egg and a salad, looks at the political scandals, reads the box scores for the Seattle Mariners, perhaps forms an opinion on the upcoming local elections, then checks the stock prices. The foregoing talk isn't necessary for the morning to "happen." The paper is always in the *genkan;* his wife picks it up and puts it there for him to get later—either on his way into the kitchen for breakfast or, on those days when he is late for his train or has to be at work earlier, for him to pick up on his way out. They—and we—take it for granted until, for some reason, we are forced to take it apart.

First of all, the man's wife does not actually answer his question. In Searle's (1969) terms, she addresses the illocutionary force of a surface yes-no question, "Where's the paper?" But the husband already knows where the paper is.

It's always there. Her assertive tone *(yo)* reinforces this. This talk is not an exchange of information.

Second, the husband does not really mean to imply that he thinks the paper didn't come. It always comes. So why does he use the negative? Is this common sense? Only to insiders, and certainly not to learners. The negative is no more common sense than is the salad for breakfast.

Third, the location called *"genkan"* is fraught with conventional meaning in the Japanese context. More expansive than the two-dimensional English translation 'door', which is a mere plane through which bodies pass, *genkan* has substance. Things happen there. Guests remove their shoes and step up into the house from it; slippers are placed neatly at its inner edge to be donned by those entering the house, while on the outer side of the same border street shoes are neatly placed facing outward so that those who are leaving can put them on as they exit; *aisatsu* are performed both by those entering and those leaving, but those *aisatsu* are strictly prescribed according to whether one is a member of *uchi*, for example, *Itte kimasu!* 'I'm going now!' and *Itte irasshai!* 'See you later!', or a visitor whose status is *soto*, for example, *Ojama shimasu.* 'Sorry to bother you.' and *Dōzo, oagari kudasai.* 'Please come in.'

The *genkan* is the intermediate territory between the outside world of social and business pretense and the inner world of home, where one can be relaxed and genuine. This territory marks the boundary between *omote* 'façade' and *ura* 'true feeling' (Lebra 1976:112). All this conventional wisdom is part of the linguistic landscape to the man who goes to pick up his newspaper in the *genkan*, whether the conventions of that location come into play or not.

There are hundreds of ways—linguistic and nonlinguistic—in which the common sense of this situation might be altered or called into question, or in which the transparent becomes opaque. The husband might, for example, be blind and accustomed to finding the paper on the right side of the shoebox, while today it's on the left, and be looking for verification that he should actually expect to find it. Imagine, in this scenario, that the wife responds using *keigo:*

A: *Genkan desu yo, itsu mo to onaji.*
A: It's in the *genkan*, as usual (distal style/*teineigo*).

Or

A: *Genkan de gozansu.*
A: It's in the *genkan* (distal style/*keigo*/colloquial *gozansu* < polite *gozaimasu*).

Such uses of polite language would rarely be interpreted to indicate that this wife views her husband as her lord and master. Far from it; most Japanese would take both these responses as symptomatic of anger, as polite style between husband and wife is indicative of sarcasm or of psychological/emotional distance. Perhaps he forgot her birthday yesterday, and she has left the paper on the concrete floor of the *genkan*. In some families, women do use polite Japanese toward their husbands, but these families are becoming fewer and fewer. If a member of such a family were to hear this exchange and respond that it was not unusual, the listener would conclude something about that person, not tell her that she was wrong or outdated or inappropriate. People who know these things can begin to respond like insiders. But becoming an insider has little to do with the linguistic code called *keigo*—or at least *keigo* portrayed as "polite language." Such highly nuanced, sarcastic, distancing, angry, or even "high-class" uses of *keigo* are not considered part of formal grammar. They certainly are not obvious to the non-native speaker.

In another possible situation, one might assume that the husband is Japanese and is truly looking for today's newspaper. But he might just as easily be an American who gets yesterday's *Japan Times* from his neighbor every morning, or that his neighbor delivers a week's worth of papers once a week—in which case there's an understood plural in the Japanese that only "insiders" (these two) know. Then again, if the same exchange takes place in a recycling center, its interpretation is very different.

In order to interpret everyday language—even language that does not serve a very communicative function—one must put commonsense trust in the linguistic landscape: what speakers know about the world and assume is normal and natural. But structural linguistics "separates speech forms from their common sense horizons" (Hanks 1996:6). Language in the structural view is a pure form with an inner logic of its own. This, says Hanks, is formalism as espoused by Saussure, Bloomfield, Chomsky, and Jakobson. What it tells us about language is that:

- Languages exhibit <u>patterns</u> (structure) across space and time.
- This patterning can be <u>abstract</u>ed. We can apply *"Genkan yo"* to any number of contexts and/or objects.
- Languages have <u>universal</u> features that enable us to make predictions about their features.
- Language is <u>repeatable</u>. We can hear *"Genkan yo"* any number of times from any number of speakers and still recognize it as the same sentence.
- Languages rely on an <u>arbitrary</u> relationship between sound and thing for meaning. We trust and rely on dictionaries and grammars to tell us what those relationships are. (Hanks 1996:7–8)

But language is also variable, locally adapted, saturated by context, never the same, and constantly adjusting in meaning to speakers' needs and wants. The line between knowing a language and knowing the world becomes blurred. This is relationality as espoused in linguistics by Boas, Sapir, and Whorf, and in the social sciences by Merleau-Ponty, Schutz, and Bourdieu.

Keigo Common Sense

Information presented in the how-to industry confirms that the formal grammar of *keigo* itself is not the central issue for Japanese speakers. Of much greater interest are situations associated with *keigo* or that call for particular language. In the classes I took at the *hanashikata-kyōshitsu*, formal instruction was kept to a minimum. Even when it was included, its function seemed to be as much to lend credibility to the enterprise as to teach. When our formal knowledge *was* tested in the *hanashikata-kyōshitsu*, the results frequently brought me up short. As we sat through numerous *keigo* quizzes, I noticed that a friend, a woman in her thirties, was consistently befuddled when asked to provide, for example, the honorific *(sonkeigo)* form of *iu (ossharu);* the humble *(kenjōgo)* form for *iku* 'go' *(mairu);* or the error in *Okyaku-sama no onamae wa nan to mōsararemasu ka?* 'What do you say your name is?' *(Mōsararemasu* is incorrect because it is an honorific inflection *[-araremasu]* attached to a humble verb *[mōs-u].)*

These were tasks that I, as a language student and a linguist, found eminently reasonable and even comforting. But most of those around me, including my friend, appeared to find such tasks frustrating and artificial.[9] They exhibited consternation at the analysis of language.[10] But at the same time, I never heard my friend err in any of her conversations with our instructors. She may have lacked confidence in or been suspicious of what educational psychologists term her "declarative" knowledge of Japanese, but she was far from inept in her "procedural" know-how. She just used common sense—and apparently took comfort in the instructor's excursus on the importance of correct *keigo*. What she lacked, in my estimation, was confidence in her own ability to apply her common sense to heretofore unknown situations. So to the extent that the *hanashikata-kyōshitsu* class expanded its participants' horizons, it served an educational purpose. But from the relational perspective, the proffered advice of how-to does not serve actually to instruct consumers in using language. Rather, it lays out familiar (to the insider) contexts that serve as frames for *keigo* usage that speakers may not have seen or heard before.

This is surely one way in which native speakers differ from non-natives, as I had demonstrated to me again and again. One aspect of the *hanashikata-kyōshitsu* that I found instructive was the constellation of contexts and other phenomena that came together in the course of a class—naturally for the Japanese participants, in edifying fashion for me. One example of this was the six-week class called *"shikaisha yōsei senka"* 'training for emcees'. A *shikaisha* in Japan is the person who chairs the PTA meeting, operates as master of ceremonies at weddings, or in general runs the social event. We were given specific training for weddings and business meetings, but we also did a unit on running outings for work associates. In our case, because it was May, and spring was upon us, we elected to role-play a get-together at a park to engage in *hanami* (cherry-blossom viewing). I learned that for such get-togethers

edifying (adj.) providing moral or intellectual instruction

there were secondary roles that had to be filled, for which the *shikaisha* was ultimately responsible: the person who made the reservation, the "treasurer" who collected each participant's contribution, the person who acted as *uketsuke* 'receptionist' for the event. There was also an agreed-upon progression for the event itself, where each person was given a chance to speak in front of the group. Each of us was expected to practice and gain control of the language forms associated with our role. My colleagues were already inculcated in the roles, as well as in the necessary basic communicative practices (who did what when). *Keigo* emerged as just one aspect of the whole package of what it meant to be a *shikaisha*.

Such conflation of language and the real world is not unique to Japan. In the West, too, conflation of formal categories is a hallmark of how-to materials. (It is, in fact, one aspect of advice literature that consistently discredits it from the academic perspective.) The conventions of *keigo* use as presented through the how-to industry are typical of the popular inability or disinclination to divorce language from its circumstances of use. The associations between language and the world that participants must have in order to purchase credibility are not something that they are usually conscious of. They derive instead from the realm of things that need no rational explanation: common sense.

Common Sense

It is remarkable how regularly the concern for prescribed behavior in Japan is overtly tied to the acquisition of common sense. In descriptions of linguistic and social convention for the general public, the how-to industry frequently uses the Japanese term for common sense, *"jōshiki." E de Wakaru Manaa Jiten* (A dictionary for understanding manners through pictures) begins: "This book is a book that assumes various scenes of social interaction and answers the question 'What in the world do I do in this situation?' from everyday etiquette to business etiquette and questions of common sense *(jōshiki)* about ceremonial occasions that you haven't been able to ask up until now" (Gendai Manaa Fuōramu 1996:1).[11] A little later, more specific advice is offered: "Carrying the so-called language of friends—that is, language usage associated with insiders or close companions—into society is outside common sense" (12).[12] *Manaa bukku* provides detailed instruction on *aisatsu*, from which the following is excerpted: "Don't neglect timing: *Aisatsu* mistimed can be labored. Normally it's best to try to be the first to say a greeting. Also, there are people who say *"Gokurōsama"* to superiors *(jōshi)*, but *"gokurōsama"* is a word that should be used to show appreciation on the part of a superior *(jōshi)* toward underlings *(buka)*. This mistake casts doubt on one's common sense *(jōshiki)*, so we want to employ due care" (Gurūpu 24-Jikan no Manaa 1996:16).[13] *Bijinesu manaa*

(Business manners) contains a section headed, "General *keigo* common sense" *(Ippan jōshiki)* (Deguchi and Minagawa 1994:160). There is even a book by the title *Atte'ru yō de okashi na keigo jōshiki* (It-seems-right-but-it's-odd: *Keigo* common sense) (Muramatsu 1990).

The term "common sense" is not intended in any technical sense in these Japanese examples. After all, common sense is what doesn't need elaboration or explanation. And yet, as might be predicted, numerous breaches of common sense took place during the 1998 Winter Olympics in Nagano, many of which are described by Nicholas Kristoff in a February 15, 1998, *New York Times* article on what happens "when cultures collide." It is fortuitous that Kristoff attributes much of the misunderstanding of social convention that took place in Nagano to differences in common sense: "From a Japanese point of view, it seems puzzling that Americans can manage to get to the moon but routinely do something silly like stand in their stocking feet where they have just stepped with their shoes." Kristoff also juxtaposes two incidents—a Japanese bath house proprietress's going into the men's bath to tell a discombobulated foreigner that he cannot go into the water in his underwear, and an American woman's going from her homestay room to the bath wrapped only in a towel—and asks in what universe of discourse these two are so very different. "It might seem odd that the Japanese would be startled by a woman wearing a towel while walking through a private house to the bath, but not by a woman running after a man in a bath house and ordering him to remove his underwear. But in Japan it makes perfect sense" (Kristoff 1998:35).

As Kristoff's observations from the Olympics amply illustrate, our most deeply held (Western) beliefs come into serious question when we attempt to transfer our heretofore unexamined American common sense to Japan. The experiences that Kristoff details are reminiscent of Garfinkel's (1963, 1967) well-known "breaching experiments,"[14] in which the breakdown of common sense makes its normative organization apparent. The difference between Garfinkel's experiments and the foreigner's experience in Japan, of course, is that Garfinkel was in control of producing and sustaining anomic environments; the foreigner does not enjoy such a luxury. Nor do foreigners always have at their disposal tools that might enable them to analyze and/or rectify misperceptions of commonsense behavior. What Garfinkel's work, Kristoff's observations, and the plight of the foreigner in Japan share is that they show in high relief the strong feeling that people exhibit when common sense— their own or others'—comes into question. People have a tendency to doubt not only the "good sense" (that is, psychological stability) of those who violate common sense, but their moral or ethical character as well.

> In conversations with clients, with superiors *(jōshi)*, or with seniors *(sempai)*, a mark of doubt about not only the speaker's but also the speaker's parents' personality and education is attached to those who cannot use *keigo* satisfactorily. Because using *keigo*

properly ratifies one as a full-fledged member of society, one wants to master correct *keigo*. (Grūpu 24-Jikan no Manaa 1996:23)[15]

It can be said that the basis of communication is *aisatsu*. For harmonious social relationships, this goes without saying, but it is also the case that in one *aisatsu* a person is judged.... It doesn't matter whether it's *ohayō gozaimasu, konnichi wa,* or some other simple phrase. Just so you do it in a cheerful, upbeat way. (Gendai Manaa Fuōramu 1996:10)[16]

Anyone can—and should—be able to use *keigo* or perform *aisatsu*. Everyone understands it. The formulas are simple, direct, and to the point. It's just common sense.

Common sense has actually proven to be a fruitful area of study for anthropologists (Geertz 1975), sociologists (Garfinkel 1963, 1967, Schutz 1962, Smith 1995a, 1995b), and even philosophers (Coates 1996, James 1907, Kant 1790, Paine 1776, Reid 1905, and most especially Rorty 1989) who seek to understand and explain the "ordinary" in human behavior and social convention.[17] A marked feature of common sense everywhere seems to be its very ordinariness: the fact that everyone knows—or is supposed to know—what it is. We all chide ourselves when we violate its precepts; we find those who fail to abide by it odd at best and malignant at worst. And yet, common sense is in fact problematic, not least of all to the outsider or non-native speaker who aims to move invisibly (without casting doubt on his or her common sense) through Japanese or any other society. It is a truism for non-native speakers of Japanese that they often find themselves at odds with what natives consider to be common sense. Or conversely, and perhaps more to the ethnocentric point, naive visitors to places like Japan often find their hosts to be completely lacking in common sense.

Common sense is also tied inextricably to ideology. The tie between common sense and ideology is more often taken for granted than it is dissected and analyzed, but it is surely the case that common sense reveals something about how people view their world, about subjective representations, about how people in a culture live their relationships, and about their beliefs and ideas (Woolard 1998). This is ideology; commonsense practice is suffused with it, which is perhaps why one so often evokes the other.

Linguistic common sense may be accessed in a variety of ways. One of these must surely be by means of the how-to industry. Books and overt instruction in *how* to talk do not predict *what* speakers will actually say in a behavioral sense, nor do they coerce speakers into a particular mode of action. But they can and do embody prevailing notions of how the world is and ought to be— common sense. Some scholars say that in this sense they are coercive (Cameron 1995, Fairclough 1989). *Keigo* how-to materials and enterprises rely on the academic and governmental accounts of *keigo* (reviewed in Chapters 2 and 3).

Keigo Common Sense

They provide an extraordinary window into the linguistic ideology of Japan and into the dispositions that Japanese people bring to the tasks of performing, interpreting, and evaluating language. In prescribing desirable linguistic and social behavior, advice literature makes assumptions about social wants and needs, about the way things have been, are now, and ought to be. One of the things that can be learned from this genre in both its popular and its government-sanctioned forms, is that language and language use are tied inextricably to the web of social convention that enables ("empowers" in current English parlance) people to navigate in "commonsense" fashion through the shoals of the real world. Through how-to industry precepts and advice, one can gain access to an understanding of just what Japanese common sense looks like, how it has evolved and continues to evolve over time, and how it differs (if we are not Japanese) from our own.

The five features of common sense enumerated by Geertz (1975) serve as a starting point for examining common sense as portrayed by the how-to industry in Japan:

1. naturalness—there will be an air of "of courseness," a sense of "it figures" cast on its reflexes;

2. practicality—there will be an implicit message that a person with common sense "is capable of coping with everyday problems in an everyday way with some effectiveness";

3. thinness, simplicity, literalness—common sense will be presented as just what it seems to be, no more and no less;

4. immethodicalness—descriptions and definitions will be inconsistent, (unscientific) (in a social scientific, linguistic sense) and "shamelessly ad hoc";

5. accessibility—any person with reason will be credited with the ability to apprehend common sense conclusions, and "not only grasp but embrace them."

Geertz approaches common sense as a very imprecise phenomenon, in contrast to the approaches of Husserl, Merleau-Ponty, and Schutz, who aim to distill "a relatively organized body of considered thought" from communal perceptions of it. Geertz's "what anyone clothed and in his right mind knows" (1975:75) characterization of common sense seems almost flippant, and yet attempts to formalize common sense all start from this unsophisticated, folksy element. Because my goal here is to lay out the linguistic landscape of Japanese common sense, Geertz's characterization is extremely appealing. The questions of whether there is a universal common sense or whether multiple common senses lead inexorably down the slippery slope of relativism are ones that I leave for others to sort out.

If evidence were needed that Japanese common sense is "shamelessly ad hoc" and eminently "accessible," it would be hard to find a clearer example than the following somewhat painfully explicit advice from *Manaa bukku:*

It can also be good to hold off

Further, in the following circumstances it is common sense *(jōshiki)* to hold off on *aisatsu:*

1. When you see your superior *(jōshi)* coming out of a bathroom stall.
2. When you observe your superior *(jōshi)* escorting a woman.
3. When you see your superior *(jōshi)* coming out of an adult video shop or a sex shop.
4. In a crowded train, when you notice your superior *(jōshi)* standing some distance away. (Grūpu 24-Jikan no Manaa 1996:16)[18]

What could be more matter-of-fact? Thin, shamelessly ad hoc, surely no one would dispute this advice. Even in the United States people politely ignore acquaintances seen coming out of bathroom stalls or sex shops! But there is more to the common sense that underlies these recommendations than meets the eye. Looking carefully at the range of common sense guidance that is available for language use in Japan, one begins to see not only that the organizing themes *(aisatsu, kotobazukai, jōshiki, ōtai, hōmon)* have changed little over time, but also that those themes can be viewed in terms of repeating words that are part of a very different linguistic landscape from that of English speakers. These themes describe a body of common sense that native speakers find irreducible. *Aisatsu* and its colleagues are keys to describing who Japanese are in the world. Borrowing from the philosopher Richard Rorty, I call this array of terminology *keigo*'s "final vocabulary."

Keigo's Final Vocabulary

[handwritten annotation: exegesis- a critical explanation or interpretation of a text, especially a religious text. (Orig. used for the Bible)]

In a philosophical exegesis on contingency, irony and common sense, Rorty (1989) introduces the notion of a "final vocabulary." In Rorty's postmodern, pragmatic approach to philosophy, a final vocabulary is the set of words that every human being uses to justify his or her actions and beliefs. "These are the words in which we formulate praise for our friends and contempt for our enemies, our long-term projects and our highest hopes. They are the words in which we tell, sometimes prospectively and sometimes retrospectively, the story of our lives." The final vocabulary is final in the sense that, if doubt is cast upon it, the user has no noncircular argumentative recourse; these words are as far as the speaker can go with language: "beyond them there is only helpless passivity or a resort to force" (73).

Rorty does not concern himself with the particulars of any single final vocabulary, because, by its very nature, it is both particular—each person's is constructed differently—and mutable—its terms are always subject to change ("anything can be made to look good or bad, important or unimportant, useful

Keigo Common Sense

or useless, by being redescribed" [1989:73]). Yet he does make an effort to pin down certain aspects of the final vocabulary by describing it as being simultaneously "thin, flexible, and ubiquitous" (giving as examples words such as "true," "good," and "right") as well as "thick," "rigid," and "parochial" ("Christ," "standards," and "creative"). There is a universality or commonality about the final vocabulary, at least in terms of belongingness; the ironist "spends her time worrying about the possibility that she has been born into the wrong tribe, taught to play the wrong language game" (75).

Implicit in Rorty's work is the notion that language—particularly individual words—constitute a unique window onto the human condition.[19] This is not a new idea. In the social sciences, an approach reminiscent of Rorty's is seen in Williams' (1976) book *Keywords: A Vocabulary of Culture and Society.* Williams' contention, like Rorty's, is that there is a pool of words that are crucial to understanding society, in this case American society. Rorty argues against any internal validity to the final vocabulary; Williams, that keywords are a critical tool for unlocking the workings of the societal whole.

The linguistic counterpart to this approach actually comes from Wierzbicka's (1991) article "Japanese Key Words and Core Cultural Values." Wierzbicka states her main thesis in much the same terms as Williams: "Every language has its own key words and…these key words reflect the core values of the culture to which this language belongs; [also] cultures can be revealingly studied, compared and explained to outsiders through their key words" (333). She then proceeds to break down words like *amae* 'dependence', *enryo* 'restraint', *wa* 'harmony', *on* 'obligation', *giri* 'duty', and *seishin* 'spirit', which are crucial to the understanding and description of Japan using so-called semantic primes in combination with a good bit of what anthropologists would call "thick description" (a term coined by Geertz [1973] to describe a method of detailed analysis that involves immersing oneself in a culture instead of assuming that one can achieve a standpoint of objectivity). In fact, if Wierzbicka's arguments were not framed by a great deal of rich sociocultural background information,[20] the semantic primes would probably not hold as much interest.

What Rorty, Williams, and Wierzbicka share is a view of vocabulary as fundamental or central to describing the world. Some words are final, as Rorty suggests, because they are as far as a speaker can go with language. They form the background against which any conversation about, say, *keigo* takes place. They are also commonsensical in Rorty's sense. When these words are called into question, there is no nonderivative way to describe the world within which *keigo* functions. There can be only profound frustration at the questioner's inability to penetrate the world as any Japanese person experiences it—common sense. Whether they agree or disagree with what *keigo* is or what it represents, Japanese speakers are bound by the available tropes of the language they speak for talking about *keigo*.[21]

Across the how-to industry, one can observe repeated uses of certain

descriptive vocabulary. I have culled from the materials discussed so far a preliminary list of words— a first attempt at circumscribing the final vocabulary of
keigo. There may be other words that readers wish to add from their own observations and experiences. In keeping with the notion that these mark out a
linguistic landscape, I have organized them according to the spatial parameters
of connectedness and of place. *Keigo* itself functions to locate speakers in a web
of communication that is simultaneously "sticky" (the nature of the connection is always salient) and highly structured (what is frequently oversimplified
as being a matter of hierarchy is better described in terms of distances of all
sorts, most readily combined in terms of horizontal and vertical axes). All of
this emerges in the vocabulary that is used to explain *keigo*'s usage.

PLACE (in/out, up/down; Japanese *"ba"*)
buka 'subordinate'
jōge 'vertical(ity)' (lit., 'up-down')
jōge-kankei 'vertical relationships' (lit., 'up-down relationships')
jō-i(sha) 'higher-ranking (person)'
jōshi 'superior (in an organization)'
ka-i (no mono) 'lower-ranking (person)'
meshita 'lower-ranking, subordinate' (lit., 'below one's eyes')
meue 'higher-ranking, superior' (lit., 'above one's eyes')
mibun 'social position'
miuchi 'insiders, relatives' (also *nakama[-uchi], uchi*)
-nai 'inside (a company, organization, household, etc.)'
nakama(-uchi) 'insiders, friends' (also *miuchi, uchi*)
sempai 'one's senior (in school and organizational rank)'
uchi 'insiders, friends, relatives' (also *miuchi, nakama[-uchi], -nai*)

CONNECTEDNESS
aite 'the other'
aratamaru 'be formal'
hairyo 'consideration'
ningen-kankei 'interpersonal politics' (lit., 'human connections')
omoiyari 'consideration, thoughtfulness'
   kikubari 'consideration, thoughtfulness'
   kizukai 'consideration, thoughtfulness'
ōtai 'reception'
shakai 'society'
shakaijin 'a member of society'
taigū 'consideration, compensation, reception'

I have not included technical analytical terms like *keigo, sonkei(go), kenjō(go),
kenson, taigū-hyōgen*. There is surely some overlap between these analytical
terms and the lists above, but the technical terms are the product of an academic argument over what language will be set apart for a specialized function.

There is a conscious commitment to placing them outside the ravages of time and popular use. The academic enterprise has laid claim on their meanings and removed them from general circulation. They were, moreover, in large part invented from Chinese morphology, not part of mainstream Japanese. Like Latin, which is set aside for scientific use in the West, these words, coined from Chinese, fall under the purview of specialists. Although virtually everyone in Japan knows what, for example, *keigo* is, and though it may have joined the ranks of final vocabulary in the eyes of some, I leave it outside this discussion.[22]

PLACE

Chie Nakane's *Japanese Society* (1970) is now more than thirty years old, but her conceptualization of *ba* 'location, frame' continues to resonate even today. It also has parallels in Western sociological theory in the workings of "social space" (Bourdieu 1991) as well as in frame analysis[23] and its offshoots (see, for example, Tannen and Wallet 1993). Human beings speak from particular locations, and "competence…is inseparable from the practical mastery of situations in which [the] usage of language is socially acceptable" (Bourdieu 1991:82). Bourdieu's assertion that "the social world can be uttered and constructed in different ways" (232) is nowhere more fitting than in the case of *keigo*. What Japanese grammarians have realized independent of Western structural and poststructural scholarship is that *keigo* cannot be given a full accounting unless speakers are placed in the web of relationships within which *keigo* functions. Those relationships include the vertical structures that mark Japanese social organizations (for example, companies and clubs). Despite increasing egalitarianism in modern Japanese society, commentators cannot ignore the fact that verticality continues to be a defining factor in Japanese organizations and society. Whether that verticality derives from the same factors as it did in the past or not is a separate question. As Japanese industry changes and there is increased mobility within the workforce, women and young people, traditionally viewed as de facto lower in rank, regularly find themselves in supervisory positions. This does not mean that they do not use *keigo*. But neither does it mean that female supervisors use *keigo* in precisely the same way that their male counterparts do. Conventions are reinvented to adapt to change, and in the case of *keigo* convention, Japan seems to be adapting quite nicely to the appearance of women and young people in heretofore unconventional roles (see Hendry 1990, Linhart-Fischer 1990, Okamoto 1995). *Manaa bukku* gives detailed instructions about the simple morning greeting *Ohayō gozaimasu* 'Good morning':

A feeling of closeness from changing one word

It goes without saying that morning *aisatsu* is *"Ohayō gozaimasu."* If the other is a subordinate *(meshita)*, it is all right to omit the *gozaimasu* and just say *"Ohayō."* Look at the other and greet him/her in a cheerful voice with a smile. If the other is a superior *(meue)*, bow while greeting.

After *"Ohayō gozaimasu,"* saying something like "Nice weather we're having," or "Cold weather we're having," adds a personal touch. Of course it's also all right to say something complimentary like "That's a snazzy necktie," but overblown praise may be taken as flattery, so exercise due caution. (Grūpu 24-Jikan no Manaa 1996:16)[24]

Other books echo themes of organizational structure in their discussions of language (such as *gokurōsama* 'good work') or posture and attitude:

> *Aisatsu* is first of all, one might say, feeling more than content. Or to put it another way, even the clumsiest speaker can acquire the ability to perform genuine *aisatsu*.
>
> At the workplace, the thing one must be especially careful of is the many phrases that one doesn't think of as rude, but which come across as rude in the business world.
>
> For example, *"gokurōsama."* This is a phrase to show appreciation for the other's labor(s), so it tends to be thought of as good to use when, for example, one's superior *(jōshi)* is leaving for the day. But from now on, this phrase has the meaning "from the superior *(jōshi)* to subordinate *(buka)*." So if it is used from oneself to a superior *(jōshi)*, it will come across as rude.
>
> They aren't *aisatsu*, but one should also avoid the *ichi-ō* of *ichi-ō dekimasu* (I suppose I can do it) and the *maa* of *maa daijōbu desu* (well, it's all right). Like *aisatsu*, use language in such a way that your superior *(jōshi)* will think of you as a "competent subordinate" *(buka)*. (Chiteki Seikatsu Kenkyūjo 1994:17)[25]

Observe that instruction does not attempt to explain the social structures to which it refers. These are taken for granted. At the same time, the intricacy of vertical relationships is not underestimated, as the emphasis on *ningen-kankei* 'personal relationships' demonstrates.

> In business etiquette, you show vertical *(jōge)* relationships *(ningen-kankei)* by your posture. It is all right for superiors *(jōi)* to maintain a relaxed posture, but the subordinate *(ka-i no mono)* should show his or her respect to the other *(aite)* by exhibiting a certain amount of anxiety and correct behavior. (Noguchi 1992:77)[26]

> In order to create good interpersonal relations *(ningen-kankei)* with peers *(dōryō)* and juniors *(kōhai)*, not to mention superiors *(jōshi)* and seniors *(sempai)*, it is crucial to understand the importance of language and *keigo*. (Shain Kyōiku Sōgō Kenkyūjo 1993:141)[27]

In Japan, vertical relations are not fraught with tension; they are expected to be harmonious. *Ningen-kankei* takes in connections of all kinds, with no need to specify whether they are superior-to-subordinate or peer-to-peer. The expectations surrounding *ningen-kankei*, including how differences are worked through and the roles of all involved, are part and parcel of common sense. When those expectations are not met, the interpretation is that there has been a serious rift in the social fabric.

Connectedness

There is no question that *keigo*'s description evolved within a society that was (and that, some say, still is) highly stratified and tightly structured, but *keigo* is much more than simply a reflection of hierarchy. In my estimation, it is in part an accident of history and an artifact of Western influence that vertical relationships took on so much of the burden in describing *keigo*. Certain features of Japanese social structure took on much more salience as Japan was challenged with the task of explaining itself in its move to modernize. Who can say whether the perceived audience for these explanations was (or is now) internal (domestic) or external (international)? Contemporary grammarians' attempt to escape the stultifying effects of the *sonkeigo-kenjōgo-teineigo* paradigm are in part a reflection of the very inadequacy of those terms. How-to materials offer many of the other features of *ba* 'place' that speakers attend to in their manipulation of *keigo*. *Keigo no tukaikata ga wakaru hon* (The book for understanding how to use *keigo*) is typical of the tendency to treat *ningen-kankei* 'interpersonal relationships'—what in the United States might also be characterized as interpersonal politics—as fundamental to smooth communication among members of any social organization: "As one member of an organization with a single goal, whether you are male or female, if you understand each other *(aite)* and can spend time together with considerate hearts, you can build wonderful interpersonal relationships *(ningen-kankei)*. Language is the basis of interpersonal relationships *(ningen-kankei)*" (Noguchi 1992:18).[28] In fact, there is often a conscious effort to divorce *keigo* from the lingering notion that it must always be associated with the constraints of inequality: "Even in workplaces where vertical relations *(jōge-kankei)* are disregarded, in order to maintain distinctions between people and the dignity of the workplace, one does not want to use rude language" (Shimizu and Arimura 1999:17).[29]

It has also been remarked that there is an overriding concern with *aite* 'other' in Japanese communication. This concern finds its echo in the quotations above and below.

When asking a superior to accompany you
"Go-issho ni mairimasen ka." WRONG
"Go-issho-shite itadakemasen ka." RIGHT
You are asking someone to go with you, so out of respect *(sonchō)* for the other's *(aite)* wish, it is better to use *Go-issho-shite itadakemasen ka*. When you do that, you show good judgment in not putting pressure on him/her to go with you, and it is no trouble for the other person *(aite)*. Similarly, we want to show consideration by asking about the other person's *(aite)* convenience before our own. (Fukuda 1993:83)[30]

When the other *(aite)* has demonstrated goodwill *(kōi)*, the best language for showing your sense of gratitude is *arigatō*. Use it with feeling. (Shimizu and Arimura 1999:52)[31]

Phrase like this make me think that Japanese culture has a lot of feeling. There's a lot of humility, consideration, and respect.

These pieces of advice reinforce the already mentioned conflation of *keigo* and features of context. The entire book *Keigo no tsukaikata ga 3-zikan de masutaa-dekiru* (You can master keigo usage in 3 hours) is organized around situational language use.

Aite need not be a superior or a subordinate. Quite the contrary, consideration for other(s)—in the sense of being able to see the world from another's perspective—is a highly valued trait in Japanese society:

> The speaker wants to think about the circumstance of the other (the listener) *(aite)* and select time, place *(basho)*, and topic of conversation. (Gendai Manaa Fuōramu 1996:13)[32]

> Especially when one has to convey one's own opinion to a person in a different position *(ba)*, the language must enter the ear of the other person *(aite)* in such a way as not to imply incompatibility. That is *keigo*, and that is why *keigo* expressions are crucial. (Uchiyama 1994:13)[33]

> **Lower self's *(jibun)* status, raise the other's *(aite)***
> What is *keigo* but a matter of politely raising the other person's *(aite)* status while lowering your own through language? And so we don't add *o-* or *go-* to matters pertaining to self. Most important here is that insiders *(jibun no naka)* include self's company and its employees. (Muraoka 1992:32)[34]

Consumers are again and again reminded to put themselves in the place of this *aite* and imagine what it feels like to be in the other person's shoes: "It is also important to make the other person *(aite)* feel comfortable....For example, even if it's for a short time, when you have to wait it can feel like forever. Put yourself in the other person's *(aite)* place and say, 'I'm sorry to make you wait'" (Shimizu and Arimura 1999:96–97).[35] Consideration for other is subsumed under the term *hairyō*, which has reflexes in more colloquial phrases such as *kikubari* and *kizukai*.

> The consideration *(kikubari)* that comes from distinguishing language use according to time, place *(bamen)*, and addressee *(aite)* is a matter of catching the other's *(aite)* true feelings *(kokoro)*. (Fukuda 1993:55)[36]

> *Keigo* is the consideration *(kokoro-kubari)*, concern *(ki-kubari)*, and care *(omoiyari)* of human relationships *(ningen-kankei)*. (Fukuda 1993:61)[37]

> It is important to show consideration *(ki o kubaru)* and ask politely, prefacing with something like *"Osore irimasu ga…"* (I'm sorry, but…). (Hinata 1989:195)[38]

Hand in hand with these notions of consideration is a consciousness of the distinction between *uchi* and *soto*. Nakane pioneered the analysis of Japanese society in terms of *uchi* and *soto*, but the utility of these terms has been further demonstrated by Lebra (1976), Kondo (1990), and contributors to Bachnik and Quinn (1994). How-to books draw an explicit connection between the *uchi/soto* distinction and *keigo* common sense:

The so-called language of friends—that is, your usage with insiders *(miuchi)* or ⟨ companions *(nakama-uchi)*—when carried into society, is outside of common se (Gendai Manaa Fuōramu 1996:12)³⁹

Distinguish between people who are insiders *(uchi)* and people who are outsiders *(soto)*

We discussed the importance of distinguishing between *uchi* and *soto* connections before. Naturally we conduct business using *keigo* toward section heads and other people who are our superiors *(jōshi)* within the group *(uchi)*, but what happens when an outsider *(soto)* enters the picture? The *uchi-soto* connection grows more complex. For example, when your superior *(jōshi)* is sitting alongside you with a client, you don't use *sonkeigo*, but rather switch to *kenjōgo* in speaking about your superior. It is the same when there is a telephone call from outside. In the business world *(ba)*, we must pay special heed to this *uchi/soto* connection. (Hinata 1989:117)⁴⁰

Although the intricacies of *keigo* use and the formal connection between certain words and relationships might require instruction, the Japanese world of *uchi* and *soto* needs no elaboration. It is part and parcel of *hairyō* in the broadest sense:

Distinguish between the *uchi/soto* connection

There are situations where people embarrass themselves by using dreadful *keigo*. More important is to acquire the know-how to understand on one's own.

There is a central difference between situation A, where one is nervous in facing another person *(aite)*, who is a client and overuses *keigo,* and situation B, where one ignores the other *(aite)* and, through rude, incorrect usage, heaps mistake upon mistake.

Language use is, on the one hand, a reflection of the relationship with the other person *(taijin)*, so it is not limited to *keigo* but includes all kinds of consideration *(hairyō)*. (Hinata 1989:24–25)⁴¹

Critics often bemoan the fact that young Japanese "carry the language of friends" into the workplace and have lost the ability to distinguish between such traditional categories as *uchi* and *soto*. But there is a difference between losing the distinction itself and making changes in its application. Because the application of *uchi* and *soto* to the workplace is a modern one (the workplace itself being a modern artifact), this harks back to Giddens' point that traditional conventions in, say, families must be consciously disembedded and applied to the situations that one encounters in a large-scale society. That those new applications might not have a firm hold or that the conventions themselves might adapt to change in other social spheres is not unexpected. But it is the job of how-to to promote continuity, and reference to commonsense practices like those around *uchi* and *soto* are reassuring to readers.

A broad overview of the vocabulary used to represent *keigo* in the popular press shows the error of analyzing it as primarily or fundamentally a matter of hierarchy. Although verticality and so-called hierarchical relationships are very much a part of what it means to find one's "place" in Japanese (or any other) society, verticality is by no means the only, or the most important, aspect of *keigo* usage.

Place and connectedness are not isolated constructs in the Japanese context, especially not in the resolution of language use. In order to know and understand *ba*, it is necessary to know and understand who else is in one's surroundings and what their connections are to oneself. This is not unique to Japan. As Bachnik points out, in drawing on the work of Heidegger, "The implications of being in the world (and of intentionality) are that everything we do (or perceive) must be from a 'placed' perspective" (Bachnik 1990:193). It is perhaps the salience of this being-in-the-world for Japanese that is so marked from our Western perspective. Although *nihonjinron* 'theories of Japanese-ness' has been largely discredited from the Western sociological perspective (see Dale 1986 and Mouer and Sugimoto 1986:168–184), from the point of view of cultural studies, its popularity as a theory of Japanese behavior must be taken as evidence that it resonates within Japan. Perhaps it is because *nihonjin-ron* explains Japan in terms to which the Japanese are accustomed—Japan's final vocabulary—and not in terms that were invented for describing something else (an artificial technical vocabulary). As my examples have illustrated, not only place, but also connections within place, are crucial when Japanese people explain *keigo* for other Japanese people. *Aite, ningen-kankei, hairyō*, and others are part and parcel of what it means to "live" *keigo*.

The Mutability of the Final Vocabulary

Rorty's (1989) goal in identifying the final vocabulary is to sketch out the argument(s) between the metaphysician and the ironist—the metaphysician, "convinced that the final vocabulary refers to something which has a real essence and that what matters is not what language is being used but what is true" (75), and the ironist, "beset with radical and continuing doubts about the final vocabulary she currently uses, because she has been impressed by other final vocabularies, vocabularies taken as final by the people or books she has encountered" (73). Rorty's purpose, of course, is to argue for the contingency of language. That is, language is not "a third thing intervening between self and reality." Rather, it is a product of time and chance (22), and the ironist is always aware that his or her way of describing the world is subject to sudden and dramatic revaluation. This stands in sharp contrast to the positivist, who sees language as gradually shaping itself around the contours of the world.

In his descriptions of final vocabulary, Rorty uses such terms as "thin," "flexible," and "parochial" and intends to discredit the notion that common sense can be universally accessed by language. Rorty is mistrusting of common sense and its role in stifling thought. For him, common sense is "the watchword of those who unselfconsciously describe everything important in terms of the final vocabulary to which they and those around them are habituated" (74).

It is perhaps not coincidental that Rorty echoes Geertz's (1975) description of common sense as "natural," "practical," "thin," "immethodical," and "accessible," because both Rorty and Geertz address the role of common sense in intellectual inquiry. But the two part company in their attitudes toward the ideology that underlies common sense. In an earlier work, Geertz (1964) pits common sense against the inquiry called science and confirms that the two may naturally clash. But the assumption that this clash is inevitable, and that the findings of some other line of inquiry will necessarily undermine common sense, is not preordained. There is much to be gained, in other words, from an exploration of common sense in cultures other than one's own.

The elements of the final vocabulary work in concert to create the fabric of how Japanese people define themselves—the linguistic landscape. But self-definition is also subject to argumentation and change. All the terms in the final vocabulary are open to argumentation. In fact, they are continually argued, even as how-to attempts to capture the unchanging essence of *keigo* use. There are factions of Japanese society that stand opposed to a greater or lesser degree to what *keigo* and final vocabulary represent. Some examples:

1. On board public transportation in any Japanese city, one can overhear junior high school girls who, speaking loud enough for those around them to hear, use "male language." My Japanese informants tell me that this performance is, at least in part, for the benefit of the surrounding adult audience and signals the girls' rebellion against traditional linguistic and cultural norms.
2. It is my understanding that at least one segment of the *burakumin* 'out caste' population refuses outright to use *keigo*.
3. Student demonstrators in the 1960s and 1970s not only shunned *keigo*, they called police officers *kimi* (a familiar form of 'you').

Such breaches are double-edged, as they serve to ratify the normative force of the very linguistic conventions they aim to undermine. Moreover, though factions of society may claim to stand in principle against what the final vocabulary represents, they are nonetheless bound by the common sense that it embodies. Endemic to the final vocabulary is that its constructs have lost their descriptive function and have taken on a direct, explanatory role—under the illegitimate, reifying assumption that they have unitary, immediate, and concrete referents (Thomason 1982:115–116). Steinhoff's (1992) work on the Japanese Rengo Sekigun (United Red Army) illustrates in no uncertain terms how constrained even counterculture revolutionaries are by the societal models and constructs they inherit. A bloody purge of twelve of its own members demonstrated haunting similarities between the Rengo Sekigun and Japanese social organization: "deference to formal authority and unwillingness to challenge it, consensus decision-making procedures that carry high expectations of subsequent participation, indirect and ambiguous means of expressing dissent, and high levels of commitment and loyalty to the group" (222–223). Normally, Steinhoff says, these practices are the hallmark of a smoothly efficient Japanese society. "The real horror of the Rengo Sekigun purge is that its bizarre outcomes resulted from very ordinary social processes enacted by quite normal individuals" (195). One can only assume that the purge was also carried out in very ordinary language. In fact, Steinhoff mentions that *amae* 'dependence'—traditionally a culturally valued pattern, and a term that might easily find its way into the final vocabulary—was rejected by the Rengo Sekigun as a deterrent to the development of strong character (207). Symbolic structures do not only constrain action. They also provide more concrete "scripts" that guide behavior in specially constructed frames. "Cultural structures, in other words, provide templates of ways in which perceptions, feelings, and thoughts are fused into patterns for action" (Bruner 1986; cited in Ben-Ari 1990:115).

There are no surprises in my list of final vocabulary. In many ways, it reinforces what social science has been saying about Japan for quite some time—such notions as *ba* and connectedness are critical for understanding and describing Japan's cultural landscape. Words like *uchi* and *soto, ningen-kankei,* and *meue* and *meshita* have long been among the anthropological and sociological tools brought to bear in descriptions of Japan. But final vocabulary goes beyond this in that it provides a way of looking at the persistence of the hold that language has on the way that Japanese people think about themselves and their language. I call my list of descriptors a final vocabulary because it satisfies Rorty's definition: it is the last recourse for Japanese people speaking about their own linguistic and social conventions. Language in this sense is so taken for granted that, if one (unkindly) presses a Japanese speaker for definitions or characterizations of any of these, one most often becomes embroiled in a circular discussion of the structure of Japanese society and what it means to be Japanese. Japanese speakers cannot step outside their language and compare it to something else any more than native speakers of English can step outside English (Davidson 1984:185).

Speakers engaged in communication, Hanks observes, carry with them "an immense stock of sedimented social knowledge in the form of unreflective habits and *commonsense* [emphasis mine] perceptions" (Hanks 1996:238). In pursuit of this dimension of language, the object is the ways in which "context saturates language" (Hanks 1996:195), what speakers take to be commonsense understanding and interpretation.

The presumed relationship(s) among *aisatsu* and *keigo, aisatsu* and *manaa, keigo* and living space are "natural, practical, simple, and accessible" for the native, confounding and anything but methodical for the outsider. My American self laughed at the notion that I would be assigned a coffee table but not a bookshelf. But the how-to industry is unabashedly unashamed of these contextual features. In how-to, the form and function of these components of communication are indistinguishable from one another, so much so that "scientific" analysis of any one paradigm—like *keigo*—apart from these other sign systems often leaves natives flummoxed.

The conflation of linguistic and other forms of social convention by the how-to industry finds its reflex in popular attitudes. How-to materials have an audience predisposed, if not to mystify, then to at least leave obscure distinctions that might undermine common sense. No matter how much one may value scientific or logical reasoning, the comfort of common sense carries a much higher premium on a day-to-day basis. In common sense people are reassured that "There is no esoteric knowledge, no special technique or peculiar giftedness, and little or no specialized training" required "...It lies so artlessly before our eyes it is almost impossible to see" (Geertz 1975:91–92). Natives do not (or will not) ordinarily see or question the bounds of common sense, because its artlessness derives in large measure from the very fact that there are no words to describe it except those that embody it. Common sense is seamlessly woven by and throughout language.

Japanese language common sense goes far beyond the boundaries of "language" as linguistic professionals know it. My experience of the *hanashikata-kyōshitsu* taught me that my pursuit of language how-to apart from other forms of social convention and divested of people's experience of it was chimerical. I kept running into "the socially constituted screen through which speakers apprehend their world and produce meanings" (Hanks 1996:83). I have tried to capture here the contours of that screen as they can be derived from common sense.

The Japanese how-to industry illustrates how common sense "determines the kinds of problems that are posed, the kinds of explanations that are offered, and the kinds of instruments (conceptual, methodological, statistical) that are employed" (Bourdieu 1991:213). Even more critically, common sense determines how problems are posed and explanations constructed. It is ironic, for example, that Western accounts of Japanese *keigo* overwhelmingly describe it in terms of an inegalitarian social structure, when assumed inequality is only one of the many factors that Japanese themselves perceive to be pertinent to the analysis and use of *keigo*. Any explanation of *keigo* in the contemporary Japanese linguistic community (assuming that that community can be said to have coherence) must come to terms with phenomena that define what it is to be Japanese. As long as Japanese leap instinctively to describe themselves in terms of *jōge-kankei, ningen-kankei, uchi* and *soto, mibun, meue* and *meshita, omoiyari,* and so on, linguistic descriptions of Japanese must also incorporate these terms. But by the same token, appropriating these terms for linguistic description need not bind Japanese agents to a single course of action. The articulation of communicative practice—of common sense and of the final vocabulary—does not deprive speakers of Japanese of their autonomy. It does, however, delineate a landscape within which those choices are typically made without consciousness or constraint, by virtue of dispositions that are the products of social determinism and that also are constituted outside of consciousness or constraint (Bourdieu 1991: 51).

It is simply not possible to speak Japanese or any other language without making a commitment to a particular view of the world in terms that may be captured in a final vocabulary that every speaker knows, simply by virtue of common sense. As Brubaker (1993:139) observes, "To speak is inevitably to situate one's self in the world, to take up a position, to engage with others in a process of production and exchange, to occupy a social space." The key is to see meaning as something that remains indeterminate until language is placed in the framework of a context—where "context" entails intersubjective contracts, ongoing discourse, and enormous background experience—all of which fall under common sense to the actors. Social actors may argue over common sense, they may fail or refuse to follow it, and the parameters of common sense may change over time, but its hold can be identified in the mundane regularities of practice that compose descriptions of everyday lives. Linguistic and social conventions that conceal themselves as common sense ensure that those functioning under their constraints need not see their machinations. By their very nature, the linguistic landscape and its associated commonsense practices are completely transparent.

Keigo from Now On

*Submitted to the Minister of Education
by the Kokugo Shingikai on April 14, 1952.*

Preface

This monograph selects those problems that are closest to us in our everyday linguistic existence and sets out those forms that are thought to be desirable for the future.

Problems related to *keigo*'s future obviously do not stop with these. In essence, problems of *keigo* are not limited to just those of language; rather, they concern whether *keigo* will be unified with the manners and etiquette of real life. Therefore, along with the growth of manners and etiquette that conform to the lifestyle of our new age, we hope to achieve sound development of a straightforward and clear-cut code of *keigo*.

Fundamental Principles

1. Up until now, *keigo* existed as it had developed from past ages with more troublesome aspects than were necessary. From now on, taking a lesson from those excesses and rectifying mistaken usage, *keigo* is something that we want, to the extent possible, to be straightforward and clear-cut.

2. Until now, *keigo* developed based mainly on vertical relationship(s), but from now on *keigo* must be based on the mutual respect that derives from valuing the essential character of each person.

3. In women's language, *keigo,* as well as euphemism, is used excessively (for example, the overuse of the polite prefix *o-*). It is hoped that there will be rectification of this point once women reflect and come to self-awareness.

4. Mistaking the spirit of service, there are those, especially in commerce, who use too lofty honorifics or obsequious humble forms. We should all take a lesson from the fact that, without even knowing it, those people miss the point of their

own and others' human dignity. It is hoped that all citizens will develop a consciousness of this point.

I. Referring to People

(1) REFERRING TO ONESELF

1. *"Watashi"* will be taken as the standard form.
2. *"Watakushi"* will be a special form for formal contexts.

   Note. In women's pronunciation, *"atakushi"* and *"atashi"* are recognized as special forms, but in principle, for men and women across the board, the standard forms are taken to be *"watakushi"* and *"watashi."*

3. *"Boku"* is a special form for schoolboys, but when one becomes a member of society one begins to use *"watashi"* again, taking care in one's speech, as is to be expected on the basis of education.

4. We wish to avoid using *"jibun"* in the meaning of *"watashi."*

(2) REFERRING TO OTHERS

1. *"Anata"* will be taken as the standard form.
2. The practice until now of using *"kiden"* and *"kika"* in letters (both public and private), too, from now on will be better served by *"anata."*
3. Rather than using the terms *"kimi"* and *"boku"* in very friendly so-called *"kimi-boku"* relationships, we want to use the standard *"watashi"* and *"anata."* Similarly, we want to switch eventually to using *"watashi"* and *"anata"* rather than *"ore"* and *"omae."*

II. Honorific Titles

1. *"-san"* will be taken as the standard.
2. *"-sama,"* a form for formal occasions, is still seen in common use, but will be used mainly in letters, for the addressee. From now on, it is also to be desired in business correspondence that *"sama"* replace *"dono."*
3. *"-shi"* is a specialized form for writing, whose purpose will be served by *"-san"* in spoken language.
4. *"-kun"* is a form for schoolboys. Accordingly, it is used for young people in general, but for conversation among members of society, in principle, *"-san"* is to be used.

   Note. A special form reserved for use among members of an assembly is *"bokun."*

5. At the workplace, when using, for example, *"sensei, kyokuchō, kachō, shachō, semmu,"* it is not necessary to add *"-san"* (whether one is male or female).

III. "-tachi" and "-ra"

1. It is acceptable to use *"tachi,"* as, for example, in *"watashi-tachi,"* in contemporary usage, when referring to oneselves.

2. *"-ra"* is written style and can be used for anyone, as in, for example, "A-*shi*, B-*shi*, C-*shi-ra*."

IV. Accounting for "o-" and "go-"

(1) CASES WHEN USE IS ACCEPTABLE

1. Cases when *"o-"* or *"go-"* would demonstrate that something belongs to the other person and could be translated as 'your.' For example,

O-bōshi wa dore deshō ka?	'Which is your hat?'
Go-iken wa ikaga deshō ka?	'What is your opinion?'

2. Cases when indicating sincere feelings of respect. For example,

sensei no o-hanashi	'the teacher's talk'
sensei no go-shusseki	'the teacher's attendance'

3. Cases where usage is fixed. For example,

o-hayō	'good morning'
o-kazu	'side dish'
o-tamajakushi	'wooden ladle'
go-han	'rice'
go-ran	'look'
go-kurōsama	'thanks for effort'
o-ide ni naru	'go' (all o-...ni naru forms)
go-ran ni naru	'look' (all go-...ni naru forms)

4. Cases when things are one's own, but there is a basis for some relationship with the other person and it is fixed usage to append *"o-"* or *"go-."* For example,

otegami (o-henji/go-henji) o sashiagemashita ga	'I gave you the letter, but'
o-negai	'request'
o-rei	'thanks'
go-enryo	'restraint'
go-hōkoku-itashimasu	'I will make a report'

(2) CASES WHEN ONE CAN OMIT (IF OMISSION IS ACCEPTABLE)

In the case of women's language, *"o-"* is attached, but in men's language it is omitted. For example,

(o-)kome	'rice'
(o-)kashi	'sweets'

| (o-)chawan | 'bowl' |
| (o-)hiru | 'noon' |

(3) CASES WHEN OMISSION IS PREFERABLE

For example,

(o-)chokki	'vest'
(o-)kutsushita	'socks'
(o-)biiru	'beer'
(go-)hōmei	'name'
(go-)reisoku	'son'
(go-)fukei	'parents'

(go-)chōsa sareta (In this case, "chōsa sareta" or "go-chōsa ni natta" is correct.)

(go-)sotsugyō sareta (In this case, "sotsugyō sareta" or "go-sotsugyō ni natta" is correct.)

V. Setting the Tone of Conversation

From now on we would like for "desu/-masu" to set the tone of conversation.

Note. This has been decided as setting the tone for general conversation among members of society and does not limit forms such as the "de arimasu" of lectures, the "de gozaimasu" of formal occasions, or the familiar "da."

VI. The Language of Actions

Honorific forms for actions comprise three forms (see Table 5).

Model 1, "-reru/-rareru" is misleading and often mistaken for a passive inflection, but because it regularly attaches to all actions and is, moreover, quite simple, it can be recognized as promising for future use.

There is no need to change 2, "o-...ni naru" to "o-...ni narareru."

Form 3, the so-called *asobase-kotoba*, should be gradually discarded from what is recognized to be plain, straightforward keigo.

Table 5.

| | Example | |
Form	*kaku* 'write'	*ukeru* 'receive'
I	*kakereru*	*ukerareru*
II	*o-kaki ni naru*	*o-uke ni naru*
III	*(o-kaki asobasu)*	*(o-uke asobasu)*

VII. Adjectives and "*desu*"

We now recognize the acceptable ending for adjectives, which until now had been a longstanding problem—for example, "*ōkii desu,*" "*chiisai desu.*"

VIII. Words for Greetings

For common usage, the set form is best when it comes to words for greetings. For example,

ohayō /ohayō gozaimasu	'good morning'
oyasumi/oyasumi nasai	'good night'
itadakimasu	'let's eat'
gochisōsama	'thanks' (after a meal)
itte kimasu/itte mairimasu	'see you later' (leaving)
itte 'rasshai	'see you later' (staying behind)

IX. Special Vocabulary for School

1. It should be noted that there is a tendency for female teachers to overuse "*o-*" from kindergarten through elementary, middle, and high school. For example,

o-kyōshitsu	'classroom'
o-chōku	'chalk'
o-tsukue	'desk'
o-koshikake	'chair'
o-kaji	'chores'

2. In the conversation of teachers and pupils, too, the principle of "*desu/-masu*" is to be desired.

   Note. This is not to hinder the use of "*da*" in familiar circumstances.

3. One feels that the convention before the war of using only *keigo*, such as "*osshatta,*" "*o-...ni natta,*" toward teachers and parents was a trifle overdone. After the war, the countermove toward using only "*itta,*" "*nani-nani shita*" is also overdone. We prefer a middle path. For example, not "*kita,*" but "*korareta*" or "*mieta.*"

X. Terminology for Newspaper/Radio

The biggest problem for newspaper and radio terminology is the use of titles. With regard to this:

1. In general, as sentences and vocabulary become simpler, titles follow suit, and the use of "*-san*" tends to be adequate.

2. The use of "*-shi*" in political news is also adequate, but it is not unheard of to use "*-ō*" 'sir', "*joshi*" 'Ms./Mrs./Miss', "*-kun*" 'Mr./Master', "*-chan*" 'Master/Miss',

Appendix 1

diminutive, and other honorific titles and terms in front-page society news, depending on the demands of time, context, day, and the matter under discussion.

3. In news about criminal suspects too, until the sentence has been handed down, it is suitable to use a title, but when, for example, it is a matter of a crime committed before police witnesses, and public opinion is united, or other similar situations, it is not uncommon to omit it.

4. In the following circumstance it is better to omit the title: Aoyama-sō Apartments (Custodian: Kōno Otsuo)

XI. Terminology for the Imperial Household

Until now a great deal of difficult special Chinese vocabulary had been used to serve as *keigo* for referring to the Imperial household. But from now on, as part of the decision to use the best *keigo* from the range of that used everyday, and as a result of what happened in August 1947, a basic understanding has been reached between authorities in the Imperial household and the media. Specifically, these forms include:

"gyokutai/seitai" 'the Emperor's person' became *"o-karada."*

"Tengan/ryūgan" 'Your Majesty's face/countenance' became *"o-kao."*

"Hōsan/seiju" 'Your Majesty's age' became *"o-toshi"* or *"go-nenrei."*

"eiryo/seishi/shinkin/ishi" 'Your Majesty's pleasure/the Imperial will' became *"oboshimeshi"* or *"o-kangae."*

Beyond this, the *"chokugo"* 'Imperial message' at the opening ceremony of the Diet became *"o-kotoba,"* and the self-referential *"chin"* became *"watakushi."* If one looks at reports in the news today, one also observes straightforward, simplified *keigo* in use of forms such as *"-reru/-rareru"* or *"o-...ni naru/go-...ni naru"* in VI, above.

XII. Conclusion

The conversation of adults in society is one of mutual equality, and yet it must contain respect.

On this point, language use between, for example, public servants and the public, or all the various workers in a workplace, should take *"desu/-masu"* as fundamental, because of its being of a form that is kind and polite.

After the war, clerks and the authorities had already put such language into practice along these lines, but from now on it is to be desired that this tendency achieve even more universality.

これからの敬語

昭和二七年四月十四日に国語審議会から
文部大臣へ建議されたものである
（三省堂編修所注）

まえがき

この小冊は、日常の言語生活における最も身近な問題を取り上げて、これからはこうあるほうが望ましいと思われる形をまとめたものである。

これからの敬語についての問題は、もちろんこれに尽きるものではない。元来、敬語の問題は単なることばの上だけの問題でなく、実生活における作法と一体をなすものであるから、これからの敬語は、これからの新しい時代の生活に即した新しい作法の成長とともに、平明・簡素な新しい敬語法として健全な発達をとげることを望むしだいである。

基本の方針

一

これまでの敬語は、旧時代に発達したままで、必要以上に煩雑な点があった。これからの敬語は、その行きすぎをいましめ、誤用を正し、でけるだけ平明・簡素にありたいものである。

二

これまでの敬語は、主として上下関係に立って発達してきたが、これからの敬語は、各人の基本的人格を尊重する相互尊敬の上に立たなければならない。

三

女性のことばでは、必要以上に敬語または美称が多く使われている（たとえば「お」のつけすぎなど）。この点、女性の反省・自覚によって、しだいに純化されることが望ましい。

四

奉仕の精神を取り違えて、不当に高い尊敬語や、不当に低い謙そん語を使う

ことが特に商業方面などに多かった。そういうことによって、しらずしらず自他の人格的尊厳を見うしなうことがあるのははなはだいましむべきことである。この点において国民一般の自覚が望ましい。

一　人をさすことば

（1）　自分をさすことば

1. わたし」を標準の形とする。
2. 「わたくし」は、あらたまった場面の用語とする。

   付記　女性の発音では「あたくし」「あたし」という形も認められるが、原則としては、男女を通じて「わたし」「わたくし」を標準の形とする。
3. 「ぼく」は男子学生の用語であるが、社会人となれば、あらためて「わたし」を使うように、教育上、注意をすること。
4. 「じぶん」を「わたし」の意味に使うことは避けたい。

（2）　相手をさすことば

1. 「あなた」を標準の形とする。
2. 手紙（公私とも）の用語として、これまで「貴殿」「貴下」はどを使っているのも、これからは「あなた」で通用するようにありたい。
3. 「きみ」「ぼく」は、いわゆる「きみ・ぼく」の親しい間がらだけの用語として、一般には、標準の形である「わたし」「あなた」を使いたい。したがって「おれ」「おまえ」も、しだいに「わたし」「あなた」を使うようにしたい。

二　敬称

1. 「さん」を標準の形とする。
2. 「さま（様）」は、あらたまった場合の形、また慣用語に見られるが、主として手紙のあて名に使う。

   将来は、公用文の「殿」も「様」に統一されることが望ましい。
3. 「氏」は書きことば用で、話しことば用には一般に「さん」を用いる。
4. 「くん（君）」は、男子学生の用語である。それに準じて若い人に対して用いられることもあるが、社会人としての対話には、原則として「さん」を用いる。

   付記　議会用語の「某君」は特殊の慣用語である。
5. 職場用語として、たとえば「先生」「局長」「課長」「社長」「専務」などに「さん」をつけて呼ぶには及ばない（男女を通じて）。

三 「たち」と「ら」

1. 「たち」は、たとえば「わたしたち」というふうに、現代語としては、自分の
   ほうにつけてよい。
2. 「ら」は書きことばで、たとえば「A氏・B氏・C氏ら」というふうに、だれ
   にも使ってよい。

四 「お」「ご」の整理

(1) つけてよい場合

1. 相手の物事を表わす「お」「ご」で、それを訳せば「あなたの」という意味に
   なるような場合。たとえば、
   お帽子は、どれでしょうか。
   ご意見は、いかがですか。
2. 真に尊敬の意を表わす場合。たとえば、
   先生のお話　　　　　　　先生のご出席
3. 慣用が固定している場合。たとえば、

おはよう	おかず	おたまじゃくし
ごはん	ごらん	ごくろうさま
おいでになる	（すべて「おーになる」の型）	
ごらんになる	（すべて「ごーになる」の型）	

4. 自分の物事ではあるが、相手の人に対する物事である関係上、それをつける
   ことに慣用が固定している場合。たとえば、
   お手紙（お返事・ご返事）をさしあげましたが
   お願い　　お礼　　ご遠慮　　ご報告いたします

(2) 省けば省ける場合

女性のことばとしては「お」がつくが、男性のことばとしては省いていえるもの。
たとえば、
〔お〕茶・〔お〕茶わん・〔お〕ひる

(3) 省くほうがよう場合

たとえば、

（お）チョッキ	（お）くつした	（お）ビール
（ご）苦名	（ご）令息	（ご）父兄

（ご）調査された（これは「調査された」または「ご調査になった」が正しい。）
（ご）卒業された（これは「卒業された」または「ご卒業になった」が正しい。）

五　対話の基調

これからの対話の基調は「です・ます」体としたい。

　　付記　これは社会人としての一般的対話の基調を定めたものであって、講演の「であります」や、あらたまった場合の「ございます」など、そのほか親愛体としての「だ」調の使用を制限するものだはない。

六　動作のことば

動詞の敬語法には、およそ三つの型がある。

型	語例	
	書く	受ける
I	書ける	受けられる
II	お書きになる	お受けになる
III	（お書きあそばす）	（お受けあそばす）

　第1の「れる」「られる」の型は、受け身の言い方とまぎらわし欠点はあるが、すべての動詞に規則的につき、かつ簡単でもあるので、むしろ将来性があると認められる。

　　第2の「おーになる」の型を「おーになられる」という必要はない。

　　第3の型は、いわゆるあそばせことばであって、これからの平明・簡素な敬語としては、おいおいにすたれる形であろう。

七　形容詞と「です」

これまで久しく問題となっていた形容詞の結び方—たとえば、「大きいです」「小さいです」などは、平明・簡素な形として認めてよい。

八　あいさつ語

あいさつ語は、慣用語として、きまった形のままでよい。たとえば、

おはよう。	おはようございます。
おやすみ。	おやすみなさい。
いただきます。	ごちそうさま。
いってきます。	いってまいります。
いってらっしゃい。	

九　学校用語

1. 幼稚園から小・中・高校に至るまで、一般女の先生のことばに「お」を使いすぎる傾向があるから、その点、注意すべきであろう。たとえば、

（お）教室　　　　　（お）チョーク　　　　　（お）つくえ
（お）こしかけ　　　（お）家事

2. 先生と生徒との対話にも、相互に「です・ます」体を原則とすることが望ましい。

　　付記　このことは、親愛体としての「だ」調の使用をさまたげるものではない。

3. 戦前、父母・先生に対する敬語がすべて「おっしゃった」「おーになった」の式ではったのは少し行きすぎの感があった。戦後、反動的にすべて「言った」「何々した」の式で通すのもまた少し行きすぎであろう。その中庸を得たいものである。たとえば、「きた」ではく「こられた」「みえた」など。

十　新聞・ラジオの用語

新聞・ラジオの用語として、いちばん問題になるのは、敬称のつけ方である。それについて、

1. 一般に文章・用語がやさしくなり、それにしたがって敬称も「さん」が多く使われる傾向があるのは妥当である。

2. 政治的記事における「氏」の用法も妥当であるが、一面社会的記事において「翁・女史・くん・ちゃん」そのほかの敬称・愛称を、その時、その場、その人、その事による文体上の必要に応じて用いることは認めざるを得ない。

3. 犯罪容疑者に関する報道でも、刑が確定するまでは敬称をつけるのが理想的であるが、たとえば現行犯またはそれに準ずるものなどで、社会感情の許さないような場合に、適宜、これを省略することがあるのもやむを得ないと認められる。

4. 次のような場合には敬称をつけないでよい。
　　青山荘アパート　（責任者甲野乙雄）

十一　皇室用語

これまで、皇室に関する敬語として、特別にむずかしい漢語が多く使われてきたが、これからは、普通のことばの範囲内で最上級の敬語を使うということに、昭和二十二年八月、当時の宮内当局と報道関係との間に基本的了解が成り立っていた。その具体的な用例は、たとえば、

　　「玉体・聖体」は「おからだ」
　　「天顔・龍顔」は「お顔」
　　「宝算・聖寿」は「お年・ご年齢」
　　「叡慮・聖旨・宸襟・懿旨」は「おぼしめし・お考え」などの類である。

その後、国会開会式における「勅語」は「おことば」となり、ご自称の「朕」は「わたくし」となったが、これを今日の報道上の用例について見ても、すでに第六項で述べた「れる・られる」の型または「おーになる」「ごーになる」の型をとって、平明・簡素なこれからの敬語の目標を示している。

十二 むすび

　一般に社会人としての対話は、相互に対等で、しかも敬意を含むべきである。

　　この点で、たとえば、公衆と公務員との間、または各種の職場における職員相互の間のことばづかいなども、すべて「です、ます」体を基調とした、やさしい、ていねいな形でありたい。

　　戦後、窓口のことばや警察職員のことばづかいなどが、すでにこの線に沿って実践されているが、これからも、いっそうその傾向が普遍化することが望ましい。

Guidelines for Expressions of Respect (*Keii Hyōgen*) in the Modern Age

Article 1 of Language Policy in Accordance with the New Age

Why consider the problems that confront "language use with a focus on *keigo*" now? Because it is a matter of extreme importance for smooth modern communication.

Keigo as it has usually been dealt with up until now (*keigo* in its narrow meaning, called *"keigo"* in what follows) comprises *sonkeigo, kenjōgo, teineigo,* and so on. But it is not the case that communication proceeds smoothly simply through the correct use of these. To begin with, in order to use *keigo* correctly, along with the suitable forms, it is important to keep certain factors in mind as we use it: when, in what context, and with regard to whom we are using it. Moreover, real communication uses a variety of expressions besides *keigo* that depend on things like the addressee and context. These include *keigo* but can be more generally thought of as expressions of respect (termed below *"keii hyōgen"*). In other words, in order to facilitate the smooth process of communication, it is necessary to cast our net to take in that larger category of expressions of respect (*keii hyōgen*), not just *keigo* in its narrow sense. In that case, it is necessary to be mindful of the fact that language use establishes the humanity, the nature of the speaker.

Starting from this kind of understanding, in "I. Communication and Language Use," we consider the guidelines for diverse linguistic usage in modern society. In "II. Guidelines for *Keii Hyōgen*," we offer an outline and a basic understanding of *keii hyōgen* as they serve to foster communication. Moreover, it is planned that from now on meetings of the Council will develop guidelines for specific *keii hyōgen* and their continued use in a section to be called "III. Modern Use of *Keii Hyōgen*," making three parts in all.

I. Communication and Language Use

1. MODERN SOCIETY AND LANGUAGE USE

In modern society, along with visible urbanization, internationalization, the information age, and an aging population, circumstances have emerged that call for the coexistence of different kinds of values.

This sort of societal change has extended its influence not least of all into people's linguistic lives. But no matter what the age, in order to build, maintain, and further human connections as the unspoken pivot of human society, it is necessary to include smooth communication. The foundation of that [communication] is that speaker and addressee respect each other, recognize the uniqueness of others, empathize with their feelings, and understand their thoughts.

There are other means besides language in which to communicate, but in a society that holds one language in common as its identity, validity comes from language. Depending on addressee, on context, and even on the smooth communication that is a product of appropriate language (language that also takes into consideration society's conventions), we can foster warm human connectedness that gives either side peace of mind. The spread of this kind of human connectedness sustains society.

Below we offer examples of some special phenomena in contemporary Japanese society, and propose the ideal language that is to be desired for each.

2. VARIOUS HUMAN RELATIONSHIPS AND LANGUAGE USE

(1) Advancement of urbanization and language use

Because of the changing structure of industry and the advancement of urbanization, there has been an enormous shift in the communal character of society as we know it. A new kind of organization that surpasses the region has arisen, and because the number of people who are associated with this unit has increased, the number of people who live their entire lives in their place of birth has diminished. Further, the social connection of people who do not know each other has increased, the solidarity and harmony of the traditional local area/region has faded in the face of growing individualism, and the human connections of regional society have become superficial. On the other hand, the expansion of secondary education and the development of transportation and communications have brought with them their own brand of human connection. In this kind of society, in order to promote breadth in the connectedness of such superficial encounters with people we do not know well, it becomes necessary for us as a country all to have the same mutual understanding of our intent to create the psychological distance that enables us not to step on each others' toes.

Still, as we emerge now from a period of rapid growth, we begin to reexamine the development of local areas, regional traditions and culture, and their uniqueness. Dialects as well have come to be reevaluated [in terms of] their place in shouldering the burden of conveying the richness of human relationships. Because of the influence of education and mass communication, standard language *(kyōtsūgo)* has come to be used widely throughout the country. But it is to be hoped that from here on our communication will be enriched all the more by both the core of standard Japanese and the dialects, which incorporate regional tradition and culture and which shoulder the burden of conveying the richness of human relationships.

(2) Gender difference and language use

Consciousness of the equality of the sexes is established, and efforts are underway to realize a society where men and women participate equally. But with regard to differences in language use that derive from gender, there is a substantial gap between those who find such differences objectionable and those who affirm their richness.

There are many languages that differentiate use by gender. The Japanese language also exhibits vocabulary and usage that depend on gender. But it is not necessary to force the notion that men must always speak like men, and women must always speak like women. In effect, everyone will be affiliated with a gender, and everyone can be satisfied with his or her own form of expression (expression that projects individual character, below called *"jiko hyōgen"*). But it is to be desired that we all choose language and topics that are appropriate to the other and to the context, so that rich communication results.

(3) Generational difference and language use

A low birthrate and an aging population, along with detachment of the nuclear family, lessen the chances for communication across generations. As a rule, most older people depend on typical traditional linguistic usage and tend to be disaffected with or criticize the new usage of younger people. Young people, on the other hand, are drawn to freshness and originality, preferring communication that is free of tradition and that distinguishes their peer group.

It is to be hoped that young people will come to recognize the value of tradition and custom and to show respect to senior citizens who have borne society on their shoulders, and that senior citizens will in turn trust younger people to carry on society in the future. Both should exhibit due consideration to believe in language in order to overcome generational differences and understand each other's minds.

(4) The development of information technology and language use

Because of rapid developments in information technology, it has become possible for the individual to share information quickly, cheaply, and easily, enabling us to communicate with others anywhere on the globe. The construction of networks that rely on new informational media has tremendous impact on people's view of communication and human connectedness. Because it has become commonplace to exchange e-mail with people one has never even met, people's sense of familiarity has also changed, compared to what it was in the past. Dependence on information technology and absorption in virtual reality has resulted in more people's communicating less, in fact, to the avoidance of communication with real people altogether. In the relentless pursuit of efficiency, we have abandoned the emotional facets of life. Thoughtless misjudgment of our proximity to others gives rise to frictions. These are only some of the problems that have arisen.

It behooves us to improve people's independent practical use of information technology. They in turn need to become conscious of the fact that communication is at the center of people's meeting heart-to-heart, and that language manifests personal character.

(5) Language use in the workplace

Service industries have grown, and language use has become a means for supporting commercial activities. Large stores and chain stores especially tend to use manuals in activities that teach or train *keigo*. Judgment is divided about the kind of hospitality/client contact that should emerge from these manuals. That is, on the one hand, the positive side [lit., face] is that it may be fair to use the same language to treat all people in the same way, as if they were valued persons, which at least will not bring out any unpleasant feelings. But the negative side is that overuse of *keigo* does not give a good impression, either. The *keigo* from these manuals does not sound like real words from people's hearts. Instruction in these manuals does not teach people how to cope with the subtle differences of real cases.

It goes without saying that a large proportion of the communication that ensues in commerce is based on relationships of trust. It is to be hoped that, rather than insisting that people base their language on manuals, they will be encouraged to use kind but descriptive language appropriate to the occasion.

(6) Mass communication and language use

It has been pointed out that the inappropriate language use that one hears on television and radio programming, in public notices and in advertisements, as well as in cartoons and game shows, has a deleterious effect on children and young people. Thus there are cases when flawed language [language associated with products or expressions that hurt people] has a negative effect on children's language use and on their relationships with others. It is thought that most people are looking for a certain standard of language from the mass media. It follows that we expect those who are involved in the broadcast or the publishing media to be conscious of the depth of the influence they have, to be all the more careful in their language use, and to have a greater awareness of the language of their fellow citizens.

(7) Fellow feeling for foreigners and language use

In recent years, the number of foreigners who have needed training in Japanese in order to reside here, as well as the number of those who study Japanese abroad, has increased, demonstrating the spread of the internationalization of the Japanese language. It can no longer be said that the Japanese language belongs only to the Japanese people. Opportunities to interact with foreigners have also become everyday occurrences for the average person.

Until now it has been the norm for the Japanese people that those with whom they speak share a culture along with its linguistic conventions, which smoothes the practical use of language—for example, euphemism, or the tendency to entrust the end of the sentence to the listener. It will be necessary now to aim for language use that does not cause misunderstanding and that is easy to understand in order to facilitate mutual understanding between ourselves and non-native speakers.

II. Guidelines for *Keii Hyōgen*

1. *KEII HYŌGEN* AND *KEIGO*

The term *"keii hyōgen,"* as mentioned before, is a generic designation to encompass *keii* 'respect', which includes the narrow sense of *keigo*. In our modern lives, when we have linguistic interaction with others, we use *keii hyōgen* as expressions of consideration that adjust to addressee and context.

In many of the world's languages there are respect expressions that underlie culture; the appropriate use of such *keii hyōgen* is necessary in any society.

In the case of Japan, it is not simply a matter of respecting superiors; there are also conventions that demonstrate empathy for others, that show by means of language an attitude of enhancing the other and humbling oneself. Those "fixed expressions" are *keigo*, and they constitute the foundation of the system that is *kokugo*. We can observe the flow of history in the changes that *keigo* has undergone, from the "absolute *keigo*" of ancient times (that is, when particular *keigo* was used for distinctive people and *sonkeigo/kenjōgo* were the norm), to the Middle Ages, when speakers became more aware of the role of listeners, to modern times, when *sonkeigo-kenjōgo-teineigo* constitute the core of *keigo*. *Keigo* can be thought of as embodying the long history of Japanese culture, as the foundation of Japanese psychology. Moreover, *keigo* has become, in one sense, a mainstay of Japanese society, even though, in another, it overemphasizes the gap between members in a vertical social structure. Finally, it is simply difficult for people to learn such complex linguistic conventions.

In 1952, in "Kore kara no keigo," the Kokugo Shingikai did away with the *keigo* of the past and set out more suitable, clearer, and simpler *keigo* for a democratic society. This was a proactive plan for that postwar society. Moreover, it is the only statement of policy ever to have come from the Kokugo Shingikai, so it has served as the basis for people's usage. The guiding principle contained therein was mutual respect, and even today we inherit the admonition not to overuse *keigo*. But it cannot be denied that *keigo* use in today's society does not always conform to these guidelines. That is, the usage set forth by the Shingikai assumed uniformity, and as it failed to recognize the variation that derives from people's relationships and context, it lacks considerations that are included in the wider meaning of *keii hyōgen*. Neither did it take up questions regarding *kenjōgo* or suppletive forms like *"irassharu"* or *"ukagau."*

In recent years, the decline in use of *sonkeigo* and *kenjōgo*, especially *kenjōgo*, is often decried. But (on the other hand,) the use of *teineigo* is thriving, and it might be said that in spoken language *teineigo* is the most generally used form (see n. 1 at end of section).

Most people seek good human relationships and desire smooth communication. In order to further those, it is thought that most people feel a need for language that takes into consideration addressee and context. People who feel that need with regard to *keigo* are quite numerous (see n. 2 at end of section). There is the opinion that such consideration can be demonstrated by *keii hyōgen* outside of *teineigo* and *keigo*, but it also goes without saying that the appropriate use of *sonkeigo* and *kenjōgo* are Japan's culture; they are crucial to the system that is *kokugo*.

The Kokugo Shingikai recognizes that *keii hyōgen* are used by all people in a personal [idiosyncratic] way, and that they make for smoother communication. We also consider it necessary to include in our deliberations of *keii hyōgen* forms the [abovementioned] use of *keigo*, which includes *kenjōgo* and suppletive forms of *keigo*.

1. In a public opinion survey (Heisei 9 [1997], January, Bunka-chō), the proportion of people who think that the *"-masu* of *tabemasu"* "is not *keigo*" rose to

85.3%. From this it can be said that there is a strong tendency to think that only *sonkeigo* and *kenjōgo* are *keigo*.

2. In a public opinion survey (Heisei 9 [1997], January, Bunka-chō), the proportion of people who said that they use *keigo* toward superiors was 86.0% , and the proportion of people who said they use *keigo* toward elders or people they respect was 79.2% and 69.7%, respectively. The proportion of people who said that they "don't use *keigo*" at all was 1.8%.

(1) Outline of keii hyōgen

When, for example, you want to borrow something, there are any number of ways you might say it. The range covers everything from the very polite *"haishaku-sasete itadake-masen deshō ka"* 'could I have you let me borrow' to the straightforward, often-used, ordinary *"kashite kudasai masen ka"* 'won't you please lend it to me', *"Okari-shitai no desu ga"* 'I'd like to borrow', or *"kashite kure yo"* 'lend it to me', *"kashite hoshii n da kedo"* 'I want you to lend it to me', and the like (refer to Addendum 2[1] below). Then again, there is the possibility of adding a preliminary phrase such as *"mōshiwake nai kedo"* 'I'm really sorry, but', *"chotto"* 'just', or explaining the reason for your action by adding, *"wasurete kita no de"* 'I forgot mine', *"Ianomareta mono da kara"* 'someone else asked me', and the like. There are ways of saying it that don't use *keigo*, such as *"kashite kure yo"* 'Lend it to me' or *"chotto kashite hoshii n da kedo"* 'I want you to lend it to me', but upon reflection, [it may be seen that] ending particles such as *"yo"* and *"-te kureru"* and words such as *"chotto"* or *"kedo"* are quite different from *"kase"* 'hand it over', and must be recognized as showing consideration for the other. The speaker, out of consideration for his/her connection to the listener or others in the speech event or the context, chooses to use suitable language. Those expressions are *keii hyōgen*.

Keii hyōgen are by no means limited to language use toward higher-ranking people. They include usage that creates distance between insiders and outsiders, expressions of gentle consideration for lower-ranking people, and straightforward usage that skips *keigo* proper entirely.

Furthermore, *keii hyōgen* takes in factors outside of language, extending to clothing, gestures, demeanor, etc. We will limit ourselves here to those things connected with language.

(2) Keigo in keii kyōgen

It can be said that this *keii hyōgen*, which takes in *keigo*, is critical, and no doubt has *keigo* as its foundation. We will outline it here.

The age-old notion that *keigo* comprises *sonkeigo*, *kenjōgo*, and *teineigo* has become commonplace, and we will use those appellations here (see n. 1 at end of section).

Keigo has the functions laid out below. These do not operate independently; in fact, many of them can be combined.

i. Raising the status of the addressee or the person under discussion

Keigo has the function of raising the status of superiors or seniors, older people, higher-ranking people to whom one is indebted or those associated with such people (n. 2). If the person to be esteemed is the subject, *sonkeigo* is used; if the speaker or the speaker's group is the subject, *kenjōgo* is used. For example, if you say *"irasshaimasu ka"* 'Are you going?' (honorific), the subject must be the addressee or someone in the addressee's group; if you say *"mairimasu"* 'I'll go' (humble), it refers to yourself or someone in your own group. Thus *keigo* functions to imply the subject. Accordingly, when you ask if your interlocutor is going to wait by using *"omachi-shimasu ka"* 'Will you wait?' (humble) *(o...suru)*, mistakenly intending it to be *sonkeigo* (when in fact it is *kenjōgo*), the subject cannot be accurately inferred.

ii. Creating distance with someone who is not an intimate

Keigo establishes distance between speakers and people they are meeting for the first time or people who are not particularly close; it distinguishes people who are affiliated with groups or workplaces not one's own; it shows a concern for not interfering with the other (n. 3). To put it another way, one rarely uses *keigo* with intimates.

iii. Demonstrating consciousness of formality

Keigo functions to demonstrate a feeling of formality. Using *keigo* with superiors or people one does not know well avoids a feeling of overfamiliarity by demonstrating awareness of formality. Even with friends or colleagues with whom one does not use *keigo* privately, when one is at a conference or some public event *keigo* is often appropriate (n. 4).

iv. Maintaining one's dignity

Keigo functions to maintain one's dignity vis-à-vis others. For example, elderly people who hold a higher place in society might still say to someone younger, *"omizu o ippai itadakenai deshō ka"* 'could I possibly have a glass of water?' or a mother might say to her child *"okake-nasai"* 'hang that up' (honorific) or *"meshiagare"* 'eat' (honorific).

Notes

1. *Sonkeigo* is used to raise the status of the person under discussion (often the addressee or someone on the addressee's side). Examples:

<u>Otōsama</u> mo <u>irasshaimasu</u> ka	'Will your father come/go/be there?'
<u>Yamada-sama</u> wa <u>okaeri ni</u> natta	'Did Mr. Yamada go back home?'
okao	'face'
kisha	'your company'
outsukushii	'beautiful'
otabō	'very busy'
goyukkuri	'take your time'

   Because *kenjōgo* lowers the status of the person under discussion (usually self or self's group), by extension it raises the status of the other person/people involved (usually the addressee or addressee's group). Examples:

Chichi ga <u>ukagatai</u> to <u>mōshite orimasu</u>	'My father says he wants to visit you'
Watakushi ga sensei ni <u>otodoke-suru</u>	'I will deliver it to the teacher'
watakushi-domo	'we'
soshina	'a small present'

   Teineigo is not limited to self or other, but rather makes the language that is used toward the other (the listener) more polite. Examples:

Yoi tenki <u>desu</u>	'It's nice weather'

Densha ga kimashita   'The train has arrived'
Kekkon de gozaimasu   'That's quite all right'

2. In a public opinion survey (Heisei 9 [1997], December, Bunka-chō), respondents overwhelmingly said that store clerks, patients, and people asking for things "are supposed to use *keigo*" toward teachers, club seniors, and older people (along with people who have greater longevity in whatever location), as well as customers, doctors, the person who is being asked (along with superiors to whom one is indebted). The figures: teachers 83.7%, club seniors 60.4%, older people 68.5%, customers 75.9%, doctors 74.7%, the person who is being asked 75.8%.

3. In a public opinion survey (Heisei 9 [1997], January, Bunka-chō), the number of people who responded that they use *keigo* "when speaking with someone you don't know (even if the same age)" was 57.7%. In another survey (Heisei 9 [1997], December, Bunka-chō), the proportion of people who responded that their language changes depending on the sex of the addressee was 34.6%, and among these 80 percent said, "I think that my language becomes more polite when I'm talking to a member of the opposite sex than it is when I'm talking to a member of the same sex."

4. From a public opinion survey (Heisei 9 [1997], December, Bunka-chō), it is clear that people respond differently to "One is supposed to use *keigo*," depending on the context. Even in companies, the proportion of people who think it necessary to use *keigo* at work when speaking to superiors is 85.9%, but that number falls to 36.2% (in the situation) when work is over and workers have gone out drinking.

(3) *Various types of "consideration" and* keii hyōgen

That many kinds of consideration can be conveyed through *keii hyōgen* is a deeply rooted belief of Japanese culture. *Keigo* is among the *keii hyōgen* that are used when speakers want to raise the status of the other or when the context is formal (for example, *"oisogashii to wa zonjimasu ga"* 'I suspect that you would be busy, but'. On the other hand, by not using *keigo,* distance between self and other is diminished, an atmosphere of frankness and a consciousness of inclusiveness is engendered, and human connections become more intimate. Yet when one makes a mistake about the connection with another or the other's state of mind, the intention of friendliness becomes presumptuous and can be taken the wrong way.

For example, in speaking with others, there are conventions for telling one's own name and affiliation, in some contexts for confirming the identity of the other, for thanking the other for favors rendered or for apologizing when one is imposing on the other, for entering the conversation or for starting it, for explaining one's reasons for addressing the other, and for how such things are carried out.

Then again, instead of using a simple form such as *"kashite"* 'lend' for what it is that one wants to convey, there are forms such as questions, negative expressions, and verbs of giving and receiving that differ only slightly in meaning but that say the same thing. The need for showing consideration can be addressed through suitable technical terms, or Chinese rather than Japanese forms, classical rather than contemporary language, because these have a higher degree of formality. Agreed-upon style is also important, as are sentence-final particles, which have a close relationship to *keii hyōgen*. Finally, the omission of *keigo* word endings allows us to shade expressions that show consideration for the addressee by trusting them to judge the language as absent in formality.

Furthermore, there are conventions for who has the right to lead the discussion or what topic is chosen, but these depend heavily on the speaker's cultural background. Even saying nothing at all falls under *keii hyōgen* in a situation where the other person does not want to be interfered with. Depending on the situation, rather than risk saying something impertinent, it is more considerate to use euphemisms. And finally, there is the kindness that is shown through understanding and respect for the other person, and that can be expressed at any time by honest regard for the actions and things associated with the other person.

In spoken language these are the primary ways in which speakers voice their consideration, but vocal quality, pitch and volume, speed, and the like are also critical to showing regard. Other elements that shoulder the same burden as language are attitude and behavior.

There are also issues of written style in *keii hyōgen*. These probably are of most direct importance in letter-writing style. Depending on the kind of letter character as well as our relationship to the addressee, we judge the level of usage and then write using the appropriate *keii hyōgen*. Other factors include the kind of paper used, the writing instrument, and the script (printed, cursive, handwritten, word processor).

Specific examples of the kinds of regard outlined here are in Addendum 2(2), below.

Note. Expressions of giving and receiving: *yaru, ageru, kureru, morau* show benefit. We classify these verbs as auxiliaries in expressions such as *-te kureru* and *-te morau*.

2. GUIDELINES FOR *KEII HYŌGEN* PRINCIPLES AND STANDARDS

As stated above, people use a wide variety of *keii hyōgen* these days. As the overview in Section I ("Communication and Language Use") states, modern society is multifaceted, and a variety of personal relationships abounds, such that it is only natural for the various *keii hyōgen* to be distinguished according to time and situation. Surely the multiplicity of *keii hyōgen* must be judged one of the richest parts of our language (see note).

Determination of which *keii hyōgen* is appropriate at any time we leave to individual judgment. It is up to each person to select the way of speaking that satisfies him/her, and to use it as his/her idiolect. To that end, we examine closely the fine shades of difference in meaning among the various ones available, and we advocate an ideal situation in which speakers correctly grasp the relationship between self and addressee, along with an ability to select the appropriate expressions for given contexts. This kind of linguistic intuition and ability to choose among alternatives is widely known as "linguistic competence," and its development is thought to be fostered in childhood; but it also has important associations with common sense and human nature in adults.

Human beings differ in their stances, their outlooks, their ages, and so forth, and nobody talks exactly the same way in any given situation. There are also degrees of newness, degrees of intimacy, the difference between whether someone is an insider or an outsider, and degrees of formality and context. Use of *keii hyōgen* adjusts in re-gard and politeness depending on all of these. It goes without saying that we should use *keii hyōgen* only when we mean it, but there are also occasions when we exploit the use of *keii hyōgen* for the sake of formality, intentionally to alienate the other, or just to inflict hurt. The intention to engage in better behavior (including language) and the reflective use of *keii hyōgen* are part and parcel of the user's sense of humanity.

At the same time that language is an individual matter, it is also social. In order to frame individual character, along with better relationships with others, it is important to use language that is suited to the other person and to the occasion, to foster capa-bility in the choice and use of *keii hyōgen*, and to manipulate these appropriately. The next Kokugo Shingikai is expected to set explicit standards for *keii hyōgen;* further-more, it is thought necessary not only to correct structural linguistic mistakes, but also to address appropriateness of use. In other words, we should organize the various *keii hyōgen* that are actually in use, set choices for clear speaking, and while explaining the reasons for various mistakes, with examples, we should establish guidelines according to anticipated contexts.

Note. In a public opinion survey (Heisei 9 [1997], December, Bunka-chō), in re-sponse to the question "How do you think *keigo* should be?" 46.9% of people said, "It is important to preserve the legacy of *keigo* as beautiful Japanese." This confirms the diversity of opinion. In contrast, 41.4% of people responded, "*Keigo* should be simplified."

ADDENDUM 1 *KEII HYŌGEN* PEDAGOGY

(1) Keii hyōgen *pedagogy in the schools*

Keii hyōgen pedagogy is not only part of *kokugo* study but has an effect on all of school life, so it is imperative to provide exhaustive guidance on this front.

We live in an era when interpersonal relations have grown superficial, so it is also critical that we foster the ability to use language in order to promote the upkeep of relationships.

Above all, *keii hyōgen* education is not simply a matter of knowing *keigo;* indeed, it is to be hoped that in their implementation people also come to reflect on the surround-ing language as well. Since young children have little call for using *sonkeigo* or *kenjōgo*, it is necessary to teach them about how language expresses respect for others and how to foster smooth communication. For young children, it is critical to nurture in school and at home the ability to choose among and to use *keii hyōgen* that are suited to con-text and addressee, as well as to establish a firm foundation in how to build good inter-personal relationships and character structure.

Note. In a public opinion survey (Heisei 9 [1997], January, Bunka-chō), in re-sponse to being asked what kinds of opportunities they had to learn *keigo*, more than 50 percent of respondents answered, "in *kokugo* class at school," "being brought up at home," or "in job training (including part-time jobs)."

To another question in the same survey, the proportion of people who re-sponded affirmatively to "It is important to deliver sufficient *keigo* instruction in school," and "It is important to include *keigo* in upbringing at home" was 77.2% and 84.4%, respectively.

(2) Keii hyōgen *in Japanese pedagogy*

Keii hyōgen are indispensable to smooth communication; they are an integral part of Japanese as a foreign-language pedagogy. It is not such a difficult problem to include *keii hyōgen* and with it *keigo* in language training. But in order to master the ability to use them properly, it is necessary to learn how they are applied explicitly and embedded in context. It follows that the difficulty of learning differs significantly, depending on whether training takes place in Japan or abroad.

Appropriate use of *keii hyōgen* requires the ability to grasp and make judgments about vertical, insider-outsider, intimate, and other relationships between the speaker and others, as well as the difference between public and private language use. As such, it is to be hoped that, depending on the student's age, native language, and native culture, teaching is carried out in the spirit of development in psycholinguistics and comparative linguistics.

Depending on the student's goals and study time, as well as the level of study (beginning, intermediate, advanced), treatment of *keii hyōgen* will vary. It is also necessary to distinguish between language comprehension and language production. Thus, in *keii hyōgen* pedagogy as intended in Japanese [as a foreign] language education, as a phenomenon used by Japanese people, it is realistic to set learning objectives with even more developed materials and pedagogy, always depending on the learning conditions.

Those who cannot use *keii hyōgen* appropriately err in language structure, and rifts appear in their human relationships. In ordinary foreign-language learning, we make special efforts to understand unskilled language use on the part of learners, and in turn speak to them choosing language that is easy to understand. But in the case of *keii hyōgen* use, it is to be hoped that there is a corresponding consideration on the part of learners.

ADDENDUM 2 EXAMPLES OF VARIOUS *KEII HYŌGEN*

(1) Ways of saying "please lend it to me"

Here we offer examples (almost all from spoken language) of forms used when borrowing something, along with levels of politeness and formality. Prefatory phrases for the examples are omitted.

Expressions	Politeness level	Formality level
Haishaku sasete itadakemasen (deshō) ka	Very polite	Very formal
Haishaku sasete itadakitai n desu ke(re)do		
Haishaku shite yoroshii deshō ka		
Haishaku sasete kudasai (masen ka)		
Haishaku shitai n desu kedo		
O-kari shite mo yoroshii (ii) deshō ka		

O-kari shitai no desu ga	Quite polite	Quite formal
Kashite itadakemasen ka [rising intonation]		
Kashite itadakitai n desu kedo		
Kashite itadakemasu ka [rising intonation]		
Kashite kudasaimasen ka [rising intonation]		
O-kari dekimasu ka [rising intonation]		

- All of the foregoing involve *kenjōgo* or *sonkeigo* + *teineigo*

Kashite itadakemasu ka	Polite	Formal
Kashite kudasai (ne)		

- All of the foregoing involve *sonkeigo*

Kashite moraemasu ka [rising intonation]		
Kashite moraemasen ka [rising intonation]		
Kashite kuremasu ka [rising intonation]		
Kashite kuremasen ka [rising intonation]		

- All of the foregoing involve *teineigo*

Haishaku shite ii [rising intonation]	Intimate +	Straightforward
Kashite itadakeru [rising intonation]	polite	
Kashite itadakenai [rising intonation]		
Kashite kudasaru [rising intonation]		
Kashite kudasaranai [rising intonation]		
Kashite chōdai (ne, yo) [rising intonation]		
O-kari shite mo yoroshii [rising intonation]		
O-kari shite ii [rising intonation]		

- All of the above are used toward intimates, no politeness

Kashite hoshii n da kedo [rising intonation]	Intimate+	Straightfor-
Kashite moraeru [rising intonation]	rough	ward, informal
Kashite moraenai [rising intonation]		
Kashite (mo) ii [rising intonation]		
Kashite kureru [rising intonation]		
Kashite kurenai [rising intonation]		
Kashite (yo, yo ne) [rising intonation]		
Kariru yo (ze) [rising intonation]		
Kashite kure (yo, yo ne) [rising intonation]	Rough	Informal

- All of the above, no *keigo*

(2) Examples of various kinds of consideration and keii hyōgen

Types of consideration	Example
1. Self-introduction; recognizing the other	*"Watakushi wa maru-maru-sha no Yamada to mōshimasu. Shitsurei desu ga, Kawamura-san de irasshaimasu ka." "Kawamura desu. Dōzo yoroshiku."* 'I am Yamada from such-and-such company. Excuse me but are you Mr/s. Kawamura?' 'I am Kawamura, How do you do.'
2. Delivering information, including weather and time	*"Oatsui tokoro, oatsumari itadaite kyōshuku desu." "Yabun, totsuzen no odenwa de mōshiwake gozaimasen." "Chokusetsu o-me ni kakatte go-aisatsu mōshiageru beki tokoro shomen de shitsurei itashimasu."* 'We are grateful for your getting together in this heat.' 'I'm sorry to have called so abruptly last evening.' 'Please excuse my introducing myself in a letter and not appearing in person as I should.'
3. Expressions of thanks	*"Wazawaza oide itadaki arigatō gozaimasu." "Osewa ni natte orimasu." "Kochira koso." "Kono aida wa gochisōsama deshita."* 'Thank you for coming.' 'We are in your debt.' 'It is we who are indebted to you.' 'Thank you for having us (for a meal) the other day.'
4. Expressions of apology	*"(Oisogashii tokoro) mōshiwake gozaimasen." "Sumimasen (ga)." "Sumanai nee." "Otema o torasemasu." "Oyaku ni tatenakute mōshiwake nai."* 'I am sorry about interrupting (when you are busy).' 'I am sorry, but...' 'I am sorry.' 'Sorry for taking up your time.' 'I am sorry I couldn't be of much help.'
5. Introductory remarks or starting a conversation	*"Chotto, yoroshii deshō ka." "Oisogashii to wa zonjimasu ga." "Atsukamashū gozaimasu ga." "Osore irimasu (ga)."* 'Is it all right?' 'I know you are busy, but...' 'It's rude, but...' 'I am sorry, (but...)'

Types of consideration	Example
6. Explaining circumstances	*"Ainiku senyaku ga arimashite (kesseki itashimasu)."* *"Ryōshin ga jōkyō shite mairimasu no de (kyūka o toritai no desu ga)."* 'Unfortunately, I have a prior engagement (please forgive me).' 'My parents are coming (so I'd like to take some time off).'
7. Right to the floor in a conclusion or declaration	Relinquishing the right to the floor (*"Soro soro..."* 'Well, it's about that time...') to the addressees in a conclusion or in a declaration; the addressee decides by urging (*"Ikō ka"* 'Shall we go?')
8. Topic selection	Topics to be avoided (in Japan, by people who are not intimates): age, married or divorced, children or no, the price of belongings, income, matters that shouldn't be mentioned in regard to distinctive physical features
9. Closing expressions	Use of ending verbs (*"Kaite kurenai"* 'Would you write it for me?') (*"Kaite kurenai ka na"* 'I wonder if you wouldn't write it for me?')
10. Expressions that build the ego of other	Positive praise for actions and belongings of the other person *"Kimi no koto wa minna homete iru yo."* *"Haru rashii sukāfu desu ne."* *"Tenisu ga ojōzu da sō de."* 'Everyone is praising you, y'know.' 'That's a spring scarf.' 'I hear you are good at tennis.'
11. *Keigo* avoidance	Abbreviate sentence close (*"Osumai wa [dochira de irasshaimasu ka]"* 'Your home [is where]?') Regard for multiple listeners (*"Maru-maru-san ga outai ni narimasu/Maru-maru-san no uta o okiki itadakimasu."* → *"Tsugi wa Maru-maru-san, uta wa XX de gozaimasu."* 'So-and-so will now sing/We'll now listen to so-and-so sing.' →'Next is so-and-so, whose song is such-and-such.')

Types of consideration	Example
12. Use of questions, negative expressions, giving-receiving verbs	*"Kashite moraemasu ka"* 'Could I have you lend it to me?' (Uses negative expressions, giving or receiving, questions); *"Kashite moraemasen ka"* 'Couldn't I have you lend it to me?' (Uses verb of giving or receiving, negative, question); *"Haishaku-sasete itadakemasen ka"* 'Couldn't I have you lend it to me?' (Uses causative, verb of giving or receiving. potential, negative, question).
13. Choice of word type, inflection	Japanese/Chinese (*ashita/myōnichi* 'tomorrow'); Modern/classical language (*itsu datta ka/itsu zoya* 'when was it'); Ordinary forms/technical vocabulary (*kanja/kuranke* 'patient'); Style (polite/ordinary/colloquial); Candid/euphemistic (*ganko da/shinnen ga katai* 'she is stubborn/she has strong faith').
14. Vocal expression	Voice quality, pitch, volume, speed, intonation, etc.
15. Written forms (for the most part, epistolary style)	Writers use *keii-hyōgen* appropriately, making judgments to select or reject sentence forms depending on the character of the letter and the relationship with the addressee.

第1 現代における敬意表現の在り方

（『新しい時代に応じた国語政策について』より）

今、「敬語を中心とする言葉遣い」という問題を検討するのは、それが現代のコミュニケーションを円滑にする上で非常に重要な事柄であるからである。

　従来主として扱われてきた敬語（狭い意味の敬語。以下「敬語」という。）は、いわゆる尊敬語、謙譲語、丁寧語などであるが、これらを正しく使えばコミュニケーションが円滑に進むというものではない。そもそも敬語を正しく使うためには、語形の適否の問題とともに、いつ、どんな場面でだれに対して使うのかという運用面での適切さが重要である。しかも、現実のコミュニケーションにおいては、敬語のほかにも相手や場面に応じた様々な配慮の表現が使われており、これらが敬語を含みつつ、全体で敬意の表現（以下「敬意表現」という。）になっていると考えられる。すなわち、コミュニケーションを円滑にするという目的のためには、狭い意味の敬語だけでなく、敬意表現という大きなとらえ方をする必要がある。その際、言葉遣いが話し手の人間性そのものを表すということにも心を致すべきであろう。

　このような認識の下に、今期は「I コミュニケーションと言葉遣い」で現代社会における様々な言葉遣いの在り方を展望し、「II 敬意表現の在り方」ではコミュニケーションを円滑にするための敬意表現の概要や理念を述べることとする。また、次期以降の継続審議によって「III 現代敬意表現の使い方」として具体的な敬意表現とその運用の指針を掲げ、全体で3部構成にまとめることが予定されている。

I コミュニケーションと言葉遣い

1 現代の社会状況と言葉遣い

現代社会には、都市化、国際化、情報化、高齢化など様々な特徴が見られるとともに、多様な価値観の共存という状況も生まれている。

このような社会状況の変化は、人々の言語生活にも少なからぬ影響を及ぼしているが、どのような時代であっても、人間関係を築き、維持し、発展させる、言わば人間社会存続のかなめとして、円滑なコミュニケーションを図ることが重要である。その基本は話し手と聞き手とが相互に尊重し合い、他者の人格を認め、その気持ちを思いやり、考えを理解することである。

　コミュニケーションは、言語以外の手段によることもあるが、同一の言語を共有する社会において最も有効なものは言語である。相手や場面、また、社会の慣習に配慮しつつ適切な言葉で円滑なコミュニケーションを行うことによって、お互いに安心できる好ましい人間関係をはぐくむことができる。このような人間関係の広がりが社会を支えている。以下に現代日本社会に特徴的な幾つかの現象を掲げ、それらにかかわる言葉遣いの望ましい在り方を述べる。

2　様々な人間関係と言葉遣い

(1)　都市化の進展と言葉遣い

　産業構造が変化し、都市化が進展したことによって、地域社会が従来有していた共同体的性格は大きく変容した。地域を超えた新しい組織が生まれ、そこに所属する人が増えることによって、生まれ故郷で一生を終える人の率は低減した。また、未知の人との社会関係が加わり、伝統的な地域住民相互の連帯感や融和感が薄まれて個々人の生活が個別化し、地域社会の人間関係は希薄になった。一方、高等教育の拡大、交通機関や通信手段の発達等により個々人の行動範囲は広がって、それぞれ独自の様々な人間関係を持つようになっている。このような社会において未知の人との接触や関係の浅い人との広範な人間関係を維持するためには、相互に踏み込まないよう心理的な距離を取りつつ、全国的に通用する共通語によって意思疎通を図ることが必要になる。

　一方、高度成長期の言わば画一的な地域開発が見直され、地域の伝統文化や独自性を再評価して外に向けて発信する動きが各地で活発になっている中で方言についても、地域の豊かな人間関係を担う言葉としての価値が再認識されている。学校教育やマスコミの影響によって、公の場では全国的に共通語が使われるようになっている現状があるが、今後も現代日本語の核としての共通語と、地域の伝統や文化を伝え、豊かな人間関係を担う方言とを使い分けつつ、地域社会のコミュニケーションを一層充実させていくことが望ましい。

(2)　性差を言葉遣い

　両性の平等意識が定着しつつあり、男女共同参画社会の実現に向けて様々な努力が行われている。しかし、性によって言葉遣いに差があることに関しては好ましくないとする考え方もあれば、むしろ日本語の豊かさとして肯定すべきであるとする考え方もあるなど、人によってかなりの幅がある。

　多くの言語には性差に基づく言葉遣いの差が存在する。日本語においても各性が特徴的に使う語彙や言語運用がある。しかしながら一般的に男性は男性らしく、女性は女性らしくといった画一的な観念を押し付けるべきではないことと同様、言葉遣いについても固定的に性差を要求すべきではない。基本的にはいずれの性に属そうとも、一人一人が自己表現（自己の人格を投影する表現。以下「自己表現」という。）として納得できる、しかも相手や場面にふさわしい言葉遣いや話題を選択して、豊かなコミュニケーションを行っていくことが望ましい。

(3) 世代差と言葉遣い

少子高齢化、核家族化等の現象によって世代間でコミュニケーションを行う機会が減少している。一般に高齢者の多くは従来の伝統的・規範的な言葉遣いに依拠して、若い人々の使う新しい言い方を批判したり否定したりしがちである。一方で若者は新鮮さや独自性を求め、伝統や規範から解放されたいわゆる若者言葉で仲間内のコミュニケーションを行うことが多い。

　若者は伝統や慣習の意義を再確認するとともに、社会を担ってきた高齢者に対して敬意を表わし、高齢者は将来の社会の担い手である若者を信頼して、相互に認め合い、言葉遣いに配慮しつつ、世代を超えて心を通わせ合っていくことが望まれる。

(4) 情報機器の発達と言葉遣い

情報機器の目覚しい発達によって、速く安く簡便に情報を交換することが個人単位で可能になり、地球上のどの地域の相手ともコミュニケーションが行えるようになった。新しい情報媒体によるネットワークの構築は、個々人のコミュニケーション観や人間関係にも影響を及ぼしている。会ったこともない人との電子メールの交換が日常化することによって、親疎の概念にも従来とは違った要素が入ってきた。情報機器に過度に依存したり、あるいは仮想空間に埋没することが習慣化したりして、生身の相手と直接話をすることを煩わしいと感じるばかりかまともに行えない人さえ増えているとの指摘もある。効率性を追求する余り心情的な要素を置き去りにし、また、相手との距離の取り方を誤って思わぬ摩擦を生ずるという問題も出てきている。

　情報機器の利用に当たっては、コミュニケーションの原点が人間相互の心の伝え合いであり、言葉が自ら人格を表すものであるということを目覚しつつ、主体的な活用能力を高めていくことが必要である。

(5) 商業場面における言葉遣い

サービス業が発展し、言葉遣いもまた商業活動を支える手段となっている。特に大型店舗やチェーン店等の商業活動では、一般にマニュアル（手引書）を用いた敬語使用が行われることが多い。このようなマニュアルに基づく接遇については評価が分かれる。すなわち、どのような相手にも同じ言葉遣いで接する公平感があり、相手を上位者として扱う言葉遣いによって、ぞんざいな物言いの与える不愉快さは生じさせないというプラス面がある一方、敬語過剰の嫌いがあること、マニュアルに依存するだけで話し手の心からの表現になりおおせないこと、画一的で相手や状況の微妙な違いに対応しきれないことなどのマイナス面もある。

　商業場面のコミュニケーションにおいても、基本的には相互の信頼関係が重要であることは言うまでもない。マニュアルを基にするにせよ、より柔軟で生き生きとした、適切な言葉遣いが行われることが望ましい。

(6) マスコミュニケーションと言葉遣い

テレビやラジオの娯楽番組や広告・宣伝、また、漫画やテレビゲーム等に現れる不適切な言葉遣いが幼児や青少年に与える影響が指摘されている。すなわち、品位に欠ける言葉や人を傷つける表現が子供たちの言葉遣いや人間関係に悪影響を及ぼす場合もあるということである。多くの人はマスコミの言葉遣いに対して、ある種

の規範性を求めていると思われる。したがって、放送や新聞等のマスコミ関係者や出版関係者は、その影響力の大きさを自覚し、言葉遣いについて更に慎重に配慮しつつ、国民の言葉に対する意識が高められるよう努めることが期待される。

(7) 外国人との意思疎通と言葉遣い

近年、日本に在住するために日本語の習得を必要とする外国人や、海外における日本語学習者が増加するなど、日本語が国際的な広がりを見せており、日本語は日本人だけのものとは言えなくなっている。一般の人々が外国人と日本語で意思を疎通する機会も日常的なものとなっている。

日本人の国語としての運用は、例えば婉曲な言い回しや、文末の判断部分を相手にゆだねてしまうなど、同じ文化に根ざした言語習慣を前提として、その文化を共有する相手と行われることがこれまで一般的であった。このような言語習慣もあるが、日本語に十分習熟していない外国人との意思疎通においては、分かりやすく誤解を与えない言葉遣いをする配慮が必要である。

II 敬意表現の在り方

1 敬意表現と敬語

「敬意表現」とは、既に述べたように、狭い意味の敬語を含む敬意にかかわる表現の総称である。我々は現実の言語生活における他者との言葉のやりとりに際し、相手や場面に応じた様々な配慮の下に自己表現として敬意表現を使っている。

世界の多くの言語にもそれぞれの文化に裏打ちされた敬意表現があり、敬意表現を適切に用いることはどのような社会においても必要なことである。

日本にはいわゆる目上を敬うばかりでなく、相手を思いやり、相手を立てて自らはへりくだる態度を一定の言語形式に乗せて表す慣習がある。その「一定の言語形式」が敬語であり、国語の体系の根幹にかかわる存在である。国語の歴史における敬語の推移は、上代の絶対敬語（特定の人物に対して使う敬語）及び尊敬語・謙譲語中心の時代から、中古の聞き手意識の出てくる時代を経て、現代の尊敬語・謙譲語・丁寧語中心の時代へという流れとしてとらえることができる。敬語はこのように長い歴史を持つ日本の文化であり、日本人の精神的な基盤にかかわるものと考えられる。そして、ある面では日本社会を支える求心力となってきたが、一方には立場の上下意識を強調し過ぎる面や、用法が煩雑で一般の人には習得困難な面もあった。

昭和 27 年の国語審議会建議「これからの敬語」は、従来の煩雑な敬語を廃し、民主主義社会にふさわしい平明・簡易な敬語を示した。これは当時の社会には画期的な提案であり、以来国語審議会が敬語について示した唯一の見解として人々のよりどころとされてきた。ここに示された内容のうち、相互尊敬を旨とすることや、過剰使用を避ける等のことは現代においても継承されてしかるべきであるが、一方には社会における敬語使用の実態に即していない面があることも否定できない。すなわちこの建議の掲げる敬語使用は画一的で、様々な人間関係や場面等の視点がないため、広い意味での敬意表現にかかわる配慮に触れていないという問題や、また、謙譲語及び「いらっしゃる」「伺う」等の敬語専用の形を取り上げていないという問題がある。

近年、尊敬語や謙譲語、とりわけ謙譲語衰退の傾向が指摘されているが、一方で丁寧語の使用は非常に普及し、話し言葉では「です・ます体」が一般的な文体として意識されていると言えよう（注1）。

　多くの人々はよい人間関係を求め、円滑なコミュニケーションを望んでいる。それを行うためには、相手や場面にふさわしい様々な配慮の表現が必要であると感じていると思われる。敬語についても、その必要性を認めている人は少なくない（注2）。丁寧語や敬語以外の敬意表現で配慮を表していこうという考え方もあろうが、尊敬語や謙譲語の適切な使用が日本の文化、国語の体系上重要であることは言うまでもない。

　国語審議会としては、敬意表現が個々人の自己表現として用いられ、コミュニケーションを円滑にするという認識の下に、謙譲語や敬語専用の形も含めた多様な敬語の使い方を敬意表現全体の中で論ずる必要があると考える。

　（注1）世論調査（平成9年1月　文化庁）では、「食べます」の「ます」を「敬語だと思わない」と答えた人が85.3％に上っている。このことから、尊敬語や謙譲語だけを敬語と思う傾向が強いということが言える。

　（注2）世論調査（平成9年1月　文化庁）では、目上の人に対して敬語を使うと答えた人の割合が86.0％に上り、年上の人、尊敬する人に対してもそれぞれ79.2％、69.7％の人が敬語を使うと答えている。どんなときも「敬語は使わない」と答えた人は、1.8％である。

(1) 敬意表現の概要

　例えば何かを借りたいという同じ内容を述べるにも、「拝借させていただけませんでしょうか」のような非常に敬意が高く改まった言い方から「貸してくださいませんか」「お借りしたいのですが」のような普通よく使われる敬意の軽い言い方、また「貸してくれよ」「貸してほしいんだけど」などのような打ち解けた言い方まで様々ある（付2[1]参照）。さらに、これらの言葉に、「申し訳ないけど」「ちょっと」などの前置きの言葉を添えたり、「忘れてきたので」「頼まれたものだから」などのように借りたい理由を説明したりすることもある。例えば、「貸してくれよ」や「ちょっと貸してほしいんだけど」は敬語を含まない言い方ではあるが、終助詞「よ」や「〜てくれる」という言い方を加えたり、「ちょっと」という言葉や「〜けど」のような言い差しの表現を用いたりしている点で、「貸せ」という命令だけの言い方とは明らかに異なっており、相手への配慮を示す表現となっている。話し手は、相手や話題の人との関係や場面などに配慮して、その時々にふさわしいものを選んで使っている。このような種々の表現が敬意表現である。

　敬意表現は必ずしも上位者への言葉遣いばかりではなく、仲間内以外の人に対して距離を置く言葉遣い、下位者への優しい配慮の表現、さらには、打ち解けた敬語抜きの言葉遣いなども含まれる。

　なお、敬意表現は言葉以外の種々の側面、すなわち服装、身振り、表情などにまで広げて考えることもできるが、ここでは言葉に関係するものに限って扱うこととする。

(2) 敬意表現における敬語

　敬語を取り囲む敬意表現が大切であるとはいえ、基本に敬語があることに変わりはない。その敬語について概要を述べておく。

敬語は、古くから「尊敬語」「謙譲語」「丁寧語」の三つに分類して考えることが一般化しているので、ここでもその名称を使用する（注1）。

　敬語には以下に掲げるような働きがある。これらは必ずしも単独に機能するのではなく、幾つかが相互に組み合わされることが多い。

① 相手や話題の人を高める

敬語は上司や先輩、年上の人、また、恩恵や負い目の関係における上位者や上位者の側の人を高める働きがある（注2）。高めたい人が主語であれば尊敬語を用い、話し手や話し手側が主語であれば謙譲語を用いるので、例えば「いらっしゃいますか」と言えばその主語は相手や相手側の人物であり、「参ります」と言えば自分や自分側を指すというように、それを使うことで、主語が示されるという機能もある。したがって、相手が待つかどうかを尋ねようとして、尊敬語のつもりで「お待ちしますか」（「お～する」は謙譲語の形）のように誤って謙譲語を使うと主語を取り違えられて正しい伝達ができないということになる。

② 親しくない人との距離をとる

敬語は初対面の人や、余り親しくない人、また、自分の属している職場や集団の外部の人との距離を隔て、相手に踏み込まない配慮を表す働きがある（注3）。逆に言えば、親しい人に対しては敬語を使うことが少ない。

③ 改まり意識を表す

敬語は改まった感じを表す働きがある。上位者や親しくない人に敬語を使うのは、改まり意識を表すことでなれなれしい感じを避けるためでもある。また、私的な場面では敬語を使わないで話す親しい友人や同僚であっても、会議等の比較的公的な場では敬語を用いることが多い（注4）。

④ 自己の品位を保つ

敬語は相手に対して自分の品位を保つ働きがある。例えば、年齢も社会的立場も上位である人が、若い人に「お水を一杯いただけないでしょうか」のように言ったり、母親が子供に「お掛けなさい」「召し上がれ」などと言ったりするのがこれに当たる。

　（注1）① 尊敬語は、話題になっている人（多くは相手や相手側の人）を高めて言うときに用いる言葉である。
　（例）「お父様もいらっしゃいますか」「山田様はお帰りになった」「お顔」「貴社」「お美しい」「御多忙」「ごゆっくり」
　② 謙譲語は、話題になっている人（多くは自分や自分の側の人）を低めて言うことによって、話題になっているもう一方の人（多くは相手や相手側の人）を高める言葉である。
　（例）「父が伺いたいと申しております」「私が先生に御届けする」「私ども」「粗品」
　③丁寧語は、自分のことか相手のことかなどにかかわらず、相手（聞き手）に対して物の言い方を丁寧にする言葉である。
　（例）「よい天気です」「電車が来ました」「結構でございます」

　（注2）世論調査（平成9年12月　文化庁）では、教師・クラブの先輩・年上の人（ともに立場、年齢の上位者）に対して、また、店の人・患者・もの

を頼む人はそれぞれ店の客・医師・ものを頼まれる立場の人（ともに恩恵・負い目の関係における上位者）に対して、「敬語を使って話すべき相手だと思う」と答えた人（教師 83.7%・クラブの先輩 60.4%・年上の人 68.5%・店の客 75.9%・医師 74.7%・ものを頼まれる立場の人 75.8%）の割合は「思わない」と答えた人に比べて圧倒的に高くなっている。

（注3）世論調査（平成9年1月 文化庁）では、「知らない人（たとえ同年輩でも）と話すとき」に敬語を使うと答えた人の割合は 57.7% であった。また別の調査（平成9年12月 文化庁）では、相手の性によって言葉遣いの丁寧さが変わると答えた人（34.6%）のうちの8割が「同性と話すときより異性と話すときの方が丁寧な言葉遣いになると思う」と答えている。

（注4）世論調査（平成9年12月 文化庁）でも、「敬語を使って話すべきだと思う」人の割合は、場面によって異なることが分かる。会社においても、上司に対して会社での仕事中に敬語を使って話すべきだと思う人は 85.9% であるが、その同じ上司と、仕事が終わって飲みに行った酒場で話すときも敬語を使うべきだと思う人は 36.2% であった。

(3) 様々な配慮と敬意表現

適切な敬意表現によって様々な配慮を表すことは日本の文化に根ざした慣用となっている。高めたい相手に対する場合や改まった場面ではこれらの敬意表現には敬語が使われる（例えば「お忙しいとは存じますが」など）。一方、敬語を使わないことで相手との距離が小さくなり、また打ち解けた雰囲気が醸されて親しみや仲間意識を生じ、人間関係が円滑になる場合もある。ただし、相手との関係や相手の気持ちのとらえ方を誤ると、親しみを込めたつもりが、なれなれしく不愉快だと受け取られることになる。

例えば、相手に話し掛けるときの礼儀に関するものとしては、自分の名前や所属を告げ、場合によっては相手を確認すること、また、相手が自分にかかわってくれることへの感謝及び相手に与える負担や迷惑の謝罪、話の切り出し方や前置き、相手と話をする理由や事情の説明などを表現するか省略するか、表現するとすればどのように言うかというようなことがある。

また、伝えたい事柄を「貸して」のように単純素朴な言い方でなく、疑問表現・否定表現・授受表現（注）等を援用することによって意味合いの微妙な差を表すことができる。用語の選択も敬意表現にかかわってくる。和語より漢語の方が、あるいは現代風の言葉より文語的な言葉の方が改まりの度合いが高いことや、専門用語使用の適否などについて配慮する必要があろう。文体的な統一も大切であるし、文末における終助詞の使い方も敬意表現と深い関係がある。また、文末の敬語を省略することによって表現をぼかし、堅苦しさを除いたり判断を相手にゆだねたりする配慮も表すことができる。

さらに、話題の主導権をだれに取らせるか、また、どのような話題を選ぶかということに関する礼儀もあるが、これは話し手の文化的背景によるところが大きい。相手にとって触れてほしくない事柄については何も言わないことが敬意の表現になることもある。場合によっては、差し出口をしない、婉曲な表現を用いる等の配慮もある。さらに、積極的に相手の言動や持ち物を褒めるなど、随時その場に応じた表現によって相手への理解や尊重を示す気配りもある。

話し言葉では以上のような配慮を音声で表現することになるが、声の調子、高低や音量、速さ等に関する配慮も大切である。その他言葉に伴う態度や行動も敬意表現を担う要素である。

　そのほか、書き言葉における敬意表現の問題がある。これは、直接的には手紙文が中心になろう。相手との関係やその手紙の性格に応じて、慣用的な形式にどの程度のっとるかを判断し、敬意表現を適切に用いて書くことになる。また、用紙、筆記具、文字（楷書か行書か、手書きかワープロか）なども敬意表現にかかわってくる。

　ここに述べた様々な配慮に関する具体的な表現の例は付2(2)に掲げた。

　（注）授受表現：「やる」「あげる」「くれる」「もらう」などの動詞を用いてなされる受給や受益にかかわる表現。これらの動詞を「〜てくれる」「〜てもらう」などのように、補助動詞として用いる表現も含む。

2　敬意表現の理念と標準の在り方

　現実に人々が使っている敬意表現は既に述べたとおり実に多様である。「I コミュニケーションと言葉遣い」で展望したように、現代社会が多様な側面を持ち、人間関係も多層的になっている以上、様々な敬意表現を時と場合によって使い分けなければならなくなるのは当然であろう。敬意表現の多様性は、国語の豊かさとして積極的に評価されるべきであろう（注）。

　多様な表現の中からいずれを適切なものとして選択するかは個々人の判断にゆだねられる。一人一人が主体的に自分で納得できる言い方を選び、自己表現としてそれを使うのである。そのためには、様々な表現の微妙な意味合いの差を吟味し、感じ取る言語感覚が求められよう。また、その時々における相手と自分との関係を的確に把握し、場面に配慮して適切な言い方を選択する能力も求められる。そのような言語感覚や選択能力は広く言語運用能力一般とかかわっており、その基礎は学齢期に培われるものと思われるが、加えて社会人としての常識や人間性という基盤も重要である。

　人間はそれぞれの立場や経験・年齢などに違いがあり、だれに対しても同じ言葉遣いで接するわけにはいかない。親しさの程度や仲間内か否かの別、また、場面や改まりの程度の違いもある。敬意表現はそれぞれに応じた礼儀や配慮を表すための言葉遣いである。元来心ある表現として使うべきであることは言うまでもないが、中には形式面だけにこだわったり、慇懃無礼に相手を疎外したり、傷つけたりするような使い方も見られる。より良い言語行動を志向して常に内省つつ敬意表現を使うということが使い手の人間形成と大きくかかわってくる。

　言葉は個々人のものであると同時に、社会全体のものでもある。一人一人が人格を形成し、より良い人間関係を築くためには、相手や場面にふさわしい言葉遣い、とりわけ敬意表現の選択能力や運用能力を身に付け、それを適切に用いていくことが大切である。

　国語審議会は次期の審議で具体的な敬意表現の標準を示すことに取り組むことが予定されているが、その場合も語形面での誤りを正すだけでなく、運用面の適切性についても扱っていくことが必要と思われる。すなわち、現実に行われている様々な敬意表現を整理して、平明な言い方を中心に複数の選択肢を掲げ、併

せて頻度の高い誤用例についてはそれが誤りとされる理由を説明しつつ、想定される場面に応じた運用の指針を掲げることになろう。

　　（注）世論調査　（平成9年12月　文化庁）によれば、「これからの敬語はどうあるべきだと思いますか」という問いに対して、「敬語は美しい日本語として豊かな表現が大切にされるべきだ」という考え方に近いと答えた人は46.9%であった。これは、言わば多様性容認に近いと言えよう。一方には「敬語は簡単で分かりやすいものであるべきだ」という考え方に近いと答えた人も41.4%あった。

付1　敬意表現の教育

(1) 学校等における敬意表現の教育

学校教育においては、敬意表現に関する教育について、国語科においてのみならず、学校生活全体を通して行われているところであり、今後もその指導を一層徹底していく必要がある。

　また、人間関係の希薄化が指摘される現在、人間関係を築き円滑に維持するためにも、言語運用能力を一層高めていくことが肝要である。

　とりわけ、敬意表現の教育も、敬語の知識だけでなく、その運用について、周辺の様々な表現とともに内省させつつ教育することが望ましい。児童生徒の日常生活において、尊敬語や謙譲語を使う場面が少なくなる傾向もあるので、相手を尊重し、人間関係を円滑にするための心遣いを、言葉でどう表現するかについては、適切に教えていく必要がある。児童生徒に対し、相手や場面にふさわしい敬意表現の選択能力・運用能力を触発・育成し敬意表現の教育を人格の形成や良い人間関係を築くための基礎と位置付けて、学校教育のみならず、家庭教育においても、日常的に行うことが大切である（注）。

　　（注）世論調査　（平成9年1月　文化庁）で敬語をどのような機会に身に付けてきたかを複数回答で聞いたところ、「学校の国語の授業」「家庭でのしつけ」「職場（アルバイト先を含む）の研修など」の三者が50%を超えた。

　　　また、同調査の別の問いでは、「学校で、敬語について十分指導することが大切だ」、「敬語は家庭でのしつけが大切だ」と思う人が、それぞれ77.2%、84.4%と高い割合になっている。

(2) 日本語教育における敬意表現の教育

敬意表現は円滑なコミュニケーションのためには不可欠な要素であり、日本語教育においても重要な課題である。敬語を含め、敬意表現の形式を学習することはそれほど難しい問題ではない。しかし、具体的な日本語の運用場面でこれらを適切に使う能力を身に付けるには、それらがどのように適用されるかを具体的に日本語使用の場面に接して学ぶ必要がある。したがって、学習環境が国内であるか国外であるかにより、学習の難易が大きく異なる。

　敬意表現の適切な使用の条件には、話し手と聞き手の上下、ウチ・ソト、親疎等の人間関係や使用場面の公私の別（改まりの程度）等を把握し判断する認知力が備わっている必要がある。したがって、学習者の年齢、母語、母文化の様相によって、心理言語学的、対照言語学的知識を基礎として教授に当たることが望ましい。

日本語学習の目的・学習時間によって、また、初級・中級・上級といった学習段階によっても敬意表現の扱い方が異なってくる。理解言語と表出言語を分けて扱う必要もある。したがって、日本語教育における敬意表現は、日本人の用いるものを対象とし、学習条件によって学習項目を選択して教材・教授法に一層の工夫を加えることが現実的であろう。

　敬意表現が適切に使えない場合は、文法等の誤りとは異なり、それが人間関係に亀裂を生じかねない結果にもなり得る。一般の外国語学習に際しては、学習者の未熟な表現には聞く側が理解の努力を払い、逆に、学習者に対しては分かりやすい表現を選択して話し掛けることが通例となっているが、敬意表現についてはそのような側面に配慮した対応が望まれる。

付2　多様な敬意表現の例

(1)　「貸してください」の様々な言い方

　一例として、主として話し言葉において、何かを借りるときに出現し得る多様な表現の形を、前置きなどを省略した形で、丁寧さや改まりの程度とともに掲げておく。

多様な表現	丁寧さの程度	改まりの程度
拝借させていただけません（でしょう）か	非常に丁寧	非常に改まっている
拝借させていただきたいんですけ（れ）ど		
拝借してよろしいでしょうか		
拝借させてください（ませんか）		
拝借したいんですけど		
お借りしてよろしい（いい）でしょうか		
お借りしたいのですが	かなり丁寧	かなり改まっている
貸していただけませんか (↗)		
貸していただきたいんですけど		
貸していただけますか (↗)		
貸してくださいませんか (↗)		
お借りできますか (↗)		
❖ 以上、謙譲語又は尊敬語＋丁寧語		
お貸しください	ていねい	改まっている
貸してください（ね）		
❖ 以上、尊敬語のみ		
貸してもらえますか (↗)		
貸してもらえませんか (↗)		
貸してくれますか (↗)		

貸してくれませんか (↗)

❖ 以上、丁寧語のみ

拝借していい (↗)	親しさ＋丁寧	打ち解けている
貸していただける (↗)		
貸していただけない (↗)		
貸してくださる (↗)		
貸してくださらない (↗)		
貸してちょうだい（ね、よ）(↗)		
お借りしてもよろしい (↗)		
お借りしていい (↗)		

❖ 以上、多くは親しい相手に使う言い方。
丁寧語なし

貸してほしいんだけど (↗)	親しさ＋	打ち解けてか
貸してもらえる (↗)	ややぞんざい	つ、ややくだけ
貸してもらえない (↗)		ている
貸してもいい (↗)		
貸してくれる (↗)		
貸してくれない (↗)		
貸して（よ、よね）(↗)		
借りるよ（ぜ）(↗)		
貸してくれ（よ、よね）(↗)	ぞんざい	くだけている

❖ 以上、敬語なし

(2) 様々な配慮と敬意表現の例

配慮等	例
1. 自己紹介、相手確認	「私は〇〇社の山田と申します。失礼ですが、川村様でいらっしゃいますか」「川村です。どうぞよろしく」
2. 天候、時刻や伝達方法への配慮	「お暑いところ、お集まりいただいて恐縮です」「夜分、突然のお電話で申し訳ございません」「直接お目に掛かってごあいさつ申し上げるべきところ書面で失礼いたします」
3. 感謝の表現	「わざわざおいでいただきありがとうございます」「お世話になっております」「こちらこそ」「この間はごちそうさまでした」

配慮等	例
4. 謝罪表現	「(お忙しいところ) 申し訳ございません」 「すみません (が)」「すまないねえ」 「お手間を取らせます」 「お役に立てなくて申し訳ない」
5. 話の切り出し方や前置き等	「ちょっと、よろしいでしょうか」 「お忙しいとは存じますが」 「厚かましゅうございますが」 「恐れ入ります (が)」
6. 事情説明	「あいにく先約がありまして (欠席いたします)」 「両親が上京してまいりますので (休暇を取りたいのですが)」
7. 断定・断言の主導権	断定・断言の主導権を相手に譲る (「そろそろ...」と相手に促し、相手が「行こうか」と決定するなど)
8. 話題の選択	避けられる話題 (日本で、親しくない大人に対して): 　年齢、既婚か未婚か、子供の有無、持ち物の値段、収入、身体的特徴相手にとって触れてほしくない事柄
9. 文末表現	終助詞の使い方 (「書いてくれない (↑)／書いてくれないかな」)
10. 相手を立てる	積極的に相手の言動や持ち物を褒める表現 「君のことはみんな褒めているよ」 「春らしいスカーフですね」 「テニスがお上手だそうで」
11. 敬語回避	文末の敬語を省略する (「お住いは... どちらでいらっしますか) 複数の相手への配慮 (「○○さんがお歌いになります／○○さんの歌をお聞きいただきます」→「次は○○さん、歌は××でございます」
12. 疑問表現・否定表現・授受表現等の援助	「貸してもらえますか」(授受表現、疑問表現の援用) 「貸してもらえませんか」(授受表現、否定表現、疑問表現の援用) 「拝借させていただけませんか」(使役表現、授受表現、可能表現、否定表現、疑問表現の援用

配慮等	例
13. 語種・文体の選択	和語／漢語（あした／明日）
	現代語／文語／（いつだったか／いつぞや）
	一般用語／専門用語（患者／クランケ）
	文体（敬体／常体／俗体）
	直截／婉曲（頑固だ／信念が固い）
14. 音声表現	声の調子、高低、音量、速度、抑揚はど
15. 書き言葉（主として 手紙文）	相手との関係やその手紙の性格に応じて、手紙文の慣用的な形式の採否を判断し、敬意表現を適切に用いて書く。
	用紙、筆記具、文字（楷書か行書か、手書きかワープロか）への配慮

Chapter 2. *Keigo* in *Kokugogaku*

1. The Japanese text reads:

   わが民族間に推譲の美風の行はるるによるもの（山田孝雄）

   思遣といふ国民性の発露であって実に尊いものである。（松下大三郎）

2. The Japanese text reads:

   ・他称敬語　他称敬語とは、己が対したる（二人称）人及己が談話の上に載すべき人（三人称）を、尊敬する時に、其の人、及其の人に附属せるもの、及其の人の動作存在等に、用うるものをいふ。例へば、「君」「御衣」「給ふ」「坐す」等の如し。

   ・自称敬語　自称敬語とは、己が対したる（二人称）人及己が談話の上に載すべき人（三人称）を、尊敬する時に、自己、及自己の動作存在等に、用うる者をいふ。例へば、「やつがれ」「奉る」「侍り」「候ふ」等の如し。

3. The Japanese text reads:

   ・素材敬語　表現素材に関する敬語。

   (1) 上位主体後　（＝敬称）。動作・状態の主体を高め、または敬う敬語。多く、話題の人物または（素材化された）表現受容者について用いられる。普通、尊敬語といわれるもの。

   (2) 下位主体語　（＝謙称）。動作・状態の主体を低め、またはへりくだる言い方。多く（素材化された）表現主体または表現主体に関係あるとされる話題の人物について用いられる。普通、謙譲語といわれるもの。

   (3) 美化語　（＝美称）。表現素材を美化する言い方。普通、丁寧語といわれるもの。対者を意識して用いられることが多いが、必ずしもそうでない場合もある。

・対者敬語　（謙称）表現受容者（対者）に対する表現主体の慎しみの気持を直接に表わす。必ず対者を予測する点が素材敬語と異なる。

4. The Japanese text reads:

   1. 尊他敬語

     他を敬う尊他敬語は、他の主体、所有、動作、状態を尊敬するもの

   2. 自卑敬語

     自卑敬語は自己の主体、所有、動作を卑下するもの

   3. 関係敬語

     関係敬語は、自己の動作の他に関係するを尊び、自己を卑しむもの

   4. 対話敬語

     対話敬語は、聴者を尊敬する為に、語を丁寧にするもの

5. *"Zokugo"* in contemporary Japanese is used to refer to slang, but in Matsushita meant the spoken, colloquial language.

6. The Japanese text reads:

・敬語法

目上の人と対話するときに、その目上の人に属する凡ての事物に就いて、此方が尊敬の意を表はす語法

例　御名前　　御両親様

・謙語法

目上の人と対話するときに、此方に属する凡ての事物に就いて謙遜の意を表はして、そして先方を尊敬する意を示すもの

例　不肖　　　荊妻　　　　茅屋

・傲語法

目下の者と対話するときに、此方に属する凡ての事物に就いて、此方の傲慢な意を表はして、そして、彼方を軽蔑する意を表はすもの

例　此方（自分）

・卑語法

目下の者と対話するときに、彼方に属する凡ての事物に就いて、此方が彼方を軽蔑する意を表はすもの

例　その方（彼方）　　彼奴（他人）

・平語法

此方と同等のものと対話するときに彼又我に属する凡ての事物に就いて尊敬の意も謙遜の意も傲慢の意も、軽蔑の意も全く表はすことなく、只平等の者に対する語遣をすること

例　我（自分）　　　　父母（人の父母）

7. The Japanese text reads:

そういう意味では敬卑等すべてを含むものとしては「待遇表現」という名称が適当と思われる。「敬語」ということばは、やはり表現主体が上位者と見なす人に用いられるところのことばに限定したいのである。しかし、そうは言っても、実は敬語の範囲を限定することはそう容易ではない。「いらっしゃる」「申し上げる」「です」「ます」「お顔」といったたぐいのことばを敬語と見な

すことには殆どの人に異論はないと思うが、「あなたさま」「あなた」「あん
た」「お宅」「君」「おまえ」「貴様」などといった人称代名詞のたぐいでは、
どれが敬語でどれが非敬語かは必ずしもはっきりしない。「あなたさま」が敬
語であり、「貴様」が軽卑語であることは少なくとも共通語の中で考える限り
言えることであろうが、それなら、ニュートラルな対称はどれかといわれて
もはっきり答えることは困難であろう。

8. The Japanese text reads:

尊敬語

いずれも、話題の人（ある人について言っている、その人）を高く待遇し、
これに敬意を表すことばである。下の図のような関係のものである。

話題の人自身、その人の所有・所属のもの、また、その人の行為や性質・状
態を言うのに使われる。

9. The Japanese text reads:

謙譲語

謙譲語はおもに自分や自分側のことをへりくだっていい、それによって相手
方の人または聞手に敬意を表する敬語である。

10. The Japanese text reads:

丁重語

いずれも、もっぱら聞手に敬意を表することばである。

11. The Japanese text reads:

美化語

いずれも、もの言いを上品、きれいにすることばである。聞手に対する意識
のもとに使われることもあるが、要するに、自分のことばの品位のために使
われるものである。

12. The Japanese text reads:

・地位・能力などをあがめる
高い社会的地位にある人、すぐれた能力や教養をそなえている人などをあ
がめて、それらの人と話すとき、また、それらの人について話すとき、敬
語を使う。

・優位者をあがめる
自分より優位にある人をあがめ、その人と話すとき、その人について話す
とき、敬語を使う。

・恩恵を与える者をあがめる
自分に恩恵を与える人をあがめ、その人と話すとき、その人について話す
とき、敬語を使う。

・人間の尊重
人間を尊重する気持で、相手をあがめ、敬語を使って言う。

13. The Japanese text reads:

2. へだての表現
・無作法か親しみか
・媒酌人あいさつの失敗

3. あらたまりの表現
   - おおやけの場のことば
   - あがめのためのへだて・あらたまり

4. 威厳・品位・軽蔑・皮肉の表現
   - 優越感で使う敬語
   - 女性は敬語を好む

5. 親愛の表現
   - 尊敬よりも親愛
   - もう一つ別のもの

   いまどき一般の家族では、母親が自分のことを「なさって...」などと言うところは、少ないだろう ... それは家庭における親の位置を絶対とし、それに対する尊敬（あがめ）の表現を、親みずから取って見せるということである。

14. The Japanese text reads:

	表現形式			内容		
	専用言語要素	一般言語表現	非言語表現	尊敬・謙譲・	ていねいなど	敬卑・尊大な ど
A	+	−	−	+		−
B	+	−	−	+		+
C	+	+	−	+		−
D	+	+	−	+		+
E	+	+	+	+		−
F	+	+	+	+		+

15. The Japanese text reads:

1. 尊敬語
2. 謙譲語
3. ていねい語
4. 美化語
5. 卑罵語とか軽卑語
6. 尊大表現
7. 今までにあげたもの以外の、各種の人の呼び方
8. 間投詞・応答詞の類
9. 終助詞・間投助詞の類
10. 一般的な語彙の選択
11. 文の構造について、話しことば的な型を使うか、書きことば的な型を使うか、ということも問題となる
12. 命令・要求・依頼・禁止・勧誘などの表現のいろいろな形の使い分け

13. 文の長さ

14. 成分を省略した文を使うか、成分を省略しない、ととのった形の文を使うか

15. 間接的な、婉曲な言い方をするか、直接的な言い方をするか

16. へりくだった表現をするかどうか

17. 前のものと似ているもので、送り手が発する言語表現、あるいは送り手の行う言語行動についての前おき、ことわり、注釈といったことばを述べるかどうか

18. 単語や文といったことばの単位のほかに、文よりも大きい単位（いくつかの文の集まり）がある

19. 目を転じると、ことばの形の要素、つまり、音の要素または表記上の要素の問題もある

20. 話しことばにするか、書きことばにするか

21. 選択の対象が言語（方言）の体系全体である場合もあり、その一部（たとえば発音のみ...）である場合もあって、その間にいろいろ程度の違いがあると思われる

22. 最も一般的な問題として、ある相手に対して話すか話さないか（書くか書かないか）、つまり言語的コミュニケーションを行うかどうかがある

16. The Japanese text reads:

23. 話の中で用いられる間投音

24. あらたまった、かたい調子、くだけた調子、強い語気の怒った調子などのことばの調子

25. 話に伴う笑い

26. 顔の表情で話に伴うもの

27. 目の動き

28. 腕、手、頭その他体の部分を使う動作で、話に伴うもの

29. 話をしている者どうしの間の物理的な距離のとり方

30. 話の中の時間的な間のおき方

31. 媒体になにを使うか

32. 字体、書体、文字の大きさなど

33. 書写の形式など

34. 書写の手段

35. 書写の材料

17. The Japanese text reads:

36. 服装

37. 身につけるものの着脱

38. 服装以外の身だしなみの類

39. 顔の表情で言語表現に伴わないもの

40. 笑いで言語表現に伴わずに現われるもの

41. 態度・ものごし・動作

42. 部屋の出入り、乗物の乗り降りなどの場合に見られる、相手を優先させる動作

43. 食事のときの作法

44. 客に対するもてなしのしかた

45. その他、交際一般についてのさまざまな行動の型

18. The Japanese text reads:

　　1. 送り手の、なんらかの対象についての一種の顧慮があること。

　　2. そうした顧慮は、つねに送り手のなんらかの評価的態度を伴っていること。

　　3. そうした顧慮、評価的態度に基づく、なんらかの対象についての扱い方の違いがあり、その扱い方の違いを反映した表現の使い分けがあること。

19. The Japanese text reads:

　　参加者

　　　　送り手

　　　　受け手

　　　　　　マトモの受け手

　　　　　　ワキの受け手

　　関係者

　　　　動作主

　　　　被動作主

　　コミュニケーションの内容

　　状況

20. The Japanese text reads:

　　1. 社会的関係の開始・打ち切りに関するもの

　　2. 社会的関係の維持に関するもの

　　3. 社会的位置の保持に関するもの

　　4. 実質的情報の受け渡し

　　5. 相手に対する強制、訴えなど

　　6. 美的価値の表現

21. The Japanese text reads:

よく、敬語は＜敬意＞あるいは＜丁寧さ＞の表現だといわれるが、その敬意とは必ずしも＜心からの敬意／尊敬の念＞だとは限らない。たとえば社員が社長のことを話題にする場合、社内では周囲を意識して敬語を使うが、ひとたび社外へ出て社長の噂をするときにはおよそ敬語など使わない、といった例はざらにあるだろう。このような社員が社長に対して＜心からの敬意＞を

もっているとは考えにくい。敬語が敬意の表現だというのはあたらない、という考え方も起こるところである。

　しかし、今のような場合でも、ともかく社内では敬語を使うということは、少なくともその場では社長に対して一種の＜敬意＞をあらわしていることだ、といってよかろう。先程見たように、話手はただ社会的な上下の関係などの把握に基づいてというだけではなく、実は、究極的には自分の意図によって敬語を使うのである。社長に話す場合でも、もしどうしても敬語を使いたくなければ、使わないという選択も―もちろんそれは何らかの"社会的制裁"を伴うかもしれないにせよ―、ありうるわけである。そちらの選択をとらずに、敬語を使うほうの選択を自分の意図で行うということは、やはり、一種の敬意の表現だといってよい。もう少し理屈っぽく述べると、敬語を使うことで、敬意を示す意図があることを表現している―少なくともその意味で、一種の敬意の表現として機能するといえるだろう。あくまでもその時・その場における＜敬意＞ではあるが。先の≪待遇的意味≫という点からは、最も狭くとった場合の敬語とは、待遇表現のうち、

　（一）≪上≫（話題の人物を≪上位者として高める≫）、

　（二）≪下≫（自分側を≪下位者として低める≫。これはまた
　　　　　≪丁重≫＝≪丁寧≫＋≪改まり≫に通じる）、

　（三）≪丁寧≫（聞手に対して≪丁寧≫に述べる）、

のいずれかの≪待遇的意味≫をもつものということになるだろう。

22. The Japanese text reads:

この待遇という語は、「あの会社は待遇がいい」とか、会社の地位で「役員待遇」などというときの「待遇」と基本的には同じで、"扱い"という意味である ... 基本的には同じ意味のことを述べるのに、話題の人物／聞手／場面などを顧慮し、それに応じて複数の表現を使い分けるとき、それらの表現を待遇表現という。

23. The Japanese text reads:

　1. 上下

　2. 丁寧 ↔ ぞんざい・乱暴

　3. 改まり ↔ くだけ／粗野／尊大

　4. 上品 ↔ 卑俗

　5. 好悪

　6. 恩恵の授受

24. The Japanese text reads:

　1. 社会的ファクター

　A. 場および話題

　① その場の構成者

　... 話手、聞手（話の相手）およびその場にいる第三者（話の直接の相手ではないが、その話の聞こえるところにいる人）のことである。

　② 場面の性質など

　... 聞き言葉か話し言葉かで言葉づかいはだいぶ違ってくる。話す場合は敬

語を使わない間柄でも、書き言葉だと使うということは間々ある...その場の構成者は同じでも、言葉づかいは変わることが少なくない。

③ 話題

その場の構成者(およびその家族など)のことか、それとも、その場にいない第三者のことか。

B. 人間関係

A のうち<その場の構成者>や<話題の人物>の間の人間関係が、言葉づかいにかかわるきわめて重要なファクターとなる。

① 上下の関係

人間関係の中でも、やはり上下関係が、言葉づかいにかかわる最も基本的なファクターだろう。

② 立場の関係

...恩恵を与える立場/受ける立場(恩恵授受関係)...権限を持つ立場/相手の権限に委ねなければならない立場(権限/従属関係)...強い(優位にある)立場/弱い(劣位にある)立場(強弱関係)...社会/心理的に、強い立場/弱い立場(社会/心理的優劣関係)...恩恵を与える立場/受ける立場と見立てる場合(擬似恩恵授受関係)...立てられるべき立場/立てるべき立場(擬似優劣関係)....

③ 親疎の関係

...親しい間柄と、そうではない間柄(知り合いではあるが親しくない場合や、初対面などでよく知らない場合)とでは当然、言葉づかいが違ってくる。

④ 内/外の関係

2. 心理的ファクター

A. 待遇意図

相手は (1) の社会的諸ファクターを把握・計算し、それにそのまま対応した待遇表現を使う。

① ごく一般的な待遇意図

最も一般的な意味での待遇意図というのは、要するに、<その人を立てた表現/普通の表現/その人を軽く見た表現をしよう>という意図、あるいは、<よい(丁寧な、品格を保った)表現/普通の表現/悪い表現をしよう>というような意図、などのことである...<社会的な「上下」などの実状に応じた言葉づかいをしよう>という意図が働くことが多かろうが...<「上下」に関して、あえて社会的な実状の通りにではなく待遇する>という話手の意図が加わる場合も、少なくない。

② 「恩恵」の捉え方

...「上下」だけでなく、<「恩恵」や「権限」に関して、社会的な実状の通りにではなく捉える>という話手の意図が加わる場合がある。

③ 「親疎」の距離のとり方

...<どの程度の距離をとるか>についての話手の意図次第なのである。

④ 「内と外」の捉え方

⑤ その他、特殊な待遇意図

…＜皮肉な表現／意地悪な表現／ふざけた表現 … など、何らかの感情・色彩をこめた表現をしよう＞という意図が働いて待遇表現が選択される場合もある。

⑥ 待遇意図が働く以前の心理状態で述べる場合

B. さらに背景的なファクター

C. 表現技術・伝達効果の観点からの考慮

25. Even in the more traditional elements the fit between Western grammar(s) and Japanese is highly suspect. The gap between traditional *kokugo* grammar (based on nineteenth-century Western grammars translated into Japanese) and later structuralist accounts (Bloch 1946, Jorden 1963, Martin 1964, 1975, Miller 1967), as well as between *kokugo* grammar and transformational-generative accounts, is a matter that generates no small amount of controversy.

Chapter 3. Inventing *Keigo*

1. Suzuki Takao is the author of the books *Tozasareta gengo: Nihongo no sekai* (Closed language: The world of Japanese [1975]), *Buki to shite no kotoba* (Language as weapon [1985]), and *Nihonjin wa naze eigo ga dekinai ka* (Why can't Japanese speak English? [1999]), among others.

2. More in-depth accounts of Japan's modernization from perspectives other than language standardization are to be found in Gluck 1985, Ishida and Krauss 1989, Miyoshi and Harootunian 1989, Robertson 1991, and Suzuki Tomi 1996.

3. Gottlieb's 1995 book, *Kanji Politics,* provides an outstanding account of the history of Japan's script reform, including the concomitant ideological issues.

4. The population was not homogeneous in any sense. Dialects *(hōgen)* were independent enough that the educational system faced a monumental task in instructing teachers and creating *kokugo* materials. Moreover, Japanese was taught as a native language *(kokugo),* not as a second language *(nihongo),* in Taiwan from 1895, in Korea and Okinawa from 1914, and in Manchuria from 1932. The indigenous Ainu language was not even considered in the standardization movement. The political underpinnings of the *kokugo/nihongo* distinction are the subject of Tani (2000), a distinction that, along with *hōgen,* is fraught with meaning even today.

5. The Iinkai apparently interpreted its charge from the government rather liberally, according to Yasuda (1999:105). Ueda had been schooled in Western thinking and took the word *"hyōjungo"* to mean the same thing as the German *"Gemeinsprach"* or the French *"langue commune"*—that is to say, as *kyōtsūgo* 'common language'. Yet the term that the Iinkai continued to use was *hyōjungo.* There is an interesting play even today between these two words. Most policy representatives are inclined to use *"kyōtsūgo"* out of sensitivity to the normative connotation of

"hyōjungo." In my experience, however, people who are unschooled in the fine points of such negative overtones are more likely to use the term *"hyōjungo."*

6. The Japanese text reads:

第二十条

「御覧なさる」、「御聞きくださる」ナドノ「なさる」「くださる」ハ、下の如く、四段ニ活用シテ、連用ニ、下二段活用ヲ混用シテアリ、ソノ如く用キテアリヤ。

将然	連用	終止	連体	已然	命令	未来
なさり（ませ）			なされ			
なさら（ぬ）			なさる	なされ（ば）	なさらう	
なされ（て）（た）（たい、たく）			なさい			
くださり（ませ）			くだされ			
くださら（ぬ）			くださる	くだされ（ば）	くださらう	
くだされ（て）（た）（たい）、たく）	くださ

い | | | | | |

7. The Japanese text reads:

口語法調査報告書以下 and 口語法分布配図 （明治 39 年 12 月）。

8. The Japanese text reads:

敬譲の助動詞わ、動作を敬って言い、又わ、丁寧にいう時に用いるものである。

先生のいわれる通り

もう来られる頃だ。

かなり高く飛びます。

また次のように、敬譲の動詞が敬譲の助動詞に用いられることがある。

お伺いもうします。

お招きいたしました。

おやすみあそばすように、

朝早くお起きなさらなら、

よく御尋ねくださる御方

御請けつかまつります。

9. The Japanese text reads:

本表は東京語の内の敬語に關するものにつきて調整したるものなり。

本表、題して特に略表といふ、是は諸種の場合に諸種の階級の者の利用する言葉づかひを悉皆網羅したるものにあらで、ただある場合々々に於て中の者が自己と同等なる者に對していふ言葉づかひ、自己よりも目上なる人に對していふ言葉づかひ、の内より最も普通なるものを適宜採録したるにとどまればなり。されば、本表中流に掲載せるものを似って直ちに東京流のいひかたを盡したるものと思ふへからず、なほ此の他に諸種のいひかた數多ありと知るべし。

10. The Japanese text reads:

常語の行には、相手が自己と同等なる場合に自己の動作又はその他をあらはす為に自己の用ゐる言葉を列記し、譲語の行には、相手が自己よりも目上な

る場合に相手に對して自己を卑下して自己の動作又はその他をあらはす為に自己の用ゐる言葉を列記し、敬語の行には、相手が自己よりも目上なる場合に相手を尊敬して相手の動作又はその他をいひあらはす為に自己の用ゐる言葉を列記したり。

本表に於ては、所謂自己は自己一人又は自己の身に密接なる関係を有する事物に限ることとし、所謂相手は一人又は相手に密接なる関係を有する事物に限ることとせり。

11. The Japanese text reads:

云う					爲る		
敬語	敬語	敬語	謙語	常語	敬語	謙語	常語
オイイニナル	オイイナサル	オッシャル	モース	イウ	ナサル	イタス	
オイイニナリマス	オイイナサイマス	オッシャイマス	モーシマス	イイマス	ナサイマス	イタシマス	

The conjugation *o-ii nasaru* has disappeared except for a reflex in the imperative *ii-nasai*. The form *o-ii ni naru* has disappeared for this particular verb, leaving only the suppletive form *mōsu* ("regular" verbs still conjugate this way).

12. Dialects *(hōgen)* hold an abiding place in the Japanese sense of itself as a state and a culture. Language has always figured prominently in Japan's self-definition (see Miller 1967, Dale 1986), perhaps most prominently in the 1930s and 1940s, when *kokka* 'national polity' rose to mythic standing in the Japanese psyche. *Kokugo* and *hōgen* were at the center of this discussion, and even today these topics help fuel Japan's internal argumentation over its history, education, and cultural studies *(bunka-gaku)*. (See Befu and Manabe 1990, Tani 2000, Yanagita 1938.)

13. The Japanese text reads:

一、長上に対しては相当の敬語を用いる。

二、自称は、普通「私」を用いる。長上に対して氏又は名を用いることがある。男子は同輩に対しては「僕」を用いてもよいが、長上に対しては用いてはならない。

三、対称は長上に対しては、身分に応じて相当の敬称を用いる。同輩に対しては、通常「あなた」を用い、男子は「君」を用いてもよい。

四、対話者以外の人に就いて語る場合、長上は勿論、その他の者にも、相当の敬称・敬語を用いる。長上に対して、その人より地位の低い者に就いて語る場合には、たとい自分より上位の者であっても、普通には敬称・敬語は用しないか、または簡略にする。

五、自分の近親に就いて他人に語る場合には、敬称・敬語を用いない。一般に当方の事に就いては敬称・敬語を用いないのを例とする。

六、受容には、必ず「はい」と言う。特に長上に対して「ええ」と言うのはよくない。

七、長上に対しては、なるべく「ございます」「あります」「参ります」「致します」「存じます」「遊ばす」「申します」「いただきます」等、時に応じて用いる。長上には「です」「もらう」「くれる」等は用しない。

八、他人の物事には「お」「御」を附け、自分及び当方の物事には用いないのを通例とする。一般的の物事にも用いないのを通例とするが、口調や慣習で用いる場合もある。

九、言語は出来るだけ標準語を用する。

14. The Japanese text reads:

日本語には敬語が多い。いや、少し多すぎるやうである。そのために、日本人でも敬語のつかひ方を知らないものや誤るものが少なくない。まして、日本人と母語を湖と異にする他方の人々、例へば大陸の人々などにとっては、日本語の敬語は、かなりむづかしくも感じられ、また、うるさくも感じられるであらう。併し、敬語の多いといふことは、一面に於いては、日本民族の特質から来たものであり、従って日本語にとってはかなり重大な特徴であるともいへる。(Translation Miller's)

15. The Japanese text reads:

大東亜の建設といふことが、現實の課題として、我々に追って 來るやうになってから、日本語がやかましい論議の對象となって浮かび上がったのは、當然のこととはいひ乍ら、慶ばしい事と云はねばならない . . . 共栄圏への日本語普及には、異常な努力と忍耐とが必要であるが、敬語法について見ても、燈鉄した知識と確乎たる政策とを似てせねばならぬこと勿論である。しかも、敬語法の現状に關しては、或人はその貧困を嘆じ、他の人はその過剰を憂へるのであるが、現在の敬語法が混乱してゐるといふ點では、いづれの見解にも一致が見出せるといふ、感心に耐へない有様である。敬語法の醇化を圖り、言靈のさくはふ大和言葉の正しい姿を得させるには、どうすればよいかといふ問題を解決するのには、敬語法のあるべき姿とは何であるかを科學的に認識するのが根本であり、此の知識に基いて現状を的確に把握し批判することがなされねばならない。(Ekoyama 1943:1–2; translation Miller's)

16. The Japanese text reads:

六　動作のことば

動作の敬語法には、およそ三つの型がある。すなわち、

語例	書く	受ける
型		
I	書かれる	受けられる

II　　　お書きになる　　　お受けになる

III　　　（お書きあそばす）（お受けあそばす）

第一の「れる」「られる」の型は、受け身の言い方とまぎらわしい欠点はある
が、すべての動作に規則的につき、かつ簡単でもあるので、むしろ将来性が
あると認められる。

第二の「おーになる」の型を「おーになられる」という必要はない。

第三の型は、いわゆるあそばせことばであって、これからの平明・簡素な敬
語としては、おいおいにすたれる形であろう。

17. According to Brown and Gilman (1960), the T/V distinction can be stated in terms of two opposing features: power and solidarity. The power semantic is nonreciprocal: the superior says T and receives V. They observe that this usage holds within a social structure in which there are unique power ranks for almost every individual, such as medieval Europe. In the case of individuals of roughly equivalent status, norms of address dictate that equals of upper classes exchange V, while equals of lower status exchange T (255–256). The solidarity semantic, in contrast, represents a state of affairs in which T is used to indicate intimacy, while V is used to indicate formality. ("The European development of two singular pronouns of address begins with the Latin *tu* and *vos*. In Italian they become *tu* and *voi*…; in French *tu* and *vous;* in Spanish *tu* and *vos* [later *usted*]. In German the distinction began with *du* and *Ihr* but *Ihr* gave way to *er* and later *Sie*. English speakers first used 'thou' and 'ye' and later replaced 'ye' with 'you'" [254]). As a matter of convenience, Brown and Gilman use "T" and "V" as generic designators for the familiar and polite pronouns in any language.

18. A more recent controversy in the Kokugo Shingikai concerned the relationship between *keigo* convention and gender (April 17, 1998, meeting: http://www.mext.go.jp/b_menu/shingi/12/kokugo/gijiroku/005/980401.htm).

19. I surveyed a wide assortment of pre- and postwar textbooks at the Kokuritsu Kokugo Kenkyūjo and found that it was around 1956 that the *sonkeigo-kenjōgo-teineigo* analysis finally gained ascendancy and was consistently included. The following are some of the textbooks that I examined (all are from series): *Koku bumpō* (National grammar [Saeki 1953]), *Kammei bungo bumpō* (Concise written language grammar [Nichieisha 1954]), *Shimben bungo bumpō* (Written language grammar: New edition [Kamei 1956]), *Kōtō-gakushū bumpō* (High school grammar [Iwai 1955]), *Nihon bumpō* (Japan grammar [*sic;* Kumazawa 1956]), *Shinkoku bumpō* (New nation[al] grammar [Miki 1956]), *Bungo no bumpō* (Grammar of written language [Hashizume 1959]). Examples of textbooks that present alternative analyses do exist; one is Iwai 1955.

20. The Japanese text reads:

口語の敬語

わたしたちが、話をしたり、文章を書いたりする場合に、相手あるいは第三
者に対して、尊敬・謙譲・丁寧の気持の含まれた表現をすることがある。こ
れを「敬語」という。たとえば、「行く」ということをあらわす場合でも、

尊敬　　①先生がそちらに行かれる。

②先生がそちらにおいでになる。

③先生がそちらにいらっしゃる。

謙譲　④あす先生の所にうかがうことにした。

⑤父も先生の所にまいるそうです。

のような表現ができる...

次に、

丁寧　⑥先生があちらにいらっしゃいます。

⑦きょうはとても寒いですね。

⑧きょうはとても寒うございますね。

⑨風が静かです。

⑩風が静かでございます。

21. Responsibility for language policy is distributed among three entities: the Kokugo Shingikai, the Kokuritsu Kokugo Kenkyūjo (National Language Research Institute), and the Kokugo-ka (National Language Section) of the Ministry of Education and Science (formerly the Ministry of Education). All of these are overseen by the Bunka-chō. The Kokugo Shingikai comprises a rotating panel of no more than fifty experts who have three-year appointments. The duty of the Shingikai is to formulate and articulate policy. The Kokuritsu Kokugo Kenkyūjo is a government-sponsored unit that carries out research in support of language policy and planning, especially as requested by the Kokugo Shingikai and/or Kokugo-ka. The Kokugo-ka is responsible for disseminating information and materials regarding the "national language," so its role in language education in Japan is central.

22. For this chronology, I relied on Asamatsu 2001b.

23. The other issues were the "information age" *(jōhōka e no tai-ō ni kansuru koto)* and "internationalization" *(kokusai-shakai e no tai-ō ni kansuru koto)* (Kokugo Shingikai 1995).

24. The Japanese text reads:

「これからの敬語では」、「基本の方針」として、「行きすぎをいましめ、誤用を正し、できるだけ平明・簡素にありたいものである。」としているが、この考え方は、現実に要請されることでもあり、豊かな言葉遣いのためにもあながち否定できない。

25. The Japanese text reads:

「コミュニケーションを円滑にするという観点、場面による適否という観点」や「単語の問題としてだけでなく、表現全体としての適切さを重視する観点」などが必要であろうとしている。

26. The Japanese text reads:

一つは、敬意表現の多様性についての配慮である。

現実に人々が使っている敬意表現は既に述べたとおり実に多様である。「Ⅰ コミューニケーションと言葉遣い」で展望したように、現代社会が多様な側面を持ち、人間関係も多層的になっている以上、様々な敬意表現を時と場合に

よって使い分けなければならなくなるのは当然である。敬意表現の多様性は、国語の豊かさとして積極的に評価されるべきである。

いま一つは、運用面の適切性について扱っていくときの配慮である。

国語審議会では次期の審議で具体的な敬意表現の標準を示すことに取り込むことが予定されているが、その場合も語形面での誤りを正すだけでなく、運用面の適切性についても扱っていくことが必要と思われる。すなわち、現実に行われている様々な敬意表現を整理して、平明な言い方を中心に複数の選択肢を掲げ、併せて頻度の高い誤用例についてはそれが誤りとされる理由を説明しつつ、想定される場面に応じた運用の指針を掲げることになろう。

27. The Japanese text reads:

私見を述べれば、語形と運用とは陳腐な比喩ながら、車の両輪であり、どちらも大切なはずである。しかも、日本語の敬語表現であるならば、やはり核となる敬語形式について（特に、今ゆれている言い方などについて）より具体的に論ずることが求められていたにもかかわらず、それが果たされなかったことは、遺憾と言わざるを得ない。

Chapter 4. The Modernization of *Keigo*

1. This is not to suggest that there was no concern for language or for *keigo* in pre-war or even pre-Meiji Japan. The how-to genre has its roots in the Confucian tradition of prescribed behavior for all stations of human existence. But before the 1950s, one rarely sees references to *"keigo"* either in educational materials for the public or in the popular press. Certainly the word existed, but it lacked depth or definition, and it was assuredly not the preferred term for looking at conventional language behavior. Much more common in the popular press were references to and guidance in *kotoba-zukai* 'language use' and *aisatsu* 'greetings, set phrases'. The word *"keigo"* might appear as one category among many, but it was left unanalyzed and referred to the repertoire of polite language and actions. Like *keirei* 'salutations' and *keishō* 'titles', *keigo* was something that Japanese people knew to be part and parcel of *sahō* 'etiquette'.

2. The topic of *keigo* and its use has, of course, made it to the World Wide Web. Some of the more interesting websites (as of August 2002) include:

   http://www.womanstaff.co.jp/bizi/bizitop.html
   http://www.jinzainews.co.jp/junction/syakai1.html
   http://kirei.net/kirei/beauty/mana501.html

3. How-to books are not unique to Japan. In fact, concern about social convention appears to be universal. One immediately calls to mind the burst of "for Dummies" and "Complete Idiot's Guide to" titles that have taken the United States by storm (McCord 1996, Theisman 1997, Tyson 1998). If Cameron is correct, "advice literature" (also known as "personal growth" and "inspirational") in Britain and America is also well represented by the "self-help" genre. On questions of language, the English-speaking public appears to be most interested these days in questions of the interrelationships between gender and language,

and to a lesser extent the language(s) and communication practices of groups like African-Americans. (In 1996 a controversy raged over the recognition of "Ebonics" by the Oakland, California, educational system, with the requisite surfeit of opinions pro and con from the media and political pundits.) Women, Cameron says, constitute an especially important market for language self-help, and it is on women's consumption that she focuses.

Furthermore, it is of more than passing interest that, in Japan as well as in the United States and Britain, the advice literature genre is paralleled by self-improvement activities—seminars, classes, and workshops—that include extensive sections on language training. American readers who work in an office setting will be familiar with the flyers that come through the mail, especially for women, that promise to instill empowering verbal communication skills. Cameron spotlights assertiveness training (AT), which has come to be known for embodying feminist principles. Yet, as Cameron notes, AT did not itself begin as a feminist practice but as a behavior modification technique for changing maladaptive behaviors. AT has now evolved into workplace communication training. The difference, Cameron observes, is that the new practice is provided by "expert" paid professionals and is concerned less with collective empowerment than with career enhancement (182).

4. The Japanese text reads:

あがり・緊張・赤顔・ふるえ・吃音
撥音・視線・会話・挨拶・会議・司会
面接・説得・冠婚葬祭・PTA

5. The Japanese text reads:

敬語は本来簡単なものだ

... しかし敬語は、言葉の約束がキチンと決まっている。ちゃんと法則とかセオリーがあるのだ。こういうものは学習して身につけてしまえば、「うまく話せない」「苦手だ」などと心配することは、まったくなくなる。

言葉は時代の流れとともに変化していく。ただ、言葉はコミュニケーションの道具だから、古いしきたりや人間関係抜きでは語れない部分がある。実はこの厄介な部分を一手に引き受けているのが敬語なのだ。

だから人々から敬遠される。

しかし、いちいち覚えるのは面倒だから逃げちゃおう－というのでは、本来やさしいはずである敬語をわざとむずかしく遠ざけてしているようなものではないだろうか。

6. The Japanese text reads:

古代には厳然とした身分の序列があった

... 身分の高い人に向かって何か言うときには、相手の動作について尊敬語を、自分の動作については謙譲語を使いました。物の状態などについては丁寧語を使いました。身分の高い人が召使などに何か言うときには、逆に敬語は何もつけませんでした。あとで説明しますが、この点は現代の敬語と大いに異なる点です...

7. Of course, the postmodernist might contend just the opposite: *keigo*'s modern role is, at least in part, to *cause* the angst associated with the array of human/interpersonal interactions that mark modern life in Japan. Since situations that require *keigo* seem to elicit anxiety on the part of Japanese speakers, one solution might be to eliminate or attenuate the requirements of *keigo* convention. This solution finds favor in certain quarters in Japan. What I offer here is the more widely accepted view that *keigo* serves as a mediator between actors and the contexts in which they find themselves.

8. The Japanese text reads:

この小辞典に収録した言葉は、約 1,000 あります。あるものは、さりげない挨拶の言葉であり、またあるものは、恐縮しながら語りかけるお願いの言葉です。またあるものは、立場の違いから、やむをえない対立関係をはらみ、なおかつ、相手との友好を壊すまいという切実な意思が、言い回しの裏に感じられます。そこには、人間関係の 1,000 のシーンがあります。

　　そのシーンでは、どういった言葉を相手にかけるかひとつで、その後の二人の関係が、良好にも、険悪にもなりうるものです。それほどでない場合も、興ざめしたり、思いがけず親密になったりするような、ささいな変化をひきおこす力をもっています。そういった変化は、ささいではあるけれど、のちにふりかえったときに、あそこが始まりだったなと思える場合もあり、恐いものです。

　　「ものの言い方」という、いいならわされた単語には、「ものには言い方がある」、つまり、「言い方ひとつで、右にも左にも転んでしまう」だから「愚かな言い方、無神経な言い方に気をつけなさいよ」という注意が含まれています。さらに、「この言い方が、望ましい言い方ですよ」という、積極的な知恵の継承があります。

　　この知恵ある「ものの言い方」を眺めていると、なかなかなもので、人間関係のシーンに対する理解が深いなあという感動があり、また、どういうわけか笑ってしまいます。この笑いは、ほんとうのことを聞いたときに、うれしくなって笑ってしまうあの笑いで、つまりここには、何かの真理が含まれているのでしょう。この小辞典で集めようと試みたのは、そういった「ものの言い方」です。

9. The Japanese text reads:

一般的に使われる敬語表現は意外とかぎられています。尊敬語と謙譲語の混同、取り違えなどよくありますが、基本的な言葉だけでも覚えてしまえば、敬語の使い方もグーンと上達するはずです。

10. The Japanese text reads:

大人の社会には敬語というヤッカイなものがあります...

　　実際、たとえばビジネス社会で、敬語の使い方がヘタだからというのでクビになった人の話はあまり聞きません。ところが、その場にふさわしくない言葉の使い方で道を誤った人は数限りなくいるのです... 社会人になれば特に「大人としての正しい言葉使い」が要求されます。

11. The Japanese text reads:

最近は、家庭内で敬語を使う習慣がすっかり影をひそめた。そのため敬語を正しくつかえない若い人が増えている。敬語廃止論もあるが、一般社会では敬語はやはり常識。

12. The Japanese text reads:

敬語が乱れている。それは尋常の乱れ方ではない。若い奥さん方がおしゃべりをしていた。ひとりが「あら、赤ちゃんにお乳をあげる時間だわ」などという。他人の赤ちゃんにあげるのではない。わが子にやるのにこういうのである。勿論当人は気が付いていない。... 現に戦後は敬語はやめた方がいい、少なくとも大幅に改革すべきだと考えている人が、殊に進歩的といわれる学者や評論家あるいは現場の教師のなかに大勢いる... 日本の敬語は日本人の心、あるいは思考様式、行動様式、価値体系、即ち日本の文化と深くつながり合っている。それにもかかわらず日本の敬語をこういった視点から考えていこうとする立場はこれまで皆無であったといっていい。

13. The Japanese text reads:

「課長！」と呼びかけて

　敬語を含むことばづかいは、慣れることが上達の一番大切なことである。一通りの基本型式がわかったところで、次のことばを声に出して言ってみよう。

　　最初は、自分の所属する職場内を敬語の慣習の場所と考えて、積極的に話し、間違ったら、その場ですぐに指摘してもらい正しく言えるようにするのがよい。そうすれば、社外の人と話すときにも自信が持てるようになる。

　　次のことばを「課長！」と呼びかけてから、声に出して何回か繰り返して言ってみよう。理屈でなく、日常の話をするときに、すらっと口から出るようにしておきたい。

(1) 課長！おはようございます

(2) 課長！今日もよろしくお願いいたします

(3) 課長！何時にいらっしゃいますか

(4) 課長！ここのところを教えていただけますか

(5) 課長！これでよろしいでしょうか

(6) 課長！ご出席いただけませんか

(7) 課長！ご都合はいかがでしょうか

(8) 課長！○○部長がおみえになりました

(9) 課長！○○商事から、ただいま帰りました

(10) 課長！提出する書類を持って参りました

(11) 課長！お荷物をお持ちします

(12) 課長！○○の件でお伺いしたいのですが

(13) 課長！何を召しあがりますか

(14) 課長！今、よろしいでしょうか

(15) 課長！私がいたします

(16) 課長！今日はありがとうございました

(17) 課長！お先に失礼いたします

14. The Japanese text reads:

電話は声の往復であり、あなたの第一声が会社のイメージを良くも悪くもします。姿がみえないだけに、話し方やことば遣いですべてを表現してしまいます。笑顔、表情、姿勢、態度が、伝わってしまうのです。

15. The Japanese text reads:

電話は、言葉と声が頼りである

電話では、相手が見えない。離れた場所にいる人と、たちどころに話が出来て、とても便利だが、相手の姿が見えない。いきおい、声と言葉が頼りとなる。敬語や、敬語的表現が、きちんとできないと、人柄まで誤解されてしまう。

16. The Japanese text reads:

① メモは用意してあるか確認する

② 伝えたい内容を整理してから電話をかける

③ 省略語はなるべく使わない

④ かかってきた電話は、ベル音3回以内に出る

⑤ 用件は3分以内で話す

⑥ 待たせる時には必ず了解を！

⑦ 人名、日時は必ず確認する

⑧ 用件は必ず復唱する

⑨ はっきりと聞き取りやすいスピードで！

⑩ 受話器は静かに置く

17. The Japanese text reads:

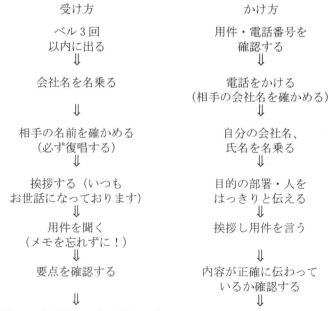

受け方	かけ方
ベル3回 以内に出る	用件・電話番号を 確認する
⇩	⇩
会社名を名乗る	電話をかける （相手の会社名を確かめる）
⇩	⇩
相手の名前を確かめる （必ず復唱する）	自分の会社名、 氏名を名乗る
⇩	⇩
挨拶する（いつも お世話になっております）	目的の部署・人を はっきりと伝える
⇩	⇩
用件を聞く （メモを忘れずに！）	挨拶し用件を言う
⇩	⇩
要点を確認する	内容が正確に伝わって いるか確認する

⇩

挨拶し、受話器を丁寧に置く。決してカチャンと置いてはいけない。

18. The Japanese text reads:

    I. 正しいか正しくないか？

    1. 課長、これを拝見しましたか？

    2. お客様のお名前は何と申されますか？

    3. 野球のことは存じませんか？

    4. 社長のことはよく知っています。

    5. 皆様、ようこそおいで頂きました。

    6. 受付けで頂いた紙をおだしください。

    II. 適当な尊敬語及び謙譲語を示しなさい。

    言う
    聞く
    見る
    食べる
    いる
    する
    やる
    もらう
    くれる

19. The Japanese text reads:

    尊敬語と謙譲語の使い方

原形	尊敬語	謙譲語
・行く	いらっしゃる	
・来る		
・言う		
・する		
・書く		
・食べる		
・見る		
・いる		

    丁寧語の使い方

原形	丁寧な言い方	一層丁寧な言い方
・あっち	あちら	
・こっち		
・どう？		
・ある		
・いいよ		
・そうだ		

「お」と「ご」の使い方

相手側のことをいうときに「お」をつける場合

・相手のからだ

・相手の健康状態

・相手の持ち物

・相手の動作

・相手の家族・親族

相手にかかわりのある自分の動作に「お」をつける場合

20. The Japanese text reads:

次のことばは大きく別けて二種類あります。自分の動作を表現するときはX、相手の動作を表現するときは○をつけなさい。

1. おります

2. ご説明申し上げる

3. いらっしゃる

4. 参ります

5. ご覧になる

6. ちょうだいする

7. 存じている

8. ご案内いたす

9. お耳に入る

10. お見えになる

11. おっしゃる

12. 申す

13. うかがう

14. お越し願う

15. ご足労いただく

21. The Japanese text reads:

どちらを選ぶか

20.「取り急ぎ御返事まで」と「取り急ぎお返事まで」

21.「失礼ですが、先生のお宅は鎌倉でいらっしゃいましたか」と「失礼ですが先生のお宅は鎌倉でございましたか」

22.「部長、課長が今日は社には戻らないとおっしゃっていました」と「部長、課長が今日は社には戻らないと言っていました」

23.「その件については、私から経緯を御報告いたします」と「その件については、私から経緯を御報告させていただきます」

24.「社長は、あの報告に満足されていたよ」と「社長は、あの報告に満足していらっしゃったよ」

25.「もうこれ以上、相手チームに点をあげてはいけませんね」と「もうこれ以上、相手チームに点をやってはいけませんね」

26.「山田先生によろしくお伝えください」と「山田先生によろしく申し上げてください」

The preferable answers are:

20. *Toriisogi <u>ohenji</u> made.*
21. *Shitsurei desu ga, sensei no otaku wa Kamakura de <u>gozaimashita</u> ka.*
22. *Buchō, kachō ga kyō wa sha ni wa modoranai to <u>oshatte</u> imashita.*
23. *Sono ken ni tsuite wa, watakushi kara keii o gohōkoku <u>itashimasu</u>.*
24. *Shachō wa, ano hōkoku ni manzoku shite <u>irasshatta</u> yo.*
25. *Mo kore ijō, aite chiimu ni ten o <u>agete</u> wa ikemasen ne.*
26. *Yamada-sensei ni yoroshiku <u>otsutae</u> kudasai.*

22. The Japanese text reads:

問題

次の言い方は適当であるかどうか、考えてみよう。

先生も　この　本を　お読みに　なったか。

（注意 [1] 親がその子に問う場合と、[2] 先生に向かって問う場合と考えられる。）

問題

次の助詞を尊敬の意を表わす言い方にして、そこに存するきまりを考えてみよう。

書く　持つ　思う　取る　起きる　助ける　受ける　きめる　見せる

問題

次の助詞に対する、尊敬の意を表わす言い方を考えてみよう。

着る　食う　死

23. The *Kokugo Nenkan* (Japanese language studies annual survey and bibliography) produced by the Kokuritsu Kokugo Kenkyūjo indicates that, in 1994, 128 titles appeared that could be classified as *gengo-gijutsu* 'language arts'. This was an all-time high; numbers have been declining ever since, presumably because of the economic recession. 1997 saw 82 new titles—still a respectable number.

Chapter 5. *Keigo* Common Sense

1. The word *ōtai* in Japanese encompasses any action that brings other into self's space.

2. The Japanese text reads:

日常の挨拶
訪問の作法と挨拶
訪問客への作法
お祝の作法と挨拶
見舞の作法と挨拶

不幸の場合の作法と挨拶
食事の作法と挨拶
一般作法と挨拶

3. The Japanese text reads:

1. 朝会ったとき
2. 日中会ったとき
3. 夜会ったとき
4. 寝るとき
5. 初めて会ったとき
6. 以後のつきあいを頼むとき
7. 出かけるとき
8. 相手を送り出すとき
9. 帰ってきたとき
10. 帰ってきた人を迎えるとき
11. 長い間会わなかった後で会ったとき
12. 先に帰るとき
13. 相手と別れるとき
14. 相手との同行を申し出るとき
15. 他人の家を訪問するとき
16. 他人の来訪を歓迎するとき
17. 相手の注意を引くとき
18. 食事をするとき
19. 食事を終えるとき
20. 相手に物をすすめるとき
21. 物をすすめられたとき
22. お礼の気持ちを表すとき
23. お礼やおわびに答えるとき
24. おわびの気持ちを表すとき
25. ねぎらいの気持ちを表すとき
26. 励ましの気持ちを表すとき
27. 驚きの気持ちを表すとき
28. 怒りの気持ちを表すとき
29. 同情の気持ちを表すとき
30. 依頼・要求するとき
31. 依頼・要求を引き受けるとき
32. 依頼・要求を断ろうとするとき
33. 依頼・要求を断るとき

34. 忠告しようとするとき

35. 相手の事柄を祝うとき

36. 相手の事柄をほめるとき

37. 相手の事柄を見舞うとき

38. 相手の病気・けがを見舞うとき

39. 相手の健康を願うとき

40. 相手の成功を祈るとき

4. The Japanese text reads:

商談の成功・不成功は言葉遣いで決まる

1. 取引先を訪問した時―挨拶と自己紹介、名刺の出し方・スイマセンは挨拶ではない。

「あ、スイマセン、私、こういうものですが」

背の高い青年が、入口にぬーと入ってきて、名刺をさし出した。

① 訪問をする場合、まず、挨拶を大切にしよう。「スイマセン」は挨拶ではない。

「おはようございます」

「こんにちわ」

「ごめんください」

これらの挨拶の言葉を、にこやかに、明るく、さわやかに、声、表情、態度、すべてを好感を与えるレベルを考えて行こう。

理想的な表情で、態度、もの腰は、テキパキと、さわやかに！

明るい表情から明るい声が出る。暗い表情で明るい声は出ない。

5. The Japanese text reads:

日常生活の中で、人間は一人では生きていけない。人とコミュニケーションを取るための、一番簡単で、有効な手段が挨拶である。

6. The Japanese text reads:

応対時の基本動作

挨拶や丁寧なことばと共に、それにふさわしい動作が伴って、心をこめた応対になります。お客様が、大切に扱われていると感じる動作は、どうしたら表現できるのか、なぜそうするいみがあるのか、考えてみましょう。

7. I am grateful to Steve Nussbaum at Earlham College for suggesting the term "bookends."

8. The *shitamachi/yamanote* distinction is a well-recognized one in Japan, most especially in Tokyo, where it refers to a traditional division between the samurai landed gentry and the merchant townspeople. It is perhaps comparable to what we in the United States might call old and new money. In contemporary Tokyo, *yamanote* dwellers view *shitamachi* residents as vulgar and déclassé, whereas *shitamachi* residents view anything that smacks of *yamanote* as uptight and snobbish. Kondo's (1990) *Crafting Selves* contains the best account of this cultural divide that I have seen.

9. The instructor's role in appealing simultaneously to people's tangled experience of language and streamlined analysis of it remains ambiguous. I believe that it is the how-to professional's job to keep a foot in both camps—for pedagogical as well as survival reasons.

10. The mystification of Japan and Japanese by means of an intellectual movement called *"Nihonjinron"* is a focus of discussion and typically severe criticism by Western scholars (Befu and Manabe 1990, Dale 1986). I do not mean to imply here that my classmates were adherents of *Nihonjinron,* only that, in their comments to me, they exhibited the same attitudes that Miller (1967:29) has commented on: "That [Japanese] is difficult for foreigners goes without saying, but much is also made of the fact that it is difficult for the Japanese themselves. This point is made over and over again in modern publications on all possible levels aimed at a wide variety of Japanese reading tastes and talents." One corollary of this attitude, I sense, is a popular belief that Japanese does not lend itself to analysis as other languages do. Hence the bewilderment that most of my classmates displayed when challenged to analyze their own language.

11. The Japanese text reads:
本書は、日常のマナーからビジネスマナー、今さら人には聞けない冠婚葬祭の常識まで、人づきあいのさまざなシーンを想定し、「こんなときには、一体どうすればいいの？」という疑問に答えた本です。

12. The Japanese text reads:
いわゆる友達言葉、身内や仲間うちで使っているような言葉づかいを、そのまま社会生活に持ち込むのは常識外れ。

13. The Japanese text reads:
タイミングを逃がさずに
　　挨拶は、タイミングを失うとなかなかしにくいもの。常に、自分が一番最初にするように心がけるといい。また、先に帰る上司に「ご苦労様」という人があるが、「ご苦労様」は上司が部下を労う言葉、こうした取り違えは、常識を疑われることになるので、くれぐれも注意したい。

14. Garfinkel's field of study, ethnomethodology, focuses on the procedural study of common sense. Early on, ethnomethodologists were faced with a peculiar methodological problem: the invisibility of common sense. How can we cause common-sense practices and commonsense knowledge to lose their status as an unexamined "resource" in order to make them a topic for analysis? Human beings take common sense and its constitutive practices for granted, unless some sort of "trouble" makes attention necessary. An early strategy of Garfinkel's was to "breach" expectations in order to generate this kind of "trouble." For example, one experiment interrupted the regular course of interaction as follows:

Subject: I had a flat tire.
Experimenter: What do you mean, you had a flat tire?
Subject: (appears momentarily stunned and then replies in a hostile manner) What do you mean, "What do you mean?" A flat tire is a flat tire. That is what I meant. Nothing special. What a crazy question!

The experiments created anger and frustration on the part of subjects, and they demonstrate in relief some of the background features that are taken for granted as commonsensical in social order (Garfinkel 1967:35–75).

15. The Japanese text reads:

対顧客、対上司、対先輩との会話で、敬語も満足につかえないようでは、本人はもちろん親の人間性・教養にまで疑問符がつけられてしまう。敬語を正しくつかえることが社会人としての基本であることを認識して、正しいつかいかたをマスターしたい。

16. The Japanese text reads:

コミュニケーションの基本ともいえるのがあいさつ。人づきあいを円滑にするためにはもちろんですが、あいさつひとつで人柄が判断されることもあります...「おはようございます」「こんにちは」など、ひとことでもかまいません。明るくはきはきとあいさつしたいものです。

17. Two central issues surrounding common sense that are relevant to arguments here are (a) its universality and (b) its relationship to ordinary language. Schutz 1962 and Smith 1995a, 1995b argue for universal principles of common sense, whereas Rorty and Geertz argue for its relativity. Where the relationship of common sense to ordinary language is concerned, Locke (1690), Reid (1905), Wittgenstein (1953), Austin (1962), and Strawson (1974) have all contributed to arguments about the viability of ordinary language as an object of logical analysis and about its role in avoiding ambiguity and vagueness.

18. The Japanese text reads:

控えたほうがいいことも

　なお、次のような場合は挨拶を控えるのも常識：

1. トイレで、個室から出てきた上司を見かけたとき。

2. 上司が女性と二人擦れでいるのを目撃したとき。

3. アダルトビデオ店、風俗営業の店などから出てきた上司を見かけたとき。

4. 満員電車の中で、少し離れたところにいる上司を見つけたとき。

19. In Rorty's view (which, he says, owes an intellectual debt to Davidson [1984]), the overriding concern for truth value and the concommitant attention to the sentence as the basic unit of analysis is no longer viable. "We often let the world decide the competition between alternative sentences...[but] when the notion of 'description of the world' is moved from the level of criterion-governed sentences within language games to language games as wholes...the idea that the world decides which descriptions are true can no longer be given a clear sense" (5).

20. Similar arguments that language constitutes a window into the inner workings of Japanese culture can be found in works that Wierzbicka cites. Other sources that support this thesis are Doi (1985), Mouer and Sugimoto (1986), Nakane (1970), Rosenberger (1992), Wetzel (1993), and White and Levine (1986).

21. There is no place outside language for talking about language. This is a rephrasing of the antirealist's contention that one cannot use language to get outside language (Post 1996). Not surprisingly, Rorty has gone on record as concurring

with Davidson (1984) about "our inability to step outside our language in order to compare it with something else" (Rorty 1989:75).

22. A very serious criticism of the focus on vocabulary is articulated by Mouer and Sugimoto (1986:134) as "linguistic reductionism." They make the excellent point that it is fallacious to identify words unique to Japanese as proof that the behavior described by those words is uniquely Japanese. I make no such claim here. Nor do I take words out of context in order to make generalizations about Japanese society or behavior. The words I have isolated here are all offered in their original contexts, and they are by definition part of a sociolinguistic dynamic that is under constant negotiation (overtly or covertly) in Japanese society. This is one of the points that Rorty drives home in his work on the contingency of language: vocabularies by their very nature are limited and limiting, and anything can be made to look different simply by being redescribed. The goal here is not to describe, but to examine how the insider describes, and to draw from repeated descriptions what is common.

23. Frame analysis is usually traced back to the work of Gregory Bateson (1972) and Erving Goffman (1974) who portrayed frames as conceptual or cognitive views of particular situations. For example, do we hear a given story as one about problems or about solutions? Our choices of frames help us to hear certain aspects of the talk around us, while enabling or causing us to overlook other parts of the conversation.

24. The Japanese text reads:

・一言加えると親しみが
朝の挨拶は、いうまでもなく「おはようございます」相手が目下なら、「ございます」を抄訳して「おはよう」だけでもいい。相手の目を見、軽くほほえみながら明るい声で挨拶する。相手が目上なら、おじぎをしながら。職場で席についている上司に挨拶する時は、上司の机のそばまで行く。
　「おはようございます」の後に、「よい天気ですね」「寒い天気ですね」などの一言をつけくわえればより親しみがます。「今日のネクタイはしゃれてますね」など、ちょっとした褒め言葉をつけくわえるもの、もちろんいいが、度を過ぎた褒め言葉は、ごますりと受け取られるので、要注意。

・タイミングを逃がさずに
挨拶は、タイミングを失うとなかなかしにくいもの。常に、自分が一番最初にするように心がけるといい。また、先に帰る上司に「ご苦労様」という人があるが、「ご苦労様」は上司が部下を労う言葉、こうした取り違えは、常識を疑われることになるので、くれぐれも注意したい。

25. The Japanese text reads:

．．．あいさつとはまず、要領よりも気持ち、といえます。逆にいえば、どんなに口下手な人でも、本当のあいさつ上手になれるということです。
　社内でのあいさつでもっとも気をつけなければならないことは、自分では失礼だと思っていないフレーズがビジネス社会では失礼にあたるケースが往々にしてあることです。
　たとえば「ご苦労様」という言い方。相手の労をねぎらうフレーズですから、自分の上司が帰宅する際などに使ってもよさそうに思われがち。しか

し、この言葉には本来、「目上から目下に」対しての意味合いがあります。で
すから自分より目上の人に使う場合は、失礼にあたるのです。

　　あいさつ言葉ではありませんが、「一応できます」「まあ大丈夫でしょう」
などの「一応」や「まあ」も避けたい言葉です。あいさつと同様、上司が「で
きる部下」と思うような言葉遣いをしたいものです。

26. The Japanese text reads:

ビジネス・マナーでは、人間関係の上下を姿勢で表わします。上位者は、リ
ラックスしたままで、かまいませんが、下位の者は、緊張感をもった、姿勢
正しい動作が相手に敬意を表わすことになります。

27. The Japanese text reads:

上司・先輩をはじめ、同僚・後輩とのよい人間関係を作るためには、言葉の
大切さ、敬語の大切さを十分理解しておくことだ。

28. The Japanese text reads:

同じ目的を持った組織の一員として、男性も女性も、お互いに相手を理解し、
思いやりの心で過ごせたらすてきな人間関係を築くことができます。言葉は
人間関係の基本です。

29. The Japanese text reads:

上下関係をきらう職場であっても、職場の品位を保つために、粗野な言葉は
使わないようにしたいものです。

30. The Japanese text reads:

目上の人に同行を依頼する
「ご一緒に参りませんか」X
「ご一緒して頂けませんか」〇

こちらから同行を依頼しているわけだから、相手の意思を尊重して、「ご一緒
して頂けませんか」とするのがよい。そうすることにより同行を押し付けら
れたわけではない、自分が判断したんだということになり、相手も苦になら
なくなる。また、自分の都合ではなく先に相手の都合をたすねるよう配慮し
たい。

31. The Japanese text reads:

相手が好意を示してくれたときに、感謝の気持ちを示す最高の言葉が「有難
う」です。心を込めて使ってください。

32. The Japanese text reads:

話し手は聞き手である相手の都合を考えて、話しを駿時間、場所、話題を選
びたいもの。

33. The Japanese text reads:

特に、立場に差のある人に自分の意見を伝えていくためには、違和感なく相
手の耳に言葉が入っていかなければならない。それが敬語であり、敬語表現
の重要さである。

34. The Japanese text reads:

自分を下げて、相手を持ち上げる

敬語とは何かといえば、自分を下げて、相手を持ち上げるていねいなことば
つかい、のことである。だから、自分のことについては「お」「ご」はつけな
い。ここで大事なことは、自分のなかには、自分の会社、その社員も含んで
いるということだ。

35. The Japanese text reads:

相手の心を快いにすることが大切です...たとえば短い時間であっても待つ
時は長く感じるものです。相手の身になって「お待たせ致しました」と言葉
に出してください。

36. The Japanese text reads:

時と場面、相手によって言葉を使い分ける気配りが、相手の心を捉えるので
ある。

37. The Japanese text reads:

敬語は人間関係における心配り、気配り、思い遣りである。

38. The Japanese text reads:

「恐れいりますが」などと、そっと聞くように気を配ることが肝要である。

39. The Japanese text reads:

いわゆる友達言葉、身内や仲間うちで使っているような言葉づかいを、その
まま社会生活に持ち込むのは常識外れ。

40. The Japanese text reads:

自分の会社内の人か会社外の人かをきちんとわきまえる

内と外の関係を区別することの重要性についてもすでにのべた。内の関係で
は、上司である係長、課長などには当然敬語を使って仕事を進めるわけだが、
外の人が関与した場合にはどうなるか。ここで内対外の関係の区別が生じて
くる。

たとえば、来客があって、上司も同席し接客する場合、上司に対して尊敬語
を用いず謙譲語を用いるようにする。これは外部から電話があったりした場
合も同様である。ビジネスの場では、この内、外の関係に特に気を配らなけ
ればならない。

41. The Japanese text reads:

内と外の関係を区別する

とんでもない敬語の使い方をして、恥をかくというのは起こりうること
である。しかし、そのことよりも、その原因が自分でわかる力を身につける
ことのほうがよほど大事である。

大事なお客を相手にして緊張して、つい敬語過剰になったり、またつい
言葉づかいを間違えたりしたような場合と、相手かまわず無礼で正しくない
言い方を重ねているような場合では、根本が違うのである。

言葉づかいというのは、一方で対人関係の反映であるから、敬語の利用
に限らず何かを表現するときにはさまざまな配慮をするものである。

21-Seiki no Nihongo o Kangaeni Kai. 2001. *Tadashii keigo de hanasemasu ka?* [Can you speak correct *keigo*?]. Tokyo: KK Besutoserazu.

Amemiya Tosiiiharu 雨宮利春. 1998. *Aisatsu jōzu ni naru hon* 挨拶上手になる本 [The book for becoming good at *aisatsu*]. Tokyo: Jitsumu Kyōiku Shuppan.

Anderson, John M. 1971. *The Grammar of Case.* Cambridge: Cambridge University Press.

Araki Hiroyuki 荒木博之. 1990. *Keigo no japanorojii* 敬語のジャパノロジー [*Keigo* Japanology]. Tokyo: Sotaku.

Ariyoshi Tadayuki 有吉忠行. 1989. *Anata no keigo doko ka okashii! Doko ga okashii?* あなたの敬語どこかおかしい！どこがおかしい？ [There's something odd about your *keigo!* What's odd about your *keigo*?]. Tokyo: Nihon Jitsugyō.

Asada Hideko 浅田秀子. 1996. *Keigo manyuaru* 敬語マニュアル [*Keigo* manual]. Tokyo: Nan'undō.

Asamatsu Ayako 浅松絢子. 2001a. " 'Kore kara no keigo' kara 'Gendai shakai ni okeru keii-hyōgen' e" "これからの敬語"から "現代社会における敬意表現" へ [From *"Kore kara no keigo"* to *"Gendai shakai ni okeru keii-hyōgen"*]. *Nihon-gogaku* 日本語学 4/20:38–47.

———. 2001b. "Kokugo-seisaku 100-nen ni okeru keigo no atsukai" 国語政策100年における敬語の扱い [Treatment of *keigo* in 100 years of *kokugo* policy]. *Science of Humanity Bensei* 32:82–89.

Asher, R. E. 1968. "Existential, Possessive, and Copulative Sentences in Malayalam." In *The Verb 'Be' and Its Synonyms,* edited by John M. Verhaar, 88–111. Dordrecht: D. Reidel.

Atkinson, Jane M., and Shelly Errington, eds. 1990. *Power and Difference: Gender in Island Southeast Asia.* Stanford: Stanford University Press.

Austin, J. L. 1962. *How to Do Things with Words.* Cambridge: Harvard University Press.

Bach, Emmon. 1967. "Have and Be in English Syntax." *Language* 43:462–485.

Bachnik, Jane M. [1982] 1990. Being in the Group: Spacio-temporal 'Place' in Japanese Social Organization. In *Rethinking Japan,* edited by Adriana Boscaro, Franco Gatti, and Massimo Raveri, 192–197. New York: St. Martin's Press.

Bachnik, Jane M., and Charles J. Quinn, eds. 1994. *Situated Meaning: Inside and Outside in Japanese Self, Society, and Language.* Princeton: Princeton University Press.

Bateson, Gregory. 1972 *Steps to an Ecology of Mind.* New York: Ballantine Books.

Befu, Harumi, and Kazufumi Manabe. 1990. "Empirical Status of *Nihonjinron:* How Real Is the Myth?" In *Rethinking Japan,* edited by Adriana Boscaro, Franco Gatti, and Massimo Raveri, 124–133. New York: St. Martin's Press.

Ben-Ari, Eyal. 1990. "Ritual Strikes, Ceremonial Slowdowns: Some Thoughts on the Management of Conflict in Large Japanese Enterprises." In *Japanese Models of Conflict Resolution,* edited by S. N. Eisenstadt and Eyal Ben-Ari, 94–126. London: Kegan Paul.

Bloch, Bernard. [1946] 1970. "Studies in Colloquial Japanese: Syntax." Reprinted in *Bernard Bloch on Japanese,* edited by Roy Andrew Miller, 25–89. New Haven: Yale University Press.

Bourdieu, Pierre. 1991. *Language and Symbolic Power.* Cambridge: Polity Press.

Boym, Svetlana. 2001. *The Future of Nostalgia.* New York: Basic Books.

Brown, Penelope, and Stephen C. Levinson. 1987. *Politeness: Some Universals in Language Use.* Cambridge: Cambridge University Press.

Brown, Roger, and Albert Gilman. [1960] 1972. "The Pronouns of Power and Solidarity." In *Style in Language,* edited by Thomas A. Sebeok. New York: MIT Press. Reprinted in *Language and Social Context,* edited by Pier Paolo Giglioli, 252–282. Hammondsport: Penguin.

Brubaker, Roger. 1993. Social Theory as *Habitus.* In *Bourdieu: Critical Perspectives,* edited by Craig Calhoun, Edward LiPuma, and Moishe Postone, 212–234. Chicago: University of Chicago Press.

Bruner, Jerome. 1986. *Actual Minds, Possible Worlds.* Cambridge: Harvard University Press.

Bunka-chō 文化庁. 1973. *Kotoba shiriizu 1: Keigo* ことばシリーズ 1: 敬語 [Language series 1: *Keigo*]. Tokyo: Gyōsei.

———. 1986. *Zoku keigo.* 続敬語 [*Keigo* sequel]. Tokyo: Ōkura-shō Insatsu-kyoku.

———. 1995. *Kotoba ni kansuru mondōshū: Keigo-hen* 言葉に関する問答集—敬語編 [Language-related Q and A: *Keigo*]. Tokyo: Ōkura-shō Insatsu-kyoku.

———. 1996. *Kotoba ni kansuru mondōshū: Keigo-hen (2)* 言葉に関する問答集—敬語編 (2) [Language-related Q and A: *Keigo (2)*]. Tokyo: Ōkura-shō Insatsu-kyoku.

———. 1999a. *Keigo kankei sankō shiryō-shū I* 敬語関係参考資料集 I [Collected data with reference to *keigo I*]. Tokyo: Ōkura-shō Insatsu-kyoku.

———. 1999b. *Keigo kankei sankō shiryō-shū II* 敬語関係参考資料集 II [Collected data with reference to *keigo* II]. Tokyo: Ōkura-shō Insatsu-kyoku.

Cameron, Deborah. 1995. *Verbal Hygiene.* London: Routledge

Chafe, Wallace L. 1970. *The Pear Stories.* Norwood N.J.: Ablex.

Chiteki Seikatsu Kenkyūjo 知的生活研究所. 1994. *Otona no manaa: Kotoba no benrichō* 大人のマナー：ことばの便利帳 [Adult manners: Language convenience book]. Tokyo: Seishun Sūpā Bukkusu.

Clark, Eve V. 1970. "Locationals: A Study of the Relations between 'Existential,' 'Locative,' and 'Possessive' Constructions." Stanford: Stanford University Working Papers on Language Universals.

Coates, John. 1996. *The Claims of Common Sense*. Cambridge: Cambridge University Press.

Comrie, Bernard. 1976. "Linguistic Politeness Axes: Speaker-Addressee, Speaker-Referent, Speaker-Bystander." Pragmatics microfiche 1.7: A3. Department of Linguistics: University of Cambridge.

Cook, H. M. 1996. "The Use of Addressee Honorifics in Japanese Elementary School Classrooms." In *Japanese/Korean Linguistics,* edited by N. Akatsuka, S. Iwasaki, and S. Strauss, 67–82. Stanford: CSLI Publications.

———. 1998. "Situational Meanings of Japanese Social Deixis: The Mixed Use of the *masu* and Plain Forms." *Journal of Linguistic Anthropology* 8:87–110.

———. 2002. "Construction of Speech Styles in a Japanese Elementary School Classroom." Paper presented at the Japanese Speech Style Shift Symposium, Tucson, Ariz., March 7–9, 2002.

Dale, Peter N. 1986. *The Myth of Japanese Uniqueness*. New York: St. Martin's Press.

Davidson, Donald. 1984. *Inquiries into Truth and Interpretation*. Oxford: Oxford University Press.

Deguchi Chikara and Minagawa Sumiyo 出口力・皆川純代. 1994. *Bijinesu manaa* ビジネスマナー [Business manners]. Tokyo: Sanmāku Bijinesu Komikkusu.

Doi Takeo 土居健郎. 1985. *Omote to ura*. [The Anatomy of Self: The Individual versus Society]. Tokyo: Kodansha.

Dower, John. 1999. *Embracing Defeat*. New York: W. W. Norton.

Ekoyama Tsuneakira 江湖山恒明. 1943. *Keigo-hō* 敬語法 [The grammar of *keigo*]. Tokyo: Sanseidō.

Fairclough, Norman. 1989. *Language and Power*. London: Longman.

———. 1992. *Discourse and Social Change*. London: Polity Press.

———. 1995. *Critical Discourse Analysis*. London: Longman.

Fillmore, Charles J. 1968. "The Case for Case." In *Universals in Linguistic Theory,* edited by E. Bach and R. Harms, 1–88. New York: Holt, Rinehart and Winston.

———. 1977. The Case for Case Reopened. In *Syntax and Semantics 8: Grammatical Relations,* edited by Peter Cole and Jerrold Sadock, 59–81. New York: Academic Press.

Foley, William A., and Robert D. Van Valin, Jr. 1984. *Functional Syntax and Universal Grammar*. Cambridge: Cambridge University Press.

Fujin Kurabu 婦人クラブ. 1932. *Fujin no kotobadukai mohanshū: Nichijō no ōtaishōreishiki no aisatsu* 婦人の言葉遣い模範集：日常の応対諸礼式の挨拶 [Language usage for wives by example: Everyday dealings, various polite phrases]. Tokyo: Dainihon Yūbenkai Kōdansha.

Fuji Zerokusu Sōgō Kyōiku Kenkyūkai 富士ゼロックス総合教育研究会 [Fuji Xerox General Education Group]. 1994. *Raku ni hanaseru denwa no hon* 楽に話せる電話の本 [Speak comfortably on the telephone]. Tokyo: Yamato Shuppan.

Fukuda Takeshi 福田健. 1989. *Mō machigawanai keigo no hon* もう間違わない敬語の本 [The book for never making another mistake in *keigo*]. Tokyo: Ronguserāzu.

———. 1993. *Bijinesu keigo ga surasura hanaseru hon* ビジネス敬語がスラスラ話せる本 [The book for speaking smooth business *keigo*]. Tokyo: Kanki Shuppan.

———. 1996. *Shikori o nokosanai tanomikata, kotowarikata: 55 no hōsoku* しこりを残さない頼み方、断り方：55の法則 [How to ask, how to refuse: 55 rules]. Tokyo: Yamato Shuppan.

Garfinkel, H. [1963] 1990. "A Conception of, and Experiments with, 'Trust' as a Condition of Stable Concerted Actions." In *Motivation and Social Interaction,* edited by O. J. Harvey (New York: Ronald Press). Reprinted in *Ethnomethodological Sociology,* edited by Jeff Coulter, 3–53. Brookfield, Va.: Edward Elgar.

———. 1967. *Studies in Ethnomethodology.* Englewood Cliffs: Prentice-Hall.

Geertz, Clifford. [1964] 1973. "Ideology as a Cultural System." In *Ideology and Discontent,* edited by D. Aptor (New York: Free Press). Reprinted in Clifford Geertz, *The Interpretation of Cultures,* 193–233. New York: Basic Books.

———. [1975] 1983. "Common Sense as a Cultural System." *Antioch Review* 33:1. Reprinted ir *Local Knowledge: Further Essays in Interpretive Anthropology,* 73–93. New Yorκ: Basic Books, 1983.

Gendai Manaa Fuōramu 現代マナーフォーラム 1996. *E de wakaru manaa jiten* 絵で分かるマナー事典 [Dictionary of manners through pictures]. Tokyo: Seitōsha.

Giddens, Anthony. 1991. *Modernity and Self-Identity.* Cambridge: Polity Press.

Gluck, Carol. 1985. *Japan's Modern Myths: Ideology in the Late Meiji Period.* Princeton: Princeton University Press.

Goffman, Erving. 1974. *Frame Analysis: An Essay on the Organization of Experience.* Cambridge: Harvard University Press.

Gottlieb, Nanette. 1996. *Kanji Politics.* New York: Columbia University Press.

Grimes, Joseph E. 1983. "Reference Spaces in Text." In *Nobel Symposium on Text Processing,* edited by S. Allen, 381–414. Gothenburg: Sprakdata.

Grosz, Barbara, Aravind Joshi, and Scott Weinstein. 1995. "Centering: A Framework for Modeling the Local Coherence of Discourse." *Computational Linguistics* 21/2:203–225.

Gurūpu 24-jikan no Manaa グループ24時間のマナー. 1996. *Manaa bukku* マナーブック (Manner book). Tokyo: Gotō Shoten.

Hale, Ken. 1983. "Walpiri and the Grammar of Non-Configurational Languages." *Natural Language and Linguistic Theory* 1/1:5–47.

Hanks, William F. 1996. *Language and Communicative Practices.* Boulder, Colo.: Westview Press.

Hannay, Michael. 1985. *English Existentials in Functional Grammar.* Cinnaminson, N.J.: Foris Publications.

Harada, S. I. 1976. "Honorifics." In *Syntax and Semantics 5: Japanese Generative Grammar,* edited by Masayoshi Shibatani, 499–561. New York: Academic Press.

Hashimoto Shinkichi 橋本進吉. 1935. *Shim-bunten bekki* 新文典別記 [Continuation of new grammar]. Tokyo: Fuzanbō.

Hashizume Kenji 橋爪堅治. 1959. *Bungo no bumpō* 文語の文法 [Grammar of written language]. Tokyo: Meiji Shoin.

Hendry, Joy. 1990. "The Armour of Honorific Speech: Some Lateral Thinking about *Keigo*." In *Rethinking Japan,* edited by Adriana Boscaro, Franco Gatti, and Massimo Raveri, 111–116. New York: St. Martin's Press.

Hill, Jane H., Sachiko Ide, Shoko Ikuta, Akiko Kawasaki, and Tsunao Ogino. 1986. "Universals of Linguistic Politeness: Quantitative Evidence from Japanese and American English." *Journal of Pragmatics* 10:347–371.

Hinata Shigeo 日向茂雄 1989. *Itsu de mo doko de mo tadashii keigo ga hanaseru hon: Anata wa mechakucha keigo o tsukatte iru* いつでもどこでも正しい敬語が話せる本：あなたはめちゃくちゃ敬語を使っている [The book to let you speak correct *keigo* anytime, anywhere: The *keigo* you're using is a mess]. Tokyo: Chūkei.

Hirst, P., and G. Thompson. 1996 "Globalisation, Governance and the Nation State." In *Globalisation in Question: The International Economy and the Possibilities of Governance.* Cambridge: Polity Press.

Holmes, Janet. 1995. *Women, Men and Politeness.* London: Longman.

Hoshina Kōichi 保科孝一. 1901. *Kokugo kyōju-hō shishin* 國語教授法指針 [Guidebook for teachers of *kokugo*] Tokyo: Hōeikan.

Ide, Sachiko. 1982. "Japanese Sociolinguistics: Politeness and Women's Language." *Lingua* 57:357–385.

———. [1989] 1991. "How and Why Do Women Speak More Politely in Japanese?" *Studies in English and American Literature* 24. Reprinted in *Aspects of Japanese Women's Language,* edited by Sachiko Ide and Naomi Hanaoka McGloin, 63–79. Tokyo: Kuroshio.

———. [1990] 1991. "Person References of Japanese and American Children." Reprinted in *Aspects of Japanese Women's Language,* edited by Sachiko Ide and Naomi Hanaoka McGloin, 43–61. Tokyo: Kuroshio.

Ide, Sachiko, et al. 1986. "Sex Difference and Politeness in Japanese." *International Journal of the Sociology of Language* 58:25–36.

Ikuta, Shoko. [1980] 1983. "Speech Level Shift and Conversational Strategy in Japanese Discourse." *Language Sciences* 5:37–53.

———. 2002. "Speech Style Shift as an Interactional Discourse Strategy: A Study of the Shift between the Use and Non-Use of *des-/-mas* in Japanese Conversational Interviews." Paper presented at the Japanese Speech Style Shift Symposium, Tucson, Ariz., March 7–9, 2002.

Ingerson, Alice. 2000. "What are Cultural Landscapes?" http://www.icls.harvard.edu/language/whatare.html (accessed 8/1/02).

Inoue, Miyako. 1996. "The Political Economy of Gender and Language in Japan." Ph.D. diss., Washington University, St. Louis.

Ishida, Takeshi, and Ellis S. Krauss, eds. 1989. *Democracy in Japan.* Pittsburgh: Pittsburgh University Press.

Ishizaka Shōzō 石坂正蔵. 1951. "Keigo-teki ninshō no gainen" 敬語的人称の概念 [The concept of the *keigo*-like person]. *Bumpō rongi 2-gō* 文法論議 2号 [Grammar issues #2]. Kumamoto University.

———. 1957. *Keigo-hō* 敬語法 [The grammar of *keigo*]. *Nihon bumpō kōza 1* 日本文法講座・1 [Foundations of Japanese grammar 1]. Tokyo: Meiji Shoin.

Ivy, Marilyn. 1995. *Discourses of the Vanishing: Modernity, Phantasm, Japan.* Chicago: Chicago University Press.

Iwai Yoshio 岩井良雄. 1955. *Kōtō-gakushū bumpō* 高等学習文法 [High school grammar]. Tokyo: Seitōsha.

James, William. 1907. "Pragmatism and Common Sense." In *Pragmatism, A New Name for Some Old Ways of Thinking,* 63–75. New York: Longman, Green.

Jorden, Eleanor H. 1963. *Beginning Japanese.* New Haven: Yale University Press.

Jorden, Eleanor H., with Mari Noda. 1987. *Japanese: The Spoken Language.* New Haven: Yale University Press.

Kabaya Hiroshi, Kawaguchi Yoshikazu, and Sakamoto Megumi 蒲谷宏、川口義一、坂本恵. 1998. *Keigo hyōgen* 敬語表現 [*Keigo* expressions]. Tokyo: Taishūkan.

Kageyama, Taro. 1999. "Word Formation." In *Handbook of Japanese Linguistics,* edited by Natsuko Tsujimura, 297–325. Malden, Mass.: Blackwell Books.

Kamei Takashi 亀井孝. 1956. *Shimben bungo bumpō* 新編文語文法 [New edition (of the) written language grammar]. Tokyo: Yamato Bunko.

Kanai Ryōko 金井良子. 1989. *Onna no miryoku wa "hanashikata" shidai "aisatsu" kara "keigo" made, shirazushirazu ni mi ni tsuku hon* 女の魅力は「話し方」次第「挨拶」から「敬語」まで、知らず知らずに身に付く本 [A woman's charm is the way she speaks: Learn it all—from conversational responses to *keigo*]. Tokyo: Yamato.

Kant, Immanuel. [1790] 1982. "Critique of Aesthetic Judgment." In *The Critique of Judgment,* translated by J. C. Meredith. Oxford: Clarendon Press.

Kikuchi Yasuto 菊池康人. 1994. *Keigo* 敬語 Tokyo: Kadokawa Shoten.

———. 1996. *Keigo no sainyūmon* 敬語の再入門 [Reintroduction to *keigo*]. Tokyo: Maruzen.

Kindaichi Kyōsuke 金田一京助. 1959. *Nihon no keigo* 日本の敬語 [Japan's *keigo*]. Tokyo: Kadokawa Shinsho.

Kojima Toshio 小島俊夫. 1998. *Nihon keigo-shi kenkyū* 日本敬語史研究 [Studies in the history of Japanese *keigo*]. Tokyo: Kasama Shoin.

Kokugo Chōsa Iinkai 國語調査委員会. 1903. "Kōgo-hō torishirabe ni kansuru jikō" 口語法取調ニ関スル事項 [Particulars of the investigation into spoken language grammar]. Reprinted in Bunka-chō 1999a, 418–426.

———. 1906a. *Kōgo-hō chōsa hōkoku-sho* 口語法調査報告書 [Report on the investigation into spoken language grammar]. Reprinted, with an afterword (unpaginated). Tokyo: Kokusho Kankō-kai, 1986.

———. 1906b. *Kōgo-hō bumbu-zu* 口語法分布図 [Spoken language grammar distribution atlas]. Reprinted, with an afterword (unpaginated). Tokyo: Kokusho Kankō-kai, 1986.

———. 1908a. *Kōgo-hō torishirabe ni kansuru jikō* 口語法取調ニ関スル事項 [Particulars of the investigation into spoken language grammar]. Reprinted in Bunka-chō 1999a, 427–454.

———. 1908b. "Tōkyō-go keigo ryakuhyō" 東京語敬語略表 [Tokyo *keigo* summary]. Reprinted in Bunka-chō 1999b, 2–31.

———. 1911. "Kōgo-tai shokan-bun ni kansuru chōsa-hōkoku" 口語体書簡文に関

する調査報告 [Report on the investigation of spoken language forms in letter-writing style]. Reprinted in Bunka-chō 1999b, 32–162.

———. 1916. "Kōgo-hō" 口語法 [Spoken language grammar]. Reprinted in Bunka-chō 1999a, 1–165.

———. 1917. "Kōgo-hō bekki" 口語法別記 [Spoken language grammar addendum]. Reprinted in Bunka-chō 1999a, 166–417.

Kokugogaku kenkyū jiten 国語学研究辞典 [Dictionary of Japanese language studies]. 1977. Tokyo: Meiji Shoin.

Kokugo Shingikai 国語審議会. [1952] 1981. "Kore kara no keigo" これからの敬語 [*Keigo* from now on]. Reprinted in *Atarashii kokugo hyōki handobukku* 新しい国語表記ハンドブック [New national language transcription handbook], 189–193. Tokyo: Sanseido.

———. 1995. "Atarashii jidai ni ōjita kokugo-seisaku ni tsuite" 新しい時代に応じた国語政策について [Regarding national language policy for the modern age]. In *Kokugo Shingikai hōkokusho* 20 国語審議会報告書 20 [Report of the Kokugo Shingikai 20], 293–321. Tokyo: Bunka-chō.

———. 1996. "Keii hyōgen no rinen to hyōjun no arikata" 敬意表現の理念と標準のあり方 [Guidelines for standards and conceptualization of polite expressions]. In Kokugo Shingikai 1998, 352–353.

———. 1998. "Gendai ni okeru keii hyōgen no arikata" 現代における敬意表現の在り方 [Guidelines for respect expressions in the modern age]. In *Kokugo Shingikai hōkokusho* 21 国語審議会報告書21 [Report of the Kokugo Shingikai 21], 345–357. Tokyo: Bunka-chō.

———. 2000. "Gendai ni okeru keii hyōgen" 現代における敬意表現 [Respect expressions in the modern age]. Kokugo Shingikai white paper, a revised version of Kokugo Shingikai 1998. Tokyo: Bunka-chō.

Kokuritsu Kokugo Kenkyūjo 国立国語研究所. 1994. *Kokugo nenkan* 国語年鑑 [Japanese language studies annual survey and bibliography]. Tokyo: Kokuritsu Kokugo Kenkyūjo.

———. 2000. "Keigo ni tsuite no ryūi-ten" 敬語についての留意点 [Points for attention regarding *keigo*]. In *Kokugo ni kansuru seron-chōsa: Mondai betsu bunseki hōkokusho* 国語に関する世論調査 : 問題別分析報告書 [Investigation into public opinion about *kokugo:* Report on analytical problems], 54–66. Tokyo: Kokuritsu Kokugo Kenkyūjo.

Kondo, Dorinne. 1990. *Crafting Selves: Power, Gender, and Discourses of Identity in a Japanese Workplace*. Chicago: University of Chicago Press.

Kraus, Ellis S., Thomas P. Rohlen, and Patricia G. Steinhoff, eds. 1984. *Conflict in Japan*. Honolulu: University of Hawai'i Press.

Kristoff, Nicholas D. 1998. "When Cultures Collide, Etiquette Loses Something in Translation." *New York Times*, Sports Pages, Sunday, February 15.

Kroskrity, Paul V. 2000. "Regimenting Languages: Language Ideological Perspectives." In *Regimes of Language*, edited by Paul V. Kroskrity, 1–34. Santa Fe: School of American Research Press.

Kumazawa Ryū 熊沢龍. 1956. *Nihon bumpō* 日本文法 [Japanese grammar]. Tokyo: Meiji Shoin.

Kuno, Susumu. 1973. *The Structure of the Japanese Language*. Cambridge: MIT Press.
————. 1980. "Functional Syntax." In *Syntax and Semantics 13: Current Approaches to Syntax*, edited by Edith Moravcsik and Jessica R. Wirth, 117–135. New York: Academic Press.
Kurihara Mikio 栗原幹夫. 2001. *Tadashii keigo de hanasemasu ka?* 正しい敬語で話せますか [Can you speak correct *keigo*?]. Tokyo: KK Besutoserāzu.
Labov, William. 1991. "The Intersection of Sex and Social Class in the Course of Linguistic Change." *Language Variation and Change* 2/2:205–251.
Lebra, Takie Sugiyama. 1976. *Japanese Patterns of Behavior*. Honolulu: University of Hawaiʻi Press.
Lee Yeounsuk イヨンスク. 1996. *Kokugo to iu shisō* 国語という思想 [The idea of *kokugo*]. Tokyo: Iwanami Shoten.
Linhart-Fischer, Ruth. 1990. "Rethinking Western Notions of Japanese Women: Some Aspects of Female Japanese Reality versus Stereotypes about Japanese Women." In *Rethinking Japan,* edited by Adriana Boscaro, Franco Gatti, and Massimo Raveri, 164–174. New York: St. Martin's Press.
Locke, John. 1690. "An Essay Concerning Human Understanding." http://www.arts.cuhk.edu.hk/Philosophy/Locke/echu/ (accessed 8/1/02).
Lumsden, Michael. 1988. *Existential Sentences: Their Structure and Meaning*. London: Croom Helm.
Lyons, John. 1967. "A Note on Possessive, Existential, and Locative Sentences." *Foundations of Language* 3:390–396.
Maher, John C., and Gaynor MacDonald, eds. 1995. *Diversity in Japanese Culture and Language*. London: Kegan Paul.
Marshall, Byron K. 1992. *Academic Freedom and the Japanese Imperial University, 1868–1939*. Berkeley: University of California Press.
Martin, Samuel E. 1964. "Speech Levels in Japan and Korea." In *Language in Culture and Society,* edited by Dell Hymes, 407–415. New York: Harper and Row.
————. 1975. *A Reference Grammar of Japanese*. New Haven: Yale University Press.
Maruyama Rimpei 丸山林平. 1941. *Nihon keigo-hō* 日本敬語法 [Grammar of Japanese *keigo*]. Tokyo: Kembunsha.
Matsumoto, Yoshiko. 1996. "Does Less Feminine Speech in Japanese Mean Less Femininity?" In *Gender and Belief Systems: Proceedings of the Fourth Berkeley Women and Language Conference,* edited by N. Warner, J. Ahlers, L. Bilmes, M. Oliver, S. Wertheim, and M. Chen, 455–467. Berkeley: Berkeley Women and Language Group.
————. 1999. "Japanese Stylistic Choices and Ideologies across Generations." In *Language and Ideology: Selected Papers from the Sixth International Pragmatics Conference,* 1:353–364. Edited by Jef Verschueren. Antwerp: International Pragmatics Association.
————. 2002. "Gender Identity and the Presentation of Self in Japanese." Paper presented at the Japanese Speech Style Shift Symposium, Tucson, Ariz., March 7–9, 2002.
Matsushita Daizaburō 松下大三郎. 1901. *Nihon zokugo bumpō* 日本俗語文典 [Colloquial Japanese grammar].

Matsūra Takanori 松浦敬紀. 1992. *Mensetsu jiko apiiru* 100 *[Danshi gakusei-shū]* 男
子用面接自己アピール 100 [Job interview personal appeal 100 (Male student
edition)]. Tokyo: Takahashi Shoten.

Maynard, Senko K. 1993. *Discourse Modality: Subjectivity, Emotion, and Voice in the
Japanese Language.* Amsterdam: John Benjamins.

———. 1997. *Japanese Communication: Language and Thought in Context.* Honolulu: University of Hawai'i Press.

McCord, Gary. 1996. *Golf for Dummies.* Foster City, Calif.: IDG Books.

McLaughlin, M. L., ed. 1984. *Conversation: How Talk Is Organized.* Beverly Hills:
Sage Publications.

Miki Yukinobu 三木幸信 ed. 1956. *Shinkoku bumpō* 新国文法 [New nation(al) gram-
mar]. Tokyo: Shintōsha.

Miller, Roy Andrew. 1967. *The Japanese Language.* Chicago: University of Chicago
Press.

———. 1971. "Levels in Speech *(Keigo)* and the Japanese Linguistic Response to
Modernization." In *Tradition and Modernization in Japanese Culture,* edited by
Donald H. Shively, 601–667. Princeton: Princeton University Press.

———. 1994. "Levels in Speech in the Japanese Language." *Asian Pacific Quarterly*
26/1:12–26 .

Minami Fujio 南不二男. 1979. *Gengo to kōdō* 言語と行動 [Language and behavior].
Tokyo: Daishūkan.

———. 1987. *Keigo* 敬語. Tokyo: Iwanami Shoten.

Mitsuhashi Yōya 三橋要也. 1892. *Hōbunjō no keigo* 邦文上の敬語 [Vernacular
keigo].

Mitsuya Shigematsu 三矢重松. 1902. "Kokugo ni tokuyū na bun no san-tai" 國語に
特有な文の三体 [Three types of peculiar sentences in Japanese]. *Kokugaku-in
zasshi* 国学院雑誌 [Language newspaper] 8:6–7.

———. 1908. *Kōtō nihon bumpō* 高等日本文法 [Advanced Japanese grammar]. Tokyo: Daiichi Shobo.

Miyoshi, Masao, and H. D. Harootunian, eds. 1989. *Postmodernism and Japan.*
Durham: Duke University Press.

Mombushō 文部省. 1941. "Reihō yōkō" 礼法要項 [Important points in manners].
Reprinted in Bunka-chō 1999b, 163–202.

Mouer, Ross, and Yoshio Sugimoto. 1986. *Images of Japanese Society.* London: Kegan
Paul.

Mozume Takami 物集高見. [ca. 1890]. "Genbun-itchi" 言文一致 [Unification of
written and spoken language]. In *Mozume Takami zenshū* 3 物集高見全集 3
[Complete works of Mozume Takami 3]. Tokyo: Ōbundō, 1935.

Muramatsu Ei 村松映. 1990. *Atte 'ru yō de okashi na keigo jōshiki* あってるようでお
かしな敬語常識 [You think it's right, but it's odd—*Keigo* common sense]. Tokyo: HBJ.

Muraoka Masao 村岡正雄. 1992. *Ichininmae no aisatsu to hanashikata* 一人前の挨拶
と話し方 [Greetings and speeches for adults]. Tokyo: Nihon Jitsugyō Shuppan.

———. 1996. *Hito ni sukareru aisatsu to ukekotae* 人に好かれる挨拶と受け答え [Be
liked by people: Greetings and meetings]. Tokyo: Nihon Jitsugyō Shuppan.

Nakane, Chie. 1970. *Japanese Society*. Berkeley: University of California Press.

Nichieisha Henshūjo 日栄社編集所. 1954. *Kammei bungo bumpō* 簡明・文語文法 [Concise written language grammar]. Tokyo: Nichieisha.

Nishida Naotoshi 西田直俊. 1987. *Kokugogaku sōsho 13: Keigo* 国語学叢書13: 敬語 [Language series 13: *Keigo*]. Tokyo: Tokyo-do.

Nishio Akira 西尾昭. 1993. *Kaisha hōmon no manaa to jiko PR: Daigakusei no shūshokushiken* 会社訪問のマナーと自己 PR: 大学生の就職試験 [Manners and self-endorsement for business visits: Employment exams for university graduates]. Tokyo: Narumidō Shuppan.

Noguchi Kazue 野口和枝. 1992. *Keigo no tsukaikata ga wakaru hon* 敬語の使い方が分かる本 [The book for understanding how to use *keigo*]. Tokyo: Asuka Shuppan.

Nomoto Kikuo 野元菊雄. 1987. *Keigo o tsukaikonasu* 敬語を使いこなす [Get the knack of using *keigo*]. Tokyo: Kodansha.

Nomoto Suien 野本翠苑. 1998. *Utsukushii bōrupen-ji no kihon renshū* 美しいボールペン字の基本練習 [Basic practice for beautiful ballpoint script]. Tokyo: Nihon Bungeisha.

Ōishi Hatsutarō 大石初太郎. 1975. *Keigo* 敬語. Tokyo: Chikuma.

———. 1977. *Keigo no kenkyūshi* 敬語の研究史 [History of *keigo* study]. *Iwanami kōza nihongo 4: Keigo* 岩波講座日本語 4: 敬語, 205–246. Tokyo: Iwanami Shoten.

Ōishi Hatsutarō 大石初太郎 and Hayashi Shirō 林四郎. 2000. *Keigo no tsukaikata* 敬語の使い方 [How to use *keigo*]. Tokyo: Meiji Shōin.

Ōishi Hatsutarō, Toyama Shigehiko, Jugaku Akiko, Yoneda Takeshi, and Nishimura Hidetoshi 大石初太郎、外山滋比古、寿岳章子、米田武、西村英俊. 1983. *Atarashii keigo: Utsukushii kotoba* 新しい敬語：美しいことば [New *keigo*: Beautiful language]. *Nihongo shimpojiumu 4* 日本語シンポジウム：4 [Japanese symposium 4]. Tokyo: Bunka-chō.

Okada Masayoshi 岡田正美. 1900. "Taigūhō" 待遇法 [Polite ways]. *Gengogaku zasshi* 言語学雑誌 [Linguistics newspaper] 1:4–5.

Okamoto, Shigeko. 1995. " 'Tasteless' Japanese: Less Feminine Speech among Young Japanese Women." In *Gender Articulated: Language and the Socially Constructed Self,* edited by Kira Hall and Mary Bucholtz, 297–328. London: Routledge.

———. 1998. "The Use and Non-Use of Honorifics in Sales Talk in Kyoto and Osaka: Are They Rude or Friendly?" In *Japanese/Korean Linguistics 7*, edited by Noriko Akatsuka, Hajime Hoji, Shoichi Iwasaki, Sung-Ock Sohn, and Susan Strauss, 141–158. Stanford: Stanford Linguistics Association.

———. 2002. "Ideology and Social Meanings: Rethinking the Relationship between Language, Politeness, and Gender." In *Gendered Practices in Language,* edited by Sarah Benor, Mary Rose, Devyani Sharma, Julie Sweetland, and Qing Zhang, 1–23. Stanford: CSLI Publications.

Paine, Thomas. 1776. *Common Sense*. http://odur.let.rug.nl/~usa/D/1776-1800/paine/CM/sensexx.htm (accessed 8/1/02).

Pakira Hausu パキラハウス. 1990. *Chotto shita mono no iikata* ちょっとしたものの言い方 [Trivial expressions]. Tokyo: Kōdansha.

Post, John F. 1996. Using Language to Get Outside Language. http://www.vanderbilt.edu/~postjf/uselang.htm (accessed 2/15/03).

Reid, Thomas. 1905. "The Philosophy of Common Sense." In *Lectures in the Philosophy of Kant*. London: Macmillan.

Robertson, Jennifer. 1991. *Native and Newcomer: Making and Remaking a Japanese City*. Berkeley: University of California Press.

Rorty, Richard. 1989. *Contingency, Irony and Solidarity*. Cambridge: Cambridge University Press.

Rosenberger, Nancy R., ed. 1992. *Japanese Sense of Self*. Cambridge: Cambridge University Press.

Saeki Umetomo 佐伯梅友. 1953. *Kokubumpō* 国文法 [Japanese grammar]. Tokyo: Sanseidō.

Sanada Shinji 真田信治. 1991. *Hyōjungo wa ika ni seiritsu shita ka* 標準語はいかに成立したか [How did standard Japanese come to be?]. Tokyo: Sōtakusha.

Schieffelin, Bambi B., Kathryn A. Woolard, and Paul V. Kroskrity, eds. 1998. *Language Ideologies: Practice and Theory*. New York: Oxford University Press.

Schutz, Alfred J. 1962. "On Multiple Realities." In *Alfred J. Schutz: Collected Papers*, vol. 1: *The Problem of Social Reality*, 207–259. The Hague: Martinus Nijhoff.

Searle, John. 1969. *Speech Acts*. Cambridge: Cambridge University Press.

Shain Kyōiku Sōgō Kenkyūjo 社員教育総合研究所. 1993. *Ningen-kankei no kihon ga wakaru hon* 人間関係の基本がわかる本 [The book for understanding the basics of interpersonal relations]. Tokyo: Business-Educational Center.

Shibamoto, Janet. 1987. "The Womanly Woman: Japanese Female Speech." In *Language, Gender, and Sex in Comparative Perspective*, edited by Susan U. Philips, Susan Steele, and Christine Tanz, 26–49. Cambridge: Cambridge University Press.

Shibatani, Masayoshi. 1978. "Minami Akira and the Notion of 'Subject' in Japanese Grammar." In *Problems in Japanese Syntax and Semantics*, edited by John Hinds and Irwin Howard, 52–67. Tokyo: Kaitakusha.

———. 1990. *The Languages of Japan*. Cambridge: Cambridge University Press.

Shimizu Shōzō and Arimura Itsuko 清水省三・有村伊都子. 1999. *Keigo no tsukaikata ga 3-jikan de masutaa dekiru* 敬語の使い方が3時間でマスターできる [You can master how to use *keigo* in 3 hours]. Tokyo: Asuka Shuppan.

Shūbunsha Henshūbu 習文社編集部. 1933. *Gendaishiki reigi sahō* 現代[式]礼儀作法 [The basis of modern courtesy and manners]. Tokyo: Shūbunsha.

Shūshoku Taisaku Kenkyūkai 就職対策研究会. 1992. *Joshiyō mensetsu shiken gōkakuhō* 女子用面接試験合格法 [How to pass the interview test (women's edition)]. Tokyo: Takahashi Shoten.

Smith, Barry. 1995a. "Formal Ontology, Common Sense, and Cognitive Science." *International Journal of Human-Computer Studies* 43:641–667. http://wings.buffalo.edu/philosophy/ontology/focscs.htm (accessed 8/1/02).

———. 1995b. "The Structures of the Common Sense World." *Acta Philosophica Fennica* 58:290–317. http://wings.buffalo.edu/philosophy/faculty/smith/articles/scsw.html (accessed 8/1/02).

Steinhoff, Patricia. 1992. "Death by Defeatism and Other Fables: The Social Dynamics of the *Rengō Sekigun* Purge." In *Japanese Social Organization*, edited by Takie Sugiyama Lebra, 195–224. Honolulu: University of Hawai'i Press.

Strawson, P. F. 1974. "Intention and Convention in Speech Acts." *Philosophical Review* 73:439–460.

Suzuki Takao 鈴木孝夫. 1975. *Tozasareta gengo: Nihongo no sekai* 閉ざされた言語・日本語の世界 [Closed language: The world of Japanese]. Tokyo: Shinchō Sencho.

———. 1985. *Buki to shite no kotoba* 武器としてのことば [Language as weapon]. Tokyo: Shinchōsha.

———. 1999. *Nihonjin wa naze eigo ga dekinai ka* 日本人はなぜ英語ができないか [Why can't the Japanese speak English?]. Tokyo: Iwanami Shoten.

Suzuki, Tomi. 1996. *Narrating the Self: Fictions of Japanese Modernity*. Stanford: Stanford University Press.

Suzuki Yukiko 鈴木雪子. 1991. *Kotobazukai to keigo* ことばづかいと敬語 [Language use and *keigo*]. Tokyo: Seisansei Shuppan.

———. 1998. *Utsukushii keigo no manaa* 美しい敬語のマナー [Beautiful manners with *keigo*]. Tokyo: KK Besutoserāzu.

Tachibana Shōichi 橘正一. 1933. *Kako yo-nenkan o kaerimite* 過去四年間を顧みて [Looking back over the past four years]. *Hōgen to Dozoku* 4/7 表現と土俗四巻七号 [Dialect and local custom 4/7].

Tai, Eiko. 1999. "*Kokugo* and Colonial Education in Taiwan." *Positions* 7/2:503–540.

Tani Yasuyo 多二安代. 2000. *Daitōa kyōeiken to nihongo* 大東亜共栄圏と日本語 [The Greater East Asia Co-Prosperity Sphere and Japanese). Tokyo: Keisō Shobō.

Tannen, Deborah, and C. Wallat. 1993. "Interactive Frames and Knowledge Schemas in Interaction: Examples from a Medical Examination/Interview." In *Framing in Discourse,* edited by Deborah Tannen, 57–76. New York: Oxford University Press.

Theisman, Joe. 1997. *The Complete Idiot's Guide to Understanding Football like a Pro.* New York: Alpha Books.

Thomason, Burke C. 1982. *Making Sense of Reification: Alfred Schutz and Constructionist Theory*. Atlantic Highlands, N.J.: Humanities Press.

Tōjō Misao 東條操. 1932. *Hōgen kenkyū no gaikan* 方言研究の概観 [Overview of dialect research]. Tokyo: Iwanami Kōza Nihon Bungaku.

Tokieda Motoki 時枝誠記. 1940. *Kokugogaku rekishi* 国語学歴史 [The history of *kokugo* study]. Tokyo: Iwanami Shoten.

———. 1941. *Kokugogaku genron* 国語学原論 [Fundamental theory in *kokugo* study]. Tokyo: Iwanami Shoten.

Tsujimura Toshiki 辻村敏樹. 1947. *Keigo settōji "o" ni tsuite, 1–2* 敬語接頭辞「お」について (1) (2) [The declension of the *keigo* prefix *"o"*]. *Nihon no Kotoba* 1:4–5, 2:2 日本の言葉 1巻4−5号、2巻2号 [The languages of Japan 1:4–5, 2:2].

———. 1963. "Keigo no bunseki ni tsuite" 敬語の分析について [Regarding the analysis of *keigo*]. *Gengo to bungei* 言語と文芸 [Language and literature], March 1963.

———. 1967. *Gendai no keigo* 現代の敬語 [Modern *keigo*]. Tokyo: Kyōbunsha.

———. 1992. *Keigo ronkō* 敬語論考 (Theories of *keigo*). Tokyo: Meiji Shoin.

Twine, Nanette. 1991. *Language and the Modern State: The Reform of Written Japanese*. London: Routledge.

Tyson, Eric. 1998. *Mutual Funds for Dummies*. Foster City, Calif.: IDG Books.

Uchiyama Kaoru 内山薫. 1928. *Kokugo dokuhon goku kyōju*. 國語讀本語句教授 [Teaching the language of *kokugo* readers].

Uchiyama Tatsumi 内山辰美. 1992. *Keigo ni tsuyoi hito no hon* 敬語に強い人の本 [The book for people who are good at *keigo*]. Tokyo: Yell Books.

———. 1994. *Keigo: Haji o kakanai tsukaikata* 敬語：恥をかかない使い方 [*Keigo:* Use without fear]. Tokyo: Nihon Jitsugyō Shuppan.

Ueda Kazutoshi 上田萬年. 1895. *Kokugo to Kokka* 国語と国家と [National language and nationalization]. *Tōyō Tetsugaku* 1:11 東洋哲学 1巻 11号 [Western philosophy 1:11].

Urano Keiko 浦野啓子. 1999. *Aisatsu ga 3-jikan de masutaa dekiru* 挨拶が3時間でマスターできる [You can master *aisatsu* in 3 hours]. Tokyo: Asuka Shuppan.

———. 2002. *Denwa ōtai toppa-hō: Ippon no denwa de jinsei ga hiraku* 電話応対突破法：一本の電話で人生が開く [Telephone success: Change your life with one call]. Tokyo: Meiji Shoin.

Walker, Marilyn A., Masayo Iida, and Sharon Cote. 1994. "Japanese Discourse and the Process of Centering." *Computational Linguistics* 20/2:193–232.

Wetzel, Patricia J. 1984. "Uti and Soto (In-Group and Out-Group): Social Deixis in Japanese." Ph.D. diss., Cornell University.

———. 1988a. "Japanese Social Deixis and Discourse Structure." *Journal of the Association of Teachers of Japanese* 22/1:7–27.

———. 1988b. "Are 'Powerless' Communication Strategies the Japanese Norm?" *Language in Society* 17/4:555–564.

———. 1993. "The Language of Vertical Relationships and Linguistic Analysis." *Multilingua* 10/4:387–406.

———. 1994a. "A Movable Self: The Linguistic Indexing of *Uchi* and *Soto*." In Bachnik and Quinn 1994, 73–87.

———. 1994b. "Contemporary Japanese Attitudes toward Honorifics *(Keigo)*." *Language Variation and Change* 6:113–147.

———. 1995a. "Japanese Social Deixis and the Pragmatics of Politeness." *Japanese Discourse* 1:85–106.

———. 1995b. "*Keigo* in Linguistic Theory." Paper presented at the Eleanor H. Jorden Festival, Portland, Ore., October 27–28, 1995.

Wetzel, Patricia J., and Miyako Inoue. 1999. "Vernacular Theories of Japanese Honorifics." *Journal of the Association of Teachers of Japanese* 33/1:68–101.

White, Merry I., and Robert A. Levine. 1986. "What Is an *ii ko* (good child)?" In *Child Development in Japan,* edited by Harold Stevenson, Hiroshi Azuma, and Kenji Hakuta, 55–62. New York: W. H. Freeman.

Whitman, John. 1982. "Configurationality Parameters." Manuscript.

Whitney, William D. [1875] 1978. *The Life and Growth of Language*. Reprint. New York: Dover.

Wierzbicka, Anna. 1991. "Japanese Key Words and Core Cultural Values." *Language in Society* 20/3:333–385.

Williams, Ray. [1976] 1985. *Keywords*. New York: Oxford University Press.

Wittgenstein, Ludwig. 1953. *Philisophical Investigations*. Malden, Mass.: Blackwell Books.

Woolard, Kathryn A. 1998. "Language Ideology as a Field of Inquiry." In *Language Ideologies: Practice and Theory,* edited by Bambi B. Schieffelin, Kathryn A. Woolard, and Paul V. Kroskrity, 3–47. New York: Oxford University Press.

Yamada Yoshio 山田孝雄. 1924. *Keigo-hō no kenkyū* 敬語法の研究 [Research on the grammar of *keigo*]. Tokyo: Takara Bunkan.

Yanagita Kunio 柳田國男 [1939] 1998. *Keigo to jidō* 敬語と児童 [*Keigo* and children]. Reprinted in *Yanagita Kunio: Kotoba to kyōdo* 柳田國男國語の将来 [Yanagita Kunio: Language and native land]. Tokyo: Iwata Shoin.

Yasuda Toshiaki 安田敏郎. 1999. *"Kokugo" to "hōgen" no aida: Gengo-kōchiku no seijigaku*「国語」と「方言」のあいだ：言語構築の政治学 [Between "national language" and "dialect": The political science of linguistic construction(s)]. Tokyo: Jimbun Shoin.

Yoshioka Kyōsuke 吉岡卿甫 1906. *Nihon kōgohō* 日本口語法 [Spoken Japanese grammar]. Tokyo: Dainihon Tosho.

INDEX

address, 8, 34, 51, 59, 66, 76, 113
addressee, 9, 13, 22, 23, 28, 29, 34, 37,
60, 76, 110, 130–138; addressee-
referent, 3; self and—, 137. *See also*
aite
advice literature, 66, 72, 103
age, 6, 14–16
aisatsu (greetings), 59, 72, 90–94, 97,
100–108, 114
aite (other [person], listener, addressee), 2, 50, 60, 85, 106, 108–
112
amae (dependence), 51, 105, 114
Amemiya, Toshiharu, 91
Anderson, John M., 12
Araki, Hiroyuki, 69
aratamari (formality), 32, 39
Arimura, Itsuko, 70, 109, 110
Asada, Hideko, 76, 91
Asahi Shimbun, 73
Asamatsu, Ayako, 63
Asher, R. E., 12
Atkinson, Jane M., 43
attitude(s) (linguistic), 13–14, 30–37,
51, 63–66, 75, 80, 92–95, 108,
113–115, 181n. *See also* consciousness
Austin, J. L., 182n

ba (location, frame), 30, 36, 37, 51, 63–
66, 75, 80, 88, 92, 94, 108, 110,
113–115; frame, 21, 79, 107; loca-
tion, 29, 39, 40, 97, 107. *See also*
frame analysis
Bach, Emmon, 12
Bachnik, Jane M., 43, 110, 112
Bateson, Gregory, 183n
Befu, Harumi, 167n, 181n
belongingness, 94, 114. *See also* *uchi/*
soto
Ben-Ari, Eyal, 94, 114
bikago (beautiful language), 23, 31, 34,
38
Bloch, Bernard, 165n
Bloomfield, Leonard, 98
Boas, Franz, 98
Bourdieu, Pierre, 44, 77, 96–98, 107,
115
Boym, Svetlana, 77, 88
breaching experiments, 101. *See also*
ethnomethodology
Brown, Penelope, 37, 59
Brown, Roger, 169n
Brubaker, Roger, 115, 116
Bruner, Jerome, 60, 84, 86, 94, 114
Bunka-chō, 48, 52, 61, 84, 113, 170n.
See also Mombushō

Giddens, Anthony, 66, 77, 111. *See also* disembedding mechanisms; expert systems
Gilman, Albert, 59, 169n. *See also* pronouns of power and solidarity
giri (duty), 105
giving and receiving, verbs of, 136, 137, 139
Gluck, Carol, 165n
Goffman, Erving, 183n
gōgohō (haughty language), 26, 43, 52, 56, 64
Gottlieb, Nanette, 43, 52, 56, 59, 64, 72, 74, 76, 90, 91, 93, 100, 165n
greetings, 40, 41, 43, 45, 56, 75, 78, 100, 111, 114. See also *aisatsu*
Grimes, Joseph E., 17
Grosz, Barbara, 16
groups, 95, 96. See also *uchi/soto*

habitus, 95, 96
hairyo (consideration), 26, 33, 36, 39–41, 92, 106, 109–111
Hale, Ken, 9, 11
hanashikata kyōshitsu (speaking classes/schools), 72, 93, 96, 99, 115; speeches, 95, 96, 98, 114, 115. *See also* education
Hanks, William F., 95–114
Hannay, Michael, 12
Harada, S. I., 7, 9
Harootunian, H. D., 165n
Hashimoto, Shinkichi, 24, 25
Hashizume, Kenji, 169n
Heidegger, Martin, 112
Hendry, Joy, 7, 13, 107
hierarchy. *See* vertical relationships
Hill, Jane H., 13
Hinata, Shigeo, 72, 110, 111
Hirst, P., 64
Hoffman, J., 19
Holmes, Janet, 13
horizontal relations, 36, 106. *See also* vertical relationships
Hoshina, Kōichi, 45
Husserl, Edmund, 103
hyōjungo. See standardization

Ide, Sachiko, 7, 13

ideology, 14–16, 32, 43, 44, 53, 63–66, 88, 102, 103, 113; modern linguistic —, 1–2, 103
Iida, Masayo, 16
Ikuta, Shoko, 13, 17
illocutionary force, 96
incorrect *keigo*, 12, 14
inflection, 47, 58, 92. *See also* morphology
Ingerson, Alice, 89
in-group/out-group. See *uchi/soto*
Inoue, Miyako, 15
insider/outsider, 98, 99. See also *uchi/soto*
internationalization, 63, 65, 170n; foreigners, 101
Ishida, Takeshi, 165n
Ishizaka Shōzō, 22
Ivy, Marilyn, 46, 66, 87
Iwai, Yoshio, 169n

Jakobson, Roman, 98
James, William, 102
jōge-kankei. See vertical relationships
Jorden, Eleanor H., 7–8, 165n
joseigo. See women's language
Joshi, Aravind, 16, 108
JR (Japan Railway), 67

Kabaya, Hiroshi, 7, 62
Kageyama, Taro, 7
Kamei, Takashi, 169n
Kanai, Ryōko, 72
Kant, Immanuel, 102
Kawaguchi, Yoshikazu, 7, 62
Kawasaki, Akiko, 7
keii hyōgen (respect expressions), 22, 23, 24, 25–28, 30–33, 38, 48–50, 55, 57, 58, 60, 62, 64, 108, 109
keishō (honorific titles), 22, 54, 59
kenshō (humble titles), 22, 28
kenson (humble), 24, 26–28, 106
keywords, 105. *See also* final vocabulary
Kikuchi, Yasuto, 7, 29, 38–41, 62, 69–70, 79
Kindaichi, Kyōsuke, 29
Kojima, Toshio, 20, 25
Kokugo Chōsa Iinkai, 2, 46, 47, 48, 50, 52, 61
Kokugo Shingikai, 53, 56, 57, 65, 76, 78, 133, 138, 170n

Nomoto, Suien, 68, 72
norm(s), 14, 62, 72, 113, 132, 133, 169n
nostalgia, 29, 33, 77, 86–88

Occupation; American —, of Japan, 56
Ōishi, Hatsutarō, 7–8, 19–21, 23, 29–34, 37, 38, 61, 69
Okada, Masayoshi, 26–27
Okamoto, Shigeko, 7, 15, 107
omote (façade)/*ura* (true feelings), 45, 65, 97, 111
on (indebtedness), 18; obligation, 76, 105; *onkei* (feeling of indebtedness), 32–33, 39, 41

Pacific War, 27–28, 56, 121; postwar society, 133. *See also* World War II
Paine, Thomas, 102
particles, 11, 17, 34, 136
popular press, 26, 72, 111
power, 40–41, 44, 46, 76
pragmatic(s), 7, 17, 42, 104
prefixes *o-* and *go-*, 13, 15, 31, 54, 58–59, 84, 110. *See also* morphology
prescription/prescriptivism, 65
pronouns of power and solidarity, 59, 169n

Quinn, Charles J., 43, 110

radio. *See* media
reference/referent, 3, 5, 21–23, 34, 37, 52–53, 111; axis of reference, 8; implicit—, 16; —, *keigo*, 22–23; —, spaces, 16
Reid, Thomas, 102, 182n
reigi. See manners and etiquette
Robertson, Jennifer, 165n
Rorty, Richard, 102, 104–105, 112–114, 182n, 183n
Rosenberger, Nancy, 2, 182n

Saeki, Umetomo, 25, 29, 86, 169n
Safire, William, 43
sahō. See manners and etiquette
Sakamoto, Megumi, 62, 65
Sanada, Shinji, 45, 47
Sapir, Edward, 98
Schutz, Alfred J., 98, 102, 103, 182n

script, 36, 44, 46, 47, 53, 81, 94; Chinese characters (*kanji*), 44, 53, 68, 165n; written style, 137, 143
Searle, John, 96
semantic primes, 105
sex, 104. *See also* gender
Shibatani, Masayoshi, 7, 9, 13
Shimizu, Shōzō, 70, 109, 110
shitamachi, 96, 180n
Smith, Barry, 102, 182n
speeches, 68, 77, 80, 93, 98; public speaking, 73–74. *See also* *hanashikata kyōshitsu*
spoken language, 1, 25, 34–35, 44–48, 51, 53–54, 60, 139
standardization (linguistic), 15, 21, 43–56, 62, 65, 76, 78, 80, 117, 165n; *hyōjungo* (standard language), 45, 47, 54, 60; nonstandard language, 14; standards, 61–63, 65, 79, 88, 105
Steinhoff, Patricia G., 113–114
Strawson, P. F., 182n
structuralism, 1, 3, 17, 19, 23; structural linguistics, 8, 98, 138; structural properties of *keigo*, 6
Sugimoto, Yoshio, 112, 182–183n
Suzuki, Takao, 43, 165n
Suzuki, Tomi, 91, 165n
Suzuki, Yukiko, 80
symbolic systems, 77, 114

Tachibana, Shōichi, 53
Tai, Eika, 48, 51, 52, 55
taigū-hyōgen, 7, 25, 27, 33, 35, 38–41, 106
Tani, Yasuyo, 165n, 167n
Tannen, Deborah, 107
taxonomy, 19, 24, 27, 31, 32; *keigo* taxonomy, 7, 31
technical, 24, 27, 32, 51, 54, 69, 77, 82, 101, 106; —, terms/terminology, 21, 26, 28, 51, 104, 106, 136; —, vocabulary, 24, 32, 69
technologicalization of discourse, 76–78, 80
teineigo (formal language), 23–24, 27, 29, 30–31, 34, 51, 60, 83, 91, 97, 109